of their own 21st century lives. The Evangelist himself created this story in 100 A.D. that had no likely factual foundation in the life of Jesus to assure Samaritans of his day that they were welcome as followers of Jesus the Galilean to join Jesus-groups despite seven centuries of violent hostility between them and Judeans. Whether selected for serious study or spiritual enrichment, this book provides fresh insights into a familiar story that will prove its enduring power to challenge and inspire readers, women and men alike."

—John J. Pilch, Ph.D., Taught Middle Eastern
cultural approaches to interpreting biblical
literature at Georgetown University
(Washington, DC) from 1993-2011;
Lecturer: Odyssey Program at Johns
Hopkins University, Baltimore, Maryland;
His most recent book is
A Cultural Handbook to the Bible
(Eerdmans, 2012)

"... each woman comes to accept that Divine help IS the only way to real peace. You have done a wonderful thing here, for women who are looking to be well. I hope this book reaches those for whom it is written."

—Bonnie Cook, Ward Choir Accompanist, Seminary
Supervisor, Fort Smith Stake;
Fort Smith, Arkansas

"There are two biblical interpretations that emerge from Jesus' encounter with the Samaritan woman at the well. The first is the traditional view based on translating *baal* as 'husband,' thereby focusing on God's redemptive and creative power to renew human life. This truth unfolds gracefully throughout the story as Kay journeys into the heartland where this Biblical event brings her life together with friends, new and old, to experience the wonder of God's transformative power. Everyday life wondrously turns into moments for personal growth. The second viewpoint is based on *baal* being translated as 'god.' This reveals the woman at the well to be an inquisitive scholar, who hungers to know and experience the truths of God. I find this translation to be present not in the text, but in the excitement and passion with which the author unfolds the story and challenges the reader to join her spiritual pilgrimage. Both interpretations of '*baal*' deepen our faith, mature self-understanding and bring others closer to God. All of this spreads out upon the pages of this book as the author's own devotion becomes contagious."

—*The Reverend Canon Ben Chase, St. Christopher's Anglican Cathedral, Bahrain; Lecturer, Retreat Leader, Mission Consultant: Yemen, UAE, Oman and Jerusalem*

"Old friends reunite for a journey to the Middle East and share unforgettable experiences as they resolve issues created by early lives in dysfunctional families. This author writes from the heart, sharing her own understanding of the Bible, as well as her first-hand knowledge of life in the Middle East. The characters are well developed, and delightful mental images come from her skill in describing the setting, the food, and especially Najila (their tour guide) and her family."

—*Carol Tilley, Interior Designer/Web Blogger*

"*The Well Women* is a well-crafted novel exploring the meaning of the biblical encounter between Jesus and the Samaritan woman at the well. The plot swirls around Kay and her friends, all of whom 10 years before had developed a love for the historic woman at the well. They now go to Palestine where they encounter Najila who becomes much more than a tourist guide. This book truly fleshes out the contemporary meaning of an ancient tale."

—*Ron Wooten-Green, author of <u>When the Dying Speak: How to Listen to and Learn from Those Facing Death</u> (Loyola Press, 2002); <u>A Fine Line of Distinction: In Search of Roots</u> (PublishAmerica, 2006)*

"If you enjoy good storytelling about people just like you and want to make better connections between your faith and life journey, this is the book for you. As you open the pages, you will soon become absorbed in the tales told by a group of extraordinary women. They discover that through honestly sharing their disappointments, disasters, and triumphs with old friends, they realize a surprising encounter with Christ that unfolds before them. Like the Samaritan woman in John's Gospel, this encounter has the power to break open the awareness of the enduring presence of a loving God. This is in spite of loss, self doubt and muddled decisions that each woman had made when they were without hope for the freeing forgiveness that only love and acceptance can bring. Whether you have ever visited the Holy Land or only dreamed of doing so, the author's superb ability to paint mental pictures will make the Middle Eastern landscape, people and customs come alive in your imagination. Then you, too, will join these women as they move from place to place, settle down, share their stories, and pull you into their experience of meeting Someone who changed their life forever."

—*Jeanette Lucinio, SP; Catholic Theological Union Emerita; Editor: Prayers for Catechists, New American Bible: Catholic Study Edition; currently Director of the Office for Women Religious, Diocese of San Diego*

The Well Women
Crossing the Boundaries

Ladine Housholder

Charlottesville, Virginia

The Well Women—Crossing the Boundaries
by Ladine Housholder

Post Office Box 4492
Charlottesville, VA 22905-4492 U.S.A.
monica@copperteapotpub.com
www.copperteapotpub.com

IBSN: Softcover   978-0-9855231-0-7

First Edition

Library of Congress Preassigned Control Number:
2012938904

Cover and water jar art created by Vevonna
Kennedy.

Contents

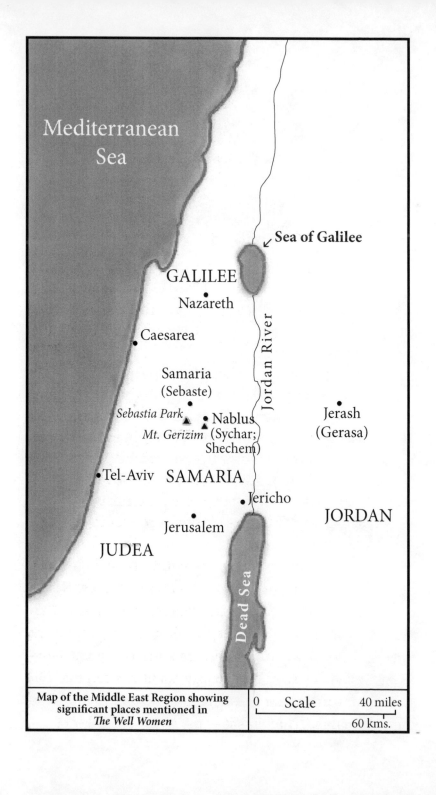

Map of the Middle East Region showing
significant places mentioned in
The Well Women

Following a Dream

K ay sat straight up in bed. There it was—that same dream again. It was something about the Samaritan woman. She remembered that much—about going to see where she had lived and what happened there.

But who were all those other people? She could have sworn that her old friends, Ruth and Norma, were there; but Norma's hair seemed to be a different color. However, the woman standing in the front looked very different than the rest of the group. Her clothes were out of the distant past. Dressed in a flowing robe and a veil, she stood in a mist with outstretched arms. She appeared to be beckoning to Kay. How very odd.

Well, of *course*, Kay thought. It was because she'd been surfing around on the Internet a few weeks ago and had discovered a site from some woman in Palestine offering tours about the Samaritan woman at the well. Looking at that site had stirred up her long-suppressed desire to know more about the original Samaritan woman and had caused her brain to fabricate these dreams. That was it—just wishful thinking.

But, Kay wondered, why the same dream three nights in a row? Was she supposed to *do* something about it? Absurd. Probably just a touch of indigestion. She rubbed her eyes, turned on the lamp by her bed and peered at her digital clock: 6:00 A.M. It was still dark outside and very cool in her room. The wind must have shifted during the night.

Kay tapped her fingers on the edge of her blanket. Then she nodded and laughed out loud. Oh, why not? What did she have to lose? What if she contacted this woman, who was called Najila something, and actually *went* to Samaria? After all, it was something she'd always wanted to do, ever since she'd first read about the Samaritan woman in the Rome study group. Wouldn't it be fabulous? But heavens, could she possible make such a trip? How would she get to Samaria or whatever it was called now? When, and with whom? Should she ask the other study group members if they wanted to go, too?

Fully awake now, Kay stretched her arms and swung her legs to the floor, excited by what had just occurred—the dream and her reaction to it. Her thoughts raced. Would it be totally *crazy* to try to assemble the old Tuesday group and go to Samaria to learn more about this woman who had influenced them all so much? Of *course* it would; but much as she hated to admit it, she wasn't getting any younger. She was still nervous about her last medical report. She was sure her oncologist would object. Maybe she just wouldn't tell her.

As she reached for her blue fleece robe and satin

slippers, she caught her reflection in the silver-edged mirror above her dresser. A slight, sixty-something woman with sapphire blue eyes stared back at her. Not another new wrinkle? So what! She pulled her robe tighter and switched off the lamp.

Kay padded through her tiny kitchen, turned on the coffee maker filled the night before, then walked through the small laundry area. After unlocking the kitchen side door, she stepped onto the porch and drew in a long breath, relishing the smell of the sea on the breeze. The morning paper lay at her feet, soggy from last night's rain; spiky pine needles clung to the plastic wrapping. She came back into the kitchen, wiped off the spotless counter, carefully removed the plastic wrapping, and spread out the paper, intending to read it at breakfast. But first, she put away the previous night's dinner dishes. Her mother had always insisted that dishes were to be washed after every meal— *never* left in the sink overnight. Kay couldn't imagine going to bed with dirty dishes in her sink.

From the pass-through behind the counter, she could see into the adjoining living room and out the large picture windows to the wet, wooden deck beyond. She was happy that nothing had been disturbed by the storm. The four fluffy, pink rhododendrons were still blossoming in their rustic clay pots; and the huge oak and evergreen trees remained upright in the front yard.

Kay moved deliberately from the kitchen into the living room; she made a point of inspecting things every morning. She caressed a small, white damask sofa, draped with warm woolen shawls in subdued pastels of soft greens, blues, and rose. The lavender one that she was knitting for her sister-in-law lay on the antique brocaded footstool near her cozy armchair. She stooped to retrieve an errant bit of yarn that her vacuum cleaner had missed yesterday.

Elegant blue and green vases vied with brass coffeepots with long, curved spouts atop small white shelf units overflowing with her favorite books: art, travel, and literature. A graceful Chinese lacquered screen stood in one corner. The effect was serene, beautiful, and inviting.

She walked back to the kitchen, poured a steaming cup of coffee, added just a touch of cream, and then went down the narrow hall to the spare bedroom that now served as her office. She sat down at her carved, rosewood desk and turned on her computer—she always checked her email first thing. While she waited for it to boot up, she paged through a small devotional booklet and found the day's entry—Jeremiah 6:16: "Thus says the Lord: 'Stand at the crossroads and look, and ask for the ancient paths, where the good way lies; and walk in it, and find rest for your souls.'"

She straightened a group of pens and some papers on her desk, flicked a speck of dust from her tiny gold clock, took a sip of coffee, then sat back and closed her eyes.

Am I at a crossroads? she wondered. What *are* the ancient paths and the good ways? Does my soul need a bit of rest? Could I actually plan a trip to Samaria? Will the other members of the Rome study group be as excited as I am about seeing where the Samaritan woman might have lived and walked?

Where *was* everybody now, anyway? The last time she'd heard from Ruth, she was in Louisville; and Corinne had been in Nebraska. But now she's in South Carolina. Norma lives in Cincinnati. She speaks Arabic from her years in Kuwait, so that would be handy. Julia's in Phoenix; Vicky's in Dallas; and Alicia, Beth, and Inez are still in Rome.

She sighed. Was this a really dumb thing to even *consider*? How would she make the arrangements? Most important, would she be physically up to the trip? That last chemo was rough. She just didn't know . . ..

Kay toyed with the small gold clock. What was that other verse she liked so much—the one where the disciples sat in the boat during a storm, and Jesus walked on the water towards them? Peter said: "If it's really you, Lord, tell me to come to you." Jesus said simply: "Come." So Peter got out of the boat. Just like that. She'd always wondered whether Peter wasn't just showing off a little for his buddies. As a fisherman, Peter probably knew that ninety-nine percent of people did *not* walk on water; yet he did it. He got out of his boat. Maybe that's what she needed to do, she thought. Just stop dithering and get out of her boat. Jesus was right there to give Peter a hand when he faltered. He'd be there for her too.

"All right, then." she said aloud. "I'll do it."

Before she could lose her nerve, she quickly opened an email, pasted addresses for her eight old friends in the "To" line, and rapidly composed an invitation:

Dear All,

Greetings from Seattle. I just had the craziest idea! Remember in our Rome study group when we read about the Samaritan woman—about her meeting Jesus at the well, him asking her for a drink, telling her she had five husbands, etc.? And how, after their conversation, she was changed and then led her village to meet Jesus, too? And how we all said that we'd love to have known this woman?

You won't believe this, but I've had the same dream three nights in a row. I'm pretty sure it's about the Samaritan woman, and now I want to see where she lived. You know this is not at *all* like me, but I have this strong feeling that it's very important for me to go to Samaria and learn as much as I can about her life and her land. There's something about her story that speaks to me.

Will you come too? It's been years since we've all been together, and some of you may not have stayed in touch with one another. So, besides learning about the Samaritan woman, this could be a great opportunity for us all to catch up. Perhaps we could even share our life stories and tell how our life has related to the Samaritan woman's story—how she might have influenced us. Unlike in our old study group, when many of us had to rush off to work, there will be plenty of time on this trip. This will be only if you want to, of course. No pressure.

Recently I was surfing on the net and discovered a site called "Woman at the Well" by Najila Danfi. She lives in Nablus, knows Samaritan history, and runs little tours around the area visiting the various places where the Samaritan woman lived. The town was named Sychar, or Shechem, in her day; but it's Nablus now, in Palestine.

If you agree, I'll see if Ms. Danfi is free to give us her tour about mid-April, before it gets too hot there, and ask if she can also arrange our airport pick-up and book some rooms for a few days at a nearby hotel. We could fly in to Tel Aviv, which is the closest airport. Of course, some of you may want to stay longer or travel on to other cities, too. My travel agent is great and can handle most of the details for us. I'll get back to you in a day or so with prices.

You know I'm too old for a midlife crisis, but this seems like something I just *have* to do. I hope you'll join me. This could be the trip of a lifetime!

Much love,
Kay

She looked up and sighed. This is *so* unlike me, she thought. I *never* do things spontaneously. What would Mother have said? Never mind. She's gone now; and besides, there's nobody here depending on me—nobody I need to consult. This may be my last big chance to do something totally outside the box—for *once* in my life. It's time to get out of the boat.

Kay proofread the letter; and, before she could change her mind, hit "Send."

"There. It's done." She smiled as she stood up from her desk.

She felt terrified but also exhilarated and *very* pleased with herself.

~2~

Full of Surprises

H alf a world away, in a small house at the end of a dusty lane, Najila Danfi stared at her silent TV. Should she get it repaired or buy a new one? Things were so expensive. Maybe she could ask Hani to find her a used one; he was such a good brother. Her mother had said she would buy her a new set, but Najila didn't like to ask.

She picked up a diminutive glass cup from the chipped gold saucer, drained the rest of the tepid, mint tea, then set the cup gently on the saucer. She ran her hand over the surface of the oak end table. The old wooden piece, with its delicately curved legs, was scratched, scarred, and really too small. She had considered replacing it but then decided it was fine. It had belonged to her Grandmother Najet, and Najila loved it. Her mother, however, strongly suggested she buy something more modern.

She lovingly smoothed the frayed, brown-striped, woolen blanket on her old, gray couch, then fluffed up a tatty, lace-edged, green and beige pillow. A mournful picture of Jesus, embroidered in red, green, blue, yellow, and black yarns hung above the sofa. This had blessed the house for as long as she could remember. Although her Gran Najet had stitched the picture, Najila found it depressing and considered taking it down. Her mother, on the other hand, loved it.

Her mother also loved pretty clothes and nagged Najila incessantly to buy some stylish outfits. Najila, however, was happy with her worn jeans and soft, cotton shirts. They were comfortable and so much cooler than the new synthetics.

Najila fanned herself with a travel magazine. Since she had passed her forty-fifth birthday, the heat seemed to bother her more; but there were still several hours before she could turn on her generator. She had been so pleased with the used window air conditioner she had found last week. She had gotten a really good price; even her mother was happy. Najila was a little annoyed, though, that local electricity still was not regular.

She stood up, stuck her feet into her old brown sandals, and wandered out to her minuscule balcony, drawn by the scent of lemon blossoms. Three large, dented oil cans served as planters for grapevines, a small lemon tree, and a bright red hibiscus bush. The cans had been a birthday gift from Ahmed, her auto mechanic. He was always so thoughtful.

Carefully, she climbed a shaky, wooden ladder up to the flat roof of her house. She decided against sitting in a white, plastic chair, now gone gray; and gazed out at Nablus. Distant lights winked as twilight began to settle softly around her like a veil. The breeze twisted her curly, black hair and carried a whiff of motor oil laced with stewed tomatoes, onions, and roasted coffee.

She sighed as she recalled the many rooftops she had stood on, seen these same sights, smelled these same smells, yet had always been an outsider. She had grown up in the tiny village of Jifna, then studied English and history under the De La Salle Christian Brothers at nearby Bethlehem University, choosing that school over the al Najah National University in Nablus. She had even taken a few tourism courses for the fun of it. After graduation, she had married Kanaan; and they had moved to the much larger city of Nablus. Each move was harder than the last.

She had met Kanaan when he was finishing medical school. He was tall, very good-looking, and extremely intelligent. She was short, had a sweet, oval face, and sparkling, brown eyes; and she laughed a lot. They had instantly fallen in love. Since she was not a local girl and was very shy, living with his family had proved difficult. His mother had been slow to accept her, especially after it became obvious that there would be no grandchildren. But, over the years, the two women had become friends.

Against Kanaan's wishes, Najila had taken a job as a teacher. She smiled, remembering that she had not been much taller than her young students. But they had loved her, and she loved them.

Then, one day, she got a call telling her that

Kanaan had dropped dead of an embolism. They had been married for only seven years. She was devastated. For many months, she was barely able to drag herself to work; every day brought new agony for her. She was so sad, so depressed, and, yes, so angry—it wasn't supposed to *be* this way.

Somehow, slowly, she pulled herself together. The regular routine of her teaching job helped a lot, plus she knew her students did not like it when she was sad. They wanted to see her smile.

After a few years, her family urged her to remarry. Instead, against their wishes, she let her maid go and sold the big house; it held too many memories of Kanaan. She bought a roomy flat across town, switched schools, and taught English to middle-schoolers. Those had been hard, turbulent years; yet she had managed. Along the way, she had lost some of her shyness, too.

However, after teaching for fifteen years, she was ready for a change. So she quit her job, even though she was not quite sure what she should do next. She rearranged the furniture in her apartment, visited friends, and took short trips. But after five weeks, she grew restless. It was not her nature to putter around at home or gossip with friends over cardamom coffee. She loved to be busy. Besides, she knew she still had something to contribute. So she sold the flat; and, in spite of her mother's strong objections, bought an old bungalow on the outskirts of Nablus. Although the little house was run down, she loved it from the very beginning. It reminded her of her parents' home in Jifna, plus there was a wonderful view of the hills above Nablus. After weeks of scrubbing and painting, she moved in.

One Thursday, after she was settled, she visited Jacob's Well, near the Old Town district. Afterward, she wanted to buy a little memento—just something to remember the afternoon. Alas, there was no gift shop, no souvenirs, nothing—only some old, gruff, Greek Orthodox monks shuffling around the courtyard, tending the flowers.

She went home and thought and thought. What if she opened a small souvenir shop at Jacob's Well? No! Never! What would her mother say? Then Najila smiled. If she could teach thirteen year olds, she could do *anything*. Besides, she still had the notebook.

A few years before, Huda, her mother, had given her an old cloth bag containing a notebook. In the notebook was a handwritten copy, done by her Gran Najet, of a first-century document. The original had been written on parchment scrolls by a woman of Samaria who described her meeting at Jacob's Well with a Jew named Jesus. Other copies had been made in later centuries.

Huda had felt that, since she was growing older, she should pass this on to Najila. Huda emphasized the book's importance and how the original documents, now in possession of a distant uncle, had also been passed from generation to generation. She told Najila that *her* mother, Gran Najet, had made a copy during a time of unrest in

Palestine; this was what she was giving to Najila. Huda cautioned Najila to keep the notebook in a safe place, as it was a valuable heirloom for their family.

When Najila first read the story in the notebook, she was amazed. She was also vaguely concerned. Huda had reminded her endlessly to always place their family first; but, since Najila had no children, to whom would she pass it along?

She bought a metal strong box for the notebook, stored it in a wardrobe in her bedroom, and waited. She loved the Samaritan woman's story and had always wanted to make it more widely known but was not sure how. Perhaps a souvenir stand was the way? So she took a deep breath and a big chance. After a hard look at her bank balance and a few sleepless nights, she decided she would do it–she would open a stand in the courtyard at the well.

Her mother was horrified; her mother-in-law was mortified. "But, Najila, why?" they wailed. "Money you need? We help. But such *shame* you bring on family. Our women not work, and especially not *souvenir* stand! Not nice girl like you! Such strange, *foreign* people come all day. Aiyee! And your *nails* ..."

Najila sighed. She knew that each of these women loved her in their own way but would never understand that this was not about money. It was about meeting a challenge, meeting people, and having fun. She knew this would be fun for her—she just *knew* it. At her age, she needed some fun.

Standing firm, she gathered up her courage, went back to the well, and persuaded the monks to rent her a space. She selected a shady corner under a large grape arbor, swept and scrubbed the stones, and tied up the grapevines. And, of course, she broke two nails.

Although he grumbled at first, her brother, Hani, built her a fine stall. He fitted it with sturdy shelves, racks, and a smoothly-sanded, olive-wood countertop and found her a high stool to sit on—for when business was slow. He even laid extra palm branches on the roof for decoration and insulation against the strong sun. As a surprise, he hung up tinkling wind chimes. "So people find you, Naji," he said gruffly.

Nervous, she set up shop but proceeded to do very well. She stocked just the right items: postcards with photos of the courtyard and the ancient underground well beneath, models of clay water jars, replicas of the brass oil lamps that hung down close to the well, and a few books about the Samaritans. She even thought to offer little bottles of water from the well—those proved to be very popular. She knew she had done the right thing when one day a bearded, old monk brought her three, fragrant, yellow roses in an old jam jar, along with a mug of strong, mint tea.

She loved chatting with all the tourists; it often provided a chance to practice her English. She felt sorry for some because they seemed to be in such a rush. A few just wanted to talk, however, and would buy something as an

afterthought. She felt like she was back in her classroom, offering a smile or a word of encouragement, as
she had to her students. She liked that.

Following this success, she decided to branch
out. Eighteen months later, she hired an assistant to
help with the stall. Then she launched a small tour
company, specializing in trips around Samaria. Hani
set up a website for her; and, slowly, inquiries were
coming in. Although he would never admit it, Hani
was secretly proud of Najila's success.

She had already guided a few people around
the Nablus area and then driven them up to Sebaste,
the former capital of Samaria. Her Bethlehem University tourism studies had proved invaluable, plus
she still had some good contacts in the department,
even after all these years. Who you knew was very
important here.

Najila had lived very frugally after Kanaan died
and his insurance coverage expired. She had banked
more than fifty percent of her earnings from teaching
and now continued that practice with her businesses.
It was difficult, but she valued her independence. By
living simply, she could manage. Even though her
mother offered repeatedly, Najila did not want to ask
her family for help.

She used Leila, the nearby hairdresser, bought
fruits and vegetables from her neighbor, Maha, and spent
very little for clothes, preferring instead to use any extra
money to help the refugees in the Palestinian camps. Although she had little, the people in the camps had almost

nothing. Her mother thought she was ridiculous for living so meagerly; Najila enjoyed the simplicity. And each small step she took gave her courage for the next.

That thought snapped her back to the present. She glanced at her watch and saw that it was getting late. She wanted to sort through some things and get a box together for the camps. Hani had promised to drive her over the next day, and she wanted to be ready.

She picked her way down the ladder and went through the living room into her small bedroom. She opened a wooden wardrobe that stood against the wall, stuck her hand into the back, and felt the metal strong box. She lifted it out, set it on the bed, then pulled out a bag of used clothing from her mother, which was behind the box.

Just then, her laptop beeped. "You've got mail, *habibati*," the digital voice chirped from the corner desk. She smiled at Hani's using the Arabic word for "sweetie" on her email.

Now what? She hoped it was not Walid, the man Mama had arranged for her to meet the week before. He was pleasant; but he had worn an ill-fitting tan suit, a wrinkled, purple shirt, and green, alligator shoes. He smoked noxious, little brown cigars and loved to eat. Not her type.

Mama. Please. She knew her mother meant well, but Najila loved her single life.

She squeezed her way to the desk and opened her email. There was the usual stuff: her brother wheedling her to help at his computer store, a note from a friend in Jifna, and one from somebody called Kay Hunter. Who was she? Najila read:

Dear Ms. Danfi,

My name is Kay Hunter. I am an American and am interested in learning more about the Samaritan woman. From your web site, I see that you offer tours of the area and are knowledgeable about Samaritan culture and history.

Some years ago, I lived in Rome and belonged to an English-speaking study group. We were fascinated and inspired when we read the Samaritan woman's story. Now I've asked the eight women from this group to join me on a trip to visit the area where the Samaritan woman lived.

Will you be free to guide us for several days in mid-April? Our plans are not complete but will include flights from America and Europe to Tel Aviv. Could you arrange to have someone pick us up at Ben Gurion Airport in Tel Aviv, as well as reserve hotel rooms in your area? Making this trip is very important to me. I look forward to hearing from you soon.

Yours truly,
Kay Hunter

Najila sighed deeply. She rubbed her forehead, her thoughts spinning. Yes, she had guided several small groups around the area but only for a few hours. Yet now *nine* women wanted a tour around Samaria— and for several *days*! She knew she had been a fine teacher and now ran a good souvenir stand; but she had never done a *real* tour. Oh, why had she ever allowed her brother to create that web site for her, saying all those things that made it sound like she knew what she was doing? Her stomach was in knots, and she felt a headache starting.

She knew a little about the Samaritan woman but not nearly enough. Today was already the twentieth of February, and they wanted to come in mid-April? That was just six weeks. Impossible! Still, the extra income *would* be nice, she reasoned. Her house and her van were old; both had roofs in need of repair. And it might not be *too* hard. She could make a simple itinerary of the most important sites, find some small bits of background information, and reserve rooms at the Morgenstern Hotel nearby. Of course, she would ask her cousin, Yousef, to pick the women up in his big taxi. Since he lived in Jaffa and had an Israeli passport, he would be able to enter the Tel Aviv airport and then drive the ladies down to Nablus. He would complain, but he would do it. She chewed her lower lip and then made out a quick list.

Ah, but my van. Can I drive the ladies around in it? I will take it to Ahmed's garage tomorrow, ask if he will fix my old transmission, give me his best price. I will bring him some fresh pitas and hummus. That always makes him smile.

She rubbed her forehead again. What do I have to lose? Besides, if all goes smoothly, this group might recommend me to other friends and then, who knows?

Perched on the corner of her bed, she exhaled deeply, then typed:

Dear Ms. Hunter,

Thank you for your pleasant email. I am happy that you have interest in Samaritan woman at the well. I am available to lead a small tour for your group in the Nablus (Shechem)-Sebaste area during the time you require. Please tell me your exact dates of arrival, length of stay, and departures, plus special room or dietary needs. I will arrange for your group to be collected at Ben Gurion Airport in Tel Aviv and will book rooms at the Morgenstern Hotel near the well. I will send a schedule and list of most interesting sites about the Samaritan woman soon.

All is calm in Nablus; the unrest of last month is now quiet. You will have a nice tour.

Best greetings,
Najila Danfi

She looked over what she had written, took a deep

breath, and hit "Send."

Najila lay down on the bed; she felt a bit faint. What had she *done*? Where would she find enough information in time—something new and different about the Samaritan woman to tell the ladies?

She sighed and ran her hands idly along the thin, chenille spread. Her fingers paused as they touched the metal box, where she had left it on the bed. Of course! The notebook! How could she have forgotten? She sat up, opened the box, and gently lifted out the old notebook. On the first page, she read her beloved grandmother's careful Arabic script:

My name is Najet Danfi, and today is 24 January 1939. Our family owns ancient parchments found in the first century in a cave near Nablus. Earlier family members, trained as scribes, made translations of these same parchments around 200, 725, and again in 1615. Historical authorities had no interest, said these were only ramblings of a simple peasant, "just some woman." But our family always kept possession.

The parchments were written by a Samaritan woman. Her name was Sapha, also from a scribe family. It is possible she was our ancestor. She was a remarkable woman who said she met a Jew called Jesus at Jacob's

Well. She wrote about that meeting during great turmoil in land.

Now, in 1939, again we face great unrest,
terrorist attacks, even massacres in our
land. Changes by the British anger Jewish citizens who turn to violence. The
ancient parchments and earlier translations are hidden in safe place, but now
I will make a new copy of 1615 translation, just in case. Though our language
is similar, some words and meanings are
now changed. It is important my family
knows what Sapha wrote.

My work is not perfect, but I write my
best.

Najet Danfi

Najila's hands were shaking. How could she
have forgotten about this notebook, this *treasure*?
This was something *very* different to share with the
ladies. It would certainly be better if it were translated, so she could read it to the women in English.
Could she do that in just six weeks, along with everything else? She flipped to the back of the notebook
and saw that there were only forty-one pages. She realized she would have to work long hours, maybe seek
help from her former English professor at Bethlehem
University. But, yes, it was possible. She had done
harder things in her life; she could do this, too.

"*Shukran, Jeddatti,*" she whispered. "Thank you,

Gran Najet."

Thrilled, Najila carried the notebook into the living room. She was so excited that she decided a small celebration was in order. She hurried into the kitchen, turned on the generator, took down Gran Najet's beloved, etched, copper teapot, and brewed a new pot of strong tea. She added two sugar cubes, crumbled up some fresh mint leaves, stirred it gently, and then found her prettiest cup and saucer and two pieces of baklava. She placed everything on a silver tray, carried it back to the living room, set it on the old, wooden table, and then switched on a lamp.

She settled herself on the sofa, poured a cup of tea, and opened the notebook. She skimmed her grandmother's and Sapha's introductory words again, then turned to the second page.

> My name is Sapha. My nephew, Moussa, some neighbors, and I are now safe in a cave above Sychar. Village elders demanded that we leave our homes on Mt. Gerizim. Fighting continues. Below us, houses and fields are burning. Not ours, yet, but perhaps soon. I cannot look.
>
> I will continue the story I started before I had to run from my house. I will tell about my meeting with a Jew named Jesus at our well many years ago. I learned later from his followers that they had all been with him in Judea where they were baptizing and he was gathering more disciples. Pharisees had heard this and were objecting. Jesus thought it best to leave and return to his home area of Galilee. He chose to travel through Samaria, some-

thing no Jew ever did.

Relaxed now, Najila laid the notebook on the sofa and took a sip of tea. She decided that guiding a tour might not be so hard. The ladies would be happy to hear Sapha's words from the notebook. Najila determined then that she would be extra-careful with the English translation—to get everything just right. She would even share the family legend that Uncle Ramzi had told her, when he explained that, although most women in the first century could not write, Sapha had begged her father to teach her. Since she had no brothers, the old man had given in but had demanded that she make her letters cleanly.

Najila savored the two baklavas, wiped the honey off her hands, and finished her tea, stroking the copper teapot for good luck. Refreshed, she was anxious to read the whole notebook. She would pack the things for the camps later.

Sapha was here now.

-3-

On Their Way

K ay looked around the cabin of the 747 and counted noses: Julia, Norma, Corinne, Vicky, and,
yes, Ruth. Good—they were all there. She gave
her seat belt another tug, as she felt the big jet lift
off. As she glanced out the window and watched the
lights of John F. Kennedy Airport disappear, she saw
her own face reflected in the glass, a little older and
thinner, but, basically, the same.

Well, why *shouldn't* she look older? She *was*
older, and the chemo had been difficult. She sternly
told herself to stop being so vain. Never mind. She
was here, and today she felt fine. Besides, though
she'd kept in touch with all of the women, and some
had kept in touch with one another, it had been ages
since they'd all been together. So there would be
changes in *everyone*.

Was it really possible that almost ten years had
flown by? Even though they had lived in different districts
of Rome, held jobs, and cared for their families, they were
also active in the international community; and they had
treasured their small study group. Once a week, they'd
met at an English-speaking church near the Pantheon to

share a simple breakfast, a brief study or meditation, and some prayers. It was the feelings of connection, of understanding, and of sharing common difficulties that brought and held them together.

Initially, they had all seemed so different. They soon learned they weren't, and they had become very close. Time, tears, and trust had enabled them to open themselves, to share their successes, and to pray for their problems. But there was never enough time to tell *everything*—to talk about their lives *before* moving to Rome.

Then, one day, for something different, Vicky had led a short study on the story of the Samaritan woman at the well from the Gospel of John. They had been intrigued by this woman—had loved her courage and forthrightness in her conversations with Jesus. At the end of the study, Kay had said, "You know, I'd give anything to have met her, gotten to know her, and heard her side of things. Something tells me that, with five husbands, she had a hard life. But still, she kept going. She knew a lot about her culture but wasn't afraid to speak her mind. I like her; she feels almost like a friend."

Slowly life rolled on; job transfers and retirements took their toll. The group grew smaller, then stopped meeting altogether. Somehow, Kay managed to stay in touch with all of them; and she never forgot her desire to meet the Samaritan woman.

She yawned and stretched her legs. Feeling slightly chilled, she tucked her blue cashmere sweater about her shoulders and straightened her black jersey slacks, happy that she'd ordered them from that exclusive travel company. They were very comfortable, and she knew they'd wash well. So what if they were a bit expensive?

She closed her eyes and breathed a prayer for their safe trip. Please, God, let everything go well: no troubles in Palestine, no lost luggage or passports— none of that. Then she allowed herself to relax, even gave herself a modest pat on the back. What a lot of work she'd done! After the initial invitation to the others and the tour request to Najila, emails had flown furiously among all of them but especially between Kay and Andrea Rowland, her travel agent. Kay had already written a note to Andrea's boss; service like hers deserved applause. Andrea had advised Kay on everything, found the cheapest flights, made all the reservations, had even booked connections and onward flights for those continuing on to other destinations. Of course, Andrea had kept Kay apprised of everything—Julia, Corinne, and Inez would take a bus to Jerusalem to spend a week there. Norma would rent a car and drive to visit friends in Kuwait. Vicky and Alicia were flying to Istanbul; and, finally, Kay and Ruth would stop in Rome to visit Beth for a few days on their way back to the States.

Poor Beth had been *so* disappointed that she couldn't join them! Her second knee operation wasn't healing well, and her doctor had strictly forbidden her to make the trip. He told her flatly that doing all the walking on such a trip would be very painful and might damage her knee even further. But Beth told Kay she'd send something via Ruth.

Kay smiled, quite pleased with herself. All that organizational work had paid off; and now they were on the plane, actually on their way. Sometimes, being a perfectionist wasn't a bad thing.

Shortly before boarding, Kay had spotted Julia Wagner in the EL AL departure lounge and went over to greet her. Julia looked cool in a burnt orange tunic that complemented her reddish-brown hair. But she was cross that she'd already gotten a spot on her new gray slacks. Kay remembered that Julia was often cross.

"Just *look* at me," she'd lamented. "After all these years of wearing only black and navy, I've finally gotten up the nerve to wear some brighter colors, even though, as you can *plainly* see, I'm still struggling with my weight. But just look—I've made a mess—*again*! I am *such* a klutz."

They'd both seen Norma Schaffer, sweet and bubbly as ever. She'd observed Julia's problem and hurried toward her, a stain remover packet in her outstretched hand. She had learned to be prepared for every emergency during her husband's Foreign Service tours in Kuwait. Wearing a long, celadon green shirt over darker green slacks, she looked good—not a day over fifty-five. But Kay noticed that Norma's face was pale, and her hair was a darker shade of red than before.

Kay hadn't seen Corinne Zartley or Vicky Bright until they collapsed into their seats across the aisle from her. Their Atlanta plane had arrived late, and they'd had to rush over to the international terminal in a taxi. They were still giggling and semi-hysterical about their wild ride.

Watching them, Kay couldn't believe so many years had passed. Now in her early sixties, Corinne had remained very slender and had the fine, porcelain skin of a true redhead. She looked comfortable in a casual, tan, cotton shirt with matching capris. A Denver Broncos sweatshirt hung over her arm. Vicky, a petite blonde of fifty-two, was immaculate in a beige, linen shirt and slacks despite the hours of flying she'd already done. A thin, light blue, woolen scarf was draped around her shoulders.

Then there was Ruth Hanford. Now that the seat belt sign was off, Ruth, who'd been a flight attendant for years, was standing near the rear galley, chatting with the EL AL crewmembers. Her short hair was almost white; and she sported trim turquoise slacks and a coral and turquoise, cotton, print jacket over a turquoise T-shirt. A big, flowered hat poked out of the turquoise tote she carried. As usual, her makeup was perfect; she certainly didn't *look* sixty-two. Kay had been surprised when, an hour before, in the airport, Ruth had seemed worried and distracted. In the past, she'd always been so zany and flippant—always the one out for a laugh. When Kay questioned her, Ruth just shrugged and said she had a lot on her mind. Then she'd suddenly hugged Kay and told her how glad she was to be there with all of them. But there were tears in her eyes.

Kay felt a little bump at her elbow. "Yes, thank you, I *will*," she said, as a pretty flight attendant offered her a glass of red wine from the beverage cart. As she sipped the wine, she pulled out her travel notebook and reviewed the follow-up letter she'd written to the group. She realized she was still a librarian at heart as she'd made their itinerary: carefully detailed sites they'd visit, and times for snacks, breaks, and shopping. She'd mentioned the weather and even made a few packing suggestions, leaving nothing to chance.

She'd done a bit of research and listed several books they might want to read before the trip. She'd even included a few discussion questions. She strongly recommended they read the story of the Samaritan woman in John's Gospel again and assigned verses from the story for each person to comment on, if they chose. For something special, she'd asked Corinne, who was clever at producing church dramas, to prepare for them to act out the Samaritan woman's whole story in John 4 as a playlet. It would be a perfect way for them to get into the spirit of the trip and to remember the woman and what she'd said and done.

Kay had also reminded them that time would be available for them to share their stories—but only if they wished. She'd emphasized that they should tell their *whole* life story even though everyone knew about the Rome years. There had never been enough time in their prayer group, since many had to dash off to work or home to small children. She smiled, recalling Julia's rapid reply—that there was no point in sharing *her* life story because there really wasn't all that much to say; and, besides, hearing that sort of thing from others always made her distinctly uncomfortable. No, thanks; she'd just be along for the sightseeing.

Fine, Kay thought. The time would be available, but she'd keep them on schedule. She glanced at her watch and realized that, with ten hours of flying ahead of her, now was the perfect opportunity to re-read the Samaritan woman's story to refresh her own memory and keep the details sharp. She reached into her bag, pulled out a small Bible, settled back in her seat, and opened to John 4:

> Now when Jesus learned that the Pharisees had heard, "Jesus is making and baptizing more disciples than John"—although it was not Jesus himself but his disciples who baptized—he left Judea and started back to Galilee. But he had to go through Samaria. So he came to a Samaritan city called Sychar, near the plot of ground that Jacob had given to his son Joseph. Jacob's well was there, and Jesus, tired out by his journey, was sitting by the well. It was about noon.
>
> A Samaritan woman came to draw water, and Jesus said to her, "Give me a drink." (His disciples had gone to the city to buy food.) The

Samaritan woman said to him, "How is it that you, a Jew, ask a drink of me, a woman of Samaria?" (Jews do not share things in common with Samaritans.) Jesus answered her, "If you knew the gift of God, and who it is that is saying to you, 'Give me a drink,' you would have asked him, and he would have given you living water." The woman said to him, "Sir, you have no bucket, and the well is deep. Where do you get that living water? Are you greater than our ancestor Jacob, who gave us the well, and with his sons and his flocks drank from it?" Jesus said to her, "Everyone who drinks of this water will be thirsty again, but those who drink of the water that I will give them will never be thirsty. The water that I will give will become in them a spring of water gushing up to eternal life." The woman said to him "Sir, give me this water, so that I may never be thirsty or have to keep coming here to draw water."

Jesus said to her, "Go, call your husband, and come back." The woman answered him, "I have no husband." Jesus said to her, "You are right in saying, 'I have no husband,' for you have had five husbands, and the one you have now is not your husband. What you have said is true!" The woman said to him, "Sir, I can see that you are a prophet. Our ancestors worshiped on this mountain, but you say that the place where people must worship is in Jerusalem." Jesus said to her, "Woman, believe me, the hour is coming when you will worship the Father neither on this mountain nor in Jerusalem. You worship what you do not know; we worship what we know, for salvation is from the Jews. But the hour is coming, and is now here, when the true worshipers will worship the Father in spirit and truth, for the Father seeks such as these to worship him. God is spirit, and those who worship him must worship in spirit and truth." The woman said to him, "I know that the Messiah is coming (who is called Christ). When he comes, he will proclaim all things to us." Jesus said to her, "I am he, the one who is speaking to you."

Just then his disciples came. They were astonished that he was speaking with a woman, but no one said, "What do you want?" or, "Why are you speaking with her?" Then the woman left her water jar and went back to the city. She said to the people, "Come and see a man who told me everything I have ever done! He cannot be the Messiah, can he?" They left the city and were on their way to him.

Meanwhile, the disciples were urging him, "Rabbi, eat something." But he said to them, "I have food to eat that you do not know about." So the disciples said to one another, "Surely no one has brought him something to eat?" Jesus said to them, "My food is to do the will of him who sent me and to complete his work. Do you not say, 'Four months more, then comes the harvest'? But I tell you, look around you, and see how the fields are ripe for harvesting. The reaper is already receiving wages and is gathering fruit for eternal life, so that the sower and reaper may rejoice together. For here the saying holds true, 'One sows and another reaps.' I sent you to reap that for which you did not labor. Others have labored, and you have entered into their labor."

Many Samaritans from that city believed in him because of the woman's testimony. "He told me everything I have ever done." So when the Samaritans came to him, they asked him to stay with them; and he stayed there two days. And many more believed because of his word. They said to the woman, "It is no longer because of what you have said that we believe, for we have heard for ourselves, and we know that this is truly the Savior of the world."

My word, Kay thought. Jesus had told this woman he was the *Messiah*! Did she understand? There they were, at this out-of-the-way, roadside well where only women came to draw water; yet look what happened. And now we're *going* there. I'm so excited! This is a dream come true!

-4-

On The Ground

K ay had actually managed to sleep a little during the flight. Perhaps the wine, and later the
Bailey's, had helped. She now felt quite rested.
Slowly, the lights went on, people sat up, stretched,
and yawned. The head purser announced that breakfast would soon be served, and they would be landing
in ninety minutes.

Ruth was in the aisle, still chatting with the EL
AL crew, happily helping them pass out washcloths
while trying to engage a steward in a chorus of "Hava
Nagila." The passengers loved it. Ruth must have
been up all night, but she looked ecstatic.

After a light breakfast of bagels, yogurt, fresh
fruit, and plenty of strong coffee, they had a smooth
landing in Tel Aviv. To Kay's enormous relief, they
all breezed through the stringent Ben Gurion Airport
customs' formalities.

As the group walked through the arrivals hall to
baggage claim, two women hurried toward them. "Hey,
you guys finally made it. *Fantastic!*" exclaimed Alicia
Corrigan. She was tall, athletic, and very fit. Her thick,

blonde hair swung around her shoulders. In cream-colored jeans, a matching top, and an elegant, tan, long-sleeved shirt, she looked much younger than fif-ty-eight. Alicia had always reminded Kay of a classic Valley Girl.

Close behind Alicia was Inez Varez. Kay couldn't believe her eyes! When she'd last seen her in Rome, Inez was a bit overweight and had always worn dark, baggy clothes. Now, at forty-seven, Inez was at least thirty pounds lighter; and her curly, dark brown hair was much shorter. She was stunning in a navy tunic and matching slacks; delicate, navy and gold, crescent-moon earrings winked from her ears. She kissed Kay warmly on both cheeks. "I am so happy to see you again," Inez said, her brown eyes shining.

Greetings and hugs were exchanged all around, to the consternation of other passengers who were try-ing to pluck their bags from the carousel rotating be-hind the women. "Ladies, we're in the way here," Kay said briskly. "Let's get our things and move outside. Our driver, Mr. Yousef, should be waiting for us. It's only sixty or seventy miles to Nablus, so it won't take too long."

After obediently gathering their luggage, they all trooped out to the curb and were hit by a blast of hot wind— a drastic change from the frigid terminal air. Kay shaded her eyes and looked across the street. Under a corrugated tin roof, a man slouched against the dented front fender of a decrepit, twelve-passenger van. He drew heavily on a cigarette as he held a sign with "Mrs. Kay" scrawled in lopsided letters.

"There's our driver," Kay said. She stepped cautiously into the lane marked "Arrival Pickup Traffic" and hurried across the street. "Are you Mr. Yousef from the Nablus Bus Company?"

"Yah, I Yousef. You Mrs. Kay?" he asked, sucking hard on his cigarette. In his middle sixties, he wore torn jeans, an old, denim shirt missing two buttons, beat-up leather sandals, and an unkempt beard. "Where you want go?"

"We're heading down to Nablus. I phoned Najila Danfi last week to confirm our plans."

"Yah, Cousin Naji say you want go Nablus, but what for? Nothing there, only big town, old ruins," Yousef muttered, flinging down his spent cigarette.

"We have a tour booked to Jacob's Well, to learn more about the Samaritan woman."

"OK, Jacob's Well," Yousef said, in heavily accented English. "But Samaritan woman? Who she is? Nobody called Samaritans anymore. Down there, all Palestinians now."

"Right. Of course," Kay said firmly. "But we still want to go. I hope it won't take too long to drive there."

"OK, lady, you boss," Yousef replied with a little grin. "You want go Nablus, we go Nablus. But, ah, small problem. Van little bit hot. Air condition broke last Thursday. Still waiting parts. Parts man say: Come back next week, then he say come back next day, then he say fifteen minutes, *insha'allah*. He always say that."

Kay sighed and steeled herself to remain calm. Then she waved to the women, who threaded their way across the busy street. Mr. Yousef raised the back of the van; and, one by one, the women piled their bags into the rear compartment. They crammed the smaller ones under the seats. "Not my new Samsonite in all that grit," Julia grumbled. "No, sir! I'll sit in the back seat and hold it on my lap. I can't *believe* this!"

"Hey, Jules," Ruth whispered, "it could be a donkey cart."

Soon everything was stowed away, and they all climbed in. Yousef slid behind the steering wheel. After several loud stutters, the engine finally roared to life. The van lurched backward, narrowly missing a catering truck. Shouting an obscenity, Yousef touched his fingers to his thumb and shook his hand at the alarmed driver. Yousef ground the gears, shot out of the airport, and sped into city traffic. Kay was afraid to breathe. Norma giggled and crossed herself. They were on their way.

5

On The Road

Careening along, they were soon hurtling down
Road Sixty-Six. The beaches and resort hotels
rapidly gave way to sparse, dry countryside as
the road climbed up from the coast. All the windows
in the van were open as the women tried to capture
the vanishing ocean breezes, but it was no use—they
were all incredibly hot.

Kay settled into the dusty front seat and tried
to get comfortable. She slipped off her sandals and
carefully tucked her trip notebook into her handbag.
All the items were ticked off on her "arrival" list.

"Hey, Kay," Ruth yelled, from the third seat,
"thanks for keeping up with us over the years and now
getting us all together again. You're always so organized. It's really good to see all you guys again. I'll try
to be on my best behavior during this trip," she said
jokingly. "I was pretty tired when we landed, but I'm
getting my second wind. That's how it always was for
me when I worked as a flight attendant. I'd be dead
after a flight, but then I'd get revved up again."

"You're welcome, Ruth," Kay said loudly, turning

around slightly. "It was easy, since you were all so helpful and replied so quickly. I had originally thought we could use this hour's driving time to catch up with one another; but we'll have to do that later, maybe after dinner—if we're still awake. With the windows open now, it's so noisy. I'm having a hard time hearing you. You'll just have to chat with your neighbor."

So, over the roar of the engine, with the wind whipping their hair, they conversed as best they could. Ruth, Norma, and Alicia compared notes about their flights; while Vicky, Inez, and Corinne scrolled through family photos for one another on their cameras. In the front seat, Kay endured Yousef's strident, Arabic music on the radio and tried to hold her knitting steady. In the last seat, Julia worked a Sudoku puzzle atop her Samsonite.

After forty-five minutes, Norma spoke loudly in Arabic to the driver. "Mr. Yousef, would you pull in at the next rest stop? I need to walk around for a bit. Thanks. *Shukran.*"

"OK, missus. *Maffi mishkala.* No problem," Yousef said. He soon swerved into the next exit lane and screeched to a halt at a small AGIP station. "Toilets behind station. Ten minutes, then we go," he stated tersely. He jumped down from the driver's side, fished out his cigarettes and cell phone, punched in some numbers, and then lit up.

"Halloo, Naji *habibati*? Yousef here," he said in Arabic. "I'm at AGIP Station, be in Nablus in forty-five minutes, *insha'allah.* We will meet at Morgenstern, OK?

Mumtaz. Good. What? Yah, womens all here. Much talking. Never stop. OK. Good. *Mumtaz.* See you. *Masallamah.*"

Twenty minutes later, they had all returned to the van. Yousef gunned the engine, shoved the car in gear, and blasted back onto the highway.

Julia leaned forward. "Thanks for asking him for that break, Norma. I was *really* getting anxious. I'm so hot, and my legs are totally cramped back here. Say, I didn't know you spoke Arabic. How handy."

Norma coughed several times before she spoke. "You're welcome, Julia. My Arabic isn't perfect, as it's been some time since I used it in Kuwait; but I still remember the important things."

"Well, Julia said loudly, "did you all notice the line in Najila's reply to Kay: about the 'previous unrest now being quiet'? I'm *very* nervous about that. I hope an ambush or shooting isn't in our future."

"Not to worry, Jules," Ruth said. "There are problems everywhere. But we're here now, all's well, and I'm gonna enjoy every minute. Relax, OK? Everything will be fine." With that, they all settled down, some even lulled to sleep by the heat.

After a while, Vicky glanced up from the map on her lap. "Look, there's the sign for the turnoff to Road Sixty. That goes near Sebastiya, the main city of Samaria in ancient times, and then on into Nablus. We're almost there."

They got themselves together: hair was combed,

lipstick repaired, and books stowed away. Kay carefully rolled up the tiny pink sweater she was knitting, and Julia happily found the last Sudoku number. As a grove of trees appeared ahead, Yousef whipped the steering wheel into a hard right turn, hurtled into the hotel parking lot, and shut off the ignition.

"We here, ladies."

Julia heaved a sigh. "Thank you, Jesus. Not a second too soon."

6

Checking In

Y ousef jumped out and opened the van's creaky
panel doors as the women peeled themselves
off the cracked leather seats. Julia handed her
new Samsonite to Alicia and then slowly clambered
out of the back seat. With a grimace she said, "Lord,
I'm so hot and tired; and my knee is absolutely *throb-
bing*! I'd *kill* for a shower."

"I'm sorry you're in pain, Julia," Norma said
soothingly. "We'll soon be inside, and you can rest."

On the eastern edge of Nablus, the Morgenstern Hotel sat a quarter of a mile back from the road.
At the end of a curved driveway, tall pine trees surrounded low, stone buildings. The reception area and
dining room were located in a new main building; ad-
jacent small cottages appeared much older. Off to the
right, comfortable sun lounges were arrayed on the
deck of an empty pool.

Norma slowly translated for them the sign over
the front door: "Morgenstern Hotel: Your Rest Our
Quest. Decent Rooms and Fine Dining."

"I certainly hope so," Julia muttered.

The front door opened, and Najila hurried down the

two stone steps to greet them. *"Marhaba.* Hello! Welcome to Nablus. I am Najila Danfi, and I am your tour guide." she said shyly. She nodded to her cousin standing behind the women. *"Marhaba,* Yousef. *Mumtaz?* Everything OK?"

"Yah, Naji," he replied in Arabic, "Everything's fine, but I'm going now home. My Sarah has fixed *baba ghanoush* and *kibbe.* She knows I like these after long drive, but she gets very angry if I am late. You pay tomorrow, *insha'allah, habibati.* Bye. See you, *Masallamah."*

"What did he *say?"* Julia whispered to Norma. "I wish he'd speak *English,* for heaven's sake!"

"I think," Norma answered quietly, "he said that Najila could pay him tomorrow, God willing, because his wife has prepared special foods: an eggplant dip called *baba ghanoush* and *kibbe*—little triangles with meat paste spread over bulgur wheat and baked—and she gets mad if he's late for dinner. Oh yes, *habibati* means sweetie; and *masallamah* means goodbye."

Overhearing them, Kay said, "Wonderful, Norma. We've just arrived, and you're already worth your weight in gold." Kay took a step back and admired Najila's black capri pants and olive safari jacket over a white polo shirt. She envied Najila's worn, leather sandals; they looked sturdy and comfortable.

"Come in, come in, please," Najila said cordially. "Everything is ready. You only need to sign this register. Then Mr. Hamid will hand round your keys, and you can go straight away to your rooms." She turned to Kay: "You are Mrs. Hunter? Your face is much younger than in your email."

Kay laughed as they all moved into the lobby. "Why, thank you, Najila. You're very kind. I needed that right now. Please, call me Kay. We're all friends, and you'll soon get to know us. So, please, use our first names."

Norma stepped forward, introduced herself to Najila in Arabic, then gently kissed her on both cheeks. Najila smiled broadly and returned the greeting. "I am most happy you speak Arabic, Norma. That will help me greatly." She looked around at the group. "I had planned for you to check in, then thought we would drive out to the well. Now I see you are hot; your journey was long, first on the plane and then with Yousef. Your faces look very tired, so I make a small change. You can have short rest, maybe shower, then we take our dinner at seven o'clock. We will meet in dining room, just near reception area. If you are still awake later, we can talk together, *insha'allah*."

"That will be perfect, Najila," Kay said. "I cannot *wait* to take off these wretched, new sandals and put my feet up for an hour—or two."

"Fine," Najila said. "Your comfort is much more impa . . . impo . . . ah, how you say . . . ?"

"Important?" Norma said softly.

"Yes, that's right, *important*," Najila said. "Thank you, Norma. I did study English in university, but I do not get many chances to speak it, so I am not always sure."

"Your English is wonderful, Najila," Norma said reassuringly. "In fact, it's amazing! You wouldn't believe all the troubles I had when I was first learning Arabic. It was always worse when I was nervous."

Najila flashed Norma a grateful smile. "Anyway, yes, your comfort is more important than my plans. We will see everything. No hurrys, plenty of time. There is bottled water in your rooms. Please drink much water; you will feel better. Your cottages all sit on the right side, just there behind the swimming pool, except for Mrs. Wagner. Mr. Hamid has given her a lovely cottage on the left side under the pine trees; it is bigger and cooler."

Julia beamed at Najila. "I'm Mrs. Wagner. How nice that *I'll* get a bigger cottage."

"If you have problems," Najila added, "please ask Mr. Hamid. He will look after you."

As the women gathered around the reception desk, Najila quickly got them registered. Mr. Hamid gave them their keys, and they made their way to their rooms. Kay watched the scene from the front steps. What an extraordinary woman Najila is, she thought. One look at our faces, and she knew exactly what we needed. How easily she changed her agenda, too. Incredible! I'm so glad I decided to come. This is going to be a terrific experience. I can feel it in my bones.

+++++++++

Key in hand, Julia viewed her cottage with disdain. The roof sagged gently, bits of stucco had broken away around the window frames, the screen door was slightly ajar, and wispy leaves nestled around the doorstep. Lord, help us! she thought. What have I gotten myself into?

Slowly she pushed the door open and surveyed the dreary interior. A rickety, painted, wooden table and a pair of worn, wooden chairs sat under the window. Two single beds, covered by thin foam mattresses, were at right angles against the walls. When she lifted a corner of the light blanket, a cloud of dust ballooned up in the late afternoon sunshine. She heaved her suitcase onto the nearest bed, igniting an even larger dust explosion.

Julia sighed. I suppose I can stay *anywhere* for four nights. Najila's probably trying to save us money, but honestly. This place is a pit! Maybe if I throw my robe over the bed, the dust won't be so bad. But I know my allergies will act up. I'll sneeze the entire night, and I won't sleep a wink!

She kicked off her sandals, slipped out of her damp clothes, and walked into the bathroom; where she took a quick shower and shampooed her hair. As she dried herself off, she wondered about the red light blinking on the water heater mounted in the corner. What if that was a recording device—some kind of special camera? She turned and made a face at the red light, then blushed and covered herself with her towel.

Barefooted, Julia padded to the bed, put on fresh

clothing, and finished off the nut bar she'd stuck in her purse earlier. She dug in her suitcase for her new, travel hair dryer. Edson, her sweet husband, had convinced her to buy it, telling her that is was very powerful and could run on both 110 and 220 volts. Plus it was small and easy to pack. She used a coin to turn the little dial to 220, walked back to the sink, plugged it into the wall socket, and switched it on. A small shock wave rippled up through her bare feet, her right arm, and across the back of her neck.

She jerked back from the sink. It's my heart, she thought. I'm having a heart attack. No! I'm being *electrocuted*! She turned off the dryer, bolted out of the door, and shouted at the top of her lungs: "Help! Help! I've been electrocuted! Help! Somebody help!"

As she raced up the path to the reception desk, Mr. Hamid came hurrying toward her, wiping his mouth and buttoning his tan suit coat. "Ah, Madam have troubles? Some problem?" he asked smoothly.

"Yes, Madam is having big, *big* problem," Julia shrieked. "I was trying to dry my hair at the bathroom sink; but when I turned on the dryer, I got *huge* shocks in my feet and in my arm—all these shocks just *raced* through my body. It was awful, *terrible*. I was almost *electrocuted*! My neck is still tingling. I'm *sure* I'll have whiplash."

"Ah, Madam, there, there. All OK. Only yesterday electrics man repair water heater in cottage. Maybe he forget to finish. Now *you* finished, eh? Ha, ha, ha, ha!" Mr. Hamid thought this little joke was enormously funny.

Julia wanted to slap him.

"Would Madam like to move to different cottage, perhaps new section?"

"Yes, Madam *would* like to move; and I will expect that everything will work perfectly. Is that understood?" Julia said sharply.

"Yes, of course, Madam. At once, Madam. I send maid to help move suitcase. Then I send electrics man to fix wiring, *insha'allah*. Come, come. I find nice, new room. Everything be perfect. Come, come, please."

In less than ten minutes, Julia was unpacking in a new cottage, while a smiling young maid hung fresh towels, opened the curtains, turned up the air conditioning, and then left.

In fifteen minutes, Mr. Hamid was back at the reception desk, assuring a newly-arrived guest that, yes, a room *was* available: very nice cottage, very good price. Please keep shoes on.

~7~
The First Supper

T he women were delighted with Najila's change
of plans. Hot and exhausted, most had showered and then fallen onto their beds for naps.
In her lovely, new cottage, Julia had enjoyed a relax-
ing bath, using the fragrant Dead Sea bath salts and
body lotion she'd discovered on the bathroom counter.
Things have a way of working out, she thought.

Just before seven, much refreshed and in casual evening attire, they all gathered near the dining
room. Kay, Alicia, and Vicky had come down earlier
to enjoy a glass of wine and the sunset from the pool
deck. Najila joined them a few minutes later and led
them all to a large, round table by a corner window.
Set for ten, the table was covered by a crisp, white cloth
centered by a low, crystal bowl holding miniature pink
roses encircled with lemon leaves. Kay noticed with
interest that at several other tables around the room,
other guests were speaking Arabic, German, Italian,
and even a little English.

"Please, ladies," Najila said, "come, come, our table
is this way. Mr. Hamid has placed us here, away from

other guests. We might even get some little breezes from the swimming pool. Please—choose your seat." As Najila stood next to the table, Kay introduced her to each woman as they sat down. When Najila had met them all, she said, "Mr. Hamid has arranged many fine local dishes for us. If you need help, I will explain. Now, please come to his nice buffet."

Ruth jumped up. "All *right* then. I don't mind being first. I'm *starving*. That little snack in the van didn't do much for me. Let's get going before those people in the corner beat us to the best bits. Come on, Corinne, hop in here behind me. Najila, this looks *great!*"

Quickly the women lined up behind Ruth and Corinne. A long, wooden table held a mouth-watering assortment of fresh salads, *tabouli* and *hummus*, steamed rice with pine nuts, fragrant platters of lamb, chicken, and beef, various sauces, dishes of tiny black and green olives, and baskets of warm pita breads. At the far end, bowls of fresh fruit stood next to rosewater pudding and *blanc mange*. A delicate, footed, silver tray displayed small cakes. After serving themselves, they found their seats. In between bites, the conversation really accelerated.

"Kay, great to see you. How are you feeling these days?"

"Najila, this is *delicious*. Please give my compliments to the cook."

"Vicky, how are your kids? Are you a grandmother yet?

"Corinne, you guys still in Nebraska?"

"As long as you're up, Norma, snag me another pita or two—just get the little ones, OK?"

"You still the tennis queen, Alicia? Are you into that new club, out by Caracalla?"

"Oh, Lord! Now I have *two* pairs of pants with spots on them; this tomato sauce will *never* come out. I am *such* a klutz!"

"Inez, are you still teaching at the girls' school?"

Seated between Vicky and Kay, Najila was happy to see the group enjoying themselves; things were going well so far. She felt self-conscious about her English, but they all seemed to understand her.

After they had all made at least two trips back to the buffet, Kay laid her fork down, carefully wiped her mouth, and turned to Najila. "That was a wonderful dinner. I want to echo Norma and ask that you give our compliments to the hotel chef. His mother would be proud of him tonight."

Najila smiled. "Thank you, Kay. I will absolutely tell him and Mr. Hamid. The new chef is young, but he tries very hard. Now, if you are all finished, we will move through to the seminar room, just behind those doors. There we will take coffee, tea, what you like. Come, come, please."

Arms around each other, they drifted into the larger room, following Najila to comfortable, beige, plush armchairs around a low, glass table. A light breeze floated in from the open door. The waiter brought tiny, baklava pastries filled with honey and chopped pistachio nuts, then poured coffee and tea. His assistant carried in a tray with ice water and glasses and set it on the table. Both men bowed slightly and then quietly departed.

When everyone was settled, Kay spoke up. "First, let me thank you, Najila, for all the arrangements you've made. Everything is just splendid."

Najila beamed. Julia sniffed but said nothing.

"It is such a joy for me to see you all again," Kay continued, her blue eyes sparkling. "I truly never thought we would all be able to reassemble ourselves, yet here we are. Najila has an exciting itinerary planned: many sites where the Samaritan woman might have lived or walked and even the actual well. As I mentioned in my second email, there will be time to tell your own life stories, if you wish. We never had enough time for this in our old study group, so we'll make time now—either during breaks or in the evenings back here. Wherever you are most comfortable. But feel no compulsion—this is only if you *want* to."

Consulting her notebook, she said, "I know this is only our first day. We've just enjoyed a wonderful dinner, and we're all tired. But I think we might share *briefly* what's happened to us since we last met. Though I've been in touch with all of you, some of you may have lost touch with each other. This will help Najila get to know us a bit, too. Then, at the end, she can tell us about herself and what she's planned for tomorrow, all right? Good. Then

I'll start.

"I left Rome a little over ten years ago. Due to very difficult circumstances, it took a while for me to get going back in the States." She paused, drew a deep breath. "Now I'm living in a small town near Seattle. I helped to reorganize our local library, I sing in a good community chorus, knit a great deal, and have a wonderful circle of friends. A few years ago, I had the dubious honor of being the first member of my family to have cancer. Following surgery and chemo, I'm now doing quite well. In the past, I've always had my life laid out. Now, I'm at a crossroads, unsure of my next step. I don't like feeling this way because I like things planned out." She colored slightly. "This is probably crazy; but my fantasy is to get a little camper, drive all over the West, and maybe start a reading program or something—while I still can."

Alicia laughed. "I can see it now, Kay—you zipping around the countryside in a blue RV, with 'Kay's Kamper' painted on a wooden shingle in the back window."

"You'll do it, Kay," Corinne said in her soft voice. "I know you will. I'd like to second what Ruth said earlier and thank you for arranging this trip. Everything is perfect! It's great to see you all again. Actually, it's like a miracle. I think of our group often. Most of the time, it was exciting to live in Rome while my husband worked there; but, sometimes, I felt out of it, you know, like the foreigner I was. So coming together in our study group every week helped me a lot."

She pushed a strand of red hair off her forehead. "Kay is always super organized and probably
wrote her thoughts down at home, but I'll just wing
it. When my husband retired in 2004, we left Italy
and lived in Nebraska awhile. First, I worked as a
secretary and, later, for the local police department on
their crisis intervention telephone hotline. Sometimes
that was hard—people had *so* many serious problems.
Even though I couldn't *see* them, I could *hear* a lot
that was going on with them by the tone of their voices
and not just by what they told me. Don't know how
much good I did—mostly, I just listened, would say
maybe one or two things. Lots of people said it made
them feel better, just to talk. Anyway, now that we're
in South Carolina, I teach religion classes for kids at
our church, ride my bike around town, and swim every day. What else? Our kids are grown, have started their own lives, my husband has recovered nicely
from some recent surgery, so everybody's fine. When
they're happy, I'm happy. As Kay knows, I'm also a
cancer survivor. Things are good for me right now,
though. Julia, how about you?"

Julia looked grim as she slipped another baklava onto her plate. She spoke very rapidly. "I'll
keep it brief because I am *so* ready to get some sleep.
Some of you might remember that I had cancer earlier, too. When Edson retired in 2002, we left Rome
and moved to Phoenix. At my yearly physical, my
new doc told me I *now* had diabetes. *What?* How
rotten was *that*? I was so upset! I mean—my diet is
fine! I still have a problem with my weight, but I'm

very careful about what I eat. When we first moved to Phoenix, I tried to go back to teaching; but it just got to be too hard. All that blood-sugar testing, taking the meds while I was at school, you name it—it was just more than I could handle. Plus, I think the stress of being in a new situation kept my blood numbers permanently off the charts. Then that young doc had the *nerve* to tell me I should exercise more. I did for a while, but my back hurt *all* the time. I was finally forced to stop. It's easy for him to say—*he* isn't the one with the sore back. Now that I'm a bit more stabilized, I volunteer at a local museum and as an adviser for my college sorority. Our daughter and son-in-law live close by, and both have good jobs. In today's lousy economy, that's saying something, isn't it? After hunting around awhile, Edson and I found a church with, you know, the kind of people we like. So that's enough from me. How 'bout you, Ruth? Ruth ... hey, Ruth ... you awake?"

Ruth yawned and stretched. "Geez, I must have nodded off. Sorry. But these chairs are great, and I'm *dead*. Dinner was outstanding, Najila. I totally pigged out, but who cares? I loved every *bite*. Anyway, I'll cut my spiel short; you guys are beat, too. Oh, yeah, before I forget, I got an email from Beth just two days before I left home. She's crushed that she couldn't make the trip—said she waited as long as she could to see how things were going; but, because her knee surgery isn't healing right, her doctor said she couldn't come. All the walking we'll be doing would kill her knee. So she sent me her story as an email attachment;

email attachment; I'll read it to you along our way. She didn't want to mess up Kay's plan for the assigned verses from the Samaritan woman's story. Nice, huh? She also stuck in a couple of photos. She looks super—sharp as ever—and sends you all her love.

"Anyway, back to me. Pete and I did the same thing when we moved back to the States in 2005, Jules, because the right church home is a biggie for us, too. Once we got settled near Louisville, since I was almost fifty, I went back to work for United for a few months to get my retirement bennies. Now I'm doing animal rescue work at a local shelter. I think God's given me a special gift of mercy. Animals are so grateful for whatever you do for them—unlike some humans I could name. And, let's see, Pete and I go to concerts, plays, and touring Broadway shows. I'd love to start doing community theater again myself, but I never seem to find the time."

Her expression grew wistful. "I still miss being a flight attendant. I *loved* that job! It encapsulated everything I needed in life: traveling to different cities, the uncertainty if we were rerouted, the camaraderie with the crews, chatting with passengers, feeling pretty in my uniform—you know, the whole thing. But you all remember how Pete is—he made me quit."

She glanced out the window at the darkening sky. "Ah, well, life goes on. I've found a neat doctor who's got me on some new medication for the old depression crap. I had a handle on it for a good long while; but, a few years ago, it came back to bite me in the pants. Some days are good. Other days, I'm *totally* whacked out. But, hey, I'm here tonight; so I'm happy." She saw Kay steal a glance at her watch. "Sorry. I didn't mean to blab my brains out. Alicia, over and out."

Alicia coughed, cleared her throat, and took a sip of tea. "I'm trying to quit smoking—not very successfully, as you can see. I grew up playing a lot of sports. So when our kids were still at home, I coached most of their teams, ran several adult tennis leagues, and did the whole jock bit. It was great because I could eat whatever I liked." She laughed and ran her fingers through her thick, blonde hair. "But, two years ago, I had foot surgery, which left me unable to do any serious exercise including playing tennis. I felt myself getting really fat and frumpy. Thank goodness, my foot's better now; although it still swells on occasion. I'm back to playing tennis moderately, and I've also become crazy *mad* about gardening: I've done a lot with the international garden club.

"We've been in Rome for ages. The kids are in college, though; and my husband's getting close to retirement. So we're looking for our next landing place. It'll be a radically new life, which is exciting but scary. So I'm weighing my options. When I was a kid, I wanted to go to med school. I'm probably too old for that now, though. I've also considered getting back up to speed in the computer world; I used to be a pretty decent systems analyst. Or maybe I'll open a greenhouse—I'm not sure. I'll get back to you as soon as I know," she said with a laugh. "Your turn, Inez."

Just then, Mr. Hamid glided over to Najila. "Madam wishes anything? More coffee or tea? Some sweets? Chocolate-covered almonds, nice, new box, very delicious."

"Yes, please, Mr. Hamid," Najila said. "Bring the sweets. Beg pardon, Inez. Now is your time."

"*Gracias*, Najila," Inez said slowly. I am *thrilled* to finally be in the Holy Land, especially with you, my dear friends." Kay loved listening to Inez's thick, Spanish accent that colored her amazing command of English. Inez's dark brown hair was shorter now, but her warm smile was the same.

"Like Alicia and Beth, we are still in Rome," Inez said. "For some years, I taught English in several different schools. Right now, I teach Spanish and English at a private girls' school. Some of the girls are hoping to study in England, America, or Spain. A few come from difficult backgrounds and are not well prepared, so we all must work harder. I want to give them what you gave me in our group—a feeling of worth. Some girls do not get that much at home. My two daughters are doing very well in junior high and college, and my husband likes his job. We are thinking to build a house." She looked down, a little unsure of herself. "I also have a dream of doing something different, maybe studying for a counseling degree and then starting a program for young women. Nothing is definite, but it runs in my head a lot."

She took a sip of coffee, then set her cup down. "It

seems that many of us are like the Samaritan woman. We have had problems, but we have moved forward. Now we are ready for another change. I think many surprises will come on this trip. Maybe that is why we are all here." She turned in her chair. "Norma, how are you?"

Norma stifled a yawn then pulled an elegant, copper-colored, silk shawl around her shoulders. Her face was very pale. "Oh dear," she said nervously, "what should I say? Oh, OK. I know. After we left Rome in 2003 and found a house in Cincinnati, I did some elementary school teaching and worked in my garden a lot. I love my flowers. Maybe that comes from my farm-girl background. Thank goodness, I haven't been back to that farm in thirty years! But I *have* moved seventeen times to different job assignments with my husband. Oh, and I have lung cancer. My doctor told me he didn't know how I was still breathing and that I certainly shouldn't take this trip, but I told him that I *was* going. Oh, and Julia, I *totally* understand what you've gone through with your diabetes medications. My chemo treatments usually gave me some trouble at first. Plus, each time, my hair grew back a darker red. I like it, though. I have a great collection of headscarves as well."

Julia looked chagrined. "*Each* time? Lord, how many chemos have you *had*, Norma?"

"Just three," Norma replied cheerfully, "but I'm one of the lucky ones. I'm still chugging along. Oh, my sofa's seen a lot of me the last five years; but, when I felt OK, my husband and I traveled a good bit. I also taught classes in my

church and gave talks to kids about life in early Rome.
I still love teaching little kids. Oh yes, and I help with
a cancer support group, too. So that's me. Your turn,
Vicky."

Vicky popped a chocolate-covered almond into
her mouth. "Yum. Well, let's see. When my husband,
Jack, was transferred eight years ago, we left Rome
and moved back to the States. Even though I majored
in theology and church history, nobody's paying much
for that these days; so I worked as a paralegal for a
while. Then I took a few years off to write a novel."

"A novel?" Julia said, as she wiped honey off
her fingers. "That sounds like a lot of work. I'd never
have the discipline. What's it about?"

"Long story short," Vicky replied, "it's about Theodora, the almost-last empress of the eastern part of
the Roman Empire. She looks back at the good old days
at the end of the Empire around the mid-sixth century.
She was the wife of Justinian, the last major emperor.
She died around 548 AD, after living the high life of
great wealth and glory. But, get this—she started out
as a real low-life, a circus dancer! Can you imagine?
Then she became an actress and a courtesan—things
no nice girl ever did. But it worked for her. She was
gorgeous and smart—had all the right stuff—and finally ended up as the emperor's wife. What a woman!
But she also had a lot of abandonment issues, though
they didn't call it that in those days. Even at the end
of her life, people kept leaving her. Finally the empire
was gone, too. The working title is *Theodora's Mir-*

ror."

"How exciting!" Norma said breathlessly. "Is it published yet? Where can we buy it?"

"Well, no, it's not published yet," Vicky replied. "I didn't quite finish it because I went back to the law profession. Our kids had started college, and we needed the money. I'll get back to the book someday. In spite of some serious health challenges, our daughter is now married and has a darling baby. Our son is finishing college. Like the rest of you, I'm thinking about what else I'd like to do with my life. It may involve teaching church history classes in a parish somewhere or more writing. Maybe I'll figure out a way to combine the two." She shrugged and smiled. "I'll just have to wait and see what turns up."

"Thank you, Vicky, that was wonderful," Kay said. "You were *all* wonderful. And we did that in just under fifteen minutes. Now we'll hear from Najila, who's been sitting here so patiently, listening to us all."

"Can I go to *bed*?" Julia whispered. "I'm *so* tired."

"Geez, Jules, hang on for another *second*, will ya?" Ruth hissed. "She's our *guide*, for crying out loud."

Najila straightened her jacket and tucked a lock of hair behind her ear; she felt rather fluttery. "*Marhaba*–hello. My name is Najila Danfi. Again I wish to welcome you to Nablus and Samaria. When Mrs. Hunter, uh, Kay wrote, asking about my tour, I was nervous and had many worries. But, after meeting you today and hearing you now, I am more relaxed. We are from different countries

but are very alike: all women, with some few bad
things but many good things, too. We will have fine
times together these next days.

"I see your heads bowing, so I will talk quickly.
I am Samaritan, born in Jifna, a small village near
here. I grew up in my parents' home, studied at Jifna schools, and married soon after graduation from
Bethlehem University, also close by. We lived first
with my husband's family then bought our own house
in Nablus. I taught school for young students. My
husband was a brilliant surgeon, a fine man. We had
no children, but we had seven happy years together.
Then, one day, he dropped down—no, how do you say,
oh yes—*collapsed* from an embolism. That was very
hard for me." Najila paused and looked away.

"But slowly, slowly, I got some better. After two
years, I sold the house, moved to a nice flat across town,
and taught middle school English for fifteen years.
Then I needed a change. So I stopped teaching, sold
that expensive flat, and bought a small house right
at the edge of Nablus. I took a big chance, opened a
souvenir stand at Jacob's Well, and, later, started my
tour company. My mama thinks I am crazy, but I *love*
my new life. Now I do what *I* want." Najila looked
around at the group and smiled. "Your eyes say you
are very tired. Breakfast begins at seven, then we
join here at nine o'clock to hear some bits about the
Samaritans. Later, we will visit the well and Sebastia National Park. We go slowly, take our time. Now,
please have some good sleep.

"I have a small surprise for you," she said with a twinkle, "but I shall save it for morning."

~8~

Meeting the Samaritans

Kay was pleased to see that—following her instructions—all of the women were wearing slacks, had finished breakfast before nine, and were assembled in the seminar room, ready for their first outing. She checked to see that their backpacks or totes contained water, sunscreen, and sun hats; most also had cameras.

Najila hurried in with Mr. Hamid. Trailing behind him, the waiters carried trays loaded with small white cartons. "Good morning, ladies," Najila said, smiling. "Mr. Hamid asked his kitchen staff to pack small boxes, so please take one. Jet lag makes you hungry at funny times. These boxes have only some breads, olives, a small apple—nothing to melt or spoil in the hot sun. We shall take our lunch here at one o'clock, so these are just some bites. Please, help yourself. Then I will tell you a little about the Samaritans."

The women quickly filed up. Each took a snack box, then returned to their seats. When the trays were empty, Mr. Hamid shooed the waiters back to the kitchen.

"I hope you slept well?" Najila asked.

Ruth gave Najila the thumbs-up sign. "Like a rock." Julia rolled her eyes.

Najila leaned against the round table at the front of the seminar room. "I want to tell you about Samaritans, so you will understand why the meeting between a Jewish man and a Samaritan woman was so unusual. I will give just the main facts, but it is nicer to sit here in this cool place—not stand outside in the hot sun.

"Long ago, about 1000 BC," Najila began, "David was king in this land. Then came his son, Solomon; his kingdom was even larger and finer than David's. Solomon had great wealth from trading and taxes: four thousand stalls for twelve thousand chariot horses, a grand ivory throne in his palace, and five hundred thousand workers to build the great Jerusalem Temple. It is said that he had seven hundred wives and three hundred concubines. Besides much wealth, Solomon also possessed much wisdom."

Alicia laughed. "He needed it to deal with all those women!"

"Yes, but it is also written that many foreign wives from other countries brought their gods and religions with them, turning Solomon away from God. His troubles grew. After Solomon died, his son, Rehoboam, and others, fought harshly; so, by 925 BC, Solomon's kingdom split into two parts: Judah in the south, Israel in the north." She paused for a sip of coffee.

"You know," Norma said thoughtfully, "the same thing happened when my neighbor died. His two daughters argued so much over their inheritance—who was going to get the furniture, the house, the dog and all—that they had this *terrible* falling out. Now they're really hateful and hardly speak to each other."

Najila nodded. "Exactly, Norma. That is *exactly* what happened, only worse. Built around 870 BC, the city of Samaria became capital of kingdom in the north and grew *very* wealthy. The southern people in Judah called all northern people 'rebels.' So Samaria was then capital of the northern 'rebel' territory." Najila's eyes shone. She loved recounting this history; but, as she glanced around the room, she saw a few heads nodding.

"I will move quickly. The north and south kingdoms were divided again and again and were finally captured by strong Assyrians; many people from the south were deported to Assyrian lands. It is said that Samaritan people descended from those northern Israelites who stayed behind. Assyrians then brought pagans or non-Jews into northern lands; there was much mixing of cultures, religions, and families through business, intermarriage, etc. This happened many times, first with Assyrians and Babylonians, then with Greeks and Alexander the Great."

"It sounds like the area slowly morphed into half Israelite and half pagan," Vicky said.

"Yes, exactly," Najila said. "Then several big things happened to create even more troubles. When Judahites—from the south, remember?—returned after their long exile in Babylon, they wanted to rebuild Jerusalem and the big

Temple. Many Samaritans offered to help, but Judahites said no. They called Samaritans half-breeds and unclean dogs and said that Samaritan blood and religion were impure because of contact with pagans. Things fell downhill from there. Southern Jews got very angry around 400 BC when Samaritans built their *own* temple on Mount Gerizim, near here. They got even angrier when Alexander the Great came with more colonization, foreign gods, and more new ideas. Jews in Jerusalem worried that their culture and religion would be lost. Around 128 BC, a gang came out from Jerusalem and destroyed the nice Samaritan temple. Relations got worse until Jerusalem Jews wanted *no* contact with Samaritans. The easy route from Judea to Galilee went straight through Samaria, took only two-three days. Yet most Jews avoided Samaria completely and journeyed the long way round."

She paused and looked at her watch. "Back then, town wells were 'women's space'—men did not go there. Also, men did not talk to women outside of the close family circle. A Jewish man would *never* speak to a Samaritan woman, *never* accept food or drink from her. This is why Jesus' meeting with the Samaritan woman was so unusual. OK. Enough. *Halas*—finished. I will say more as we go along. You will remember better when you see the actual sites, *insha'allah*."

"Great!" Ruth declared. "Thanks, Najila. You've really got that history stuff down. Sounds to me like Jesus and the Samaritan woman were two people in the wrong place at the wrong time."

"That was *fascinating*, Najila!" Kay declared.
"I now have a much clearer idea of everything that led
up to the meeting at the well. You're *still* a terrific
teacher, my dear, if you can hold the attention of this
group for ten whole minutes at this early hour. Now,
since we'll be going out to the well soon, I've asked
Corinne to do something a bit unusual. Corinne,
you're on."

Corinne came to the table carrying a duffel bag.
"Kay and I thought it would be fun to read the story
from John 4 as a little playlet before we see where it
all happened. It's easy because John wrote it in such
a dramatic style—Jesus and the Samaritan woman
are in the foreground, the disciples in the middle, and
the townspeople in the background. Plus there's lots
of dialogue, even different scenes. To make it more
authentic, I brought along a few fabric remnants to
help you feel more like the characters." She opened
the duffel bag and pulled out pieces of colored cloth.

Julia's face grew very red. "Oh, I could never do
that!" she blurted. "I'm no Meryl Streep, for heaven's
sake! Do I *have* to?"

"Hey, as long as it doesn't involve makeup,"
Ruth said, with a laugh. "Mine was perfect this morning, so I'd hate to mess it up."

Corinne smiled. She'd heard all these objections before. "Julia, because you speak *extremely* well, I'd like you
to be the narrator. I have this *special* blue fabric for you.

Kay, Ruth and Norma, you can be the disciples. I have brown and beige pieces for you because you're always on the dusty road. There are also some bits of cording you can use for belts. Alicia and Vicky, will you be the townspeople? I have bright, striped pieces for you because you were merchants, tradesmen, etc. Here's more cording. Inez, I'd like you to be the Samaritan woman. Here's a big piece of green cloth for your robe and a smaller, beige piece for your veil. And, Najila, you can be Jesus—your accent is perfect—so here's a big piece of dark brown cloth and some cording."

The women were quick and creative with the small fabric remnants. These were not *real* costumes—just an impression, a suggestion. Despite a few more complaints, even Julia got into the spirit. Some draped the piece over their shoulders, some tied it around their heads, and others around their necks. Inez deftly arranged her larger piece as a cloak, with the smaller one over her hair, partially covering her face, like a veil. "I've seen this done before," she said.

"Now, if you'll just group yourselves," Corinne instructed, "in the right order: narrator, Jesus, the Samaritan woman, disciples, and townspeople. That's good. OK, here are your scripts. Before I left home, I made copies of the text from my Bible and highlighted your lines. You'll find your character's name at the top right. If I were doing this for a kids' class, I'd probably type it out like a regular script; but this'll work. You guys are all smart. Hmm, Julia, since you'll carry the story along, I want you to stand up in the *front* here; so everyone can *see* you. That's it, perfect. After all, *you're* the one who keeps the action rolling. I'll be the prompter; and I'll be right behind you, if you need me. Just read slowly, and you'll be fine. OK, everybody ready? Lights, camera, action! Take it away, *Julia!*"

And, so, for the next eight minutes, the women read their parts, tentatively at first, then with growing conviction and expression. Slowly, they were transformed. They *became* the characters in the story at the well. As a town merchant, Alicia mimed selling cloth to Vicky; as disciples, Kay and Norma argued among themselves; and as the Samaritan woman, Inez spoke boldly to Najila. After the townspeople, Alicia and Vicky, read their final verse: "'It is no longer because of what you said that we believe, for we have heard for ourselves, and we know that this is truly the Savior of the world,'" there was total silence.

Julia sighed, laid the script on her lap, and pulled the blue fabric tightly around her.

Finally, Ruth spoke. Her eyes glistened with tears. "*Awesome*, Corinne. Thanks."

"You're welcome. And Norma, thanks for collecting the fabric and the scripts. Perfect."

Najila stood up. "Thank you, Corinne. It was exciting to hear the story that way. It became lively for me. Now, please gather your things. You will find the ladies' room near the hotel front entrance, and my van is outside. We shall leave in ten minutes. I will tell you my surprise out by the well, *insha'allah.*"

　　　Norma smiled at Julia. "It means 'God willing.'"

~9~

Surprising Sapha

N ajila parked across the street from Jacob's Well, in the shade of several pine trees; the sun was already very warm. When they got out of the van, Vicky and Norma took photos of the beige, stone wall surrounding the ancient well site. To the right of the entrance, a small, faded sign in English, Hebrew, and Arabic revealed that this was Jacob's Well and also a Greek Orthodox monastery. A hand-hewn, wooden door in the wall stood partially open.

The group followed Najila through the door and into a small, cobblestone courtyard shaded by olive trees, oleanders, bougainvillea, fragrant, white jasmine, and grape vines. Tall, red cannas and pink roses offered luxuriant color, a welcome contrast from the gray dust on the road outside the walls. Behind the fronds of a small palm tree, a low, stone fountain splashed with cool water.

"What an oasis of peace this place is," Norma said as she sniffed a tiny rose.

Opposite the entrance, the skeleton of a tall, half-finished church rose at the rear of the courtyard. Blue, metal scaffolding showed that work was ongoing. The roof and walls were in place, as well as a rough altar table under what would become the central, cross-shaped window. A few wooden benches were scattered behind the altar.

In front of the altar, two small, white, concrete structures stood about eight feet apart in the center of the church, like miniature guardhouses. Each roofed structure was about four feet wide by ten feet high and had an arched doorway that provided an entrance to stairs leading down to the actual underground well area, twelve feet below the surface.

Najila gently urged them forward. "Come, come," she said, "we must go down to the well before other tourists make it too crowdy, ah, no, *crowded*. When we come back up, we will find a shady spot to sit. I will tell my little surprise."

They followed Najila through one of the arched doorways and carefully descended the stone steps down to the well. Kay had to catch herself to keep from slipping on the mossy steps. When they got to the bottom, they saw that they were in a shadowy, crypt-like room. It was cool and smelled damp. The only illumination was from ornate, hanging, brass oil lamps and a few bare bulbs dangling overhead. "This is like a *time* warp," Alicia whispered. As her eyes adjusted to the dim light, she glimpsed beautiful, sacred icons hanging on the rear walls.

And, then, there it was. In front of them was Jacob's Well, *the* well where the Samaritan woman had met Jesus. Norma quietly moved next to Kay and gave her a little

hug. "This is so *exciting*." she said softly. "I feel like
the Samaritan woman or even Jesus himself might
walk down those steps this very *minute*."

Around the well opening was a small, raised,
stone platform that supported a wrought-iron framework; at the top of the frame was a large hook and
pulley. A length of coiled rope ran through the pulley;
the end of the rope was tied to an ordinary, galvanized
metal pail.

Julia sniffed. "Would you look at *that*? Not even
a nice silver pitcher—just some old, beat-up bucket.
Honestly."

"Actually," Vicky murmured, "that's probably
pretty appropriate."

As they gathered around and peered down into
the well, a gray-robed monk emerged from a dark corner. Using the metal crank, he carefully unwound the
rope, lowering the bucket. He then reversed the pro-
cedure, drew up some water, poured it into a footed,
stone container, and nodded to Najila.

Norma was wide-eyed. "Why, that's just like
the big flowerpot I bought at Home Depot last month."

Najila gestured toward the well. "Please, take
a drink, ladies. You may use that small cup there
on the corner of the platform. The well water is very
pure. Local people call it *living* water and say it is
quite healthful."

Julia made a face. "Eeww! I'll bet we wouldn't want
to know what's living *in* that water." She took the cup from
Vicky, looked into it without drinking, then passed it to

Inez.

As the others were having their drink, Najila softly shared some history about the site. "Already in year 333, a traveler called the Bordeaux Pilgrim identified this well because it was very close to Joseph's tomb. The Pilgrim wrote of a large Byzantine church built over this well, cross-shaped, with the four sides like four points of compass. Crusaders later rebuilt the Byzantine church and enclosed the old well in a crypt under the main high altar. Sadly, that church was destroyed in 1187. Parts still make up the crypt or lower level—where we stand—of the unfinished Greek Orthodox church, begun in 1914—what you see in the courtyard. This well is over one hundred feet deep and still flows."

Slowly, they moved around the small space, studying the icons. After they had taken photos of one another by the well, they reluctantly made their way back up the steps.

Ruth blinked and looked around as she came out into the sunshine. "Totally *awesome*! I can't *believe* I just stood by the same well and drank the same water as Jesus did. Too much! Hey, isn't that your stand over in the corner, Najila? Could we have a few minutes to do some shopping? I want to pick up a little gift for Beth; I know she'd love something from here. Kay and I will see her in Rome on our way home."

"Yes, no problem. My helper is looking after the shop today. She can show you what you like."

The women walked to the corner and clustered around Najila's stand, eager to buy postcards, small bottles of well water, and maps of the area. Ruth bought a replica of a small, ancient, clay water jar for Beth and then took a photo of Najila holding it, with the other women gathered around her. Somehow, the familiar act of shopping brought them back to the twenty-first century, after their profound experience down at the well. Vicky hugged herself, awed by the biblical significance of what they'd just seen.

When Najila observed that they were finished, she led them to benches shaded by grapevines. "We shall take a small rest here, and I will tell you my surprise. You know now that Samaritans are very old and isolated peoples. Even today, many still use the same language and writing as our ancestors did thousands of years ago. Maybe you also know that in the last fifty or sixty years many ancient scrolls were found in caves around this area." She paused and smiled. "Our family has owned a similar scroll for centuries."

Najila's eyes were sparkling. "In 1939, my grandmother, Najet Danfi, made a new copy of this scroll, a document originally written by a first-century woman at a time of great trouble in our country. This woman said she had met a Jewish man called Jesus at Jacob's Well—here. Her writings were copied by ancestors of our family, all professional scribes, around 200, in 725, and in 1615. There was again violence here in 1939; so my Gran made a new copy, just in case. She hid her notebook in a small bag and,

later, gave that to my mother. Last December, Mama
gave the bag to me for safekeeping; I put it away in
strongbox in my wardrobe. I became busy and did not
think about it." Najila blushed slightly. "Happily, I
saw this box six weeks ago, on the same day as Kay's
first letter arrived. I thought to make an English
translation for you; my professor at Bethlehem University helped me. He is British and was *very* strict;
he corrected me endlessly! First I did a word-for-word
translation, and then he suggested better ways to say
things. I worked very hard to get everything right.
You would like to hear some?"

"Oh, my *word*! Yes, of *course*," Norma said excitedly. "What a gift! What a *wonderful* surprise!"

Najila then read her grandmother's introductory notes—about the finding of the parchments, who
wrote them, and about her transcription. "I should go
on? You are tired?"

"Good heavens, no!" Kay exclaimed. "Please go
on, and don't skip a *thing*. This is *incredible*!"

Najila smiled. "Because my Gran Najet made
the copy, I love it. I will go on, but please tell me when
you have had enough. Here is what Sapha, herself,
wrote":

> Time is short. From my window, I can see
> smoke billowing up. A neighboring village
> is set alight. I thought I would have more
> time. My eyes and nose tell me otherwise.
> Ah, but my hands. It is painful to write
> after so many years of weaving and tying

knots.

My name is Sapha. When I was a girl, my father trained me as a scribe for his business. Thank God my nephew, Moussa, is now here to write when I cannot. He is young, but he forms his letters carefully.

My small house stands halfway up on Mt. Gerizim, our holiest place, normally so quiet and peaceful. But now, in this thirteenth year of the reign of Nero, there is great unrest. I fear we are heading towards revolt. Two days ago, Hala, my neighbor, told me that young Jews are raging through the countryside, angry because of unbearable restraints and taxes. Last week in Jerusalem, Gessius Florus, that brutal Roman procurator of Judea, brazenly stole temple funds, then imprisoned and crucified Jews who objected or resisted.

Troubles break out in Galilee to the north, in Judea to the south; roads are never safe. Hala says Roman troops pour out of Caesarea, across the plains of Samaria. They destroy our villages, farms, and fields, as they head down to Jerusalem. Caesarea is a beautiful city. How can such ugliness come from there now?

And we Samaritans? We are caught in the middle. Again. Always. What will these young men, from both sides, do when they reach Jerusalem? How many will fall in the fighting? All their mothers will weep when they get that news. Will this ever stop? Will it be worth the cost? The young men do the fighting; but when the battles are over, the old men sit round the table, do the talking, make the agreements. Why can't they talk first and avoid the dying?

Enough of my musings. The smell of smoke grows stronger. I am afraid. I have waited so long to tell my story of meeting a Jewish man at our well. I can wait no longer. I want to tell who he was, what he did for me, for my people. He was so kind, so gentle, knew so much about me. He seemed like a prophet, perhaps even the Messiah. Ah, if only he were here now. He would know what will happen to us.

That day at Jacob's Well, the midday sun was scorching. I approached alone with my water jar, and there he sat. When he spoke, I knew. He said...

Najila paused. "There is a break in the writing; but then, it goes on."

My nephew, Moussa, some neighbors, and I are now safe in a cave above Sychar. The village elders demanded that we leave our homes on Mt. Gerizim. Fighting continues below us; houses and fields are burning. Not ours yet, but perhaps soon. I can't bear to look.

I will continue the story started before I have to run

from my house. I will tell about my meeting with a Jew named Jesus at our well many years ago. I learned from his followers later that they had all been with him in Judea, where they were baptizing; and he was getting more disciples. Since the Pharisees had heard this and objected, Jesus thought it best to leave and return to his home in Galilee. He chose to travel through Samaria, something no Jew ever did. Being tired because of the long journey, he stopped at the edge of our town, Sychar, by the well that Jacob had given his son, Joseph. Jesus' disciples went to buy food in the village.

I had walked slowly out to the well to get water for our household. The sunlight was blinding, and it was very hot. My robes were pressed to my body. As I walked, I thought about my life, my future. I was so unhappy. It was all so different from my childhood. My early life in my parents' house was calm and peaceful; ours was a happy home. In spite of being born a girl, I was cherished by my parents. Nothing from those years could have prepared me for all that I would face, all that I would lose. That day, I felt I was drowning in sorrows as my life overflowed with heartaches, separations, and losses.

Through death or divorce, I lost five husbands; so I lost my homes and possessions. I became very poor. I buried four babies. They were so small; I held them only a few hours. Each time, it was harder, more painful. Before I met Jesus, the house where I lived was not my own, nor were the children I looked after. I had no children, no sons. Without husband or sons, I counted for nothing. I was a Samaritan, a woman, many times married, and I had no sons. I was nothing.

Then he spoke to me. He asked me for a drink. Imagine: a Jew, asking me, a Samaritan, for water, for anything. I was astounded. He just said, 'Give me a drink.' There were no rude remarks because I was a Samaritan, no sly glances because he might have heard about me, just 'Give me a drink.' He needed a drink, and I could give it to him. In spite of all I had lost, I still had my water jar. I could give him some water; I could still share that. I could have chosen to turn and walk away, fearful of this man, of what he might think. I did consider that. But I was so astonished by his question, his asking me for a drink, that I chose to stay, to give him the water. What he told me later was to change my life."

"There is much more in this notebook," Najila said, "and I will read you small bits as we visit other sites." She looked around at the group. "As I mentioned, in ancient times, the town well was a gathering place for women, to meet friends, share troubles, and tell stories. Today, we are all friends, we sit at Sapha's well, hear her story. As Kay said, maybe you will want to tell your story, too. Now we shall take a break, walk around, have some snacks. No need to rush. We have plenty of time today."

Kay's heart was racing. But do I? *Do I?*

~10~

Water is Life

While Norma snapped close-ups of the roses and jasmine, some of the women wandered around, studying the church interior. Others sat on the benches behind the church altar and ate from their snack boxes. Julia enjoyed one of the nut bars she'd tucked into her purse for emergencies.

Kay sat on a low, stone bench beneath the grape arbor; tall roses bloomed behind her. She felt such a kinship to Sapha; they had both experienced so many losses. Now she sensed an overwhelming urge to talk, to get a few things out—things she'd never spoken aloud to *anyone*. Talking about her personal life was difficult for her, but this seemed like a good time. She *had* considered this when she'd made the trip plans and had even jotted down a few notes, so as not to forget. She'd assigned herself the first few verses in the biblical account of the Samaritan woman before she'd written to the other women. She opened her snack box, nibbled a fragrant, lemon biscuit, and waited.

"Najila I can't *believe* all this stuff!" Alicia exclaimed, as they strolled back and sat down near Kay. "I'm totally blown away, not only that your grandmother transcribed it, but also that Sapha wrote it in the first place. It's just *incredible*."

Najila nodded. "Yah, it was a big surprise for me, too." She took a sip from her water bottle and recalled her own excitement when she'd first read Sapha's words. She'd felt *so* proud, thinking that maybe Sapha was actually her ancestor. Now she was sharing her words with these women. Gran Najet would be *so* pleased. Najila was pleased, too. Things were going well, and she felt happy. If only her mama could feel the same.

Kay picked up a fallen rose and nervously plucked off a few petals. "Najila, I was so moved by what Sapha wrote, where she said she had had so many losses and felt she had nothing to give. That fits me perfectly. Since this is such a beautiful place, I'd like to tell my story now if you don't mind. Do we have time?"

"Yah, there is plenty of time," Najila replied. "We have all morning here. I would like to hear your story, Kay."

Kay turned to Alicia. "Would you ask the others to join us? We've all shared so much in the past. Now is no different." At Alicia's wave, the women returned to the benches and looked expectantly at Kay.

Kay drew a deep breath. She couldn't *believe* what she was about to do; this was *so* unlike her. She *never* unburdened her soul to others; her generation just *didn't*. Her mother had always said that dirty laundry and family matters were best kept at home. But now it was time.

She squared her shoulders and sat up straight. "Ladies," she said, "remember when I said that, during this trip, we could share our life stories if we wished— that it would be just like old times, only we'd have more time? I'd like to tell my story now, in this lovely place. Feel free to stop me to ask questions or make comments."

Julia rolled her eyes. She fiddled with her shirttails and shifted nervously on the bench.

"Ooohhh, Kay," Ruth said devilishly, "you're gonna tell us everything, like when you were a rotten little kid, and then grew up, and had boyfriends, and all that mushy stuff? All *right!*" The whole group burst into laughter.

"Well, yes and no. I'm going to tell the important parts of my life's story, but I reserve the right to be selective," Kay said primly, relaxed now. She smoothed out a wrinkle in her lightweight, denim slacks and patted her face with a small, lace handkerchief. The smell of the roses on the wall behind her was intoxicating; she could hear the little fountain bubbling in the corner. Slowly, something began to rise and break loose in her heart.

She smiled. "You'll not be surprised to learn that I first made notes and then wrote down every word of my story at home. It's always been important for me to get things right. But after the little play, then hearing Sapha's actual words, I see that every last detail of my life isn't important. But a few threads *are.* So, for the first time ever,

I'm going to wing it."

"Yayyy, Kay!" Alicia said as she waved both hands.

Kay laughed. "Most of you know that I'm an intensely private person, and it's hard for me to speak about my feelings. But after hearing from Sapha, about her life and losses, I want to, no—I *need* to. The first verses from Sapha's story in John's Gospel fit me perfectly: 'It was about noon. A Samaritan woman came to draw water. Jesus said to her, "Give me a drink."'

"We're all here," Kay said, as she looked around the group, "sitting by that same well, and it's almost noon. Back then, Jesus sat down by this well and asked the original Samaritan woman, possibly an ancestor of Najila's, for a drink of water, nothing more. We know the rest of the story: What started out simply, quickly grew into something much more. My life's been like that too.

"When I was preparing for this trip, I studied the Samaritan woman's whole story at some length. I noticed that verses four to twenty-six were between Jesus and the woman, verses twenty-seven to thirty-eight were about the disciples, and verses thirty-nine to forty-two were about the Samaritans. But the Samaritan woman is even mentioned there, too. Do the math, ladies. While the others rate only three or eleven verses, she gets *twenty-two*."

"Kay, you're too *much*," Ruth said, laughing. "Only *you* would think to count those verses."

"But that's important," Vicky affirmed in a serious tone. "Women just didn't *get* that kind of coverage in most biblical stories. That's telling us that something out of the ordinary is happening."

Kay nodded. "Thank you both. I also observed that there were no miracles—no healings, and no raisings from the dead. Jesus just asked her for a drink. It never even says she *gave* him one. Then they had this incredible conversation about water and worship. Later, of course, there's the part about discipleship. I want to focus on the first part where they just talked with each other. The most important things seemed to be the idea of living water and that Jesus accepted her just as she was. Plus, he didn't criticize her about the five husbands; and she didn't apologize. Then she was so excited, she *had* to spread the word—maybe this man was the *Messiah*."

Kay's blue eyes grew bright as her words flowed. "His words, his acceptance and his affirmation were like cool water on a hot day for her. They transformed her, gave her courage, made her believe in herself, and gave her a new life. I want to tell you who has done that for me."

Everyone, even Julia, leaned forward slightly. This was a *new* Kay.

"The first person to give me real affirmation was my dear grandmother, my father's mother. You see, in order to attend a better elementary school, I lived with my grandparents in town during the week for the first and second grades. My mother, a former teacher, thought our little country school wasn't good enough. She was determined that I was going to have the best education available in our area. I was *delighted* to have my beloved grandmother all to myself then. Grandma Caroline was everything a grandmother should be: a kind, loving woman. My years with her are my most cherished childhood memories.

"When I got a bit older, I returned to the country school. Since my brothers and I were all born two years apart, my mother was very busy with four children under eight, plus helping my father run our farm and stockyards near Centerville, South Dakota. She was also very strict. Her parents were hard-working Presbyterians and had instilled in their eight children a strong work ethic, the value of education, and the importance of family.

"My father was an only child and an easygoing man. As children, we could always count on his support. Now that I am an adult and a parent, I realize how difficult it was for my mother to be the primary disciplinarian. My mother loved us and was affectionate, but she was very strict. We all adhered to her rules and schedules. There was only one way to do things: *hers*." The remaining rose petals fell, crushed from Kay's hand.

"No wonder you're such a stickler about timing," Alicia said. "You learned all that from your mama. But, hey, being punctual is not a bad thing."

Kay nodded and brushed away a fly. "Being the only girl and the oldest, I looked after my younger brothers a great deal. As each of us grew old enough, it was expected that we would begin to assume certain duties of running the house. My parents were certainly believers in equality, as there were no 'boy-jobs' or 'girl-jobs' in our home. Each of us made our own bed, cleared the table, washed or dried the dishes, dusted, ran the vacuum cleaner, weeded the garden, or mowed the lawn.

"When I was eight, my dear Grandmother Caroline died suddenly. I was *inconsolable* for weeks. Some time later, Grandpa Joe moved to Clearlake, in western Washington, to be near family. He persuaded my parents to join him. So when I was ten years old, we moved from Centerville to the Pacific Northwest. I can't remember feeling sad about leaving the farm. In spite of all Mother's rules and the frequent tension between my parents and Grandpa Joe, I would call my childhood happy. My parents were quite strict, but they weren't harsh. We all knew we were loved. Even though there wasn't much money, our parents provided us with toys and sports gear that the entire family could enjoy: equipment for basketball, volleyball, softball, croquet, and even archery.

"We had such fun on Sunday afternoons playing board games together, listening to radio programs and eating popcorn and homemade ice cream for a light Sunday supper. Mother had taught high school music before she married and had private voice and piano students after marriage, so there was always music in our home. We often had sing-alongs on Sunday afternoons. Because my parents remained close to family members, I grew up knowing my aunts, uncles, and cousins on both sides; we've stayed in touch through letters and reunions. These contacts gave me a deep sense of family continuity, an important foundation for my later life."

"Do you know how blessed you were, Kay?" Vicky murmured. "Strict or not, at least your parents were *there*."

"Yes," Kay said. "I realize that now. Plus I had good church training, as my grandparents and parents were members of the Congregational Church. As we grew, my brothers and I became active, too. We attended Sunday school, sang in the choir, and were in youth groups. Our church life was an extension of our home life, really. I loved it. My parents entertained friends from church with children our ages; often those kids were schoolmates also."

She walked over to a blue, metal gate nearby and gently tapped the thin iron rods that tapered to sharp points at the top. "Then things began to change. My relationship with my mother started to deteriorate as I entered adolescence. I had always been very independent, and my mother and I met *head-on*. It was a terribly traumatic time for me. I felt guilty over the chasm developing between us. I felt like I was losing her; or, at least, our relationship. I felt *awful*."

"Well, of *course* you were independent, Kay," Julia said, as she finished her nut bar. "You *had* to be, because you were doing all that stuff: tending your little brothers, doing chores around the house, your schoolwork, and church activities. All that took independence."

Kay nodded. "Still, I'm sad that my mother and I never really became friends. I have a great deal of admiration for her because of all that she accomplished: graduating from college and becoming a teacher, in spite of the difficulties she encountered, like losing her mother at seventeen. However, she was also very controlling and was quick to express her disapproval in very strong terms if my behavior did not come up to her expectations. There was *never* any room for error."

Julia sighed heavily.

"Do you s'pose," Alicia asked, flipping her hair off her neck, "that because your dad was pretty lenient, she felt she had to be even tougher?"

"Perhaps," Kay said, as she came back and sat down. "Or she found it difficult to accept the fact that I was growing up—was not a child any more. I really don't know. Whatever, it made life *very* stressful for me. During this time, I did not question anything I had learned during my religious schooling. I continued to attend church and the youth group and to sing in the choir. After I finished college, I married Howard Hunter. Even though I soon knew it was a mistake, we managed to build a reasonably pleasant life for nearly five years."

"Was he your mama's choice," Inez asked gently, "or did you marry him against her wishes?"

"He was *not* her choice; and, as to the other, I have often wondered. At any rate, at that point, our son, Chris, was born with a severe heart defect. No one who has given birth to normal, healthy children can ever know the *extreme* stress that a child with a physical defect places on a family. Howard and I had the anxiety of not knowing from day to day whether our child would live or not plus the pressure of astronomical medical bills. It took so much time to care for him—to make sure that his medications, his food, and his activities were right—and I was usually the one who did all that. Our daughter was born three years later, and she didn't understand all the attention her brother received. She told me later that she didn't realize the severity of his problem until she was in her *twenties*."

"Aiyee . . . ," Najila said sympathetically. "How very sad for you all."

Kay looked somber. "I struggled with the question every parent asks when this happens. Why *me*? What did I do wrong that brought this plague upon my child? Many people, trying to be helpful, offered the usual cliches: 'God does not give burdens to those who can't handle them.' or 'God has his reasons. We don't know why, but we shouldn't question him.' I grew angrier and angrier when people said these things. I did *not* believe God had his reasons, and I didn't think that I was able to bear this burden more than anybody else!" Her voice rose sharply.

"Howard wanted nothing to do with organized religion; but I was attending the Congregational Church in Tacoma, where we were living. The minister of that church was a wonderful man and teacher who helped me to understand that the people who made these hurtful remarks were basically kind and truly meant well but just didn't know what else to say. Like me, he did not believe that God sent burdens to selected people. He also helped me to discern that questioning 'why?' was healthy."

"What wonderful gifts!" Norma exclaimed. "He gave you hope and understanding."

"Absolutely. So when Howard and I eventually divorced, I again leaned on this same minister for guidance. Since Howard refused to seek counseling, there was not much the minister could do except to offer me support in whatever decision I made."

Ruth's face was a sea of emotions. She spoke haltingly. "You were lucky. A little help can be a lot of help. Still, that had to be a *really* hard decision."

Kay nodded. "After the divorce, I found it very difficult to live on my own and support two young children. I worked as a school librarian in the Seattle area and eventually got my master's degree in library science. There were still *huge* medical bills. By and by, with a lot of fortitude, Chris finished college in western Washington and found a good job. He was actually the one who encouraged me to apply for the position in Rome—because the salary and the benefits were good, and he knew I'd enjoy the travel. He was able to work for a number of years, but then his health problems increased."

She paused and took a deep breath. "Most of you know this next part, but Najila doesn't. So I'll tell it all. At the time, I was employed in an international school library in Rome; but I returned to the States because Chris's health was deteriorating. His medical problems were so overwhelming; he had to struggle each day just to get around and to breathe. Our doctor said that surgery was not possible. I *knew* that. I didn't want him to suffer so, yet it was agonizing to see him slipping away. Chris's death was so traumatic for me! The pain was actually physical, and I was severely depressed for months."

Ruth slipped her arm around Kay and whispered, "Depression is horrible. Believe me, I know."

Kay nodded, then continued slowly. "We all expect our parents to precede us in death, but things are *totally* out of sequence when our child dies before us. It's just not supposed to *happen* that way. Over the years, I've had many opportunities to examine, test, or reject my beliefs; and I firmly believe the worst disaster that can befall a parent is the death of a child. Chris lived to be thirty-three years old. His death, all those years ago, is still a painful memory." Her voice was choked, and her eyes were bright with tears.

"Then there was my own reaction. I had never experienced depression before, so I didn't know what was happening to me. After weeks of insomnia, horrible crying jags, being angry all the time, feeling useless, worthless, and incredibly sad, plus having no appetite for food, friends, or activities, I knew something was *very* wrong with me. I finally went to my doctor; and, after listening carefully, he explained to me that I was depressed and why. He prescribed some medication that slowly helped."

She sighed and studied her hands. "But, you know, I've often wondered: Was there something *else* I could have done? If *only* I'd sought a different doctor, if *only* I'd been more agressive on his behalf, perhaps Chris wouldn't have died."

"Oh, Kay," Najila said gently, "I asked myself a thousand, no, *million*, times why I left our house, went to my teaching job the day my husband had his embolism. Did I not notice his pale face that morning? If *only* I had stayed home or insisted that he rest at home instead of going to his office. For many months after his funeral, I made myself crazy asking those questions. Finally, a friend said that we cannot, no, we *must* not stand in the way when God calls. That seemed very hard at first; but, slowly, I found consolation."

Kay wiped her eyes and nodded to Najila. "Then the losses started mounting up. In the two-year period following Chris's death, first Mother died, and then two of my nephews died of AIDS. I still do not believe that God sent these burdens to me and to my brothers and sisters-in-law. But the losses were devastating. There were just so *many* of them, so close together. Had I done something for which I was being punished? Probably not; but, oh, it *felt* like it! In those dark times, I felt so lost. I didn't know where to turn with my pain, grief, and my anger. It was almost unbearable." Tears were rolling down her cheeks. Ruth handed her a tissue.

Silently, a yellow butterfly settled gracefully on a rose next to Kay's head.

After she regained her composure, Kay blew her nose and smiled ruefully. "Like that butterfly, slowly I began to come out of my cocoon. Gradually, I was able to accept the love and caring that came through my family and friends. Over time, I let go of the grief and began to find a little joy. It seemed to take forever. But, somehow, it happened.

"I have often thought of Job and all the disasters that befell him, yet he never wavered in his belief. I can't say that I never wavered in my belief, yet I *do* know that there is a Higher Power that helps me find answers for the questions I have. It isn't always what I want, nor do I always recognize the answers to my prayers. It isn't always in the time frame that I want. However, when I am still and quiet and not trying to solve everything myself, often the answers come. That's living water. I *know* it."

Najila reached quickly in her bag for the notebook. "Kay, listen."

I met Jesus at one of the very lowest points in my life. When we first began to talk, I knew he was a Jew because of his speech and his robe. I came to the well at noon hoping only to find some quiet. But I found much more. I realized his acceptance of me as a woman and a Samaritan. We weren't even considered 'real' Jews even after all we suffered when the Assyrians came. I know the stories about the things our people lost then, how hard it was to be sent away from all they had ever known. They said it was even harder to come back, start over, and not be accepted by the other Jews. But Jesus didn't care that I was a Samaritan woman or that I'd had five husbands. As we talked more, I realized he knew everything about me. All those things that had bothered other people didn't seem to matter to Jesus. He just wanted a drink, and I gave it to him. He gave me a new life.

"You know," Vicky said thoughtfully, "for centuries, writers have criticized the Samaritan woman, calling her everything from a 'fallen woman' to a 'five-time loser.' They were all wrong! She was just like *you*, Kay. She had so many losses! She came to the well wanting only peace and quiet, but *look* what she *got*. She met *Jesus*!"

Kay smiled. "It took me a long while to recognize the help and the new life I was being offered. I feel much better now, but I still need time alone to talk with and listen to God. Each day I make time to walk by myself—to think about things that are troubling me or problems that I am facing. The combination of exercise and time for quiet reflection often give me a solution I hadn't previously considered. The answers that *don't* work are because I rush in with my own solutions. It's my lifelong struggle for complete control, but listening to and heeding God's word is essential for me. Alas, those lessons do not come easily; nor are they always remembered."

Just then, an old Greek monk shuffled out of the blue gate. After raking up the dead leaves and flowers that had fallen by the wall, he slowly bent down and collected them in a torn burlap sack.

"That's me," Kay said, "always tidying up, always trying to control everything. How futile and what a waste." She looked at her watch. "I know everyone's ready for lunch, so I'll finish up quickly. I used to be reluctant to talk about personal problems, and I always felt uncomfortable when someone else started airing theirs. But I know that friendships deepen when you care enough to share experiences. Someone else may have an insight that has eluded you.

"For instance, I attended a grief group for people who had lost someone close and dear to them. It was led by a professional grief counselor who, herself, had experienced the trauma of her mother's murder, a crime as yet unsolved. When she shared that at our first session, everyone visibly relaxed. I realized that we were all more at ease with our grief because we found others had the very same feelings. We had *all* experienced the pain, no matter whether the death was a spouse, a sibling, a child, or a close friend. Losing a person, or even a pet, that you love, causes the same feelings. It was the *sharing* and then the acceptance that enabled us to move on."

"And that's so comforting, isn't it?" Vicky said.

Kay took a bite from her lemon biscuit. "After my cancer surgery and the chemo, I sat down and evaluated my life. Cancer makes you do that. It's a *huge* catalyst. I realized that the beginning of my life was really quite good; and, in spite of the bad things in the middle, I have it in my power to make the last third good also. So I looked at where I'd been, where I was, and where I still wanted to go. Then I made a decision.

"I'm at a crossroads, but I am not going to stay there. I'm going to move on. Therefore, I won't focus on what I *don't* have—my losses or my medical problems—but rather on the things that I *do* have, that I *can* do. I want to spend my energy doing things I love, like reading, library work, singing, knitting, and traveling. I especially love spending time with good friends like you because you all give me so much affection and understanding." Kay's blue eyes twinkled.

A sharp gust of wind shook the branches over their heads, causing leaves to cascade down around them. Kay laughed. "What did I just say? All that poor monk's work for nothing! Maybe that's the real point of Sapha's story: Many things *are* beyond our control; but no matter how many losses we have, we can still do something nice for someone—find somebody new who needs love. We can pass on the same caring we received, once we let go of our grief and *our* agenda. So, that's it, dear friends. Thank you for your patience."

Julia shook her head. "Gee, Kay, that wasn't so bad,

after all. And here, all this time, you always looked so organized, so *together*. Yet you've had *lots* of problems ... just like *me*."

"That took you only twenty-two minutes and four seconds, and you never checked your watch *once*," Ruth stated briskly. "You're really lightening up." Kay smiled her thanks as she bent to pick up the rose petals around her feet.

"*Shukran*, oh, I mean—thank you, Kay," Najila said. "I will never forget what you said about not staying stuck and that we should do things *we* want. Now I want to eat. We will take our lunch then have a rest. Later, we will drive to Sebastia National Park to see a palace, the Temple of Augustus, a big tower, and the Roman theater. We will return here again, *insha'allah*."

As the rest of the women stood up, Ruth leaned close to Kay. "So, were *you* the one who initiated your divorce? What was *your* last straw?" Kay recognized the pain in Ruth's eyes. "Yes, and I'll tell you later. Come see me after lunch."

~11~

Sebastia Park

The women filed out of the courtyard behind Najila, climbed into the van, and were soon on their way back to the hotel. They were quiet as they pondered Kay's story. In the front seat, Kay felt more relaxed than she had in months. It was as if she'd washed away a huge burden of sadness there at the well. How long had she been holding onto all that? she wondered. Far too long.

Najila pulled into the hotel lot and chose a shady spot for the van. Although they proclaimed they weren't hungry, the group did fine justice to the lunchtime buffet. Naps were on everyone's agenda; even Najila put her feet up and dozed a bit in a staff room.

Shortly before four o'clock, they reassembled in the reception area, refreshed and eager, then headed outside to meet Najila at the van. She looked cool in olive green capris, an orange shirt, and a bright orange sun hat. "Hello again, ladies. Your rest was pleasant, I trust? Jet lag is hard. First day is fine; but on the second day, one needs sleep. Now we drive out to Sebastia National Park, only six miles or so. This is one of the biggest tourist sites, so we will take time, go slowly—half today, half tomorrow, OK?"

After they found their places in the van, Najila turned to them. "All buckled up? Then we go." She steered the van carefully out onto the dusty road. In the front seat, Vicky took videos of a small flock of sheep as they passed the turnoff to Mount Gerizim. In the back, next to Julia, Corinne said quietly, "I know I've told you before, Julia; but I want to say again how much I really appreciated all you did for the club in Rome. My job was easy because you left everything so well organized." Corinne had succeeded Julia as secretary of the International Women's Club when Julia had moved back to the States.

Julia beamed. "Well, ah, gee, thanks, Corinne. That's sweet of you. Most people don't bother with such niceties anymore."

From the driver's seat, Najila spoke loudly. "Behind us, several roads come together—the road from Jordan Valley, the road to Sebastia National Park, and one other—to make a big crossroads. Centuries ago, all cities were built near important roads, with good water supply, and up fairly high. These things all gave good defense against enemy attacks. All three are here."

We're at a real crossroads, Kay thought. I love it.

"This whole region," Najila continued, "is called central highlands. Now we pass by Mount Ebal at right, Mount Gerizim on left. Perhaps you can see the community of Kyat Luza on the lower slopes? A small group of Samaritans live there. Mount Gerizim is almost three thousand feet above sea level and seven hundred feet above this valley we drive through. The Samaritan temple, built around 400 BC, was on top. We will drive up to see the ruins in a day or so." She swerved around a donkey cart. "Good—traffic is light today."

Norma laughed and pointed to the donkey's hennaed mane. "Look! His hair is the same color red as mine. And past him, those terraced hillsides, with little olive trees and grapevines and that old man trimming them with that curved blade thing—why, it's just like in the *Bible*."

"Yah," Najila said, "the gound is very rocky here, so farmers use what land and tools they can. Perhaps it still looks like first century. Sapha might have seen those same things, too."

After passing the small Arab village of Sebaste, they turned into the entrance of the Sebastia National Park. Najila circled several times until she found a space under a large palm tree. As they all got out, she said, "If you need them later, restrooms are over there, just behind that big, wooden platform. I will buy our group ticket at the kiosk near the gate then meet you at the platform in some few minutes, OK?"

Corinne and Ruth were whispering and giggling together as they climbed out of the van. "Here, let me take that second tote," Corinne said. "You don't need to schlep everything yourself."

"I've *got* it, girl," Ruth said. "Just be sure you've got

all the props in your bag." From her smaller tote bag, Ruth pulled out a floppy, turquoise sun hat and clamped it firmly on her head.

Vicky followed the group up the six steps of a large, new, wooden platform. "Wow! Terrific overview of this whole place!" she exclaimed. Laborers could be seen in several areas below them, digging, hauling, and mounting stones; hammering was heard in the distance. A thin haze of dust lay over the entire area. Another group of tourists passed by near the platform; Norma heard bits of German, Italian, and Arabic. There was obviously a great deal of international interest in this site.

Soon Najila joined them. She moved to the far edge of the platform and pointed to a distant spot. "The old Roman stadium is over there, but it is closed now for maintenance. We can look from here. It was built during time of Herod when Samaria was a big Roman city. Many races, games, and other events were held there. Six hundred and fifty feet long, and two hundred and thirty feet wide, it lay outside city walls. You can see a few columns still standing.

"Now we go down and take a short walk. We stop first at Palace of Israelite Kings, also called *Beit-Omri* or House of Omri Palace. Then we pass by Temple of Augustus, look also at big Hellenistic Tower from Greek times, then take a rest at Roman theater. By each place, I shall tell you a bit of history. When I talk too long or you are tired, please give me sign, OK?"

They followed Najila off the platform and down a path, gradually climbing a small hill to the palace ruins. "Here is our first stop. This big pile of rocks and rubble was once a very large palace, started in 880 BC by King Omri. First he buy, no, sorry—*bought* this hill from Shemer. The name then became *Samaria*—first for the city, then the whole area. After Omri died, his son, Ahab, made more construction. Perhaps he wished to impress his wife, Jezebel—yah, famous Jezebel. She was a very fine and fancy Phoenician who brought worship of her own gods with her. Archeologists have found over two hundred beautiful Phoenician ivory fragments here: statues, throne decorations, and much more."

Najila took a sip from her water bottle. "Other kings gathered even more wealth; there was much luxury up here. Many Old Testament prophets later complained that kings worshiped idols, forgot about God of Israel. Look in the books of Isaiah, Jeremiah, Hosea, Amos, and Micah. You will find harsh criticism of Samaria. The large city surrounding here was destroyed and rebuilt many times. Local people were invaded, occupied, or deported by Assyrians, Babylonians, and Greeks. With so much destruction, rebuilding, and shuffling of people in and out, some Samaritans married foreigners. Later, Israelites in Jerusalem called those people half-breeds and unclean, said they were not *real* Jews, wanted no contact, would *never* eat or drink with them. You can see why Jews would not go through Samaria by Sapha's time. Now we will walk to Temple of

Augustus."

"Incredible!" Vicky declared. "I thought I knew something about Old Testament history; but seeing it, *standing* on it, I can almost hear all those voices talking to us. I feel the rumblings of another story— maybe something that took place earlier than my first book."

"Hey," Ruth said brightly, "you could do a prequel to *Theodora's Mirror*—call it *Jezzie's Belles*, or something—make it one of those saga deals that run over many generations. You need ideas? Just ask me. I'm *loaded!*"

Najila laughed. With a wide sweep with her arm, she gestured to more ruins of the same, silent, sandstone near the palace. "Later, Herod the Great changed the town name from Samaria to Sebaste and built a very big temple, both in honor of Emperor Augustus. Part of the palace next door was discovered under temple foundations. Of that temple, now only a few columns and this large staircase are left–only these fourteen long, wide, stone steps."

"Very impressive," Julia said, as she climbed slowly up the stone steps. "Herod was into looking good, making the big splash, the right guy in the right place. This must have made a *spectacular* grand entrance for old Augie."

Norma and Corinne laughed and snapped photos as Ruth swanned dramatically up and down the steps. "Stairway of the stars!" she said. "Ya know, I'll bet even back then there was probably some poor slave who ran up these stairs when he shouldn't have and got clobbered—the wrong guy in the wrong place. I'll also bet that some engineer worried himself sick about column strength, cost overruns, and construction deadlines when this joint was built. Now look—the only things left today are the front steps. Wonder what I'll leave behind?"

They backtracked on the same path until Najila turned off the path then led them up another small hill. "This is the Hellenistic Tower. Originally, a large wall surrounded the palace, ending just there." She gestured with her foot. "During Greek or Hellenistic times, this wall became the foundation for the tower, which was built later. This tower still in fine condition; construction was very good in those days. Come, now I show you *best* ruins in park. Then we will stop for a bit."

"Not a moment too soon," Julia said with a groan. "My knee is *killing* me! I've just *got* to sit down." As she limped a few yards further, she saw that the path curved and opened to the remains of a small theater built into a hillside. The seating area was bordered by olive trees and small, scrubby bushes, while piles of rocks and broken column pieces lay scattered to the right and left. Julia noted that the center section of seats and the open stage area had been cleaned and repaired.

Najila stood under an olive tree near a tier of stone seats. "Since you are here for the Samaritan woman, I will usually show you places she would have seen. But this theater was built a little bit later, in the third century after Jesus. Like most big Roman cities, Samaria had its theater. Look—here original seats survived; others, over there, were restored in this century. Fine people sat here, in lower sections up front—these fourteen rows of seats—with narrow aisles to divide them. Cheap seats, standing areas, were up there, against the hill. Now we will take a rest under those shady olive trees. I *love* to sit there," she said shyly, "and dream about early plays. This is my favorite spot in the *whole* park."

Ruth looked around. Would this work? she wondered. When Kay had written her earlier emails, telling them they could share their life stories during the trip, Ruth had been very apprehensive. She didn't want to tell them *anything*. How could they ever understand what it had *really* been like at her house when she was growing up? Oh, sure, years ago, she'd told Corinne and Kay a little about her past, but not the other women. She didn't want them to know how messed up she *really* was. Who needed to rake through that old stuff anyway? She was so over all that.

But a few weeks ago, when she'd been leafing through her family photo albums, intending to get them organized, an idea began to take shape. Why not tell the highlights of her story and make it more fun by showing a few photos of the important people and places in her life? That could work. Carefully, she'd removed some photos, put them in a plastic folder, and stuck it in her suitcase. When Najila had mentioned this morning that they'd visit a Roman theater, Ruth had dug out the folder and thrown together a few simple props to tell her story like a play.

She loved being dramatic. Besides, doing this might take her mind off her worries, as in, what to do about Pete. She hadn't slept well for weeks; her stomach felt like she'd swallowed a brick. She was going to have to come to a decision soon. Talking to Kay after lunch had helped some; but, still, she wasn't sure. She wasn't quite ready to decide yet.

Ruth glanced around again. There were shade, benches, and even an old wheelbarrow jammed behind a tree.

Perfect. It was the right place; and she was the right person.

Finally.

~12~

If You Only Knew

W hile the group found seats and arranged themselves on the shady rows, Ruth had a quick
word with Najila. A few curious tourists wandered into the stage area, stared at the group briefly,
and then hurried off, eager to get back on their air-
conditioned tour bus. Ruth beckoned to Corinne, and
they walked under the olive trees. As Corinne held
the tote bag, Ruth pulled out several articles of clothing, a piece of white fabric that looked suspiciously
like a hotel bed sheet, a magazine, and the thin, plastic folder.

"Hey," Alicia yelled from the third row, "what
are you guys *doing* over there? Will this be a major
production?"

"Cool it," Ruth shouted back. "Najila just
agreed that I could do my story like a little play, and
Corinne's my stage manager. Relax and chat with
each other for a minute 'til we're ready, OK? Pretend
you're hearing the overture, like 'Helloo, Ruthie,' or
something."

"I just wish they'd hurry up," Julia mumbled. "It's
so hot! I'm dying! These stone seats are so bumpy and

hard on my back." She opened her tote bag and took out her water bottle and a nut bar.

Soon Corinne came onto the center stage area pushing the dusty green wheelbarrow; a rough board was laid across it. "We wanted to roll out one of those broken column chunks so Ruth could sit on it, but no way. Even those little pieces weigh a *ton*. Luckily, this wheelbarrow was parked over there in the weeds. We'll get it back by nightfall." She bowed and exited stage left amid much clapping and whistling.

Quickly Ruth entered, carrying the magazine and the plastic folder; she laid both in the wheelbarrow. She was dressed in an old, white shirt, rolled-up jeans, and white sneakers with crew socks. Her hair was pulled into dog ears by two red scrunchies; she looked about fifteen.

"While the rest of you guys were napping this afternoon, Corinne and I were working this up. Najila mentioned earlier that we were gonna visit an old Roman theater, so I thought it might be a good place for my story. But, man, the setup here is beyond my wildest dreams! Some of you guys know that I used to do some little theater stuff in Rome; but I was usually just an extra—part of a crowd scene. Now's my chance to do a solo act and be a star, so I'm going for it." She made a little bow then picked up the magazine.

"In her email, Kay asked me to talk about verses nine and ten of the Samaritan woman's story. That's the part where the disciples are in the background, going off to buy food. You know, some goat cheese and pita bread, maybe a little jug of wine—stuff like that. Jesus and the Samaritan woman are in the foreground, by the well. Jesus said that if she'd known the gift of God and who he was, she'd have been asking *him* for the water. Then there's that line: 'Jews do not share things in common with Samaritans.' Najila told us why Jesus shouldn't be asking a Samaritan for a drink. Then he says if she really knew who *he* was, she'd be asking *him*. Say *what*?

"That really rang a bell with me because, as a Samaritan, Sapha probably *always* felt like an outsider, somebody who didn't belong. Yet here was Jesus, not only talking to her, but also being the one who spoke first. And get this: Her answer was a question—'What? You're asking *me* for a drink? Get *real*. I know the rules, the laws, what you people think of us, how you avoid us, even going around our territory, and taking the longer route. I know I'm not OK, not good enough. You're a Jew and a man; I'm a Samaritan and a woman. You people even think all Samaritan women are unclean from *birth*.' Yeah, Sapha knew all that stuff."

"Wonderful commentary," Vicky observed dryly. "The Bible—according to Ruth."

Ruth laughed loudly. "Thanks. I thought it was pretty good myself. Anyway, this all fits me perfectly because there's so much stuff *wrong* and out of place. Most of those folks in the story didn't know who or what Jesus was. I sure wish *I'd* known who he was and what he was offering me earlier in my life. I could have used a little living water back then," she said with a sigh. "But after hearing Kay's story, I realized that I *did* have some, a lot actually, only I didn't recognize it. So all day, I've been thinking about it. Now I'm gonna *show* you. Pretend that this," she said as she held up the magazine, "is my family photo album. I took the most important pictures out so you can see them better. They always say a picture's worth a thousand words, anyway. I'm gonna do my story in three acts. Since Kay's probably already timing me, Corinne's gonna hold up her hand as a one-minute warning when I need to finish an act. We're a good team. Oh yeah, feel free to boo and hiss whenever. Ready, Corinne? Hit it."

Corinne ran out, held up a sign that read, "Act One," then hurried off.

Ruth perched gingerly on the wheelbarrow board, crossed her legs, and prayed she wouldn't tip over. "This is a low-budget show, no program or anything; so I'll just give you a little background about my family. My parents were both from Michigan: My dad was born in Detroit and my mother in Grand Rapids. Here's the first photo: Dad was in his early twenties—Mr. Devil-May-Care, good-looking, lots of dark, wavy hair, a canary yellow convertible, a good gypsy violinist, and a daddy's boy. I'm pretty sure he ran around with women and stuff."

"Woo-*hoo!*" Alicia yelled. "What a fox!"

"I don't know too much about Mama," Ruth went on, "because she died when I was only nine. I *do* know that, before she married, she worked as a nurse at a local hospital. Here's Mama in her white uniform. Look how slender she was." Ruth held up the second photo.

"And so pretty," Norma added sweetly. "I remember those pointy nurses' caps. My aunt in Pittsburgh had one of those." Julia rolled her eyes.

"Here's the third shot, of my folks when they were wed in a Presbyterian church in Washington, DC, in 1947. They were both thirty-three." Ruth held up the next photo and grinned. "And here's Mama, holding me a year later. Wasn't I just the *cutest* little peanut? I was the baby boomer, born in 1948, in Detroit, in the section of town where the Slavs live: Polish, Hungarian, and Czech. My brother came along the next year, then a sister in 1951, with our youngest sister arriving in 1954. Mama had me when she was thirty-four and my youngest sister when she was forty. Here's Mama with all of us," Ruth said, as she held up another picture.

"Poor thing! She looks exhausted," Corinne said from her seat in the first row. "I've got a photo of my mom with about seven of us kids, and her face looked *just* like that."

Ruth laid the pictures in the wheelbarrow. "Yeah, well, having four kids in six years took a toll. Mama had rheumatic fever when she was a girl, and her heart was weakened on account of that. Maybe having the four of us ran her heart down even more. I remember her often saying, 'Ruthie, Mama's got to go lie down.' Her heart would begin to flutter, so she'd have to rest. Her doctor told her that because of her enlarged heart, she shouldn't have kids; but she had me, anyway. Then he said she shouldn't have any more. But back then, in the late forties, early fifties, things were different. And she had the other three."

Ruth glanced up at the hillside behind the theater; the sun was beginning to set. "I still remember my mother as being the most loving woman. The other kids in our neighborhood often came over to get chocolate milk 'cause their mom didn't buy any; mine did. She was always nice—never yelled at them–they loved being there. Billy, our paperboy, even came to her for some counseling about whether he should go to college or not. She was never too busy to listen to any kids, no matter how tired she was.

"Without a shadow of a doubt," Ruth said with a big smile, "Mama was the first person to teach me about what love meant and who God was. Every night, before I went to bed, she would be with me as I said the 'Now I lay me down to sleep' prayer. Mama also took us to Sunday school every week while she went to the adult classes. Some people from the church had offered to come by our house and pick us up. Here's the four of us kids one Sunday," she said, as she held up another picture.

"My dad would grump around in the kitchen in his underwear with a cup of coffee, readin' the Sunday papers. Meanwhile, we four little kids would be runnin' around, screamin, jumpin' on the bed, and fightin' while my mother was tryin' to get ready. Then we'd all go to Sunday school.

Her favorite hymn was 'The Old Rugged Cross.'"

"No wonder!" Julia declared. "She had *plenty* of them."

Ruth laughed. "Yeah. Well, anyway, our church was pretty fundamental and conservative; it was a small branch of the mainline Presbyterian Church and was very evangelical. They were always having revivals and altar calls, begging people to walk down the aisles and accept Christ as their Savior. Once, in Sunday school, our class even had a contest on who could memorize the first chapter of Genesis from the King James Version. I drove myself, studied day and night. I was the winner, the *only* one who did it. Seemed like a big deal," she said proudly.

"It *was* a big deal, Ruth!" Vicky said. "That's a really long chapter. Yayy for you."

Ruth chuckled. "I know you find this hard to believe, but I was a very sensitive little kid. I cried very easily. Even then, I loved animals and would fall apart, crying hysterically, on a summer day when there would be a storm and baby birds would blow out of their nests. I would bring them to Mama, wanting her to take care of them. I was also a very serious student—studied like a maniac. Even when I played, I was always trying so hard to win that I never had much fun."

Her expression grew wistful. "But, you know, I don't think Mama had a lot of fun either. I kept her diaries after she died. In the last one, she lamented a lot about my dad who sometimes told her she wasn't much of a wife. He'd have these long periods of silence—wouldn't talk to her for, like, two weeks. He'd just go around like a thundercloud, grunting answers. I used to think he suffered with melancholia—you know, as a young guy being Mr. Flash; and then having four kids, never making much money, etc. Maybe it was even worse, like maybe he was depressive."

"At my house," Alicia said grimly, "that was called a hangover."

"Yeah, well, later he had plenty of those, too. But here's what else I think: that it was tough for my dad, with four kids, to put food on the table, pay the bills and stuff 'cause he was a self-employed optician. See, first he worked out of our basement but later bought a little cinder block building about a mile from our house. Even though he worked hard, there was never much money at our house. Here's a shot of his shop," she said, as she showed another photo.

A warm wind swirled the ancient dust behind the wheelbarrow, while a chattering group of desert sparrows sifted through the underbrush, foraging for crumbs. Ruth nibbled at a hangnail, sighed, and then spoke very softly. "My mother died suddenly while we were getting ready to go to Sunday school on March 17, St. Patrick's Day, 1957. I heard this big thud. We were usually pretty rambunctious, so I thought that maybe one of the little kids had slammed their head against the wall. But I had this feeling.

"I went looking for my mother. When I went into the bathroom, there she was, on her back on the floor, with her head resting up against the bathtub. She was breathing heavily, and her eyes were open. I didn't know it at that time; but a blood clot had formed in her heart, then broken off, and gone up to her brain. She died en route to the hospital. That afternoon, when my dad came back from the hospital, our next-door neighbor was there, comforting us kids. I didn't really understand what was happening. My dad came into the room. With a big sigh, he said, 'Ruthie, Jesus took Mama to heaven.' Those words will always, *always* ring in my mind. All I could say was, 'Who's gonna take care of us?'"

"How terrible!" Najila whispered. "You were so young to lose your mama. What then?"

Ruth's face was drawn. "Well, after that, everything was kind of a blur. Though I was only nine, I can still remember the funeral. So many people came 'cause everybody loved my mother. And there I was, trying to rein in my little sister, Betsy, who was only two and a half. She was running all over the funeral home, racing around in her little pink dress and patent leather shoes. As the big sister, I was trying to make her behave. I don't think I cried much. I just kept asking 'Who's gonna take care of us?'"

"So, who *did* take care of you?" Alicia asked gently.

"Well, at the beginning, my dad looked after us as best as he could; but there were a few years when we were left on our own an awful lot. Some of those years are pretty hard to recall; but I do remember that my life got very difficult, very quickly."

"Uh-huh," Vicky muttered. "I know that song."

"Summers," Ruth went on, "my dad would take us kids to his optical shop. We'd run around like little savages. We'd go to the meat market and beg for heels off the salami. Then we'd go into the back yard of my dad's shop, where there was an untended garden plot that still produced a few vegetables. We'd pull up carrots and eat them with mayonnaise on sandwiches. Because he went to a nearby bar frequently, we were always going in there, looking for Daddy. He had his hands full!

"After a while, we met this lady, Arlene. She lived next door to his shop. She felt sorry for us, I guess, and invited us kids up to her apartment and often fed us. Time passed. Arlene and her hubby, Gordon, were fighting a lot. One day, old Gordie bopped her in the face with a telephone. She said, 'That's it! I'm out of here.' So after Arlene left Gordon, my father wooed her; and they married. See, he really needed a mother for us kids. She came into our family when I was eleven."

"So, how was she?" Julia asked. She tucked her nut bar wrapper into her bag and moved further into the shade.

"Actually, at the beginning, Arlene was OK—fine really," Ruth said as she waved another picture. "This one's kind of faded; but you can make out Dad, Arlene, and us four kids. We're still smiling here. For the first three years of Arlene's being there, things were pretty good. She

cooked meals, sewed clothes for us, stuff like that. But
as we started to move into puberty and began to think
more mature thoughts, it became too much for her.
She loved babies, little kids, and dogs, probably 'cause
they'd give her adoration and love, and, mostly, do as
she said. But any questioning of her decisions or authority *whatsoever* would get us in a heap of trouble.
She would just shriek at us at the top of her lungs."

Ruth picked at her thumbnail. "Since I was the
oldest, I had the smarts to know how to play her. So
I was perfect, every day, in every way. I didn't say or
do *anything* wrong. I was quiet, never questioned her
authority, did my homework, and went to church. I
played her game. I was spared, but the other kids got
hit with a belt a lot. As we grew, so did her frustra-
tions. My father started drinking. She was *always*
screaming at us, *always* calling him on things, *always* putting him down. The more she nagged and
screamed, the more he drank; the more he drank, the
more she screamed! And, so, the house was in a constant turmoil." Ruth's voice had risen considerably.

Najila's kind eyes reflected her concern. "How
terrible for you kids but sad for Arlene and your papa,
too. How did you survive such a stormy life?"

"Well, see, each of us kids had our own role. My
brother, Joey, was a star Little League pitcher and Michigan State Marble Champion. Karin was quiet and aloof—
off in her own world. Betsy was the youngest and very
pretty. She got kind of wild—you know, climbed out the

window on bed sheets, ran around, attracted all kinds of guys, wore super short skirts, that kind of stuff.

"I was the serious, studious one. I didn't want to hassle with Arlene. So I became a person of rigidity and conservatism—never made waves. Then, too, we were poor: I had only two pairs of socks, two skirts, and three blouses, which I wore in rotation. But I never complained. Worst of all, I began to have this hideous cystic acne. Huge bumps would erupt, and they'd become horribly infected. This took a big toll on my self-esteem. I didn't have much in the first place, and Arlene sure never helped me. My sister, Karin, took this picture of me, crying over my face in the bathroom mirror. Not a pretty sight," Ruth said glumly, as she showed the photo.

"*Ay Dios mio*! You poor thing," Inez said sympathetically.

"So," Ruth continued, "because I was ashamed of my appearance, my wardrobe, my complexion, and our house with its old, ugly furniture, I just applied myself *totally* to my studies. I got great satisfaction from getting perfect scores. I would stay in the john with the door locked, sitting on the pot, with the lid down, like a chair. I would read out loud, figuring that it would saturate my brain better. Consequently, I was the darling of every class. The teachers absolutely *loved* me and often chose me to be their special helper. I received glowing report cards, with excellent comments about my study habits, as well as my personality. One time I brought home six As on my report card, but Arlene couldn't have cared less. She just said, 'Well, that's what you're *supposed* to get.' That really hurt. I had a stomachache for days.

"Later, I became a co-op student. So while I was still in high school, I also worked part time at a Detroit bank. I took dictation and typed. Of *course* I was really a good little secretary, and of *course* I excelled. I was even voted best business student in the senior class. Before I graduated, Mrs. Lloyd, my drama teacher, tried to help me arrange financial aid for college. But by then, I was just totally burned out from four years of studying so hard. Besides, there was no money—we often didn't have the thirty-five cents for *lunch* money. So I just slipped through the cracks."

Absently she brushed her cheek with her index finger. "Because of my acne, I was also shy with the guys—had not one date in high school, sat home on prom night, told myself I didn't care. But I did.

"As you might imagine, I was also very active in my church. I was there every time the doors opened, did all the altar calls—the whole bit. I also worried constantly about my salvation. I *knew* I was a Christian. But I never felt I was a *good* enough one, or even a good enough *person*. I must have believed that everything Arlene screamed at us was true. Oh yeah, she took care of us and all; but she was never like my mom. Even though I was totally committed to my faith, because I was so unsure of everything, my coming to the light spiritually was pretty gradual—unusual for a Protestant evangelical. So there I was, dedicated to my studies, my church, and to doing everything *perfectly*. It was the *one* way I could feel good about myself and try to maintain some control in my life."

She got up, walked behind the wheelbarrow, and kicked at the dust with her toe. "At the same time, things were flying out of control at home. The fighting between my father and Arlene was at *bombastic* proportions. Sometimes she even tried to use me as a marriage counselor, as in—'Tell Daddy I'm sorry that I burned his supper' and that kind of crap. By this time, my dad was pickled every day. While he never abused us, he withdrew from us, was so quiet, rarely talked to us, and acted like he had no role in our lives. Arlene was screaming constantly, every day, *all* the time. I guess he felt he had nothing to say—she said it all! I can remember lying in bed at night, listening to them scream at each other."

"Oh Ruth," Norma said quietly, "those must have been *very* hard times for you."

"Yep," Ruth said, her mouth in a straight line, "but I couldn't let it show. Besides, who would have cared anyway?"

Corinne pointed to her watch and held up her index finger to remind Ruth to finish the act.

"Got it," Ruth said. "Anyway, Arlene gave me a set of luggage for my graduation gift. Only *she* went to the ceremony; my dad didn't go. That hurt, too. So the day after, I was out of there. I *had* to leave. I felt like I was

suffocating! I didn't care where I lived. I just *had*
to get out of there! Very soon, I went full time with
that bank in their letter-of-credit department and
then in their audit department. I lived with friends,
took the bus to work, and started pulling in a salary.
Many people helped me then and reached out to me
big time."

"You were a very brave young woman, with
much courage," Najila murmured.

Ruth rubbed a hand across her forehead as
if trying to erase those sad memories. "Yeah, well,
maybe," she said. "It was either that or go *completely*
nuts. Our house was turning into a living *nightmare*.
At first, I kept asking myself: If things are so bad between them, why don't they just get a divorce? Then I
tried to change things—tried to get Dad to stop drinking, tried to get Arlene to stop screaming—but nothing was happening. Then I'd get mad at myself for
failing. I did the 'if only' thing for months on end. My
face got worse. Then I started getting depressed. Everything just seemed so impossible. Finally, I just *had*
to get out. I felt terrible that I had to leave the other
kids behind—it was like I was abandoning them—but
I couldn't help it. I had taken care of them, protected
them, for so long. Now, for the first time in my life, I
knew I had to take care of myself *first*."

"Yay, Ruth!" Alicia shouted.

Corinne ran out to center stage and held up a
sign: "End of Act One."

Ruth stood up and bowed amid warm applause.

"Thanks, guys. Gimme a few minutes to get ready for the next act, OK? Take a seventh-inning stretch."

While Kay and Corinne held up the sheet, Ruth hurriedly changed. She pulled out the scrunchies, combed her hair, and donned a pair of horn-rimmed glasses. Then she tucked in the white shirt, rolled down her jeans, and slipped into a short blue jacket.

"Why, that looks just like one of our waiters' jackets," Norma whispered. "It has the same *buttons*. How sweet that they loaned it to Ruth."

"You do what you have to do," Corinne said with a wink. Ruth nodded, and Kay and Corinne exited slowly with the sheet. Corinne's sign said: "Act Two."

Ruth walked to the center and leaned against the wheelbarrow. "Geez, I didn't mean to run off at the mouth so much; but I guess I needed to say all those things. Who knew? Anyway, now that I got through most of the bad stuff, it won't be so heavy duty; and I'll zip along faster. Oh yeah," she said, as she gestured towards her jeans, "and these were my 'working girl' clothes for the first few years. Pretend I'm wearing a dark skirt, OK?

"So, right after graduation, I moved out of the house. I lived with the families of three different high school girlfriends; they were all terrific to me. Near my twenty-first birthday, the third friend helped me to find a better job, buy my first car–a brand new, 1968 Rambler American—and get a studio apartment for eighty-five bucks a month. I was on my own, finally. Here I am with my Rambler. I *loved* that car! That's my apartment, just behind me," she said proudly showing another photo.

"So how *was* it?" Vicky asked. "Did you *feel* free?"

Ruth made a wry face. "Actually, no because Arlene *still* couldn't let go. She'd call me on a nightly basis and would talk nonstop for *hours*. Sometimes I'd put the phone down, do the dishes, pick the phone back up; and she'd *still* be there, yakking about what an SOB my father was, how he should be ashamed that he's a human being, and on and on and *on*! She was constantly ragging about him, the neighbors, my siblings, whatever. I hated it."

Julia laughed. "Now we know why old Gordie used a phone as his assault weapon."

"Yeah," Ruth said, "I'm sure you're right. Anyway, here I was in my twenties. I still had this really active cystic acne. But at least I had a job, was involved in other organizations, and was still totally devoted to my church. By this time, I was working for a law firm as a legal secretary. I worked very hard; so, of course, I was very, *very* good at what I did. I was very conscientious, ambitious, and serious-minded; yet I had a good sense of humor and was quick-witted. My bosses always liked me.

"Through my church, I met some College Challengers, eventually joined their national staff, and did five years with them in California. I just hitched a U-Haul to that little Rambler and drove out there. At first things were cool. I thought they were all so wonderful and that I had a calling. See, I figured if I went into full-time Christian service with my business skills, then I could give God my eight hours a day at work *plus* all my time at church. What's not to like?"

"But," Kay said thoughtfully, "I've always heard that College Challenge was a pretty aggressive, evangelistic, somewhat legalistic organization."

Ruth laughed bitterly. "You heard right. I was great at my job; but outside the office, I was constantly living with guilt. It was so real and tangible! I didn't have consistent daily devotions, like the Challengers *wanted* me to. I didn't polish off five books a month, like they *said* I should. I was not a soul-winner, like they *wanted* me to be. I felt that I should be witnessing to everyone I met. And when the depression came back–big, funky, black holes of it, sometimes for two weeks at a time—a few of the CC-ers even suggested it was a spiritual problem—that I was demon obsessed." Ruth's eyes were brimming.

"Oh, for heaven's *sake!*" Julia said sharply. "What a bunch of self-righteous hypocrites! The Inquisition: Part Two. But, Ruth, have you never thought there might be a connection—that you and your dad might have both suffered from the same thing?"

"Yeah, I did, but not 'til years later. Anyway, the best part about the job was that I found a Christian plastic surgeon who performed a dermabrasion—like sanding—on my face. It alleviated the depth of the scarring but didn't prevent further eruptions from boiling up from within. It helped some but not enough. Anyway, no matter how

hard I worked at that job, again, it was never good
enough. Pretty soon—the growing depression, the
burden of guilt, that whole thing—I just couldn't take
the pressure anymore. After five years, I knew I had
to leave; so I did. And that's when things really started looking up."

"Another step out of Stucksville?" Vicky asked
with a grin.

"Yep. First, I temped awhile in the LA area.
One day, while I was eating my lunch outside, near
the John Wayne-Orange County Airport, I watched
these big planes fly over my head. I remember seeing
their bellies go by, thinking how much I would like to
be in one of those airplanes, working as a flight attendant. I would *love* to do what those girls did. I mean, I
could serve soda and peanuts. That's when this little,
budding thought came into my mind about doing just
that—learning to be a flight attendant. But at my age
and with my looks? No *way!*"

Ruth's eyes were shining. "Then came one of
the major turning points in my life. I stopped caring
so much about *other* peoples' opinions, and I decided
to go for it. Long story short, after much badgering, I
got my foot in the door at Air Cal, worked in marketing and personnel, and then jumped at the chance for
a flight attendants' class. Another dermabrasion followed; and, at thirty-one, I got accepted into a class.
My dream was coming true!"

"How exciting!" Inez exclaimed. "You were so
persistent!"

Ruth blushed as she waved the next picture around.

"Here I am in my Air Cal uniform. I did that job like a crazy person! I was just *so* grateful. It was a validation of *me*. Alas, sixteen months later, Air Cal had big financial problems. I was laid off. Soon after that, Western Airlines hired me. They were in deep financial trouble, too, and wanted only experienced flight attendants who'd been previously employed by other airlines so that training could be abbreviated. Again, I was thrilled!

"While I was based in Salt Lake City with Western, I found a doctor who specialized in acne scarring. After one look at me, he told me that he could give me a new, controversial medicine, called Acutane, which had just been approved by the FDA. I had the blood tests done, assured him I wasn't pregnant or ever wanted to be; and he started me on the treatments. Thank God, Acutane finally stopped the oil production and eruptions. There were some side effects; but after the two-month treatment, the oil flow finally slowed down. I was never again bothered with cystic acne. I still have oily skin but no more acne. Part of my long nightmare was over. The depression still lurked around, but at least my face looked better."

She walked to the edge of the stage area, then turned back and flashed a big smile. "Better yet, shortly after I finished the Acutane stuff, I got my very first boyfriend. He was a ticket agent at the LA Airport. When I met him, I was thirty-three; and he was forty-nine. He was handsome, smooth, a confirmed bachelor, and a *total* weasel! Only I didn't see that at the time. I was looking better but was *incredibly* naive. I can't tell you how much I was *thrilled* by his attention. Being with him was the most spine-tingling time I'd *ever* spent! I became totally *enraptured* by this guy. To be sought after by somebody was paradise for me. Nobody had ever sought me—for *anything*! Here we are at a party," Ruth said, as she held up another picture.

"Wow, you looked great," Alicia said. "Love your outfit. You're right. He was really handsome."

Yeah," Ruth said with a bitter laugh. "I strung myself along for *six* years. It took me that long to admit to myself that this was a man who treated me as though he were a lover, but he only wanted me around for a day or two. He'd see other women during the week, usually when I was away on a flight. I was *so* dumb."

"Handsome or not," Vicky muttered, "he was a jerk and a rat."

Ruth nodded. "I tried to witness to him, but God was anathema to him. He was pretty much interested in just one thing. I know now that I must have represented an enormous challenge to him because I never succumbed entirely, ah, you know—we never went all the way. Actually, I should have been hospitalized in a psychiatric place because I was so *obsessed* with this guy. But he would have made a lousy husband. We'd be divorced by now—if I hadn't killed him first. But guess what? After six years, I unloaded him. When I finally admitted he was Mr. Wrong, I got up my courage and said, 'Bye, I'm out of here.' Another step forward for old Ruthie!" She danced a little jig in front of the wheelbarrow.

The women cheered loudly as Corinne gave the one-minute warning sign again.

"Gotcha," Ruth said hurriedly. "So, after five roller-coaster years with Western Airlines, they were purchased by United, where I was until I retired. During my last year with Western, I met Pete, my future husband, on a luau bus trip in Hawaii. Here we are, stuffing our faces at dinner," she said, as she showed another photo.

"We had a commuter marriage for a while. After a few years, I took a leave of absence from United and joined Pete in Rome, which is, of course, where I met all of you. OK, that's it for Act Two. Don't go away. Stage crew, I need you for a minute."

Kay and Corinne hurried out and held up the sheet while Ruth stripped off the jacket and shirt, rolled up her jeans, and slipped on blue leather sandals and a bright flowered blouse with a matching sun hat. Corinne gripped the "Act Three" sign in her teeth as she and Kay walked the sheet to the side.

Ruth strode around the stage area. "OK, guys. This is the last act, and it's gonna be short and sweet. Not long after we arrived in Rome, I was still crying all the time—not able to think clearly. Thank God, I found some real help for my depression. A friend put me onto a good shrink who gave me medication, and it worked. I still have some depression but not like before. Both the medication and also my inner hope as a Christian helped. I realize now that God is not an unfriendly grandfather, ready to club me with a stick. He forgives me again and again. Plus, I don't live under the burden of blaming myself for everybody who doesn't want to know or embrace the truth. As I'm growing older, I'm mellowing out. I don't get as excited or upset over the things I used to. I'm calmer, and I can think clearer. Is that the medication talking? Who knows?"

She sat down again on the wheelbarrow board. "I can see that my life span is lessening, life is passing, and time is going by so quickly. Like Kay, I want to make the very most of what I have left. I blew my entire *youth* on worrying, depression, and sadness— all those wasted years, wasted tears, full of fret and upset, the stomachaches, and the headaches—all of it. Now I've come so far, maybe the hard way, sometimes with the help of medication. Now I refuse to be drawn into unnecessary expenditures of precious emotions. Like Sapha, I've got a new life! Before, I was a chief worrier because I always felt so responsible. But guess what? Almost everything that I ever worried about, wrung my hands over, and tried to make preparations for, never happened—well, almost."

Corinne spoke from the side. "My grandmother used to say that exact same thing: Ninety-five percent of the things we worry about never happen, and the other five percent you couldn't do anything about anyway."

"She was right," Ruth said. "Anyway, once I felt better, I started to do more fun stuff. First I joined the prayer group where I met you all, then the international Garden Group, and after that, the Drama Group. That's where Corinne and I got to be friends. We did several shows together, and I even sang in one—God help us all." She flashed a photo. "Here we are, in a mirror, getting made up for a play. *I'm* the prettiest one," she said, laughing.

"After Pete retired and we moved from Rome to Louisville, I had to start over again. I'm big into animal rescue work. I've made some new people friends, too. If the time is right, I try to tell them about Jesus and what he's done for me. It's up to them, whether they believe this and act on it. I'm not responsible for their choices any more. What a relief! So now, I'm going for all the gusto I can get. I feel bad that I waited so long to figure this out—you know, realizing the gifts Jesus wanted to give me. However, I'm not spending too much time moaning about wasted years. Everything in my past contributed to the way I am today. Now, spontaneity is more my bag—laughing, being silly, and doing dumb things. Before, when I was a kid, I never, *ever* wanted to stand out. I always wore dark colors, and never raised my hand. Now, I'll be the only one to wear a hat, spray silver sparkles in my hair, or put glitter on my face."

"Take *that*, Arlene," Julia said.

"Yeah. I really love pretty clothes; and I'm sure that's why. But speaking of taking, I'm sure Pete's had to take a lot, you know, what with me being up and down all these years. Things have been alternately rocky and rosy for both of us, but we're still together after twenty-five years. We have lots of differences: He's a Type AAA and an accountant, while I'm more laid back and a wannabe actress. The main thing we have in common is God."

Ruth's face clouded over as she picked at her thumbnail again. "But I'm not gonna kid you guys: Some days I think I may have to *kill* Pete because he makes me so crazy! I mean, nobody's perfect and *everybody's* got issues; but he's just so rigid and has so much *anger*. Sometimes, I just can't stand it! I've changed, moved forward in my life; but I don't think he has." She drew an X in the dust with her sandal. "I came to the Holy Land for the usual reasons but, also, because I'm trying to make a decision. You can all guess what that is. Should I or shouldn't I? What will I do if I do? How will it affect both of us?"

"Well," Norma said softly," if it helps, I can tell you that being left is really devastating."

Ruth had tears in her eyes. "Thanks, Norma. I'll remember that. Before I came, I prayed that on this trip I'd get some answers—some direction. I think I just have. I'm not perfect either; but I want to enjoy my life more and have a good time, while my health and my mind are still good. I'm positive that if God is *for* me, who can be *against* me?"

Vicky spoke from her second row seat. "You know, Ruthie, maybe it's time for *you* to be for you, too. You've been against yourself for so long; maybe it's again time to put yourself first. How many times did you tell your passengers, 'In case of an emergency, put on your *own* oxygen mask first'?"

Ruth laughed. "Roger that, Vick. I'm so grateful for all the people God sent me along my way, especially you guys; you've been so accepting—so supportive. All those losses and trauma in my early life, all that doubt and guilt: I felt like I was in the Sahara Desert, dying of thirst. God really *has* sent me help, even if I haven't always recognized it. Sapha didn't realize right away who Jesus was, yet he still gave her his love and acceptance. He's given it to me, too. I *know* that beyond a shadow of a doubt. Now, as I understand and accept myself, maybe I can pass that along–you know, help other folks do that for themselves."

"Even Pete?" Alicia asked, with a faint smile.

"Yeah, maybe," Ruth answered slowly. "I'm still not sure yet, though. I have to think about it some more. Anyway, here's some closure trivia: My siblings have had their ups and downs—been in and out of marriages, work, trouble, and other stuff. Arlene passed on a few years ago—actually had a heart attack while she was on the phone—so Dad moved to a nice senior place. He's sober, gets better food, more exercise, new friends plus his doctor's got him on some antidepression meds similar to the ones I take. They're working for him."

She hopped off the wheelbarrow and spread out her hands. "So, that's it, gang. This morning, I sat by Jacob's Well, which has been giving water for over two thousand years. The Lord's been my shepherd and has sent me help

for a long time, too. I didn't always recognize it because it was so gentle, or right in front of me, like all of
you. The College Challengers would fall down dead if
they heard me say this; but, sometimes, I think maybe
God isn't always in church. Instead, he's right here
with us, in you and in me. I know that God's not gonna fail me. I *know* this."

She took off her sun hat and bowed with a
flourish. Loud clapping and cheering erupted from all
the women as they stood up and slowly prepared to
leave the theater. While Kay gathered all the clothes
and props into the two tote bags, Corinne returned
the wheelbarrow to its home under the olive trees. A
brave sparrow hopped onto the edge, hoping for a tid-
bit. Corinne smiled and fished a bread crust out of her
pocket for him.

As Ruth moved off the stage, Inez came over and
gently rested her arm on Ruth's shoulders. She spoke
softly in her lilting Spanish accent. "Everyone's situation is unique, Ruth; but I was also in such a place
earlier in my life. I was ready to divorce my husband.
Things were *very* bad between us. Sometimes he was
so critical and unpleasant to me, and at other times
he ignored me completely. He was never home—was
always running around with his friends—while I was
busy with our two little girls, my job, and our home.
But you see, I grew up in a house with no peace and
in a country with no peace. I did not want that for
myself, for my girls, or my marriage—I did *not*. So I
got some professional help. Then I started thinking
about what I really liked about my husband—why I

was attracted to him in the first place. I started talking to him. We would talk and talk, sometimes for hours. Slowly, we came to know and understand each other. Things are still not perfect, but they are much better now. Maybe you can try this. Do not close a door that will be impossible to reopen."

Ruth gave Inez a quick hug. "Thanks for sharing this, Inez. I really value your opinion, and I'll think hard about what you said. Now we'd better join the others. Don't want them to leave without us.

"Hey, you guys, wait for us," Ruth shouted. "We're right behind you. Kay, how much time did I take?"

~13~
Family Ties

The other women paused a short distance from the theater. Hugs and tears were exchanged when Inez and Ruth joined them. Ruth finally pulled herself away, ran her fingers through her hair, and wiped her face on her shirt sleeve. "I have to tell you guys: This was one of the hardest, but the best, afternoons of my entire *life.* I've never said most of that stuff to anybody, *ever.* Well, OK, Corinne knew about my depressions, 'cause I told her in Rome, but all my early years? Geez, I really spilled my guts, didn't I? All that crap about my family—I hope you weren't too disgusted or bored out of your minds. Anyway, I'm dead; and I'm starving! Is it time to eat yet, Najila?" She danced around, still buoyed from the excitement of releasing all those pent-up emotions.

"Ruth, your story was *astounding!*" Kay said sincerely. "And it only took thirty-three minutes and twenty-four seconds."

Amid much laughter, Najila said, "Now we will walk down to the car park and then drive to our hotel. We should arrive back by six-twenty. You will have some time to relax before dinner comes at seven, like last night, OK?"

Driving back, they encountered little traffic and were soon at the hotel. Ruth jumped out first. "Man!" she exclaimed. "I really need a shower. After all those costume changes out there in the dust and all that blabbing, I'm a mess. See you guys at dinner. Don't make me wait," she said. She dashed across to her room, shirttails flying. The others followed more slowly, still amazed at her story. Kay shook her head. She found it hard to believe Ruth had lived through all those experiences.

Najila checked the inside of the van, then locked it. As she walked into the lobby, Huda Danfi, a shorter and slightly older version of Najila, hurried over to her. "Aiyee, Naji," Huda said in English, "you finally back. I wait almost one hour. Where you were? Why so long, so late? Hamid say you be back long time before."

"Ah, *marhaba*. Hallo, Mama. I just finished a tour with ladies out at Sebastia Park. We started at Jacob's Well this morning. My day was very long; it was very warm out there. Please, Mama, sit down. My feet are very tired."

"*La*, Naji, no, no. No time for sit," Huda announced, trying to hide her irritation. "Tonight very big party for Rania. All family coming, my new friend, you invited, too. Change clothes fast, please, then drive with me."

"Ah, Mama," Najila said haltingly, "I told the ladies I would have dinner and spend tonight with them. Besides, with so many people there, Rania will not notice if I come or not. She only talks about her travels, her shopping, or herself."

"*Naji!*" Huda shouted. "Do not speak bad about your Auntie Rania. Why you so *hard*? First you teach, then you do souvenirs, now tours with these women— these *foreigners*! They more important than *family*?" Huda's dark red curls shook with indignation.

As Julia hurried through the lobby on her way to the ice machine, she heard Huda's impatient voice. She *knew* that tone; it was the same as *her* mother had used.

"No, Mama, family is *always* important; but I see our family often. These women are only here for four-five days. I have my job, they pay me money, I try to do a *good* job. You come too, Mama. The ladies are very nice ...." Her voice trailed off.

"Is this how it be, Naji? Always take more cares for tourists, for *foreigners* than *family*? Bah! Same, same. Just like your *papa*!" Huda flung over her shoulder as she huffed out the door.

Oh, Mama, Najila thought. Why now?

~14~

Drink Up!

The air was laced with fragrance of exotic herbs and spices. Dinner was again a tempting buffet: The long table displayed a tantalizing array of salads, vegetables, rice, fruits, and desserts. Tonight's single main course was a huge platter of steaming *St. Peter's Fish*, browned to a turn, with a coverlet of tomatoes, onions, garlic, and bread crumbs and garnished with bright green parsley sprigs. A large group of Italian hotel guests were already in the line, pointing to the table and loudly arguing about the variations in Mediterranean cooking.

"Man, just *smell* this place!" Ruth exclaimed. "Thanks, guys, for getting here on time; so I don't have to wait. I'm starving! No more carrot and mayo sandwiches for me. C'mon, Corinne, you go first tonight; so I won't always look like Miss Piggy."

Corinne laughed and joined the Italians in the line; Ruth and the rest of Najila's group followed. They served themselves quickly and took the same seats they'd occupied the previous evening. Their table was now covered with a pale yellow cloth; the low, crystal bowl held a fresh arrangement of floating red and yellow hibiscus blossoms, surrounded by waxy, green plumeria leaves. They ate quietly, feeling the heat and the jet lag. Najila was right: The second day *was* the worst.

At length, Kay folded her napkin and pushed back her chair. "Ladies, this has been an extraordinary day. I'd love to sit up with you and discuss it all at greater length; but my doctor made me swear that if she let me come on this trip, I'd get myself to bed early. I still need to write a few postcards and catch up in my journal, so I'll take my leave and see you in the morning. Najila, what's the agenda for tomorrow?

Kay noticed that Najila's eyes were red and puffy, and she hadn't seemed herself during dinner.

Najila licked a bit of baklava honey from her fingers. "Ah, tomorrow," she said slowly. "Yes. First we return to Sebastia National Park to visit the Roman Forum, the basilica, then the small church of John the Baptist, maybe the colonnaded street, and one-two other things. In the late afternoon, we will drive up to Mt. Gerizim. We will be outside a great deal, so best to wear cool clothes and bring water. We will come back here to take our lunch, but maybe you wish to pack small bites from the breakfast buffet."

"Terrific!" Ruth declared as she rose from her chair. "Sounds like a plan to me. I'm heading out to the pool deck to kick back and enjoy the stars. I deserve it because I *am* one. Who's coming?"

"I should get to bed, too," Norma said as she pulled her shawl around her shoulders, "but I'll join you for a bit. I've loved every minute of today, but I'm fading fast. So don't be surprised if I slip away." She laughed nervously then coughed a few times.

"Night, night, Kay. Sleep tight," Ruth said as Kay headed toward her room. While Ruth led the rest of the group outside, Najila remained behind to have a word with Mr. Hamid.

"Would you look at that?" Alicia said, as they moved onto the deck. "Those cushy armchairs are here now. I could have *sworn* only the plastic ones were out here earlier. I'll bet those nice waiters did that during dinner. Listen, I've been really good all day; but I'm absolutely *dying* for a cigarette. I'll sit over there, on the other side; so my smoke won't bother you guys. I'll just have one," she said with a husky laugh.

They all sank gratefully into the comfortable chairs. Soon small tables, glasses, ice water, chocolate almonds, and an ashtray for Alicia materialized magically as the two waiters moved soundlessly around the deck. "Amazing what a ten-dollar bill can do," Ruth whispered. "The short guy loaned me his coat; so I just paid the rent, so to speak.

"Those men worship you, Ruth," Norma said as she arranged her shawl and reclined in the plush armchair. "I saw you talking to them before dinner. They were over the moon." She tipped her head back. "My, but would you just *look* at that sky? It's so black, yet there are so many stars. Isn't that the Big Dipper over there?"

The group grew silent as they leaned back to gaze up at the glorious night sky. A gentle breeze ruffled the pine trees behind the pool, rousing a solitary bird who peeped in sleepy protest. Water trickled onto an unseen rock near the kitchen garden. The scent of night-blooming jasmine caressed them like a silken veil.

Alicia cleared her throat. "Hmm. Anyone up for a little bedtime story? I know we've heard two already today, but this black night is a perfect setting for me. Some of you know about my earlier life; but, Inez, you and Julia, and, of course, Najila, weren't in Rome back then. So it's probably best if I tell everything."

"Oh yes," Inez agreed. "I would love to hear your story, Alicia. Please leave nothing out."

"Just don't take three forevers, Al," Ruth quipped. "I need my beauty sleep, OK?"

Alicia laughed and then took a long drag on her cigarette. "Got it. I'll get right to the good stuff. When Kay emailed the verses she wanted me to consider, I thought there was nothing that pertained to me. It's that part where the woman asks Jesus who he is and how he'll get water without a bucket. Then he tells her that if she drinks this well water, she'll still be thirsty; but *he* can give people water that will gush up like a spring and give them eternal life—whatever *that* means.

"Later, I realized how this part really *does* resonate

with my life. I counted at least fourteen references to drinking: bucket, well, water, drank, drinks, thirsty, spring, etc. The Samaritan woman misunderstood Jesus' previous statement, saw only the things he *didn't* have, and worried that he didn't have the right equipment to draw water or the right family connections. Who *was* this guy anyway? What did he mean about water being able to change one's life? It all sounded like a puzzle to me."

The red ash from Alicia's cigarette glowed near her face, revealing a rueful smile. "Turns out, those lines are incredibly appropriate for me; since drinking played such a huge role in my early life at home—with my family of origin. Plus, for years, I wrestled with the puzzle of who I am. The good news is, I think I'm onto some answers. Anyway, it's getting late; and, even though Kay's not here timing me, I'll cut to the chase and start with the night my life really changed. In fact, it almost *ended* that night, too." She stubbed out her cigarette and crossed her long legs. Idly she twisted a strand of thick, blonde hair around her finger.

Julia stifled a yawn as she selected a chocolate almond. "Give me a *break*, Alicia. I'll bet nothing bad has *ever* happened to you. You've always led a charmed life—been the golden Valley Girl." Julia tried to sound neutral, but her tone held a slight edge.

"I wish," Alicia said with a sigh. "You might change your mind when you hear what I have to say. Looks can be deceiving."

She folded her hands on her lap and took a deep breath. "It was late spring. We were living in Rome, and I was pregnant with our third child. I'd been hospitalized several times earlier for placenta previa, a condition where the baby keeps trying to be born too soon. I woke up one night, feeling awful, and realized that I was covered in blood. I had been bleeding off and on for weeks, so I guessed what was happening. I was terrified! That night, there was so *much* blood! My husband rushed me to the nearby emergency room, where they stopped the bleeding— but just barely. Later that night, when things were under control, the attending doctor told me I'd have to spend the next four months lying flat on my back in the hospital if I wanted to save the baby's life *and* my own. Lying still and flat was crucial, plus I had to hope that I didn't bleed anymore so that when the baby was large enough, and I did go into labor, he or she would be able to survive.

"Four *months*?" I cried. "You must be kidding! I've got two other little kids at home, my husband is *not* Mr. Mom, plus I have a *ton* of things lined up for the summer: I've got guests coming, and I'm running a big tennis tournament. I can't just lie around here and do *nothing*." Then this suave, black-haired, Italian doctor looked at me sternly through his gold-rimmed Gucci glasses and said, 'Signora, I do *not* kid you. If you do not do this, you will surely lose this baby. You will be responsible for your baby's death and possibly your own. Can you stand that on your conscience?'"

"By this time, I was semi-hysterical from the pain, the fear, and, let's face it, the frustration. With my schedule, how could I just check out for four months? But after I calmed down a bit, I realized that that was *exactly* what I had to do. My decision to do so was the key to my being here today."

"How frightening for you," Najila said compassionately. "What a hard choice! But you held two lives in your hands that night."

"Right," Alicia said. "I was *so* scared. I mean, I was just *shaking* with fear. It hit me that I could very well *die* in the next few hours. Nothing like this had *ever* happened to me before. In the past, I'd always prided myself on things going according to *my* plans, *my* agenda, having everything together."

"Too bad Kay's not here," Ruth said, as she poured a glass of ice water. "Same deal."

Alicia nodded. "At that point, I recognized that I was not in control of my life. I realized that I had to give everything—the fear, as well as my life—over to God; or I wouldn't be able to make it. So I took a deep breath, and I did it. I turned *everything* over to God. The realization of God's nearness was almost instantaneous; it was an *incredible* moment for me. Even sitting here tonight, I can still feel that amazing warmth—like I was being cared for. I know that sounds weird, but I don't know how else to describe it.

"And so, as the days and weeks went by, I found that

the more I asked God for help, the easier it was for me to do what the doctor ordered. For instance, it became easier to lie on my left side; so the baby would get the most oxygen. It became easier to move as slowly as possible when it was time for a bathroom break or a shower. Once I made the *decision* to do these things, everything got easier. Somehow, I had all this new patience and a new attitude."

"That is the hardest part, is it not?" Inez said. "Help always comes at just the right moment but only after we have decided to let go of *our* plans."

"For sure," Alicia said. "And some of the best plans, the best help, was what *you* guys did for me while I was flat on my back during my hospitalization. *They* know what they did; but, Najila, you, Inez, and Julia weren't there. So I'll fill you in. I thought it was just a ho-hum study group, but they became my lifeline."

Alicia spoke quickly as she enumerated what everyone had done. "First, Kay made up a huge schedule—of course—and meals appeared for weeks in my kitchen for my husband and kids, and very often for me in my room; since Italian hospital fare is questionable at best. Norma cared for my flowers and my garden, Beth and Ruth drove my two older kids back and forth to school, Corinne and Vicky cleaned my house and did the laundry, and they all came to see me as often as they could. They brought news from the outside and, sometimes, even those fabulous chocolate biscotti! They would pray with me or give me spiritual books to read. Kay even asked me to write little book reviews for her because she was too busy to do it herself."

Julia chuckled. "Oh, Lord! Doesn't that sound just *like* Kay?"

"What else?" Alicia said hurriedly. "Oh, yeah, Ruth came up several times to help me wash and style my hair and do a bit of makeup—to make me feel pretty and not just this huge, pregnant blob in my oversized pajamas. You guys didn't even know you were acting out the Samaritan woman's story; but if all that wasn't a spring of water gushing up, over and over, the Spirit helping me to live, I don't know what is. Telling somebody you'll pray for them is fine, but doing laundry and making supper for their family is putting *feet* on those prayers."

Ruth burst out laughing. "Geez, Al, I'd forgotten all about that! Remember the day when I set that yellow, plastic basin on the bedside table, to wash your hair while you hung off the side of the bed? We were tryin' so hard to be careful; but I got so much shampoo in your eyes—and then I knocked over the basin? What a mess! I thought we'd both split a gut! I've never laughed so hard in my *life!*"

"I think of that every time I wash my hair, Ruthie," Alicia said. "Anyway, making that decision, to turn everything over, was the most important thing that's happened to me in my life because it eventually brought me back to God. Oh, sure, early in my life, I thought I *was* religious. I did all the 'right' Catholic stuff. It was all ritual but no relationship.

"During my hospitalization, when you all helped me in so many ways, you were leading me to God—showing me his love up close and personal—giving me living water. I loved talking and reading about this kind, benevolent God. All those books you brought were the best. Those readings helped me to reconcile the judgmental God of my childhood with the Lord who, through his grace, now allowed me to face every day. But I have to tell you: Those months in the hospital should in *no* way be viewed as a literary vacation! I often felt so frightened; and, because I was isolated in a private room at the end of a long hall, there were lots and lots of hours when I was very much alone."

"Ghastly," Julia said, "but I hear you—big time. Early in my marriage, when Edson and I moved to another town, away from my family and everybody I knew, I felt really alone and isolated, too. I was afraid I'd never have another friend again."

"Ah, thanks, Julia," said Alicia. "I know now I would never have been ready to change had I not been so desperate. Looking back, I realized I had spent a good part of my life feeling isolated and alone, different, and *very* much out of step. During all those weeks and months while I was lying in that bed, I had lots of time to think back over the paths I'd taken. I tried to determine the causes of my isolation—the roots of my feeling so different from the rest of my siblings and the world." Alicia took a deep breath, hesitated, and then plowed on, grateful for the darkness. "It was a combination of things, but the main one was that I'd been sexually abused by my father when I was a little girl."

Julia inhaled sharply. "Oh, *no!*"

"*Ay Dios mio!*" Inez whispered.

Alicia nodded, her mouth a grim line. "Yeah, it's true. Even though I covered it up, blocked it, and sublimated it for years, I know there were many times when he abused me. Plus, he threatened to punish me if I told. Maybe I should give you a little family background."

She crushed out her cigarette, stood up, and began to walk slowly along the edge of the pool deck. "I was born in Illinois, near Chicago; but we moved out to California when I was about two. My family was Irish, well off, and well educated. Education was always a big part of my life, too; and I'm grateful for that. All my grandparents were college graduates: teachers, lawyers, a Chicago stockyards owner—they did OK. During his life, my dad actually made quite a lot of money as a wool buyer. He had two private airplanes, and we went lots of places. He was one of four kids, and Mom was one of nine. Her family was very close; they all got together at least once a year. However, my parents chose to move to the West and be away from all of that. Mom told me before she died that her parents were not thrilled with her choice of a husband. Maybe they saw things she couldn't."

"You and Kay have a lot in common," Norma said.

"For sure. Anyway, in my immediate family, I had

two sisters and one brother. My oldest sister, Paula, was adopted at the age of four because my parents were told they could never have children. Then, of course, they had the rest of us: Carol, Johnny, and myself in thirty-three months. Paula died at thirty-eight from an alcohol and drug overdose, Johnny died at forty-five of liver failure, and Carol is on her second marriage."

"Lots of trauma in your family," Corinne said gently. "That's tough for anyone."

Alicia sat down and lit another cigarette. "You don't know the half of it. Anyway, one of the reasons for my isolation was that we lived on ranches, in the middle of absolutely godforsaken nowhere. First we lived in California. Then, when I was about seven, right before Christmas, we moved to Arizona. Something must have happened between my parents—or maybe my dad wanted to diversify, to get into something different—but he bought a piece of property with a guest ranch on it. Suddenly, we found ourselves in this new home.

"I'm not sure if my father envisioned purgatory or hell when he commanded Mom to run the ranch on her own, but it was definitely a penance. We were about fifteen miles out of town. Except for guests, we had little interaction with people. My siblings and I attended school in town, but we couldn't have friends over after school. It was deemed too far away. Besides, they couldn't have ridden the horses or swum in either of the pools because they weren't guests and weren't covered by our insurance; or so I was told." Alicia gave a bitter laugh and took a long drag on her cigarette.

"I have forgotten my flashlight, so it is hard to read the notebook just now;" Najila said, "but I remember Sapha saying how alone *she* felt, how hard it was for *her* to be accepted by citizens in a new town, each time she would move with her husband. And after her third marriage, the townspeople criticized and gossiped about her endlessly, saying she was a fallen woman or had an unclean spirit. Nobody ever asked *her* for the truth."

"Incredible!" Vicky exclaimed. "Sapha lived so long ago, yet she could be one of us!"

"Yup," Alicia said. "Being shunned and ignored is tough, no matter when you live. Anyway, when I was about nine or ten, in the fifth grade, my father bought a second ranch in the Blue Mountains of eastern Oregon. So we lived in Arizona during the winter months and in Oregon during the summer. Dad's main job as a wool buyer was very seasonal; he would travel at least six or seven months out of the year. When he was gone, we had no contact with him whatsoever; so my mother was totally in charge. This was in the pre-email days, remember; there were no phones on our ranches then. People wrote letters to make their reservations. Mom managed the ranches, took care of the guests, supervised the housekeeping and ranching staff, ordered all the supplies, kept the books, took care of the house and us kids—did it all.

"But, when Dad would come home, we would all have

have to do what *he* asked us to do, or yelled at us to do. Uh, you see, my dad had another problem—the bane of many Irish—alcohol. So he wasn't always as calm, cool, or predictable as we would have liked him to be. I should have wanted him around all the time, but it wasn't happening. His departures were usually accompanied with a huge sigh of relief. Some of you know what I mean." She twisted the strand of hair tightly around her finger.

"You got *that* right, Al," Ruth muttered.

"Strangely enough," Alicia said, "in spite of all this, I was a very happy child. There was lots of interaction with guests from different places, many sports activities, pretty much a total outdoor environment. We had horses and tennis courts in Arizona, and the Oregon ranch was actually a camp in the summertime. We'd have boys for six weeks, and then girls for the next six weeks, usually about twenty kids a week. They slept in cabins, and each cabin had a counselor. We had a natural hot springs pool with a river running through it, which made for great swimming. There was no TV or other modern digital things, either. We played volleyball, badminton, cards, and rode horses. So in that way, it was very happy."

"So that's why you're still such a sports buff?" Julia asked.

"Yeah, probably. And, as the youngest in my family, I usually got away with murder. I learned from the mistakes my older siblings made and didn't often get caught. I was always the sweet and compliant one. My mom would always say: 'Just bite your tongue and do whatever you have to do to get along. That's another jewel in your crown in heaven.' I've done that most of my life."

"Huh," Ruth said tartly. "I'll bet your mom did a fair amount of that herself."

"Absolutely. All of us kids helped Mom on the ranches. We all had our jobs to do, which went from making beds to fixing breakfast and cleaning up for seventy or eighty people: breakfast, lunch, and dinner year round. So it was not always fun and games. But it was expected of us, so we just did it. There was a housekeeping staff, of course; but we kids still had to do a lot. Summers were great, though. There were all those campers!

"But I have to tell you—the end of the first Oregon camp session was very tough for me. I remember that when it was time for the kids to leave, I got an anxiety attack and had to go hide. I was completely *overwhelmed* with grief. I didn't realize that our time together was such a transient thing; it was my first big lesson in loss. I had made such close relationships with these kids, and then they left. It's still hard for me to say good-bye."

"Long ago," Inez said, "I realized that I had to hold my friends lightly. One of us either moved away or turned away. Either way, it is hard, no?"

"Yeah," Alicia said sadly. "There were a lot of good things in my life but also a lot of awfulness. As I said, my father was an alcoholic; and my mom was an enabler. I'll spare you the details, but those of you from alcoholic families know. My parents didn't get along very well; and, later, my mother was left to raise all of us on her own. As a parent now, I know what an *incredibly* hard job that was. She must have been worried *all* the time!"

Najila laughed softly in her chair. "Oh, pardon me, Alicia! I am not laughing at you, only thinking of Sapha when she wrote of *her* worries—about her husbands' absences, about trying to understand the kind of water Jesus was offering her, how he would get it since he didn't have any bucket with him, and, really, who *was* he, anyway? What village did he come from? Who was his *father*? What did he *do*? And, particularly, who was his *family*?"

"Well," Alicia said, "I can definitely relate to the 'what did your father do?' part. Being a financial success was second only to your IQ number around my house. The Irish, at least in my family, peg their members as 'bright' or 'not bright.' The horror is wondering how you've been defined. Status and success depend *totally* on it."

She blew out a puff of smoke and shifted in her chair. "So that brings me to the darker part of my story, one that's really tough for me to talk about; but I want to tell you anyway. I mean, about the abuse issue. For most of my life, I had a hard time knowing who I really was—my true identity."

"Uh-oh," Julia whispered to Corinne, "here it comes."

Alicia took a long drag on her cigarette before she

spoke. "As an adult, I've realized that there are a lot of things I don't remember from the time I was about four or five until I was almost twelve or thirteen. That led me through a quest to understand why I couldn't recall much from that period and what could have happened to me. Years ago, I sought counseling and psychological help on this issue on several occasions. After a few sessions, one psychiatrist recommended that unless I was totally falling apart, it was probably better not to be regressed or hypnotized to help remember the trauma. Let's face it: My biggest fear was that I would discover I'd been sexually or physically abused by my father. I questioned my brother before his death, but he didn't want to talk about it."

Vicky raised an eyebrow.

"So for a long time," Alicia said slowly, "it was a big mystery. I am now convinced that this is exactly what happened, but I couldn't delve into it for many years. It's something that I totally blocked from my consciousness. I didn't want the feelings that I had about this issue to filter down to my kids, so I tried to be more loving towards them. For a while, that seemed to work, without my having answered those questions about my past. But, later, I started to have such *horrible* nightmares about all of it."

Ruth whistled. "Geez, Al. Here, I always thought you were Miss Golden Girl—so beautiful, so smart, so totally *together*; yet inside, you were just as shaky as I was. Maybe you should find another doctor and try again. Seeing a shrink was one of the best things I ever *did*. Making the decision to get help was hard; but, after I went, I wished I'd have gone sooner. Listen, Al, you had to let go of control once before in your life. Maybe it's time to do it again."

"Thanks, Ruth," Alicia said. "Actually, I've already done it; I'll get to that in a minute. Sorry, guys, I realize I'm meandering in my story; but whose life is ever in a straight line? I'll finish telling you about my family, then I'll come back to some decisions I made, OK?"

"Goodness, Alicia," Norma said gently. "How brave you've been through all of this."

Alicia looked at her watch. "Yeah, well, thanks. Listen, I know you're all tired; so I'll move it. But, first, I have to back up a few years. Religion was very much a part of my early life. I went to school with the nuns until I left California in the second grade. I went to Catholic high school first in Little Rock, Arkansas, and then near Chicago. My mother said the Rosary nightly, we all attended Mass weekly, and I attended catechism classes the years I wasn't in Catholic schools. That was the biggest gift that Mom gave me because I was born into a faith that has been the mainstay of much of my life.

"However, I *did* walk away for a time. I was a lapsed Catholic for many years because I found the hypocrisy within the Church and all that *organization* very repulsive to me. It became very convenient for me to say that it was *not* something I wanted to do. I was a freshman at an all-girls Catholic school and had to go to all the classes and religious services, but I didn't have to believe *everything* they taught us."

"Gosh," Julia said, "you were pretty young to make that decision. Was it hard? I mean, didn't you feel *guilty*?"

"No and no," Alicia responded quickly. "I might have been young, but I wasn't blind. I suppose part of it was normal teenage rebellion, but another part was deeper–questioning why my parents fought so much in spite of going to church so often. That didn't compute, in my mind anyway. I thought belief in God was supposed to bring you peace and harmony. Didn't happen at our house. And get this: Once, during confession, when I said I'd had impure thoughts after kissing my boyfriend, the priest asked how long the kiss had lasted. I thought: And why is *he* interested? Now I can understand that he was just trying to figure out how much trouble I was in. But, then, I saw it as something totally stupid. So it was a convenient excuse to walk away.

"Sometimes I longed to return; but my standards dictated a total commitment, not just to the Ten Commandments, but also to Catholic dogma, real or imagined. In my twenties, I was not living what I considered an appropriate Catholic life, so I just didn't return. A cop-out? Maybe. As a young adult, I can remember hoping that there would be *some* time when I could go back to a life with God because I felt it to be so calming."

"Calm is comforting, isn't it?" Vicky said softly.

Alicia sighed. "Yeah, but my life had taken a different spiral. My lifestyle and choices, in my mind anyway, precluded a relationship with God. I married a guy who was a Catholic but not a practicing one, so we didn't attend church. Religion just wasn't a part of our lives then. You know, even though we're in the twenty-first century, it *still* bothers me that the Church is *still* so patriarchal—so male dominated. I doubt that, unlike the Episcopal Church, the Catholic Church will ever allow women to become priests. And guess what? Same deal in most Irish families—men rule. However, women are the backbone, the strength, and almost always the intelligence of the family."

"Hey," Ruth said sharply, "it's the same in Pentecostal families, too Trust me on this."

"I love it!" Alicia said, laughing. "Anyway, my mom was definitely the backbone at our house. Because of her strength, discipline, and organizational skills in running everything, we kids were pretty secure. But, like you, Ruth, by the time I was about fifteen, things were beginning to fall apart—I mean, really crater. This had been building for some time. My dad was gone six or seven months a year, so then things would be fine. But when he was home, they got worse and worse. I didn't know any different; so, at first, I thought it was normal."

Alicia was now twisting her hair very tightly; her voice grew tense. "Then, one night, this one *awful* night, my father and brother were having a horrible, just a *horrendous*, physical fight. By this time, these went on quite a lot in my house. My mother was trying to stop them, but she couldn't get in the middle of it. Somehow, I finally got my father to stop hitting my brother. My dad suddenly told me that he was leaving. I begged him not to go. He said if I wanted to go with him, I had to leave with him right then. The situation escalated. It was *terrible*! I can *still* smell the alcohol—feel his anger and my fear and panic. I knew that our family was breaking up, but I couldn't make the choice to go with him because I knew that my mother was the more stable person. I was *terrified* of him! Still, I didn't want him to leave."

She relaxed her hold on her hair. "Long story short—he walked out. A few days later, Mom, my brother, and I packed up our suitcases, left the ranch, and moved to another house. We decided that, finally, it was time to break the ties and try to have some sort of a happier existence for ourselves From then on, we were 'systematically excluded' from my dad's life."

Vicky punched the air with her fist. "All *right*! What a big step for your mom! I mean, to just up and walk away, after all those years, coming from the kind of family that she did. Good for *her*."

"Yeah," Alicia agreed, "it *did* take a lot of courage. It was not an easy time, of course, because my father then decided he wouldn't give us any money. Even though Mom had a college degree, she had no way of earning an income— now that she wasn't running the ranches anymore.

So we all went to work: my brother at a gas station and Mom and I at a clothing store, where I modeled and sold high-end fashions. We all got a practical, hands-on education in a hurry. Like overnight."

"But, Alicia," Julia exclaimed indignantly, "you said your mother was one of *nine* children! Why didn't any *family* members help out?"

Alicia grew thoughtful. "You know, I don't believe inadequate financial care would have even *occurred* to my mother's family. My father had made a *lot* of money. They would have assumed that he would be decent and provide for his family. Divorce never happened in their family. It was always just called 'a separation.' Why not be civil? Or maybe they thought when she married my dad and moved west, that was it: A done deal.

"My oldest sister got married young, and the other one was in college. So, for my mom, my brother, and me, it made for a very different experience. We had always had an upwardly-mobile existence, living on the ranches and flying wherever we wanted on my dad's planes. For that time, I'm sure he was considered a very, very wealthy man. There was nothing that we ever wanted for. In fact, there was an excess of all things"—she laughed bitterly—"especially alcohol.

"Let me tell you, in very short order, we went from having *everything* to having *nothing* but each other. Now there was very little money. Of course, I couldn't appreciate it at the time. This was much better for me.

I wish my mother had made that choice for us many, many years before. She felt a commitment to stay married to my father because of her faith. Towards the end of her life, we had many discussions about this. The man she married at twenty-one was not the drunken alcoholic who beat her years later. I think she should have left earlier; but, given the time, which was the 1960s, she would not have gotten support or encouragement from any priest, or certainly *didn't*, as far as I know."

"Geez, Al," Ruth said softly. "That must have been really rough for you all."

Alicia nodded. "Yeah. It was. Anyway, our sheltered existence was now over. I continued to do as well as I could in school; it was expected of all of us. We were told that we had genius IQs and that there was absolutely no reason for anything but straight As. We all performed, because we were told we could. I don't remember ever having to study or really work too hard to get those grades. Because of moving from place to place, it would take a while to get settled into the new environment, make friends, and all of that. I was usually a cheerleader and was popular. I also always felt that I was different from my siblings.

"I wanted to get out on my own, so I popped into fast forward mode. I graduated from a Catholic high school near Chicago and from Arizona State University with a BS in business in three years each. I just didn't want to *be* there; I wanted to start *living*! Mostly, I wanted to be outside the realm of my parents' influence. I laughingly say that I was brought up in a repressed, Irish-Catholic home: There was a lot of laughter, but there were also lots of tears and unspent anger that we were not allowed to voice *whatsoever*. Now I just wanted to get out from *under* all of that.

"Years before, my dad had set up educational trust funds for us kids, to get us through college; but he hadn't made provisions for graduate school. He died of liver failure when I was nineteen, just after I finished college. So I scraped together some money and took off for Europe, where I studied art for a year. I took classes in drawing and graphics at the *Accademia dell' Arte* in Tuscany, threw pots at Deruta, and took Italian classes at the University of Stranieri. On weekends, we visited different cities and learned about the art of Italy. Fantastic! I loved the freedom of expression there. In fact, I loved the whole European scene: the pace and the laughter. After that first experience, I wanted more. I came back to America, applied for, and was accepted at, the American Graduate School of International Management, near Phoenix. I tested out of many of the classes and finished the two-year program in one."

"You know, Al," Ruth said solemnly, "we could be clones, except you're really a brainiac. Who *knew*?"

Alicia laughed. "I was looking for my identity back then, too. Maybe that's when I first began to want to return to the Church. I didn't want the hypocrisy, but I desperately needed the calm and the love my faith had provided me earlier. I just didn't know *how* to come back."

"So, it took almost losing your son for you to take the step, right?" Corinne asked.

"Absolutely. Before all that, I worked in the computer field in several different European locations and married my husband at the last one. We had our first two kids, and then I had the terrible experience of almost losing my baby. You know, it was during those four months that I really had, no, *took* the time to slow down and reflect. I saw that much of my early life had been spent rushing around and probably running away from stuff: blasting through school and college, spending that time in Italy, and hustling through grad school in a year. I needed to be busy, to be in control.

"Another step forward happened soon after I got out of the hospital in Rome. An American neighbor invited me to join her Rosary and Bible study group. The group was small, and I felt comfortable with these women; saying the Rosary was an old habit for me. The Bible study thing was new, but I loved the learning part. Like you guys, these women were also very kind and accepting. They'd all had their own problems in life but had found new ways to deal with them. Plus, they helped me enormously with parenting issues. Since their kids were all turning out well, I figured this was a sign they were doing a lot of things right. We shared some personal things, but I never told them *everything*—you know, the abuse stuff. I just couldn't. Besides, I didn't want them to think badly of me. Dumb, huh?"

"No," Julia said softly. "Looking good is *so* important."

Alicia rubbed a hand over her forehead. "Things were cool for a while. But, then, my whole past came back with a vengeance! For years, I'd had a lot of really bad dreams—OK, nightmares. They were like seeing horror films, and I was the star. I would wake up, night after night, in a cold sweat—sometimes screaming. It was terrible, and I wanted them to stop. So I made a big decision—actually two." She reached over to the table for another cigarette.

"The first decision was that I made an appointment to see a counselor. Her name was Jan, and she was highly recommended by a friend. Jan was also an American living in Rome, in her fifties—a wonderful woman. She let me talk and talk, say everything, and tell her all my fears, anxieties, and worries. For the very first time, I told her *everything*. I kept nothing back. I felt I could trust her totally; and, besides, I felt it was time."

"Sometimes," Ruth said, "spilling your guts is the only way to get from A to B."

"Absolutely. Then it was Jan's turn. She asked me if I really *wanted* to change my life and if I was willing to do the work required to do so. In other words, would I persist? When I agreed, we got busy. She helped me to look at what really happened and told me I had to *embrace* my innocence as a child—a *powerless* child. She told me over and over that I was *not* to blame, that there was nothing wrong with *me*, that I had not somehow *caused* these things to happen, and that I had not been a '*bad*' girl. I'd always thought: 'If only I'd been a better kid, my dad wouldn't have abused me, or become an alcoholic, or left us.' She helped me to forgive my dad, my mom—why hadn't she stopped him and protected me—and, finally, to forgive myself.

"Then she gave me some tools: writing, meditating, and visualization. She knew I played a lot of tennis; so she suggested that I write down all my thoughts, fears, anger, dreams, etc. on little strips of paper, then roll these strips into balls. She said I could either visualize hitting these little balls completely out of the court into the stratosphere, where they wouldn't harm me anymore; or I could actually hit the balls on a real court. I told her that this was the dumbest thing I'd ever heard of. 'Fine,' she said. 'Just try it.'

"So, I thought, what the heck? What have I got to lose? I'd sit in my chair in a shady corner of my garden, listen to the birds, get all relaxed, and just sink down into my mind. Some days, I'd just meditate there and hit balls only in my head. Other times, I actually got out on the court, took one of these little paper balls out of the my pocket, tossed it up, and whacked it. I mean, I hit the *snot* out of it! That felt so good that I took out another ball and did the same thing. I just kept coming back, doing it over and over. You know, I got to where I could calm myself, even after a bad nightmare, by doing this in my mind. After some months, the nightmares started getting less and less. Then, one afternoon, I took all these little balls that I'd saved, went outside to my back garden, laid them on a flat rock, and burned them. Watching that smoke curl up was pure *heaven*! All that bad stuff that had happened and all my anguish about it—the whole thing–just floated up and away. I sat down and cried my eyes out. When I stood up, I felt like I'd lost fifty pounds!"

"Oh, Alicia," Inez said, her Spanish accent very thick, "your spirit is so strong and determined. Not everyone can make that work. I am very happy for you."

"Thanks," Alicia said. "I just figured it was all or nothing. My second big decision flowed directly from that afternoon. I decided not to keep dwelling on these things but to let them go, just like that smoke, and move forward. I couldn't change what happened to me when I was little. I could change my reaction to it, now that I'm an adult. After all, I was supposed to have all this brainpower. Why couldn't I use some of it to clean out my *own* head?

"Through all of you, your love, help, and support, I saw God's love—in real time and with real people. So when I made my first big decision, to do the bed-rest thing, the right thing happened— Kevin was born almost at full term. Later, when I made those other big choices—to get help by seeing a counselor and, finally, to let go of the bad stuff— more right things happened; and I could move on. I know that I *was* a victim of abuse. But holding onto that hurt now—being angry, resentful, and all that negative stuff—only hurts *me*. My dad's been dead for years, so there's nothing I can do or say to him any more. So why should I keep hanging onto all that old anger and let him keep *on* hurting me?"

Julia was amazed. "Wow, Alicia! You lost your childhood, your family life, your father, two siblings, and almost lost your son and your own life; but you *found* God and yourself. Sounds like you're *way* ahead of the game."

"Yeah, I think so. Plus, I feel much better now than before. My experiences in the hospital, with the counselor, and with all of you guys *completely* changed my life. Now I've got a relationship with Jesus in *faith*, not just rituals. I've since talked with other women who've been abused. It's so common yet so devastating and painful to discuss. But once we start talking, we can start healing. It's our secrets that keep us sick."

"Besides," Corinne added, "people are persuaded by the changes in us, not by what we prescribe for them."

"Exactly," Alicia said. "Now, I don't worry anymore about those boundaries that I thought separated me from others around me. Come to think of it, Sapha and Jesus broke social, religious, and cultural barriers and crossed a number of boundaries. At the beginning, she questioned him about sharing her Samaritan water jar. People have often considered *her* to be the one out of bounds, but she wondered why *Jesus* was. I love it."

"Sapha met Jesus by the Samaritan well," Najila said. "You met him in your hospital room, Alicia. You both became sources of healing."

Alicia put out her last cigarette and stood up. "Thanks, Najila. I hope so. And thanks to you all, for listening and just being who you are. Your friendship is such a treasure for me. Sleep well. I know I will."

Ruth moved quickly to Alicia's side and gave her a hug. "You're one strong woman, Al. It took a lot of nerve to do what you did and then tell us about it. You're *tops* in my book. I'll walk you back, OK? It's dark, and you're a lot older than I am. I don't want you to fall."

Alicia burst out laughing. Arms entwined, they hobbled down the path to Alicia's cottage.

~15~

Back at the Park

They arrived at the park just after 9:00 AM. Najila was happy to see that her favorite parking spot was still free. "Good. My van will not get so heated under those trees. OK, ladies, when everyone is out, I will tell you one-two things, then we take a short walk." The women climbed down from the van, clutching their tote bags and water bottles. Kay looked refreshed after her early night; Ruth and Alicia whispered happily together, sharing incidents from their early years. Corinne and Norma nodded attentively as Julia explained about her bum knee; and, finally, Inez and Vicky closed the van doors.

"We now stand," Najila explained, "in the parking lot of Sebastia National Park. This was the former town square, or forum, of the old city of Samaria. In any early Roman city, the central forum was busy commercial center with many shops, businesses, and offices enclosed by arches and surrounded by columns. In ancient times, there were twenty-four columns. Today, only seven columns still stand on the western side of this lot. You can see some column bases. Across the way is another souvenir shop. We will stop there later, *insha'allah*."

Kay laughed. "Downtown: first century AD. Wait, Najila, let's get a group photo by those pillars over there." Kay asked a passing tourist if he would take a photo of the group. When he agreed, she quickly arranged the women around a rocky outcropping so that the seven tall columns were visible behind them. A low, green mountain range rose behind the columns; puffy, white clouds dotted the bright blue sky. "Yes, fine," Kay said, as she stood back and carefully surveyed the group. "That should make a good shot for your Christmas card, ladies. We each have our own pillar, well, almost."

"I'm the short one," Norma said with a giggle, pointing to the single, half-size column. "That's me to a T—sawed off but still standing."

With Kay's camera, the tourist, a German by the sound of his accent, took shots from different angles. "*Ausgezeichnet*—excellent! You can choose from several pictures."

Najila thanked him graciously. "Now we will walk to the basilica, ladies. Another group comes very close behind us."

Just after Najila passed a pile of decorated column segments, Ruth stopped. "Hey, guys. Look, up there, at the carvings on those big top sections. See all those flowers and palm fronds? Can't you see some poor apprentice, sweating under his master's stick in the workshop nearby, scratching out all those intricate designs? Yet here they are,

are, two thousand years later. Amazing! Do you suppose he ever thought about that?"

Alicia made a wry face. "Oh, Ruth! More likely
he was focused on getting through the next two *hours*
until lunch."

Walking to the right out of the parking area,
Najila led them to another group of columns. She gestured with her foot. "The original building was very
big, but now only small bits of this basilica remain. In
ancient times, a town basilica was a most important
building, a meeting place for rich people, with offices
for city officials. Sapha might have seen such a building, when she came to Samaria with her husband for
business."

"Upscale location," Vicky observed. "These
must have been similar to our administrative buildings or courthouses of today. Trust the lawyers to
snag the best real estate!"

Najila pointed to a large mound of rocks and
rubble. "See there—many large column chunks, bases, and tops? They are called capitals. Columns, or
pillars, divided this basilica into three parts: a main
section, then two side sections with an aisle to divide.
Businesses and offices went right round the open main
section. While we walk, I will show you a small altar
added later. Many buildings here were used for other
purposes throughout the centuries. Now we will visit
a nice small church, John the Baptist. Come, please."

They dutifully fell in line behind Najila as she led

them up the left side of the park. "It is a bit steeper to walk up this side, but maybe we will not meet so many other tourists here yet. This is the *opposite* direction than most tour guides take; but, sometimes, I *like* being opposite. Just ask my mama. Ah, Julia, your knee is bad for you today. Please walk slowly, take time. No hurry. There are benches in front of the church to rest."

"Thanks, Najila," Julia said. "I don't know *what* I've done, but this trick knee of mine is acting up again. I'll be fine, really. I'll just take it a little slower. You all go on; don't wait for me. I'll catch up."

Ruth came up behind Julia and put an arm around her. "Here, Jules, lean on me. I have trouble with my knee sometimes as well, so I know how tough that can be. I slipped once, runnin' up the steps of a plane in a downpour; all my weight was on that leg." She laughed. "I've never been the same since!"

Julia's eyes widened with surprise. "Why, why—thank you, Ruth. Most people *never* offer to help me. They can't be bothered. If they only *knew* what I go through! I'm sure I can make it up this hill, but I really appreciate your help."

As the path wound up past more ruins and little groves of trees, Vicky said, "Najila, I have a question. A few months ago, I read an article by a guy named Pilcher, or Pitcher, or something, in a magazine called *The Bible Today*. It was about the Samaritan woman going on from here to Africa and later being called Photina. What do you know about this?"

Najila came to a halt under a large tree. "We will stop here for a minute. Yes, Vicky, I *do* know some bits about Photina; and I meant to tell you. But I forget, no, sorry, *forgot*, until now." She waited until the rest of the group caught up and gathered around her in the shade. "This is what I know about Photina, a later name for the Samaritan woman. One day, when I first opened my souvenir stand, a nice old monk came out to help. I think he only wanted to sit and visit, but he had interesting tales. He sat under the shady grapevines and told me that, many centuries ago, his Eastern Orthodox Church took the Samaritan woman's story from John's Gospel and changed it a bit. To them, she is Photina, which means 'enlightened one' or 'shining with light.' They are very devoted to this woman. Even now, the Eastern Orthodox Church celebrates her feast on April 2.

"The old monk told me a legend that says she went from here and preached the good news about Jesus in Carthage, North Africa. She also had two sons and five younger sisters. There were tales of torture and possible martyrdom of all these people. One story said Photina died in prison; another said she drowned in a well."

"Gross," Ruth whispered. "But ironic, too."

Najila went on. "Yah, this old monk told me that most people in the Western tradition do not know about Photina, but she was very important for the Eastern Orthodox Church. She is part of a bigger group of powerful helpers against the lust demon. Another story says she was much honored for healing trembling and shaking diseases, like palsy or Parkinson's. Just before he went back inside, the old monk told me that, though this story started in John's Gospel, it was changed some and took new life. The story still inspires people, depending on their needs. I like to think Sapha got more courage after she told villagers and friends about Jesus. Maybe she lived in other towns, told even more people. Carthage is about fifteen hundred miles from Samaria by ship on Mediterranean Sea but farther if she traveled overland by caravan. She started in Samaria, but it is possible she did not stay there forever. Perhaps she went on to other places."

"Of course," Norma said. "After all, look at us. None of us is where *we* started."

"You know," Vicky said, "like so many stories of earlier saints—Mary, the mother of Jesus, settling in a village above Ephesus; James possibly going to Spain; Mary Magdalene maybe ending up in France; etc.— the actual details are lost to us. But I'm *convinced* that the legends around these figures always have a kernel of truth at their core."

"Well, *my* legs are shaking like Jell-O," Julia said with a grimace. "I could use a little healing myself. Where's Photina when we need her? Are we almost there? I've just *got* to sit down."

Najila led them out onto the path and up the hill. "Yah, soon we will have a rest. I will talk as we move along. Tradition says that John the Baptist was killed on the other side of the Jordan River, and his head was hidden here. The original small church was built in seventh-century Byzantine times and eventually became an important pilgrimage center. During the Middle Ages, it became part of a monastery and was later restored and enlarged."

At a curve in the path, they came upon the remains of a small church built into the side of a hill. The front wall of the roofless church was solidly constructed of intricately-shaped, weathered sandstone. Above the doorway was a long lintel, which had obviously been repaired and remounted. Several carved, wooden benches were situated under nearby trees.

"OK. Here we are," Najila said. "Julia, sit here on this nice shady bench. Look, here is even a small pillar to rest your leg." Julia sat down gratefully on the nearest bench and fanned herself. Ruth glanced around. "Nice place. Too bad the roof's gone. Hurry up, you guys. Let's go in and have a look."

~16~
A New Call

As Ruth led the way, the group climbed the three worn, stone steps onto what had been a porch or front entryway of the early church. "Oohhh," Norma exclaimed, "look at those huge thistles and all that tall grass! I used to know their real names, but I can't seem to remember much these days. I'll just take some quick photos and identify them when I get home."

Alicia paused on the steps and waved her arm in a wide arc. "Can you *believe* the possibilities here, Norma? Over there, next to the wall, we could plant some oleanders and bougainvillea and, in front of them, stick in a row of ice plants. With a couple of Weed Whackers, we could have this place shaped up and looking great in no time!"

Norma giggled. "Wouldn't that be fun? I'll bet there were some church ladies, just like us, who did exactly that—thirteen hundred years ago! Do you suppose sunflowers and petunias would do well here?"

Entering through the tall doorway, they saw that, twenty feet in front of them, a crude altar stood on a slightly raised platform, surrounded in the back by a curved wall, creating a primitive apse. A single column, the remaining interior support, rose near the outer wall. Norma quickly took several photos and then started coughing. Breathless, she came back out and sat down on the wooden bench beside Julia.

"I hope you don't mind if I sit here with you, Julia. I'm really pooped today, and I need to rest a bit. It makes me so angry that I don't have the energy I used to, but that's just how it is. I'm happy I could make this trip at all. So we'll sit here, *outside* the church, just like the old men who always did that in my hometown. They were sweet, but they could never quite get *inside* the doors."

"Hah! I knew guys just like that when I was a kid, too. It probably went against their religion," Julia said, laughing. "Of course you can sit here; I'm happy for your company. Now that I'm sitting down, my knee's feeling a little better. Here, have a nut bar. I always carry a few with me, for when I need extra energy."

While Julia and Norma chatted in the shade outside the little church, Kay arranged the other women for a group photo in the altar area, their bright shirts providing a colorful contrast to the pale stone blocks. She seated Najila in the middle, on a three-foot column fragment, then placed the others around her. "You're our leader, Najila; so you belong in the center. Ah, Ruth, a little to the left, please. There, fine. I'll take the first photo of you all, then, Corinne, you and I can swap places, so you can take another photo that includes me. We'll get Julia and Norma on our way out. Gracious, but it's hot up here! Let's do this quickly and then get out with the others in the shade."

Several more photos were shot, then the group filed out and down the steps. "Inez, scooch over, will you?" Ruth asked. "Here, Kay, you can squeeze in between us. I'm all over the fact that the Israel Parks' Service provides benches at these sites. Being a tourist is hard work."

They all relaxed on the benches under a cluster of olive trees near the church's entrance, the wall behind them providing a backrest. Most drank from their water bottles and shared snacks; Norma threw a few nut bar crumbs to a tiny brown sparrow hopping near her.

Julia laughed nervously as she wiped her hands on a tissue. "Guys, my heart is starting to pound. It's not just the heat. That probably means I should do my story now. Until thirty seconds ago, I didn't want to say *anything*, at least nothing you'd want to hear. But it's nice up here. Is that OK, Najila? Do we have time? I promise I won't talk too long. I don't want to bore you too much," she said in a rush.

"This is your trip," Najila said gently, "so you ladies can choose the agenda. Sometimes talking, telling stories, is more important than seeing old stones. Stones are interesting but dead. We are alive. Take your time, Julia. We have nice shade to rest. See, even a small breeze comes up the hill for us."

Julia's face grew very red; she spoke very rapidly. "First, I have to say how much I related to Sapha because we were both victims of so much misunderstanding. But her actions, following all those harsh words, all that criticism—especially from her family–and then all her new courage after she talked to Jesus, have been *so* inspiring to me. I know *all* about criticism from family. The verses Kay gave me even include a family member. It's where the Samaritan woman asks Jesus for this special water so she won't be thirsty anymore, but he tells her to go call her husband and come back. Say *what*?

"Short, mysterious, and a little weird, huh? First, there's all the stuff about water, then a lateral arabesque to her husband. What was *that* all about? Sapha probably thought Jesus meant the kind of water one could drink, and she wanted some to quench her thirst. Even better, maybe she hoped Jesus would magically fill up the water jars at her house; so she could bag all those hot, boring trips to the well. She would have been all over that! Then he brings up her husband. Why would he flip from the subject of water to her husband?"

She looked off in the distance. "I've often wondered whether he was testing her, to see if she'd tell him the truth. And another thing: Maybe when John wrote his Gospel, he used a symbolic or code language that meant something to his community but means zip to us today. Since it's so far in the past, there's no point in speculating because we'll never really know." Julia paused for a breath. "I'll tell you right from the get-go that I usually *hate* doing personal stuff. Hearing other people's troubles or airing

mine makes me *really* uncomfortable, but the stories
we've heard so far weren't too bad. Besides, my life
isn't all that interesting anyway." She fanned herself
slowly with a tissue and took a swig from her water
bottle.

"Like you, Ruth, I was a baby boomer, a small-
town girl, born in the late forties in the southeast
corner of Idaho. Farming dominates the economy, as
does the railroad that runs through it. Idaho State,
my alma mater, is there as well. My parents met
while both were working for a large railroad company,
which was, and still is, the major family employer. As
with you, Alicia, alcohol did a *big* number in our family. My brother is recovering, while a favorite uncle
is still in denial. Alcohol also took my dad's father
when Dad was only thirteen. Mom's folks lived in our
town and were very dear to me; I have only the best
memories of holiday family gatherings with them.
But Dad's mother? She was quite a character—not a
very warm person."

"Well," Vicky said, as she took a small chunk
of bread from the snack she'd thrown together from
breakfast, "if your dad's father, your grandfather, was
an alcoholic, that must have made your grandma's life
pretty miserable."

"Yeah, she was one tough cookie. Maybe
that's why. It makes me laugh now to think of this;
but, despite being married to railroad men with
strong personalities, the women usually called the
shots. They touched base with the husbands only
to affirm decisions. They'd never admit it, but I observed this on many occasions. This probably resulted from the men being on the road so much and might

explain my strong streak of independence."

Alicia sipped her water. "Of *course* the womenfolk had to run things if they were dealing with a bunch of drunks! Otherwise, they'd have all ended up in the poorhouse. Been there, lived it."

Julia pursed her lips, then attempted a smile. "Luckily for me, I spent twenty-two happy years growing up in this lovely little town. In my eyes, it was a storybook-type community and way of life. For several years, I was the only child and grandchild in my family. But I was eager for a sibling and was happy when my brother, Dennis, was born; I never felt I was put in second place. Even though he's seven years younger than I, we're very close, as was our extended family. The whole gang got together frequently; these gatherings usually involved food— no doubt part of my ongoing weight problem. Family movies reveal everyone stuffing food into my mouth, with me looking like a young sparrow." She sighed.

"Food is often equated with love, is it not?" Inez asked, speaking carefully. "Maybe your relatives were trying to make up for you not being the only child. The food might have been nice, but I imagine the attention felt even better."

"I suppose," Julia said, as she rolled the ends of her shirttail between her fingers. "But, sadly, my resulting chubbiness became the subject of great concern for my mother, grandmother, and aunts. They talked to me, to my mother, and to each other. They presented me with diet plans and endless suggestions for losing weight. They all thought *theirs* was the magic cure, the silver bullet. They all wanted me to be thin *so* badly. The men just bought all of us kids ice cream cones when nobody was looking; and, naturally"—she smiled ruefully—"I ate mine. Even now, I'm overly concerned about the opinion of my family, friends, or neighbors. I always want to 'look good'—to be perfect. I'm so hard on myself and always worry about how others view me. I know it's silly to worry about that so much, but it's so hard not to." She swatted away a persistent fly.

Najila tapped the notebook that lay in her lap. "Hard family words were painful for Sapha, too. She wrote that her women relatives never let her forget her many husbands and babies she lost, as if those things were *her* fault. Such criticism was *very* difficult for Sapha, since her family was so kind and loving when she was young."

"Man," Alicia muttered, "the more things change, the more they stay the *same*."

"I can't *believe*," Julia said, "that Sapha had to deal with the same stuff we do. Now that I think about it, I'm positive that my early, very mediocre, school record was a result of my self-consciousness about my size because when I dropped the weight in high school, I was suddenly an honor student. Consequently, high school became a neat experience. The school was small and overcrowded, but who cared? I was into every activity I could sign up for. Daddy encouraged me to enroll in speech classes so I could gain self-confidence. In fact, I became a championship debater by graduation. Because our family finances were tight, I could only enroll at the local university. I'd wanted to go to law school after getting a bachelor's degree, but that never happened. I helped out with expenses as much as possible by doing steno work for the railroad, but it still wasn't enough to float the law school boat. But I did meet Edson, my future husband, at the university.

"Let's see—what else? Oh, yeah, then there was my religious background." Julia shook her head at the memories. "We were a strange stew at our house. Daddy's side has Catholic roots all the way back to Ireland and Scotland. Mom's folks were different. Her mother was Catholic, although this was her converted religion. Her parents, who were Scottish Protestants, sent her to Catholic 'finishing' school. Grandpa's people were Masons who affiliated with the Episcopalian Church, as many Masons do. Plus, many railroad officials were Masons. My grandparents let their kids decide. So Mom and one uncle chose Catholicism, while another uncle saw being a Mason as his ticket to promotion. I was sent to the Benedictines for elementary school; those nuns had a more humanistic view of life. Fortunately, I avoided the horror stories of many students of that era."

Norma coughed slightly. "Goodness, Julia, your family *was* an interesting mix. You know, my family would *never* have sat down with even Protestants, let alone *Masons*. Yet, here we are: Anglicans, Catholics, and a Pentecostal. It doesn't matter, does it? We're all just friends together."

Julia nodded then took a bite of her nut bar. "But some of my early impressions about religion proved to be faulty. As I was growing up, we were active in the Catholic Church, went to Mass every Sunday, and even went to the novenas. Daddy got there when he could because he had to spend lots of weekend time with the labor union. Until the last few years, I thought his faith was firm, although not public; I knew he was proud of being Irish Catholic. But after Mom's death, Daddy revealed that he questioned the Catholic Church in many areas. Before he died, I learned that he was very angry with the Church over the death of Pope John Paul I—he held the hierarchy responsible. This was pretty strange and uncomfortable for me and shook my own faith to the core."

Alicia cleaned off her sunglasses. "I remember when that happened. Weird, wasn't it?"

Julia sighed. "Yeah. Alas, the only fly in this ointment was, and has been, my weight problem. It was fussed over and focused upon constantly. Somewhat later, I found out that I had had an under-active thyroid gland. My doctor gave me a new kind of medication that helped. Then, for six wonderful years, I was blessedly thin. I felt my parents' pride even more during this time and was able to come out of my shell somewhat."

Inez patted Julia's arm. "Oh, Julia, you felt your parents were proud of you *only* when you were thin? How *sad* for you."

Julia pulled the ends of her loose cotton shirt around her, although the morning was very warm. "Yeah, well, kind of. Anyway, my very first job during high school was as a carhop at a drive-in. I had just lost my weight and was looking good; but Mom was *petrified* that I would gain it back, since I was working at a restaurant. Nope. Once you've made twenty-seven cones for screaming Little Leaguers and smelled grease all day, food loses its appeal. I also played lots of tennis that summer. The next summer, after high school graduation, I changed even more. I got a job as a chambermaid at a nice hotel in the mountains. It was my first solo time away from my parents. I learned all sorts of new swear words, new hairstyles, pleased only myself, and was no longer a Momma's girl. You could say I grew up a little."

Norma spoke up quickly. "I know how that feels, Julia. When I was forced to be on my own, I grew up, too. You just *have* to, don't you?"

Julia threw Norma a grateful smile. "Not long after I graduated from college, Edson and I married. A few years later, I had our daughter; there were some bad complications. Then, with new discoveries about thyroid treatment, my doctor said I absolutely *had* to stop taking those earlier pills. Soon my weight shot up. My body's just been a yo-yo most of my life. Again, it became a source of worry and, no doubt embarrassment, for my parents; and, let's face it: for me too. Fortunately, by this time, I had carved out a niche for myself in many other areas."

She sighed, picked up the nut bar wrapper that had fallen to the ground, and stuffed it in her pocket. "So now, on most days, I'm able to deal with my feelings of being imprisoned inside my own body. Fortunately, my parents helped me to cope and to be as outgoing as I am. Probably, in my formative years, they were afraid that being large was my lot in life; so they encouraged me to develop my *mind* and what was on the inside."

"But I have to tell you," she said, as she blinked back tears, "it's been hard, especially since my mom was tall and thin. I couldn't help comparing myself to her, wishing I looked more like her—and a secret part of me believed that she wished the same thing. There! That's the first time I've *ever* said that out loud! I've never wanted to admit or accept that. You guys will understand; you know how hurtful words from family members can be. Mom told me that her parents, particularly her mother, were embarrassed about *my* mother's height. They commented on this to her, too, as if it were her fault, like Najila said about Sapha. Now I ask you: What can anyone do about her *height*? But looks were *super* important in my mom's family."

Najila shifted down the bench, into the shade. "I know painful family words, too, Julia. My family did not understand my getting a teaching degree. They spoke their upset very clearly. I was *not* following Mama's steps. Plus, other things I did pulled our family into a most unhappy spotlight: first my souvenir stand and now these tours. Appearances are very important for us, too. But, while some small part of me *does* care, a bigger part does *not* care. I know what I want, and I do it. It is *my* life." She colored slightly and lifted her chin high.

"Woo-hoo, *Najila!*" Alicia cheered.

"I've always wondered," Vicky said, with a little grin, "if Jesus' family gave him a hard time, too, once he started his ministry. After all, he wasn't following in Joseph's footsteps, becoming a carpenter and taking over the family business. He was just going from town to town preaching, talking to people, and doing some healings. I'll bet they asked him plenty of times: 'When are you going to straighten up? Be like Joseph? Get a *real* job?—with the 'and stop making the rest of us look like idiots' implied."

Julia laughed and then wiped her eyes. "Terrific! It's one of those things the Bible never mentions; but I'll bet it happened just like that. Anyway, as I said, while I was in college in my hometown, I met the guy who later became my husband. Edson's still my best friend. We seem like opposites because he's very quiet, while I'm far more outgoing. But we're soul mates in so many ways," she said shyly.

"So, after I graduated with a degree in elementary education and science, I taught one year in the public schools before marrying him. Then, to my horror, we moved all the way to New Mexico; so he could attend grad school. I was miserable! When we returned to Idaho for two years, I happily settled back into my comfortable and familiar 'cradle.' Then we moved to Phoenix. Six months later, I woke up one morning and wondered what in the world I had found so appealing about that little town in Idaho. A few years after that, we moved to Rome, I met all you guys, and I've never looked back. Throughout my career, I've had some good teaching jobs, especially at the International School in Rome, where I taught kindergarten. I've met some nice people; and most of my life has been fun, productive, and fulfilling. It was only when all the medical emergencies started happening in 1995 that serious ruts appeared in the road." She took a sip from her water bottle and mopped her face with a tissue.

"For Najila's sake, and in case you guys don't remember, here's a short list," she said, as she ticked off the items on her fingers. "First, my father nearly died during a serious operation. Soon after that, Edson and Mom were both diagnosed with cancer. Hers was a really fast-growing kind; and, sadly, she died before hearing the good news about Edson's remission. Not long after Mom died, our daughter, Elise, developed clinical depression while she was in college. I returned to the States to look after her for six months."

Corinne ran her hand through her sandy red hair. "I'll bet the stress of her dad's cancer and losing her grandmother was just too much. That would be hard on anybody."

"*Exactly* what I told her doctor," Julia said strongly. "Then Edson had a minor stroke, eventually requiring surgery on both neck arteries. He was later diagnosed with diabetes. Then, suddenly, the cancer returned; and he had to start taking some very aggressive medications that changed his body and his personality. Then Daddy had a heart attack, had a pacemaker installed, and then had shoulder surgery. I went back to the States again to help him."

"Merciful heavens!" Kay said. "I thought my family had problems! That must have taken enormous strength, Julia. How did you cope? How did you ever *survive* all that?"

Julia was silent for a moment as she looked down at the ground. "How did I cope? I actually did fine until the fall of 1999. My faith and all your help and prayers carried me through. But, sometimes, it was hard as heck! And, by that October, everything just went south. I still don't know exactly what happened to me. I lost faith, got mad at God, got desperate, despaired, and then was ashamed of despairing. I was a wreck for months—totally exhausted. I had some health problems of my own. I'm sure I soothed myself with food, too.

"During all that, friends thought I was being so strong. Hah! They just couldn't see the battle raging under the surface. I had a talk once with our priest, and that helped some. But, by early spring, I was a basket case! I was just tied up in knots about Edson because his test results were all over the charts. So, for a while, I didn't do anything—didn't pray, didn't even go to church—nothing.

I just rested. You know, I did the 'Be still and know that I am God' thing. Then, out of the blue, I got the idea to start praying again. Life seemed a little brighter; I was able to go on. Somehow, whatever I needed, it was there. I'm still a little nervous about the future—as in, will I have to carry multiple crosses? Will I ever have a 'happily ever after'?"

She took several deep breaths and straightened her shoulders. "OK, enough of the maudlin stuff. Let me tell you something really neat that happened to me ages ago, before I met any of you. I call it my faith-changing encounter. I was the church secretary, and we were hosting a ladies' luncheon one day. More women appeared than we had prepared salads for. The priest and some ladies prayed that we'd have enough, and guess what? I witnessed a miracle that day! We had enough, and there were leftovers. Plus, the topic of the video presentation was the miracle of the loaves and fishes! The priest said he was sure it was meant for me, as he knew I'd been searching. Right then, God became a real presence in my life, not some mystical being of my youth. Jesus was real to me. Having a God who took my hand—well, that got me through. During the tough times, it's easy to forget; and, believe me, I've forgotten a *lot*."

"I understand that," Kay said. "None of us could have survived all our losses without help from a power higher than our own."

Julia reached into her tote bag for another tissue; although they were sitting in the shade, the temperature was climbing. "Here's something else that was tough. After we had come back from Rome, Edson and I decided to leave the Catholic congregation with whom we had worshiped for several years. After lots of praying and soul-searching, we joined an Episcopal group—we just weren't being fed at the other place. You can imagine what a *huge* step this was for me, given my closeness to my parents and my strong Catholic upbringing. But all those talks with Daddy, hearing his later views about the Church, gave me permission to change. It was the right thing for us. And guess what? It was all right with Daddy, too."

"Good, Julia," Najila said, smiling broadly. "You did what *you* wanted."

Vicky brushed some breadcrumbs off her slacks. "Well, look at us here today. We come from different towns, different churches, and we're different ages. One size *doesn't* fit all. I love that line about 'My Father's house has many dwelling places.' We're all in this together, but we don't have to be carbon copies. This might sound heretical in some circles, but it's not as important where you sit on Sunday morning as what you do after you *leave*."

Julia laughed. "I've sure learned that through teaching little kids. They don't care—they just accept and play with whoever's around. More recently, as I've been active in several professional education associations, in church-related activities, and a social sorority, the friendship offered by those women has also been a great source of strength. There is lots of variety in those groups, too; but they've all been equally helpful to me.

"Anyway, as I told you the other night, we left Rome for good in 2003, moved back to Phoenix; and, after a short classroom stint, I became a children's docent at the local natural science museum. Working with kids is great. They keep things real and help me keep my head on straight. And, after some searching, we found an Episcopal Church near our house."

Julia leaned forward, and her voice became strident. "But, then, in 2005, everything went south again. I was diagnosed with early stage breast cancer. I felt like my whole world was collapsing—as in, oh *no*, now it's *my* turn. I had surgery and did the chemo and radiation things. I'm still battling the awful side effects of the heavy-duty follow-up drugs they put you on. I'm positive those have messed with my thyroid, too. Now there's this new issue of diabetes. My weight's still a problem; but, hey, once I'm off these drugs, maybe I'll feel good enough to get out for a walk, start swimming again, and even hit a few tennis balls. Then I'll be able to drop some pounds for sure. Wouldn't my mom love that?"

She sighed and looked around the group. "I'm glad I came on this trip. All you guys look really great and seem to be doing so well. Now that I'm about done with this whole cancer thing, I'm not sure what I can or should start next. While I was recuperating, I spent a lot of time with my needlework, reading, watching old movies, working on Sudoku puzzles—that kind of stuff. Now I think I'm ready for something else. I used to say that my ambition in life was to keep learning; but during the cancer ordeal, that had to take a backseat. I just wasn't up for anything except getting through the day. Recently, though, I joined a women's group called Spiritual Journey. I'm hoping they can give me some direction. So, that's it, folks. *Finito*." She looked at her watch. "Lord, I'm *so* sorry! I can't *believe* I talked about myself for so long. I'm sure your eyes are crossed from boredom."

Several more sparrows flew down, pecked deftly at Vicky's breadcrumbs, then fluttered up into the olive trees overhead. No one spoke as they watched the busy birds.

Finally, Kay looked over at Julia. "Thank you for telling us your life's story, Julia. I loved it; and it was most definitely not boring, probably because I related *so* much to what you said about the critical words from your mother. You know, I often had the same thing from my mother, too. Those words were so hurtful when she spoke them. I have mulled them over and over on many of my walks and have come to the realization that, although they were painful to me at the time, I don't think she *meant* them to be. She was just very busy with four small children, always had a lot on her mind, and probably didn't consider how her words would affect me. I know she loved us, and she meant well."

"Same here, Jules," Ruth said as she dug around in her tote bag for her lip gloss. "Actually, I had both kinds of moms. My own mother always said kind and loving things to us; but my stepmother, Arlene, was a total one-eighty, a world-class criticizer. I can still hear her, screaming at us kids: *'This is for your own good.'* I guess, in her heart, she thought it was. In her own way, she meant well, too. But, hey, Jules, don't let your mom's comments keep pulling you down. Stop trying to be so perfect, so hard on yourself. Geez, *you're* the one with the science degree. Run the numbers. Your life is slipping by so fast. Don't waste it on stuff that doesn't matter. Cut that ball and chain, release your death grip on those injunctions from your parents. They meant well, but they might have been wrong. I know now that my stepmother, Arlene, was wrong in her treatment of us kids. So I've let it go, moved past it. You could try that, too, Jules. God loves you, and *we* love you—and we're the first team."

Julia wiped her eyes and smiled wanly. "Oh, you guys! What a support you are! I don't know what I've done to deserve friends like you. No, wait, that's wrong. I *do* deserve good friends. See, I'm learning already. Do you think I really could? I mean, like, change myself and move on? I guess I could try. What have I got to lose?" She laughed as she tried to stand up. "Now, I've *got* to move on because my leg is completely asleep. Shall we go, Najila?"

As the rest of the group rose off the benches, Alicia stepped close to Julia. "Listen, Julia, I *loved* your story; and I want to echo something Ruth said. Your mom is gone now and isn't here to do it anymore; but you're doing a fine job of keeping her words going twenty-four/seven. You know what? You can stop. You've *got* to let go of all those voices of your mother, your grandmother, your aunts—all those *judges* in your head. Put them to rest. Stop letting them control your life. You've dragged that burden around long enough. It'll take a little practice, but I know you can do it. Trust me on this. Now I've got to ask Najila something, so bye. See you back at the van." Alicia strode rapidly down the hill.

Corinne picked up her tote bag, took a drink from her water bottle, and then put her arm around Julia. "You've been like a sister to me for years, Julia; so I think it's OK for me to say this. We've been together for almost four days now, counting travel time; yet who has mentioned your weight or your looks? Which one of us has said one *word* about that? *You're* the one who has mentioned it repeatedly in one way or another. We've just heard all the things your family wanted for you, and most of it had to do with your weight. Since your mom got so much criticism about her looks from her mother, she probably felt it was necessary, or even her duty, to try to improve or change you. But *did* it? She meant well, but did it help? No. All it did was hurt you. By focusing on it so much yourself now, you're continuing to hurt yourself."

Julia slumped back down on the bench, pulling Corinne down with her. "Oh, Corinne! I wish I had a sister like you. But see, I guess that putting myself down is a symptom of my want-to-please personality. I feel the need to be accepted, to fit into as many molds as possible.

I know that the need to please seems to dominate my life. Maybe this comes from my weight problem, sort of 'If I please you, you won't notice me from the chest down!' I just can't seem to *help* it," she said glumly.

Inez hurried by in front of them then suddenly stumbled. "*Ay Dios mio*! There is a small stone in one of my sandals. May I sit here for a minute, Julia, and take it out?"

"Sure, Inez," Julia replied. "Here, I'll move over." Corinne stood up. "Meet you at the bottom, Julia. Remember: refocus. Our little secret, OK?" Corinne winked at Julia and moved off to join the rest of the group.

Inez removed her right sandal, shook it vigorously, and then slipped her foot back into it. "Ah, much better," she breathed. She turned and smiled at Julia. "That stone gives me a chance to tell you that your story was wonderful! You also said several very important things."

"It was, and I *did*?" Julia ask incredulously.

"Yes. First, you told us about how your family criticized you endlessly but how Sapha's words and actions have been so inspiring to you. You also said that, because of that miracle about the salads, Jesus was now real to you. If you *really* believe that, you can do yourself a great kindness and break the cycle of how you think about yourself."

"You mean it's time to reboot? Just like that? But *how*? I mean, what do I *do*?" Julia looked puzzled.

Inez laughed, her brown eyes flashing. "You get a new life. I did this, and I know you can do it, too. Your mamma, your aunts, and all those relatives are gone now; but your husband is still here. Go call him. Talk things over with Edson, get *his* advice, then believe him. *Believe* that he accepts you as you are. Call your *husband*, Julia, and *not* your parents. You are fine just the way you are. You are fine just *because* you are. You see, Julia, I had a long problem with my weight, too; but once I learned to think of myself as a powerful adult who could change things in her life, and not the helpless child I once was, with so many problems at home, then I was able to turn my life. Once you change how you think *about* yourself, you will want to do more good things *for* yourself. Then you will feel better. Come, let us join the others. I will walk with you."

"Thanks, Inez," Julia said eagerly. "You've helped me so much this morning. I'm not sure I can do it all, but I know I *want* to."

As they walked slowly down the path, Julia's thoughts were jumbled. All these women were her good friends and had just told her the same thing: Stop cutting herself down, quit replaying her mother's criticism a thousand times a day, and, mainly, think of herself as an adult. Sounds good, even sounds possible.

Then, slowly, those old familiar feelings kicked in.

Oh, *right*! Stuff like that might work for others but not for *her*. How could a few simple changes like that make *her* lose weight?

Fat chance.

~17~

Little Shop of Gifts

F urther down the path, Najila turned and waited for Inez and Julia to catch up. "Thank you, Julia. Your story was very honored, no sorry, *honest*. It was hard for me, too, when I took charge of my own life. But once I took my first step, next steps became easier. You are a strong woman, Julia. I know you will do this, too."

Najila raised her voice a bit to include the other women. "Now, we will all take some steps and walk back to the gift shop near the car park. You can find many nice books, maps, T-shirts, even sun umbrellas. The walk is easy, all downhill. Take your time. Kay, could you start? I shall come straight along with Inez and Julia."

Glancing at the group, Najila was happy to realize how much *she* was enjoying these stories. It was also getting easier to lead this tour, to show them where Sapha might have lived and share her writings. If only Mama would understand. Ah, well, maybe she never would. Mama came from a different time, different generation. *Halas*—finished.

"Right, ladies," Kay said briskly. "I'm always ready

for a little retail therapy. Follow me."

After a leisurely walk down to the parking area, the group paused and chatted in front of the gift shop; while they waited for Julia, Najila and Inez. Julia moved slowly, favoring her knee. "Well, I'm finally here, girls," she said, slightly out of breath. "I can't wait to see their wares. This is the first real shopping chance we've had. I'm excited!" Norma and Corinne chose to go back to the viewing platform for more photos, but the rest hurried into the shop.

Kay looked around, astonished. The shop was beautifully arranged—spacious and bright, with well-stocked, wooden bookshelves lining two long walls. At the back, three large windows revealed a beautiful panoramic view of the whole park. In front of the windows, an attractive reading area was furnished with comfortable, maroon leather armchairs; low, wrought iron tables surrounded a dark red, Oriental rug. Tall, leafy fichus trees flourished in each corner. Throughout the shop, display tables held a wide selection of souvenirs: cups, key chains, spoons, T-shirts, hats, maps, guide books, and even multicolored sun umbrellas, as Najila had promised. Several Italian tourists were browsing through the Arabic and Jewish folk music CDs, which were arrayed in a large rack near the cash register, next to a smaller rack of colorful postcards. Soft, classical music provided a serene atmosphere.

"If I'm dreaming, don't wake me," Kay whispered

to Vicky. "This is my idea of the *perfect* gift shop: comfy chairs, good music, books everywhere, and everything well organized. Delightful!"

Julia mopped her forehead with a tissue. "Oohh, feel that cool! You didn't *tell* us there would be air conditioning here, Najila."

"Yah, you never know when there is enough power for the air conditioners; so I thought not to say. It does feel very nice. Alicia, back on the left wall, there are several books on plants and flowers in Palestine."

"Wow, would you look at all this loot?" Ruth raved, as she stood in the center aisle with hands on her hips. "I could go bonkers in here, or at least do a lot of damage to my plastic. So many cute T-shirts, and there are even some coffee mugs calling my name. Where should we start, Corinne? Hey, what's that music?"

"Hmm, I think it's Mozart," Corinne answered. "Imagine hearing a Mozart symphony out here at the back of beyond. Wait, I want to look at some of those CDs on that rack. Whenever I travel, I always try to buy folk music of whatever country I'm in. Then, when I'm back home and cleaning house, I throw on a CD and dance around with the dust cloth. Makes the time just fly!" She began searching through the rack while Ruth agonized over the coffee mugs.

Norma came in and then walked to a table in the center of the shop; many items had been marked down. "Look at this! Here's a little book called *Israel: Past and*

Present. This spiral binding is great; but it also has plastic overlays with the artists' ideas of an ancient place on top of contemporary photos of the same sites, to give you a feel for how it looked centuries ago. I'm getting one of these for my Sunday school kids right now. They'll love it. Look at this, Ruth. Right here in the middle is a photo of a Roman theater, just like where you told your story. With the overlay, it seems much larger and even shows how the top rows of seats would have looked. I just *love* this!"

Julia moved slowly around another table nearby. "Have you guys seen all these great guidebooks? There are two on Sebastia/Samaria; and they're small—perfect to tuck into my suitcase. What do you think, Najila? Are these any good?"

"This place is amazing," Vicky agreed. "I just saw a sign that said, 'Josephus: New Edition.'" She strode quickly to a side table and picked up a thick volume entitled *The New Complete Works of Josephus*. She studied the back cover. "Think of it, Kay. This guy, Josephus, was a historian in the first century; so he could have been a contemporary of Sapha's. Who cares if this costs a hundred and eighty-four shekels? I'm *buying* it."

Just then, Najila passed by. Kay glanced at her then back at Vicky. "Are you thinking what I'm thinking? Najila could do the same *thing*. She could publish Sapha's writings, and perhaps we could help her. Let's go talk to her now." Vicky smiled broadly. "Absolutely. Najila's *got* to do this. Lead the way."

They caught up to Najila. Each put a hand under her elbows and steered her back to the reading area. "Sorry, Julia," Vicky said hastily over her shoulder, "but we're stealing Najila for a minute. She'll be right back. Better yet, come and hear our proposition." They settled Najila in an armchair and then seated themselves. Several of the other women joined them.

Najila looked alarmed. "Something is wrong? Someone is hurt? What can I do?"

"Nothing's wrong," Vicky said soothingly, "and nobody's hurt. But Kay and I were just thinking ... oh, *you* tell her, Kay."

Kay smiled at Najila. "Seeing all of these historical books in here made us think that possibly *you* could publish Sapha's writings. You could take all the things from your Gran Najet's notebook, rework them a bit, and put them into a book. You are the *perfect* person to do this, Najila! You're a teacher, you know a lot about the Samaritans and about the area around here, plus you can include all the history of your family translators throughout the centuries. You could tell how your Gran Najet made her copy back in 1939, on the brink of World War II, and so on."

"Today is a *perfect* time," Vicky continued. "Women's issues are hot now, and you can do a great service by publishing Sapha's writings. What she wrote has been so helpful to all of us; it's bound to help other readers, too. You could sell the book in your own shop, places like this, in bookstores, or maybe even over the Internet." Vicky looked around the group. "And we could all help Najila, right, ladies? Kay's a great librarian, so she could be your research assistant, Alicia can do the computer stuff, Norma and Corinne can supply photos, I'll help you with some of the legal details. There's your whole team right here!"

Najila looked dazed. "Oh, but, I could never, I am not, how could I ..."

"Stop right there," Julia said firmly. "If I can get off the dime, so can you. Besides," she said with a twinkle, "just *think* how fussed your mama will be!" They all burst out laughing.

Najila looked very happy. "I think I should read you something from Gran's notebook. It seems to fit." She took the notebook out of her bag, opened it, and read:

At the well that day, Jesus surely must have known what all Jews knew, that one usually did not have more than three marriages in a lifetime. More than that cast suspicions on the person's morals. When I met Jesus, I was not living with a husband; he was a relative but not a husband. Naturally, the neighbors knew this. In small villages, there was no privacy. But they still talked.

Yet Jesus, who as a Jew, was not supposed to talk to me at all, said nothing derogatory or accusing. He even gave me two small compliments. I will never forget them. He said I was right and that what I had said was true. How healing it is to be listened

to and to be told | was right. He did not criti-
cize or judge me. He only wanted a drink and
to talk a bit. He did not assume that anything
was wrong with me.

After | told him the truth—that, yes, | did have
five husbands, | felt so free. | could have lied
to him about it and covered it up; but | did not.
And then he gave me those words of praise,
telling me that | was right and that | had spo-
ken the truth.

"You know," Najila said as she closed the notebook, "long ago, when I first read Gran's notebook, I
think, no, sorry, *thought* to write something; but then
I put it away. Now you tell me that I am right and
should do this. But I can do it *only* if you all help me.
Oh, but, I do not know. Mama will ..."

She looked at her watch. "Aiyee, we must go
and see the next site before lunch; or the afternoon
sun is too strong. We will see the colonnaded street,
important place for first-century shopping."

"More *shopping*?" Alicia and Ruth asked simul-
taneously. "We're *there*."

~18~

To Tell the Truth

As they hurried out of the shop, Kay asked, "Does everyone have everything—wallets, credit cards, and all your purchases? I would hate for us to leave anything behind, as I don't imagine we'll be coming back here."

Vicky chuckled. "Kay, we really appreciate your care and diplomacy in looking after us."

"I'll second that," Ruth added fondly as she gave Kay's shoulder a squeeze. "I left my backpack on a tour bus once and had to go through hell and high water to get it back. If Kay had been along, that never would have happened."

On the sidewalk, Najila gestured toward the parking lot. "The distance is not very far; but, since Julia's knee is bad today, I will drive. Then it is only little ride to hotel for lunch." The women all got into the van quickly. As Najila climbed into the driver's seat, her cell phone rang. She glanced at it, sighed, and turned it off. "Mama. She will want to know what I am doing, where we are. I will call her—*after* lunch." She backed carefully out of the parking lot and drove slowly along the left exterior rim of the park.

Julia glanced out the window and saw that the road was uneven and unpaved, covered with coarse gravel. She heaved a sigh of relief. "Lord, am I glad I didn't have to walk over *that!*"

At a narrow curve, Najila pulled over to allow a grizzled old shepherd to pass with his flock of brown and black sheep. A scruffy little dog darted in and out, expertly keeping them together with a well-aimed nip at the heels or a sharp bark. Najila waved and called out a greeting to the shepherd. "This is a national park, but sheep still have right of way. Some customs are quite old." She parked near the ruins of a large stone gate at the end of the road. The women got out, clamped on their sun hats, and followed her up the street.

"Come, I will tell you small bits as we walk. This colonnaded street starts near western gate, just behind us. Here, you see the street is quite wide; but it becomes narrow at the other end, closer to the forum. This street was built at the end of second century/ beginning of third, when Sebaste was enlarged as Roman city; so it was not here during Sapha's time. We all like to shop, so I thought to show you. In early times, this street was *very* grand, with much luxury: fine shops and stalls on either side, where olive trees now stand over there. In ancient times, along both sides of this street, there were six *hundred* tall stone columns; but most have fallen in earthquakes. Good stones were carted away for Nablus houses. The columns once lifted a very large roof, creating a shady marketplace."

"We're at the *mall!*" Alicia exclaimed gleefully. "Merchants were big into marketing even back then. The cooler you were, the more shekels you'd spend!"

"Oh, Najila, it's still enchanting up here," Norma said as she took several photos. "I can see why the Romans picked this spot. I would love to have lived here."

Julia squinted down the road. "Guys, I'm trying really hard; but I just can't *imagine* that this quiet, dusty, tree-lined track was once a bustling boulevard, jammed with stores and shoppers."

"Close your eyes, chicks, and picture this," Ruth said as she danced around in the street. "Instead of those gnarly, old olive trees, I see a butcher shop, next to the fruit shop and the baker's stall. Across the street is a wine shop, with cute little tables out front ..."

"... and a cute little waiter out *back*," Vicky added wickedly.

"And then," Alicia went on, undeterred by the laughter, "there's an exclusive ladies' boutique with elegant, linen robes and gorgeous, silk veils and maybe a little counter with trendy, gold earrings and bracelets towards the back. Then, over *there*, is the hairdresser's, next to the sandal maker's; and *way* down there, near the end, sits the villa of Lady Sophia's Academy for Refined Young Maidens."

"Yeah, and what *exactly* were they teaching those girls?" Julia asked, with a crooked smile.

"Honestly, you all have the *wildest* imaginations,"

Kay said. "We should put you in a road show."

"Whaddya mean *'should'*? Ruth retorted. "We *are* the road show. Speaking of, here comes another flock. I'm hopping up on this wall to watch them—the shade's good under these trees. There are even some column chunks you guys can sit on. Park it right here, Jules."

"Julia, wait, *wait*," Kay said, as she opened her tote bag and hurried over to where Julia was starting to sit down. "You don't want to get those nice slacks all dusty. Here, let me brush that off for you."

"Oh, Kay, you're the only person in the entire *world* who travels with a whisk broom in your tote," Julia said, laughing. "But if I have to sit on a column, clean is better. Thanks. You're always so good to us."

"Anyone else, as long as I have it in my hand?" Kay asked, as she glanced around. "No? Fine. But if you need it, just ask."

Najila made a mental note: Buy small broom for van.

Corinne looked thoughtful as she picked up a pebble from the road. "This is pretty amazing, when you think about who was here before us. In the past few days, we've seen a castle built by the Assyrians, a tower built by the Greeks, this street built by the Romans, near a community built by the Samaritans and now part of modern Palestine. I'll bet you could dig down with just a *spoon* in this road and uncover *incredible* history! Lots of stories here."

"I'm making a story about these sheep," Norma said

breathlessly, as she hurried over to capture photos of the second flock passing by. "Aren't they just the *cutest* things? Seeing them here gives it such a biblical feel. Oops! There's a little lamb trying to escape."

Inez set her bag next to a column fragment. She leaned against the rosy-beige stone wall and checked her watch. "I had thought to wait; but the mix of all those cultures—and that little sheep running off—are a good introduction. So I would like to tell my story here. We have a little time before we have to be back for lunch. I will sit here so you can all hear me, but I might get up and walk a bit, too. That helps me when I'm nervous. Is that OK, Najila?"

"Yah, plenty of time," Najila replied, as she glanced at her watch. "We have an hour or so before we take our lunch. It is very nice up here. Please tell us your story, Inez."

Inez wiped tiny beads of perspiration from her forehead with a large white handkerchief, then perched on a rough, stone block under the olive trees. Sunlight filtered through the branches above her, highlighting her stylish, honey brown hair curling softly around her face.

She smiled at Julia. "Though it was hard for her, Julia spoke with so much honesty earlier this morning. As I heard her story, I realized that I want to do the same thing."

Ruth and Alicia sat on the wall across from Inez. Holding her sun hat in front of her face, Ruth whispered,

"Man, I love her Spanish accent and those dark eyes—and how I envy her all that beautiful *clear* skin! Those dark green slacks and matching beaded T-shirt have *got* to be a chi-chi Italian label, too."

"You know," Alicia whispered back, "Inez lives way on the other side of Rome; and, since the study group doesn't meet anymore, I *never* see her. She's really changed; she's so *slim*. What's she done? How has she dropped all that weight?"

Overhearing them, Inez smiled her gratitude. "What Najila just read us at the gift shop, about Jesus giving Sapha two compliments—that was the part that Kay gave me. When the Samaritan woman told Jesus she had no husband, he said, 'Yes, you are right, for you have had five and the current one is not your husband; what you've said is true.' Jesus knew a lot about Sapha's past, but he did not criticize her for anything. She told him the truth; and he gave her two compliments: first, saying that she was right and, second, that she spoke the truth. To look back on my life, I saw that this had happened to me *many* times. God knows all about my past but does not criticize me. I have also received many compliments from the people around me. So I want to focus on those things: telling the truth and compliments."

She spoke slowly, choosing her words carefully. "Like this place, I am a mix of cultures and beliefs. My early story is full of harshness, violence, and abuse; but there has also been light and hope for me, especially in the

past few years. I was born in the small country of El
Salvador, with beautiful geography but many political
problems. Those problems had a great impact on my
life, as I saw how difficult it was to fight for justice.
During the civil war there some years ago, thousands
of people died: some of them because they objected to
the repression of the government and, others, because
they lived in denial and tried to maintain the old order
of things, which was very unfair for the majority of
people. A lot of civilians, who had taken no part but
were in the wrong place at the wrong time, died as
well. Many people just disappeared, never to be found;
others were tortured and exiled. Some of these people
were my teachers and friends. It was *very* hard."

"How *terrible* for you!" Norma said.

Inez looked sad. "Human and civil rights in my
country were not respected, abuse was rampant, and
there was a long cycle of violence. Nobody seemed to
care, and it appeared as though no one was really in
control. The papers said one thing; but, on the ground,
in our schools, neighborhoods, and town, there were
other realities. We did not know what or whom to believe. It was hard to know *what* the truth was; this became a metaphor for my life. I remember my mother
saying that she would *kill* me if I joined the opposi-
tion. I do not think she literally meant that, but I did
not appreciate it. As a young person, I was an idealist
who wanted to fight for justice. I know now that it was
not meant for me to participate and die in that war."
She twisted her watch around her arm.

"What I did have to participate in was my family. We were six at home: my maternal grandmother, my father, my mother, my older half-sister, from my mother's side, my older brother, and me. Things were often very harsh at my house; no one was really in control. Often that felt like a war to me. There was little truth and much violence and abuse. Actually, there were many times when I thought I might die there, too. Let me explain.

"At our house, my grandmother—I called her Mamafina—was like a second mother to us; and that was good. She was a person who was constantly working: cooking, cleaning, shopping for groceries, and taking care of us in every way. She had separated from my grandfather while my mother was very young and then tried to do the impossible to make my mother happy. Personally, I think Mamafina made things too easy for my mother. My mother got married, had a child—my half-sister—and then began to have issues with alcohol when she got divorced. Sometime later, she met my father and had another child, my brother. By the time I was born, she was drinking even more. Our family became dysfunctional. Her drinking affected all of us as a family. That was bad—very, *very* bad."

"Yup," Alicia said, "with an alcoholic in the house, *everybody's* affected. There's no escaping, nowhere to run."

Inez nodded. "I was the youngest and often felt that my brother and sister acted out their anger about this situation in many ways. I was frequently the target of their abuse, which came in many forms. They would play wicked tricks on me, lay traps for me, lock me up ... you know. Some of the abuse was direct and sudden; some was more drawn out. All of it was painful."

She smiled as she fingered a tiny cat charm dangling from a thin, gold chain at her neck. "But my father ... ah, my father. He was a kind and gentle person—always very relaxed. He was very important in my life. I would say he was my hero, as he tried to protect me from the temperamental outbreaks of the rest of the family. Unfortunately, he had his own problems with gambling. Plus, he did not have a stable job for a long time; so I had little sense of security. People in our family did not always tell the truth; so, again, I often did not know *what* the truth was. My childhood was sad and lonely. I did not have many friends, so I invented some imaginary ones. At the time, they seemed real and true to me. I gave them up when I was seven or eight because I thought I might be crazy or, at least, *look* that way. Two ideas were in my mind a lot then. One: I wanted to run away. The other: I wanted to die."

"That's *awful!*" Julia said vehemently. "Little children shouldn't have to feel this way."

A pale green olive leaf floated down onto Inez's shoulder. She nodded. "You are right, Julia. I was not a very good student in elementary school because I was always absentminded and daydreaming. I guess I was trying to escape. Oh, I could tell you many more details of my childhood, some of which would make your hair curl; but they are just too hurtful." She shifted on the stone pillar as she clasped and unclasped her hands.

"She may *think* she's sparing us the details," Alicia whispered to Ruth, "but her body language says it all. Plus, the tougher the topic, the thicker her accent. No wonder!"

Inez began to stride back and forth in front of the wall. "When I became a teenager, my role in the family turned around. I experienced some major changes, and my life got worse before it got better. I went from being an invisible, unwanted child to being the young adult who took care of the emotional issues of my brother and my mother. There was her alcoholism, of course; but my brother also had several unhappy love affairs, could not hold a job, was in trouble with the police when he stole some money, and so on. They both found the truth of their situations difficult to face. So they wanted me to do it for them. I became their rescuer and began to carry their burdens, but I was too young for this task. I hardly knew what the truth was for myself, let alone for *them*."

Ruth jumped off the wall and gave Inez a big hug. "Man, I thought I was the only one who wore the junior shrink hat at home. You too, huh? Here, have a tissue."

Inez hugged Ruth back and went on. "By the time I was in high school, I had developed many symptoms of codependence and overeating. I also became aware that my life had some other major problems. I had some serious self-destructive behaviors, like abusing myself with strenuous diets and fasts. Once, I even hurt myself with a shaving blade. I had suicidal thoughts, but I did not have the courage to kill myself. Daily a battle flamed inside my mind: to live or to die. I never told anyone—I could not. Besides, who would have believed me? Or cared?"

Ruth nodded. "Uh-huh. I hear that. *Totally*."

"I was prone to chemical addictions," Inez continued. "I had this friend who also had alcoholic parents and a dysfunctional family, and she drank alcohol and took pills. So I tried them a few times with her. I know now that I was playing with fire—perhaps trying to die. I was very lucky that I *did not* die. I guess my desire to live was greater than my tendencies towards self-destruction. Instead, I became an overeater. Food didn't seem quite as dangerous, at the time, anyway; and it was *so* much more readily available and socially acceptable."

Several women laughed. Julia bit her lip.

Inez kept walking. "Even during those horrible war years, organized religion was still socially acceptable in my country. My parents, both Catholics, did not practice religion; we had few conversations about God at home. As a child, I had studied in a Catholic school with nuns; most of what I knew about religion, I learned there. We had all the rituals like baptism, First Communion, and the other sacraments; but there was very little about love. So I believed in a God who punished us for every single mistake. In my childish way, I blamed myself for my mother's drinking. She would drink, then quit and be sober, sometimes for many months or even years. Then, she would start again;

and I thought it was my fault. I did not think God cared about me personally; he was absent in my life. As a very scared child, I was afraid of a lot of things; so, naturally, I was afraid of God. I did not know the truth about him, either. Even today, I am still not always sure. I want to believe, and sometimes I think I do. But ..."

She stopped pacing and spread her arms wide, palms up. "In spite of that, I have had several strange religious experiences that I still cannot explain. One of them happened when I was only eight years old. It was Good Friday; and, when I woke up that morning, I had a small cross on the tip of my middle finger. I was puzzled, as no one had drawn that perfect cross. I asked Mamafina, but she could not explain this to me. The memory of this event stayed with me; I am not sure whether it was a dream or whether it really happened. Then, some years later, I had two very important dreams."

She sat down and took a drink from her water bottle. "When I was a teenager, I became an atheist for about six years, until I was twenty-one. When well-intentioned people tried to talk with me about God, I would not listen; I was very stubborn. But my refusal to believe in God changed a little when I had a very vivid dream in which I saw the need for God in my life. However, at the time, I did not pay much attention."

Julia leaned closer as Inez continued in a soft voice.

"Then I had a second dramatic dream—almost like a relevation. In this dream, I was in a very strange place where I had the ability to see the future. I was given the best choices that anyone could have in her life. Pictures were in front of me like a deck of cards. I was shown myself married to the man of my dreams, I was shown as an intellectual who had won the Nobel Prize and who had achieved fame and fortune, and I was shown many other things that people wish for. Then, I was shown that something very important was missing. Without that missing element, nothing, absolutely *nothing*, could make sense. There was no real happiness. It seemed like God was the missing element—was more important than anything else. There were no words, only the understanding. At the time, this seemed like an absolute truth. I cannot describe my feelings about this. I was moved and humbled, all at once. I wanted to believe—*so* much."

"I find it interesting," Corinne said, as she fanned herself with her sun hat, "how many different ways God uses to speak to us. I usually blow off my dreams, thinking they're the product of too much pepperoni pizza before bedtime."

Inez laughed, then started pacing again. "I have jumped ahead of myself, so I must back up a bit. My mother had been sober for many years; life was much better for us as a family. However, when I was fifteen, our lives took a bad turn because she started drinking again. This fact impacted all of us very dramatically. I had a religious crisis; and that is when I became an atheist, as I told you. I was *so* tired of my fear of God and was *so* disappointed by the events. I prayed and prayed for God to help us, to change my mother, and to stop her drinking; but he did not. So I turned my anger and frustration towards God. Oh, yes, and during that time, another way that I dealt with my mother's alcoholism was by working very hard on my studies." She smiled at Ruth. "I, too, received a sense of security when I excelled."

Ruth sighed. "Inez, I *know* we are twins; or, at least, we both used the same coping strategies. What else did you do?"

"I worked," Inez replied quickly. "I had many different jobs. I always worked in the summer as a shop assistant while I was in high school to have some extra money. When I graduated from high school, in 1979, I could not enter the public university; it had been closed by the government because of the civil war. So I decided to do a year of secretarial studies, which turned out to be a good idea because, after getting a job as a secretary, I could then afford the fees of a private university. I paid for my studies by working in many places. I also got life experience and met many different kinds of people. I worked for a small news agency, for the symphonic orchestra, then a few years in educational television in public relations, where I was in charge of the personnel department."

"Gracious," Kay said. "The media and then musicians? You certainly had a broad spectrum of experience."

Inez leaned against the stone wall. "Yes, I was

lucky; and I learned a lot. Anyway, after that second dream, my attitude about myself slowly began to change. It did not happen overnight, but the changes started then. I knew I had some talents and some intelligence that I could put to use to improve my life and perhaps help others. I finished my university studies in my country, received a Fulbright Latin American Scholarship for students at American universities, and completed my master's degree in educational psychology, in 1991, at a university in the south of Illinois. I met my husband soon after arriving in America; we married six months later. After two years, we moved to another university, where he found his higher education; and I tried to find a Higher Power through a Twelve-Step program.

"Slowly, I started to believe in God again. My change from being an atheist to a believer was very gradual, and I am *still* not always sure. For so long, my ideas about God were contaminated by false conceptions. I had felt God was a punishing and vindictive being. It was not until I started my journey in a Twelve-Step group for my food addiction that I started to grasp a more accurate knowledge of my Higher Power—that God is all about love and forgiveness. I try to believe in a Higher Power that is here with me; my life has been improving steadily ever since. When my husband accepted a job in Rome, I joined your study group. You have helped me so much."

"Many people," Norma said sweetly, "have such mistaken ideas about God. He wants to do good things and give love, goodness, and peace to all his children. But, for some people, it's so difficult to accept. However, I've heard many parents say the same things about *their* children."

Inez laughed. "Yes, and as I learned about love, truly unconditional love, from you and from my friends in the Twelve-Step group, I discovered that I cannot love other people unless I first love myself. I learned that I do not need to eat or to use any strange substances to ease the pain and fill myself. I can take care of myself, do good things for myself, and fill myself with love instead."

Vicky looked wistful. "How perfectly you've stated the problem and the solution. I wish my mom could have known this."

Inez nodded. "In the years before my encounter with the Twelve-Step program, I had many problems. Because I was addicted to food, I weighed over two hundred and thirty pounds. I had lost some by the time I moved to Rome, but I was still heavy. I was also a codependent, in that I took care of other people's problems at the expense of my own. Sometimes I even enabled them to stay sick themselves. I was often very depressed and had many difficulties with my husband. Worst of all, I hated myself. I felt out of control, had no self-respect, had no self-confidence, was a people pleaser, and was very passive."

She went on, her accent not so prominent. "I was able to find a Twelve-Step group in Rome, so I kept going. Happily for me now, I don't have suicidal thoughts anymore; and I am not depressed. My marriage is more fulfilling. I am more comfortable with my mistakes because I know that they are a part of learning. I am still a perfectionist at heart, but I am working on it. I can also feel love and forgiveness towards others. I can see that the people who hurt me were also victims and that everything was a chain reaction. Most of the time, I think my Higher Power loves me. So that helps me to love myself—to stand up for myself. I am also more aware of my rights, so I am learning to relate to other people in a much healthier way. To quote St. Francis, there is now forgiveness instead of hatred. There is pardon instead of resentment. That is something so important for my own girls who are now fourteen and twenty. They are growing up in a much more loving environment.

"Another way I am learning to take care of myself is through therapy. I was fortunate to work with a Christian friend of mine. She is full of love and truth; she told me that God is truth and that the truth will set me free. That is why I liked it when Jesus complimented the Samaritan woman for telling the truth."

Corinne plucked an olive leaf from a nearby branch. "Isn't it funny how people love to invent slander, rather than taking the time to look for the truth? Sapha endured a lot of gossip because of all those marriages, but I wonder what the *real* story was. Earlier, she said that she had no male children."

"Well," Norma said, "I lived in the Middle East for

several years; and, even now in some of those countries, the woman's not being able to have children is a frequent reason for divorce. I had several friends in those same circumstances. So, in order for Sapha to have any kind of security, she would *have* to continue to remarry—to have a husband's protection."

"True, true," Vicky said, "but some scholars say that Sapha didn't actually *have* five husbands but that that was a symbol for something else—like five different rulers or five different gods over that territory."

Najila's eyes blazed. "Puh! They can believe that if they *want*," she said sharply, "but I think Sapha really *had* five husbands. Nobody would make *that* up! All those husbands were necessary so she would not have to go to the streets, just to eat. Besides, others in Samaria and Judah, higher born than Sapha, married five times and more. Fancy Roman wives, many in the Herod family, changed husbands like changing sandals. Sapha got the bad news."

Norma tucked her camera in her shirt pocket. "Maybe you mean bad *press*, Najila; but I'll bet you're right."

"I'm sure it was difficult back then," Kay said earnestly, "for a woman to live alone and support herself around here. It still is. But look at you, Najila—you're *doing* it."

Najila frowned. "Um, well, yes, you are right. It *is* very hard, with such talk and criticism and so many side looks, mostly from my family. Sapha wrote that people thought she was inventing tales to cover her lacks as wife. *They* said she failed and was a shameful and wicked woman."

"Criticism from family is a knife in the heart, isn't it?" Julia said in a subdued voice. "It's the *worst*. It was then, is now, and ever shall be. Amen. I read this book once about stuff people say and do, telling you it's for your own good. I wanted to barf."

"I have read a similar book," Inez said, "and that has made me be really careful with what I say to my own daughters. There is a difference between criticism and truth. Telling the truth, especially to myself, has become so important for me. Consequently, I do not have the self-destructive behaviors of the past. I do not need them now. I *know* I am a codependent and that I still need to do a lot of work to improve, but I also know that I am moving in the right direction. I do not have the desire to die anymore because I have so much now to live for. The better I feel about myself, the more I see myself helping other people. Who knows? Perhaps, one day, I will even be able to help the people in my country. After all those years of war, a few things were achieved that benefited the country. Our worst enemy is ignorance; that will take many more years to overcome. It is a long, slow path."

She smiled and started walking again. "But, at least, the process has started; and that is how I feel about my life. My journey of change has often been painful. I had to own my dysfunctional family, my denial, and my addictions. I did not know who I was or what I felt. I did not know *what* the truth was. I was confused about my beliefs; and I was constantly fighting with myself most of the time, no matter *how* good other people told me I was. I was very self-destructive.

"The difference is that now I know the truth. I know that I have choices, and I am choosing *not* to be a victim. As I am trying to believe and learn the truth about God, I am also learning the truth about my family and myself. I have even gained some confidence. A few years ago, along with ten other teachers, I got the nerve to quit my job. We had problems with our school supervisor, and I decided it was no use for me to continue working in an abusive environment. We told the owner of the school the reasons, but they would not hear from us. So let *them* deal with it now!"

"Yayy, Inez," Alicia shouted. "Way to go!" Everyone cheered and applauded loudly.

Inez blushed. "I have learned that I am set free now, to live a better life and not to have to repeat all the destructive patterns of behavior of my childhood. Several years ago, my mother and I reconciled; we had a good relationship until the day she died. I am *so* grateful for that. Perhaps because of my own difficult background, I have always loved psychology. Although that is what my degree is in, it was hard to find a job in that area in Rome. So, for the last few years, I have been teaching Spanish and English in a small girls' school in the suburb of Rome. It is very rewarding; as most are not the spoiled, rich-girl type one *can* find in private schools. Rather, they are smart and sensible girls; and I love seeing their transformation into more confident people. I share many of my own books and my Spanish music with them, and I compliment them very often because I know how good compliments make *me* feel."

"Well, see," Corinne said, "you're using your psychology training after all."

"Yes, I guess I am. I also have some projects that I hope will become a reality. I would like to get another degree or certificate and start doing some counseling. I want to help people know and be able to speak the truth about themselves—to free themselves and stop whatever destructive cycles *they* are in.

"I can truly say I was the victim of long years of abuse. It came in the form of war and terror within my country. It also came from those closest to me who should have been protecting me. Through my various encounters with my Higher Power and a lot of help from my counselor and friends, I am slowly coming to believe—at least, I am *trying* to. One of the best things I have learned is to love and forgive myself. This has changed my life." She gave a small bow and flashed a brilliant smile. "I hope you all find the same things."

Ruth slid off the wall and reached for her tote. "Wow! And I thought I had a horrible childhood! You've come a *long* way, Inez."

"Yes," Najila said, "compared to you, Inez, my life was *very* easy, like a walk in the dark."

Kay stood up and gave her slacks a flick with the whisk broom. "I couldn't agree more. It's '*park*,' Najila; but your English is fabulous anyway. Let's go to the hotel, shall we? I'm ready for lunch and a nap. I'm sure I'll dream about Inez and her wonderful deck of cards."

As the group moved off, Julia lingered behind, her face a study of emotions. She glanced around to make' sure they were alone. "Good story, Inez; but I just have one quick question. You said you had previously weighed over two hundred and thirty pounds, but I can see you weigh a *lot* less than that today. How did you lose it? Did you take pills? Is it easy to keep it off? What do you do on a daily basis? Do you have to think about it a lot?"

Inez sat back down and smiled at Julia. "Thanks. I *have* lost about sixty pounds. Well, let me see. I lost the weight by eating sensibly, cutting out sugar and most white flour products. Those things are very addictive for me; they make me want to eat more of *everything*. I was a vegetarian for about a year; I still do not eat beef. I drink a lot of water, and I exercise several times a week. But, no, it is not easy. And, yes, I think about it and have to make those decisions every day. Should I eat this good thing or just a little bite of that bad thing? After all, who will *know*? On this trip, the buffets are hard, too, because everything is right there in front of you. Some days are easier than others, but I know that I only have to worry about what I eat *today*. It is not as hard as it once was, but I have to watch it *every* day. However, two years ago, when I made that first big decision—that I was *fed up* with how I looked, and I had it in my power to change—then the daily decisions got easier, like Alicia in her hospital bed. Oh, yes, one more thing: I stopped doing fat talk."

"*Fat* talk?" Julia exclaimed. "What the heck is *that?*"

"I have stopped mentally punching myself—stopped making those little digs about how *fat* I look in a particular pair of jeans, what a *bad* girl I am if I eat this slice of cake, how wonderful life will be, once I am *thin*–things like that. Instead, I give myself compliments; I even write them down in my journal. I also compliment my husband, my daughters, my students, my neighbors, and my friends. They all love it, of course. It is easy, once you start. It may sound like a small thing, but it works for me."

"So, basically," Julia asked pensively, "you just substitute *positive* statements for negative ones? That's *all?*"

"Yes. That's right," Inez answered. "I am what I eat *and* what I say. Now I like myself more, I am healthy, and I feel better. I do not want to go back to my old life *ever*! But I *do* want to go to lunch. Let's join the others!"

~19~

Mt. Gerizim

N orma pushed the book off her chest and glanced at her blue travel alarm. Heavens, almost four o'clock! *I've got to get up. Kay so likes us to be punctual, and I don't want to miss anything.*

As she threw off the light blanket and started to sit up, she was rocked by a wave of nausea. She thought for a moment. *Was it those cucumbers or that lamb stew she'd had for lunch?* Whatever, she was not going to worry that it might be anything else. She would see her doctor once she got home; those new pills just weren't sitting right. She stood up carefully and squared her shoulders, determined to enjoy the day. They'd already seen so many exciting things; she wouldn't have missed hearing all of Sapha's revelations for *anything*. What a treasure Najila had in that notebook!

She fished her scuffed, tan oxfords out from under the bed and quickly slipped them on. After she ran a comb through her dark red hair, she swiped on some peach lip gloss and then hurried out the door and down the shaded path that connected her cottage to the parking lot. Kay was standing by the door of the van; it looked as if everyone else was already inside.

"Wait, wait, I'm *coming*," Norma called, as she ran towards Najila's van. "Don't leave yet."

"It's all right, Norma. Take your time," Kay said calmly. "I just got here, too. We're all a bit slow getting started this afternoon. I think everyone's here now, Najila; so we're ready." Kay climbed in behind Norma and pulled the van's door shut.

"The other day, we saw Mt. Ebal and Mt. Gerizim when we drove to Sebaste," Najila said, as she drove onto the highway. "Now we will go right up on Mt. Gerizim. There is more traffic today, so I will talk about the sites once we are there, *insha'allah*. First we will see ruins of Samaritan temple, then I will tell you some bits about Samaritan beliefs."

They began a slow ascent of the gently sloping mountain called Gerizim. After a short time, Najila pulled over to a viewing area, shut off the engine, and turned to face the group. "This is about halfway up, so we can stop here. We are now forty miles north of Jerusalem. This mountain, Mt. Gerizim, and Mt. Ebal, over there"—she pointed—"make the sides of an important east-west pass. The town of Nablus, where our hotel is, sits in between. You remember that Mt. Gerizim is about three thousand feet above the sea. Not so high like the Rockies or Alps, I think, but high for this land." She consulted a small note card in her hand. "It is formed of Eocene limestone, which makes dark gray color on the upper slopes."

Vicky was busily writing down Najila's explanations, while Corinne and Norma took photos out the van's windows. "What's Eocene limestone, for heaven's *sake*?" Julia muttered.

Alicia pointed up. "It's obviously some kind of gray rock. Google it when you get home."

"In ancient times," Najila continued, "both mountains were very important. There was an east-west highway in the valley at the base of mountains, crossed by north-south highway from Jerusalem to Galilee near Shechem. Like guards over this valley, both mountains could be fortified, securing the roads in time of attack. There was also a good water supply from Jacob's Well, making settlements possible since ancient times. Now we will go up to the old Samaritan temple." She drove slowly up the winding mountain road, and soon they pulled into a parking lot at the edge of a large and well-preserved site. "It is only a short walk. You can manage, Julia?"

"Heavens, yes, Najila. I'm fine. But thanks for asking. I'll just take it slow."

"Oh, look," Norma exclaimed. "Those Italian tourists from our hotel are getting out of their bus across from us; and isn't that the German man who took our photos up at the church of John the Baptist, standing over there by a taxi? Looks like everyone's trying to get in here before closing time."

"My, but this site is huge!" Kay exclaimed, as they

climbed out of Najila's van. "What a spot they chose
for their temple. This view is *fabulous*!"

"Even then, church guys knew the best real
estate agents," Vicky mumbled.

Separating the parking lot from the site, a new,
metal fence enclosed a vast area. In the distance were
ruins of what appeared to be a large fort or castle. A
square, stone tower stood to the right side of the fort;
a roofed, wooden viewing platform was at the opposite
end. Workmen were busy in a lower area. A green,
metal fence gate stood open, allowing access to the site
via a new asphalt sidewalk. To the right of the gate,
a large, blue sign displayed careful white lettering in
both Hebrew and English.

Alicia strolled over and read slowly out loud:
"'Archaeological Site of Mount Gerizim. This site
was excavated and restored by the Staff Officer
of Archaeology for Judea and Samaria.' That's
interesting, Najila; but we're in *Palestine*. How come
the sign isn't written in Arabic, too? How does that
make *you* feel?"

Najila looked over her shoulder, stepped close
to Alicia, and whispered, "*occupied*." She smiled as
she adjusted her shoulder bag. "But, I decided long
ago that I will not be sad about problems like that. I
enjoy my job and want to keep doing it, *insha'allah*.
We learn to deal with things, how to work around
them."

Nearby, Ruth chuckled. "I learned the same
thing, working for the airlines."

As they walked along the sidewalk, Najila explained

about the site. "More excavation work goes along to develop this as a national park, like Sebaste. Signs are up, fences are in, and some sidewalks are done; but the main area is not yet finished for close-up viewing. Oh yes, that second sign, by the gate, said no photos allowed; but when your cameras stay down low, inside your hand, I see nothing."

Julia laughed. "So *that's* how it works! I love it."

A bit farther down the walk, Najila stopped at a metal fence. "Just here"—she indicated—"you see a fine example of a very old olive press, comes from Greek times, maybe third or second century BC. The site manager told me this press will be moved soon to better location, where it is easier to see."

Standing close to the fence, Kay poked her camera through the chain links and quickly took several photos of the round, stone press. It was about a foot high and four feet in diameter, with a deep groove or trough in the middle. There was a little opening in one side, where the freshly-pressed oil would have flowed out into a waiting container. A smaller, flat, round rock, perhaps the grinding stone, lay nearby.

"I use olive oil in everything," Vicky said, "so I'm glad I can just zip into a deli and not have to mash my own in a deal like *that*. Looks tough."

Soon the sidewalk turned, and they entered the actual site of the temple ruins. Since it was close to five, the workmen were starting to clear up. "*Mumtaz*, oh, sorry, good," Najila said. "Now there is not so much noise or dust.

Come, we will walk and look closer. You cannot
see them all, but there are many layers in this site.
Around 400 BC, after problems with the peoples of
Judah, Samaritans of this area built their own temple
up here. It was *very* beautiful, similar in design to the
temple in Jerusalem, but was destroyed around 110
BC by the Jewish leader, John Hyrcanus. When he
smashed the city of Shechem down and destroyed this
temple, his importance rose with religious leaders in
Jerusalem who hated the idea of *any* temple outside
of Jerusalem."

"Give me a *break!*" Julia said as she walked along
slowly. "They were probably just whining because of
lost revenues from temple taxes and tourism. What
else is new?"

Najila laughed heartily. "Oh, Julia, you have
such good humor. Later on, the Roman Emperor
Hadrian built a large pagan temple to honor Jupiter,
around 135 AD, over the ruins of the first temple.
That temple of Jupiter had a very big stairway—three
hundred steps—to make it easy for people from town
to walk up for worship."

"*Easy?*" Julia exclaimed. "Three hundred steps
uphill? Just for *church*? I'm glad *I* don't have to do
that. My poor knee would never make it. No, wait, I
mean, well, *maybe* I could if I walked really slowly ...
oh, forget it."

"The Byzantines," Najila went on, smiling, "built
their church up here around the year 490, on top of ruins
of first two temples. At first, local Samaritans complained
that this Christian church sat on top of their old temple.

Around 529, they made a big revolt; but it was put down harshly by the Byzantines. One hundred years later, when Muslim Arabs came, they seemed like *liberators,* as Samaritans were tired of the Byzantines and their heavy ways."

Corinne stopped and looked around her. "Can you even *imagine* how hard it was to haul those huge stones up here in wagons or on sledges, to build that early temple, four hundred years before *Christ?*"

"Yes," Norma said with a little giggle, "and local scroungers have been hauling them back *down* to town ever since. I've noticed some pretty unusual foundations around Nablus."

Najila beckoned them forward. "Now we go to the viewing platform on left. You can look out over whole site." They followed her down the sidewalk, then up three steps onto a spacious, new, planked platform. A well-designed, wooden roof provided welcome shade from the afternoon sun. With a nod to Najila, a lone workman finished brushing off the smooth benches lining the inside, gathered his tools, and left.

Julia laughed as she chose a corner bench. "Look, Kay, a guy after your own heart! He's got his own little broom. Wow, this is *great*! Even though I'm sitting down, I can still see out and all around me. Clever design."

"That archaeological staff officer did that just for you, Julia," Alicia said sweetly. She patted Julia on the knee as the rest of the group found seats.

Norma coughed several times. "My goodness, Najila, it was just one thing after *another*, wasn't it? All those layers, all those different kinds of churches on top of each other through the centuries. That whole thing reminds me of the Russian wooden dolls my grandmother used to have. First there was a big one, then you opened it and inside was a slightly smaller one, then smaller yet, and so on until you got down to the last little bitty one. From the first to the last, they were all smiling; but they were also hiding what was deep down inside them. Now, all around us," she said, waving her arms, "archaeologists are doing the same thing: digging down, one layer at a time, uncovering ruins and deep, hidden things, and seeking all those ancient people who lived and worshiped up here."

Najila walked to the edge of the platform, then turned to look at the group. "Exactly, Norma. What a good thought! Even today, Samaritans hold many of the same beliefs about worship as their ancestors. For them there are four principles of faith: one God; one prophet, Moses; one holy book, called the Pentateuch— first five books of Old Testament—and one holy place, here on Mt. Gerizim. They also believe that *taheb*, or Messiah, son of Joseph, will be a great prophet like Moses and will appear on the Day of Vengeance and Recompense. They observe just seven holy days from the Torah and do not celebrate Hanukah or Purim. New Year is celebrated fourteen days before Passover; and, on Passover Eve, there is a *very* big sacrifice of lambs and male goats, still held nearby. Samaritans are governed by their high priest; observe Sabbath, purity rules, strict marriage codes; and practice circumcision. Oh, yes, and Sapha even wrote that she spoke to Jesus about worshiping on this mountain; but he said the time would come when the place of worship—on a mountain or in Jerusalem—wouldn't matter but that the Father seeks those who will worship in spirit and truth."

Inez sighed. "It is *so* beautiful here, Najila. Those words about true worship not being in a place but in spirit and truth mean a lot to me."

"Yah, I like to come up here to sit and think. Now we should go, as tonight we will have a special dinner in Nablus. Have you any questions?"

~20~

Seeking Such People

N orma laughed nervously. "Yes, one. May I tell my story now, Najila? You said we'd have dinner out, but it's just five o'clock now. I won't talk too long, so we'll be able to get back to the hotel and change in plenty of time before we need to leave, OK?"

"Fine, Norma; we have time," Najila said graciously. "I made reservations at Cousin Adnan's restaurant. And I will call him just before we leave the hotel, so he makes everything ready. No problem."

Kay started to look at her watch but changed her mind. Did it *really* matter if they were *precisely* on the dot? She smiled and allowed herself a small sigh of relief.

"I know we've been sitting here awhile," Norma said, "so if any of you want to walk around or take photos, I won't mind. It's just that, well, I *have* to tell my story up here."

"Are you *kidding*?" Ruth said quickly. "You guys can take off if you want to, but I wouldn't miss this for *anything*. So dinner's a little late. Big whup. Go for it, Norma."

Norma found a lozenge in her purse and popped it in her mouth. She cleared her throat and took a deep breath. "What Najila just said is perfect for my story: I have been to religious services on mountains and in Jerusalem; and, like Sapha, I haven't always understood what I worshiped either. But, some years ago, I had an experience that completely changed my life. So that's what I want to tell you—about all the people who helped me and did things just like Jesus did. You know when he said to his disciples: 'Do this in memory of me'? Well, those people did that. They helped me when I needed it most. They understood. They *got* it, and then they gave it to me."

She pushed a strand of dark red hair off her forehead and sat forward on the bench. "Here's what happened. My encounter with Jesus was touched off by a dramatic incident, some thirty years ago now. I'd been married for thirteen years and loved my husband very much. I'd known him for eight years prior to our marriage. I even remember the day that I first met him—I was fifteen."

Norma made a wry face. "After we married, the years just flew by. We were very happy, or so I thought. Then, one day, he told me he wanted a divorce and that there was someone else in his life. I felt my life had ended. I was beyond hurt—I was *devastated*! We were living in Kuwait—that was before I met you all in Rome—and were part of the U. S. Foreign Service family. My husband put me on a plane for the States. Because I was a dependent spouse, I had no choice in the timing of my departure or where I was going. I said good-bye to the one I loved and the life I loved, not realizing at first that Jesus was offering me a better life, like he offered Sapha. There I was, in my mid-thirties, sent to live in a small, empty house in the Washington, DC suburbs—alone, no car, no job, and no nearby friends; since most of my friends were overseas. It hurts to remember, even now." She coughed slightly and pressed her hand to her chest.

"Sapha knew hurt, too, Norma," Najila said softly. "Perhaps now is a good time to hear this part." She opened the notebook and read:

> Even though the pain is sharp, I must write the truth about my marriages. My first husband, Shedeur, much older than I, had died. His brother, Shelumiel, then took pity on me; and we married, according to the ancient law that said when a man dies, his brother must marry that man's wife and raise up children to honor the memory of the dead man. Shelumiel was also older and was very unkind. We both tried to do our duty; but, after I lost four babies in three years, he divorced me. What good was I to him? I was worn out from all the pregnancies, so I was relieved.
> During our marriage, I had met some of his business associates. After the divorce, one of them, Samuel, asked my brother for my hand. Since I had returned to his house to live, his wife was only too happy, as it meant one less mouth to feed. Though I feel shame to admit it, I was very

attracted to this man. Samuel was a wealthy trader. He showered me with gifts and luxury. I couldn't believe my good fortune; but even if he had been a pauper, I would have loved him. He was everything my first two husbands were not: young, handsome, and kind. Even though we had no children, he professed that his love for me outweighed his lack of sons. We moved to Gerash, where his business was, and were very happy—so I thought.

Then, one day, after several years of marriage, he informed me that, since I had burned his dinner on several occasions over the past few months, he wanted a divorce. I was numb with shock. In my heart, I knew there was another reason. I suspected it was because a colleague of his, who owned many businesses, had recently died; and his pretty wife had flashed her eyes at my husband. Here was a chance for him to gain even more wealth, a young wife, and perhaps even a child. He ordered the servants to pack up my things, wrote out the bill of divorce, and sent me back to Shechem. I was desolate in a silent house, with no husband, no children, and no friends—only the cold stares and whispers of neighbors. I cried until I could cry no more.

Norma blinked back tears that threatened to slide down her cheeks. "Oh, my. Oh, my goodness. Poor Sapha."

"Poor *Sapha*?" Julia exclaimed shrilly. "How about poor *Norma*?"

A long ray of the setting sun slanted under the roof above them, illuminating Norma's dark red hair with a fiery brilliance. Ruth wrapped her arm around Norma and offered her some tissues.

Norma smiled at Ruth, then wiped her eyes and straightened her shoulders. "Before I left, a priest friend overseas had advised me, upon my return to the U. S., to join a prayer group. In those days, I had no idea what a prayer group even *was*. When I arrived back, I was a stranger in a strange land. I felt totally abandoned, like an orphan, a widow, a leper, all rolled into one. Like Sapha, I cried daily, sometimes hourly.

"But then, one day, I finally got tired of that. So I took the priest's advice and found a prayer group. Then, through those wonderful people in that group, Jesus somehow came to me and gave me so much help, so much support, so much hope ..."

"So much living water?" Inez asked.

"Yes, exactly," Norma answered. "You'll appreciate this: That group was within walking distance of my house. Great, huh, since I had no other means of transport. Here's another thing: About a year before the breakup, I'd been given a prayer card. The prayer was about asking God where I was to serve in his vineyard. I'd always wanted a family and children, but that wasn't happening. I didn't know

know *what* my vocation was. I kept asking Jesus: What is my job here? What's my life's work? The prayer card seemed to fit the situation, so I kept praying it."

"You know Norma," Kay said tentatively, "I think I might need that same prayer. I'm certainly having a hard time knowing what *my* next vocation is."

"I'll jot down a copy for you when we get back to the hotel," Norma said. "I still have it in my Bible. Anyway, when I was in that empty house, with no TV, I would have these long conversations with Jesus. I remember reading that part in John's Gospel where Jesus talked a lot with Sapha, telling her: '*True* worshipers will worship the Father in Spirit and truth and indeed the Father seeks such people to worship him.' So I wondered if Jesus was actually seeking Sapha there at the well—you know, *looking* for somebody like her to do his work. It obviously didn't matter to him that she'd had five husbands; he surely knew about the three marriages thing. But he also knew her circumstances; he knew exactly *why* she'd had five husbands. He didn't criticize or condemn. It just didn't matter. Because he knew all this, she decided that Jesus must be somebody really special, like a prophet, maybe even the Messiah. I mean, he sure made her feel special, didn't he—talking to her about important religious topics, like salvation and places to worship?"

She coughed again and took a sip from her water bottle. "So, after a while, I got to thinking: Maybe I was being sought, too—being *prepared* for work I would do later.

Although I didn't know it at the time, that's exactly what happened. The prayer group did know about Jesus, though. They prayed for me, and I prayed for them and myself. They said that since Jesus was a prophet, he knew exactly who I was and what I needed."

Alicia looked surprised. "Wow, Norma! You never talked about this in our Rome group."

"I know—probably because that group was a bit different than the one in Washington. Anyway, guess what? The new prayer friends were right! I got a car, a job, and more education; the classes I took enabled me to teach in a nearby Catholic school. My life began to fill in for me. After all, I had thirty-five children in my classroom; who could ask for more? I even planted some flowers at my little house. Jesus and I continued our conversations. I asked my returning overseas colleagues to speak to the children on various subjects. The kids loved it and so did the speakers. Then, one day, about six years later, I asked a certain Foreign Service officer, named Jerry, who'd been in Israel, to speak to my class about the Old Testament. Well, the rest is history."

Ruth waved her sun hat. "Ta-*dah*! Yay for you."

Norma laughed. "Since both our spouses had left us, Jerry and I obtained annulments and were married shortly thereafter. Again, I found myself making preparations to go back overseas. Jerry had a son, so that made me part of a family again. Later, when his son went off to college, we headed to the Middle East. Then our place of worship became very different—in community rooms, private houses, wherever we could squeeze together. But who cared? We worshiped as a group, and we knew that God was there with us. We became like each other's family.

"Speaking of worship, I think Sapha was pretty nervy when she asked Jesus about the right place, since the Jews believed one thing and the Samaritans another. Each claimed that *theirs* was the right place, and each tried to destroy the other's temple from time to time. It's just like my little students fighting over their corner of the sandbox. Honestly, people can be so hardheaded and opinionated about religion. Don't I know! My own family and the neighbors around us were *just* like that—small-town folks, with small-town ways. They all thought *their* ways were the best.

"You see, I was born and raised in a Polish-Slovak area of rural western Pennsylvania, where, two generations back, entire communities had moved from Eastern Europe to work in the mines and steel mills. The culture I grew up in was very Catholic, very ethnic, and very, *very* insular. I wanted *out* of all that; so, as soon as I got my BA, I moved to Maryland and taught in a public school. Like you, Ruth, I felt I *had* to get out."

"I hear ya, Norma," Ruth said. "And I'll bet you ate lots of cabbage and kielbasa at *your* house, too."

"Yes, and pierogis as well. I still love those." Then Norma reddened slightly. "I know this sounds terrible, but I told Jerry once that the best thing he ever did in marrying me was to keep me from having to move back there as a divorceé to take care of my parents. That was just the expected thing: If a daughter was single or divorced, aging parents were *her* responsibility. Period. No questions and *no* exceptions."

She stood up, straightened her pale green shirt, and walked to the edge of the platform. "In fact," she said with a wide sweep of her arm, "these hills and pine trees, minus the ruins, of course, remind me of where I grew up. When I was little, my grandparents lived near us and spoke little English; one grandfather didn't even know my *name*. They were not unloving people, but that's just how things were. Affection of any kind was not shown. As I grew older, I was sad that our relationship was not close. But I had the freshest fruits, vegetables, poultry, beef, pork, and fresh eggs, too, sometimes still warm from the hens. I didn't have my first store-bought egg until I was twenty-one. Then, and only then, did I appreciate what I'd had earlier."

"Well, I wasn't in your shoes," Vicky said, "but that all sounds pretty *good* to me. Like Inez said, maybe they thought that providing food *was* affection. For people from their background, food probably was a *big* blessing."

"Oh, I know. Plus, both my folks had many siblings; so there was a slew of cousins. Who could keep them all straight? My mom was from a Polish-American farm family; she went to school only as far as the third grade. Dad's parents were from Slovakia. He'd lived on a farm, too, and went as far as the eighth grade. Later, he worked in a steel mill; but farming was all-important.

"My parents never took vacations, never went to the movies, and never visited Pittsburgh, the nearest city. About the only place we went was to church on Sundays, where the Mass was in Latin and the sermon was in Slovak. That was our place of workship; and, as far as my family was concerned, there was no other. They had little interest in people who believed differently. We lived in the country, with no other kids around. My only sister was six years older than I; so, when she graduated from high school and left home, I was very lonely, especially in the summers. In essence, I had no neighborhood. So I learned how to be self-sufficient—I *had* to."

"I know that song," Alicia said with a smile, "and *all* the verses."

Norma cleared her throat several times. "Looking back, maybe it wasn't all bad. Hmm, I need to stop talking for a minute and have some water. Najila, tell us what happened next with Sapha. How did she manage after her husband sent her back to Shechem?"

"Wait, I will find the right place," Najila said. "Ah, here.

> Life became very difficult. My brother did not want me back with his family. His wife begged him to find me another husband. My brother knew Elisaph, a caravan merchant, the brother of my

third husband, Samuel. By offering to pay a good amount of money, my brother arranged for us to marry. We were reasonably happy; and, praise God–I was even able to conceive a child. I was overjoyed at the thought of being a mother at last. But it was not to be. While Elisaph was traveling to the desert land of the Nabateans, he was set upon by bandits, robbed, and killed. In my anguish, I lost the baby.

So, in the space of two years, I had been divorced, married, with child, then again widowed and mourning the deaths of my husband and my baby. My grief was extreme, as was my poverty; as all our money was invested in Elisaph's last caravan. Once again, I was penniless. I was still in Shechem, so my brother arranged a marriage once more, this time to Asriel, cousin to my first two husbands. Asriel was a businessman who grew and pressed olives in addition to his other interests. We lived in a small house on the edge of town; I planted my first garden–some vegetables and a few flowers–and tried to enjoy the peace, hoping it would last. We lived comfortably in our little house. Three years later, Asriel was killed when a wagon loaded with barrels of olive oil overturned, crushing him beneath.

I then lived with my uncle, Kohath, my father's brother. He was not my husband; but, at least, it was a roof over my head and food. In return, I cared for his children and helped in the house. His wife, Milcah, scorned me worse than a slave. She ridiculed me constantly, said I was not a good woman or a real woman; since I could hold no husband or babe. It was shortly after I moved into my uncle's house that I came out to the well and met Jesus. My chores included getting our water. So, while Milcah was preparing the noon meal, I would often leave the house at midday, to escape her carping tongue. Other women drew water in the mornings or evenings, stopping to exchange gossip. I craved only quiet.

Ruth groaned. "Man! Milcah sounds just like Arlene, two thousand years earlier. Some things *never* change!"

Inez brushed away a fly. "Goodness, what a hard life Sapha had! What a survivor she was! We all are, though. We have been made stronger by our experiences. Sharing our stories affirms that."

"Well," Norma said brightly, "that's certainly true for me. Anyway, I began to tell people about my terrific new life, too. When Sapha did that, she even forgot her water jar to go to town to tell her neighbors about Jesus. I'll bet people could see that she'd changed: The townspeople saw the healthiness of her soul and her peace. Before, she must have looked *so* sad, so exhausted and rundown; her face must have reflected that. But after she met Jesus, she probably stood straighter and looked more relaxed and happy. She began a new life and then passed that along to the townspeople. St. Francis once said: 'Preach the Gospel at all times; use words if necessary.' Sapha didn't have to say much; the change in her was obvious."

Norma came back and sat down on her bench. She covered her mouth with her hand and tried not to cough. "Unfortunately, there were some changes going on for me, too. In 2003, when Jerry retired from the Foreign Service, I learned that I had lung cancer. Funny, because I'd never smoked, nor had Jerry."

"But," Corinne said, "you grew up near coal mines and the belching smoke stacks of Pennsylvania steel mills, right?"

"Goodness, Corinne, you're *so* perceptive! I wish I listened *half* as well as you do. Yes, you're right. Anyway, I've had chemotherapy and lost my hair three different times and have had surgery and two different radiation batches, five years apart. Jesus and I still talk each day."

"But, in *spite* of all that," Julia said haltingly, "you *still* seem so happy, Norma. Uh ... don't you ever worry about *dying*?"

"Sometimes, sure. But I don't *obsess* about it. I want to enjoy every day that I can and keep doing the things I like, for as *long* as I can."

Corinne laughed. "I think we all worry, Julia. When a car swerves too close to me on my bike, I get a chill; but I still keep riding. Part of me is still ten and a daredevil, I guess."

"You bet," Ruth added. "When your number's up, it's up. In the meantime, do your best and enjoy every day."

"Thanks, all of you," Norma said. "I do, and I am happy. It's been eight years since my diagnosis, and people often comment that the cancer must be the worst thing that ever happened to me. I say, 'No, cancer is *not* the worst thing.' It's hard to explain that being alone and abandoned was the worst thing—until my conversations with Jesus started, that is.

"I'll admit, since retirement, much of my energy has been spent fighting the disease. But when I feel OK, I love putting together programs for local schools about children in different countries. I still love to travel. We've done some great archaeology cruises to Turkey and Greece. Don't laugh, but I also like to cook Eastern European foods. Since we usually had a cook in the Foreign Service years, I couldn't use the kitchen much; but now I'm a whiz at making stuffed cabbage. I'm also proud to tell you that I've won—ta-*dah*—several ribbons at the Kentucky State Fair for table decorating: you know, setting a table with flowers, candles, pretty china, etc."

Kay leaned back and shook her head. "Norma, you're *amazing*! I'm so impressed by your ability to stay involved, and to always be so cheerful and sunny, even after surgery, three rounds of chemo, and all the other medical issues you've gone through. I know what that often does to people—how it can make them grumpy, depressed, or constantly worried about themselves. You're definitely *not* like most people."

"Oh, Kay, you're sweet to say that. Some folks think I'm sort of silly, a ditz even; but I really *am* happy. Ever since those first conversations with Jesus in that lonely Washington house, I have seen him and myself with new eyes. I saw what he did for me and then learned what I could do for myself. So each time something special happened, it gave me courage to try the next thing. Plus, I saw how *lucky* I was, compared to lots of other people I'd see in the clinics and on the wards."

Ruth pulled out a loose thread on the edge of her flowered sun hat. "Huh. I suppose you've even forgiven your ex, Mr. Rat?"

Norma shrugged. "Yes. It wasn't easy; but I knew I had to, so I did. Then I felt a lot better. Believe me, I'm not perfect. Sometimes I gripe and fuss. Although I dearly love my stepson and my nieces, I *wish* I could have had children. I plan to take the issue up with the Almighty when I see him," she said with a laugh.

"In the meantime, I stay busy. I've always been an avid reader. One of my volunteer jobs in Louisville, after retirement, has been to keep the parish library organized. That way, I get first dibs on the new books. When I can, I go to daily Mass and attend retreats at a center near us. I've been co-facilitator in a scripture-sharing cancer support group. We always pray for life—earthly or eternal. Since that very first prayer group, I've continued in such groups. They have all been full of incredible people, just like you. I was so happy that I found your group in Rome. Once my doctor told me, 'I don't know how you're breathing,' meaning, biologically, I shouldn't be. Then he said, 'Oh, I know how—it's all those prayers.'

"So, here I am, still puffing along. God put adventure in my soul and gave me the emotional and physical equipment to move with my husbands seventeen different times to different states and countries. I was never homesick, maybe because of my solid background. God sent me out into the world to seventeen different 'villages.' Like Sapha, I've been able to leave my old life behind. I'm so lucky and have been given so much. You know, a few years ago, I never dreamed I'd see you all again; yet here we are, in this special place where Sapha's and Najila's people worshiped. Maybe I'm still breathing just so I could be here with you today."

She glanced at her watch. "Done. And it's not quite six. Let's head back to the van, shall we? A quick shower, my new outfit; and I'll be ready for a night on the town!"

Najila wiped her eyes. "What a wonderful story, Norma! Now I will tell *you* something. Before you all came, I had such worries about leading your group. I thought I would not know enough. But I have learned so *much* from you. You are all *gifts* to me."

"What a lovely thing to say, Najila," Kay said as she stood up. "I think each of us came on this trip with many concerns and misgivings, yet look how things are turning out! Thanks to you and Sapha, we *all* know ourselves a little better."

Kay gathered her things and started down the steps of the platform. "I also know that I'm really looking forward to tonight's special dinner. My mouth is already watering for that fresh *zaatar* bread you've told us about, Najila. Shall we go?"

~21~

Dinner at Adnan's

Traffic was light; Najila drove quickly back to the hotel. Almost before the ignition was turned off, Alicia yanked open the side door and hopped out. She started toward her cottage, then turned and offered her hand to help Julia down.

Kay got out and meticulously checked her watch. "Let's see. It's now almost six-thirty. Can we meet in the lobby, say, in forty-five minutes, by seven-fifteen?"

"Fine," Najila said. "I will call Cousin Adnan, tell him we arrive at seven-thirty, *insha'allah*. Then he makes everything ready for us. He is very excited we are coming to his place."

Ruth elbowed Alicia in the side. "All *right*, then! I'm gonna jump in the shower, and I'll meet you back at the bar for a quickie, OK, Al?"

"You're on. Last one there buys!" Alicia shouted as she hurried down the path to her cottage. As she stepped inside, she glanced down at her right foot, now red and puffy. Oh brother! Would you look at this? she thought. This stupid foot *would* have to swell now. I thought that dumb tennis injury was over. Tough. I'm wearing my new shoes anyway. I'll just pray I won't be like Cinderella's sisters.

Thirty minutes later, Alicia and Ruth hurtled into the bar, almost colliding in the doorway. "Beat ya," Ruth exclaimed. "Nyah, nyah, *you're* buying." She was still fastening the brilliant, crystal buttons on the shoulder of her hot pink tunic and "arranging" the waistband of her silver gray slacks. The tiniest bit of shower foam was visible behind her flashy earrings.

"Did not, *did not!*" Alicia shrieked. "It was a dead heat, and you *know* it." She flipped her long, blonde hair to one side, secured it with a large gold clip, and smoothed down the beading on the front of her beige, silk pantsuit. This was all done in one swift motion, born of years of dressing the kids first, herself last, nanoseconds before dashing out the door. Carefully, she bent to loosen the straps of her slinky and treacherously high-heeled sandals.

"Ladies, *ladies*," Kay admonished as she swooped in, dressed in a flowing, sky blue caftan. "I'm the oldest, so I'll break the tie and buy a round for all of us. That will solve everything."

Amid much laughter, seats were found and drinks ordered. As the others gathered, Ruth passed among them with the small silver dishes of almonds and green olives she'd seen on the bar. With a towel draped over her arm, she still loved playing "flight attendant."

Vicky slipped in and gave her order. She perched on

the arm of a sofa, while she sipped a glass of white wine. After adjusting the sleeves of her pale pink, raw silk jacket, she leaned forward to remove a lint fleck from the matching slacks. She checked her makeup in a pink compact.

"Vick, you look *terrific!*" Ruth whispered, as she offered the dish of almonds.

Soon Norma entered, scrubbed and radiant in a shimmering green caftan. She was followed by Inez, chic in a silver lamé jacket over a fire-engine red, sequined cami and black palazzo pants. Corinne came in quietly, wearing a stunning cinnamon-colored top, edged with iridescent green and gold braid over dark green slacks, the colors a perfect complement to her red hair.

Inez hesitantly opened her red silk handbag and removed a knotted silver necklace. "Can someone help me untangle this?" she asked.

"Sure, Inez. Let me see it," Corinne answered. At a table near the bar, she immediately set to work and began to unsnarl the necklace.

Julia limped in slowly a few minutes later, elegant in a royal blue, linen dinner suit. "Goodness, Corinne. Where did you learn how to do that? I can *never* fix my things. I *always* have to ask Edson. You've got magic fingers."

Corinne blushed. "No big deal. My Gran just taught me a few tricks on rainy afternoons."

Najila was puffing as she hurried in. "Sorry, sorry. I am *so* late!" She dabbed at her damp face with a tissue and greeted the bartender with a wave.

"Relax, Najila, you're not late," Vicky said as her eyes widened. "Get a load of *you*! You look *fabulous*—like something out of *Vogue*. Turn around, so we can see the back of you."

Shyly, Najila did a small pirouette. Her long top in stretchy, thin Lycra knit had a beautiful pattern in black and dark gold, with a bit of orangey-red. A gold ring held gathers at the décolleté. Under the top, she wore sleek, black leggings with gold/bronze rivets at the ankles. Sparkly gold sandals, burnished gold, dangly earrings, and a beaded, gold evening bag completed her ensemble. She had even applied a bit of makeup and swept back her dark curls with a bronze headband.

"*Dyn-o-mite!*" Ruth exclaimed. "Where did you *get* that outfit, Najila? *Tres chic!* It's a whole new you. If you bought those things around here, we are going shopping *to-morrow!*"

"*Shukran*, oh, sorry, thank you," Najila said modestly, her eyes shining. "My Auntie Rania brought these back from America last week. She has good taste; but, ah, different—more exotic than mine. Oh, but, I do not know ... I feel so open, oh, sorry, *exposed*. Mama would have *fits* if she saw me! You *really* think this looks all right ... for somebody my age?"

Kay laughed. "*Your* age? Good heavens, Najila! What are you, all of forty? You're young enough to be my daughter, and she wears things like that all the time. Besides, you're very petite and have a lovely figure, so why not show it off a bit? After all, this is a special night for all of us. Live a little! Ruth, bring Najila a glass of wine, please. Let's have a toast."

As Najila accepted the glass, Kay raised hers. "To Najila, for guiding us to find Sapha, the Samaritans, and ourselves."

"And to our new lives," Norma added quietly, as the women all sat down.

Najila chose a place next to Julia. "Thank you, Kay and Norma." Najila smiled as she sipped at her drink. "Thanks to you all. I have also found many new things on our trip; some very surprising." She gently swirled the golden chardonnay in her glass and then took another drink. "You all make it so simple. I hope my next group is as nice." She looked at her watch. "We must go straight away. I will call Adnan, tell him we come at seven-thirty—that actually means seven forty-five. No problem. I just find my keys." She took one last swallow, set her glass and some shekels on the bar, waved again to the bartender, then led the group outside.

Quickly, they all piled back into the van, careful of their finery. "Hey, guys," Julia said as she pulled the door closed, "I'm not used to being this festive; but we clean up pretty good, don't we?"

Najila drove slowly through several dark streets and then up a slight incline on a winding road to the edge of Nablus. Soon she turned into a graveled parking lot, and everyone got out. Sheltered by tall pine trees, the small restaurant was almost hidden from view. A halo of soft light glowed from behind the building. The green-painted signed above the door said "Adnan's Fine Restaurant" in Arabic, Hebrew, and English.

As Kay walked closer, she saw that masses of pink roses, planted in large clay pots, were twining up trellises on both sides of the entrance. She inhaled deeply, captivated by the fragrance, and decided immediately to do pots on her deck, once she got home. Roses would be lovely around her kitchen door.

As the women started up the steps, the door flew open; and a short, stocky man burst out, arms widespread. His gray, linen suit was well tailored to his ample frame; his black mustache was large and *very* bushy.

"Naji, how you *are, habibati?*" he exploded. "Where you been? Such long time no see you." He enfolded Najila in a smothering bear hug then held her off a bit. "My God! Look at you. You are knock over, no, no, knock *out*! Rania been shopping again, eh?" He laughed uproariously then stepped back, extending his arms again. "Ah, sorry, sorry. Welcome, ladies. Welcome all. I am Adnan, Najila's favorite cousin. Welcome to my restaurant. Tonight you my honored guests. Come in, come in."

With Najila on his arm, he paraded them proudly through the restaurant. She waved gaily at several friends and would have stopped to chat, but Adnan pulled her firmly along towards the side door. "I make special table out in garden for your ladies, Naji," he whispered.

"Best place. Boys work all day, set up. Not want your ladies think we pheasants."

Najila laughed. "That's *peasants*, Addie. But no problem. I know. *Shukran*. Thanks. *Mumtaz*. Very good."

As Adnan held the door open, they stepped into an enchanted, walled garden filled with trees, flowers, and splashing fountains. Delicate fairy lights twinkled from the branches above, while soft spotlights shimmered on the pale, creamy blossoms of the plumeria trees. Thin poles held small lanterns that swayed on a light breeze in front of pink oleander bushes. Four round tables were covered in snowy white cloths; a large, gold candle in a glass chimney stood in the center of each table. Pink rose petals were strewn near the candles.

The women were stunned. This was so lovely and so unexpected! Finally, Norma spoke—first in Arabic and then in English. "Oh, Mr. Adnan, this is not only beautiful, it's *magical*. I've never seen such a *gorgeous* garden!"

"You like?" Adnan crowed, pleased that Norma spoke Arabic. "*Mumtaz*. Good. I am happy. Come, come. Ah, here, this your table. Ten places, like you ask, Naji. Few other tables in garden, but maybe no other peoples come tonight. Business little slow these days; but now you ladies here, everything fine. Come sit here, please. I send boys to take orders."

As Najila introduced the women to him, Adnan seated each with a flourish. Then he turned and clapped his hands. Immediately three uniformed waiters emerged through a rear door and surrounded the table. They were very handsome and bore a strong family resemblance.

"Good evening, ladies," said their leader. "My name Abdullah, this my brother, Nader, younger brother, Zaidoun." He indicated the men to his right and left. "We your table team tonight. Anything you want, just ask; and we do, OK? Mr. Adnan make very special menu for you tonight, since you from America. We start with drinks first. I start here, with this lady." He extended his hand toward Norma, who ordered a glass of white wine in Arabic. Abdullah beamed. "*Shukran*, Madame." Norma smiled up at him. "*Afwan*, Abdullah. You're welcome."

Ruth rolled her eyes. "Sell mah clothes, I'm goin' to heaven! Don't you just *love* it? This is going to be a night to remember!"

"I'm so glad I could make this trip," Norma said happily. "Today has been totally *wonderful*—first seeing all those sites, then getting to tell my story, and now this tonight. Thank you for arranging this for us, Najila. I feel so blessed to be here. Actually, I feel blessed just to *be*–anywhere at all!"

Drinks were soon served, accompanied by a tempting array of appetizers: almond-stuffed olives; plates of *kibbe*—small triangle-shaped bulgur wheat pastries filled with a mixture of ground beef, onion, pine nuts, and cinnamon—and wedges of warm, flat *zaatar* bread, kissed with an aromatic blend of thyme, sumac, sesame seeds, and salt, which were used to scoop up the thick creamy *labna*, a dip made from strained yogurt.

"If I'm not careful," Julia said, "I won't have room for the main course." As she bit into her second *kibbe*, she noticed the side door opening. Three people started to enter, then stopped. "Najila, look," Julia whispered. "We've got company."

Najila drew in her breath sharply, as she saw that the new guests were her mother, her Aunt Rania, and a man with his arm around her mother. "There is Mama and my Auntie Rania," she whispered to Julia, "but who is that, that *man*? I have never seen him; I do not know him; I wonder if he is; I hope he is not; what if he …?" Najila's face registered her shock.

"Geez, Najila," Alicia said softly from across the table. "You sound just like Mother Superior at my old high school. Relax. Maybe your mom's got a new beau. So what? Wouldn't that be nice for her?"

"Besides," Julia added, "then she wouldn't be in your face and on your case so much."

A tall, striking brunette, exquisite in a sleek black caftan, glittering with extravagant silver and gold beading, stood in the doorway; she was accompanied by a shorter woman with dark red hair and a tall man. "Ai-yee, look here, Huda. Isn't that Naji with all those women? Halloo, Naji!"

The brunette waved, then strode briskly to their table. "Naji, *habibati*. Sweetheart, how *are* you? You look simply *stunning* in that outfit! Stand up, and let me see you. Yah, fits perfect. At first, I didn't think it was at *all* your style when I saw it in Saks last week; but when I showed the salesgirl your photo and described you, she said it would be perfect. I hate to admit it, but she was right. You *do* look good in something with a little more, ah, flair. You never *know*, do you?" she trilled. "These, ah, ladies are your *tour* group, Naji? Very nice to see you all!" Carefully, Rania lifted the hem of her caftan and took a small step back.

Alicia leaned over and whispered to Corinne. "Rania's a real pro at left-handed compliments. I wouldn't want to be her *enemy*."

"Ladies," Najila said as she stood to greet the newcomers, "this is my Auntie Rania. Her house is in Nablus. She says she lives there but is hardly ever home; she is always traveling. Here is my mother, Huda Danfi. She also lives in Nablus. Auntie Rania, Mama: These ladies are my group. We have been seeing Samaritan sites: Jacob's Well, Sebaste National Park, and Mt. Gerizim. I have told them Sapha's story; some ladies also tell their own stories. We all learn much."

Huda gave her a small hug. "Halloo, Naji. You looking—ah—*different*. Oh, and hallo to all ladies. I am happy to make your quaintness." She then turned and shyly laid her hand on the tall man's arm. "And, ah, here is friend, Maher Musallam. You not meet him yet, Naji; but Rania introduce us at dinner some weeks ago and, ah, Maher stop to take tea some few times and now ...." Her voice trailed off, as a slight flush crept up her cheeks.

"And *now*," Norma said slowly in Arabic, "why don't you join us for dinner? We have plenty of room at this table. We'll all just squeeze in a bit, and then we can visit better."

Huda looked sharply at Norma. She was very surprised that this American woman spoke Arabic.

Najila smiled. "Yah, Mama, Auntie Rania, and Maher—please join us."

"Oh, but," Huda sputtered, "I not know really, I not think, I mean, this your *business* dinner, yah, Naji?"

Najila smiled at her mother. "Come on, Mama. We are all friends; there is plenty of room. No worries. Live a little." Najila waved to Abdullah. Quickly, three more chairs and place settings were brought. The group shifted slightly; and Huda, Rania, and Maher sat down.

As Najila began to introduce the ladies, Kay spoke up. "Najila, perhaps it would be simpler if we each said our names and where we live now. Then *you* don't have to do all the talking."

"Ah, yes," Najila agreed. "Very good, Kay. Abdullah, take the drinks' order, please."

"Yah, Madame," he said, with a smile. "Right away, Madame."

Kay shook her head in wonder. How gracefully Norma had rescued a potentially embarrassing situation, she thought. It must be all that diplomatic corps experience.

It looks like Najila and Huda are *both* in for some changes. Life is full of little surprises.

After the group had introduced themselves, conversation turned to the weather, the beauty of Adnan's garden, and the sites they'd seen the past few days. Seated next to her, Norma continued to converse with Huda in Arabic, complimenting her on her dark green caftan, highlighted by gleaming emerald earrings. They discussed issues of tailors, the difficulty of getting good housemaids, and how to make the best baklava. Huda even smiled when she glanced up and saw that Norma's dark hair was the same color as her own.

To the right of them, Inez and Maher chatted easily in English and Spanish. She inquired about his international business interests, and he asked about her teaching. They laughed when they discovered they'd both been in Milan recently. Kay admired his suave courtesy and dark good looks. Huda was a lucky woman.

Across the table, seated on either side of Rania, Alicia and Ruth expertly held their own with Rania's grandiose pronouncements and prolific name-dropping. Her eyes grew wide as Alicia and Ruth traded humorous anecdotes of vacations in Capri, the risqué wall paintings in Pompeii, and ferryboat rides to the Borromeo Islands in Lago Maggiore. Alicia stretched out a tennis-tanned hand and glanced at her solitaire diamond. She polished it casually with the corner of her napkin. "Just a little birthday surprise from my husband."

While they talked, a young guitarist took his place on a tall stool at the rear of the garden. The warm night air was soon filled with the romantic sounds of his music. "Ah, listen, Maher," Inez said in Spanish, "a bossa nova—my favorite rhythm."

Just then, Abdullah came up to Najila. "Madame is ready for dinner? Yes? *Mumtaz*. Good. OK, boys. We start." He returned to the kitchen, picked up two platters, then led the procession. Nader and Zaidoun followed, each carrying two dishes to the table, then going back for more. They brought *shish taouk*—grilled chicken with garlic—rice with pine nuts, and small bowls of yogurt to spoon over the rice. There was a platter of fragrant *warak enab*—stuffed grape leaves so time consuming to make but so delicious. There were silver trays of sliced tomatoes and cucumbers on young romaine lettuce leaves; several dishes of *tabouleh*—bulgur wheat dressed with finely-chopped tomatoes, parsley, mint, and lemon juice; *hummus*—the creamy paste made of mashed chick peas, garlic, tahini, lemon juice, and cumin; and, of course, more green and black olives. Adnan kept his eye on everything but said little to the waiters. They knew their jobs, and he was happy to leave them to it.

"Yes, I think I *will* have another glass of wine, thank you," Kay said to Nader as he made his way round the table. "A bit more sparkling water also, please. I didn't drink much today, and now I'm quite thirsty."

They ate slowly, savoring the delicious foods; and

they all talked a great deal. After the main course had been cleared away, sweets were brought in: *ma'amoul*, little cookies filled with dates and nuts; baklava; and *moghly*, a creamy rice pudding. Sugar-coated almonds were passed with the delicate gold cups of strong black coffee.

Finally, Norma laid her napkin beside her plate and cleared her throat. She spoke first in Arabic and then in English. "Najila, thank you *so* much. This was a perfect choice for our big night out. I can't remember when I've enjoyed a meal so much. It's such a gift to be here tonight with all of you in this wonderful place, delighting in so many of my favorite foods and getting to meet some of your family and friends. I'm just sorry Beth and Sapha couldn't be with us." She waved to the group standing by the back door. "Thanks to you also, Mr. Adnan, and to Abdullah, Nader, and Zaidoun. You all did such superb work. You made this night a huge success."

How good Norma is with everyone, Kay thought. Her house staffs must have *loved* her! All the ladies clapped as the four men emerged from the kitchen and took a bow. Huda and Maher looked a bit surprised but then joined in the applause.

Rania raised a carefully drawn eyebrow and turned to Alicia. "Clapping for waiters? But, why? They are only, ah, workers."

Najila smiled as she stood up and hugged her cousin. "*Shukran*, Addie. It was the best dinner ever! Your garden is beautiful, such a perfect place. Now we must go. Today was long, and we have more places to see tomorrow. Maybe some shopping, too. You never know," she said as she winked at Ruth.

While the group gathered their belongings, Ruth slipped back to the kitchen. "You guys were *terrific!*" she exclaimed. "My husband always says: 'Don't forget the little guys.' You were the *big* guy, Mr. Adnan. The best." Adnan beamed, his mustache quivering with delight. Abdullah, Nader, and Zaidoun all bowed and looked very pleased.

Slowly the group, which now included Huda and Maher, filed out of the garden, through the main dining room, and into the parking lot. Flashing a dazzling smile, Rania waved a hasty good-bye to them and then descended upon surprised friends at their table.

As Najila unlocked the van, Corinne asked softly, "Najila, could we drive back up on Mt. Gerizim, just a little ways? I'd love to see it at night—if it's not too late." Alicia looked at Corinne's face. "Story time, eh?"

"Yah, fine," Najila agreed. "Tonight is very beautiful; and, look, a big moon comes out. Just one minute; I will tell Mama."

Corinne smiled, then climbed into the van, followed by the rest of the group. Huda and Maher were still standing by his car, as Najila walked over and explained where she was going.

"Najila," Maher said, "perhaps your ladies would like to see small pine grove on Mt. Gerizim, just above big Roman theater. Very quiet there now, with good view of Nablus; lights very pretty at night. I can go first, and you follow me, OK?"

"Yah, fine, Maher. I have some blankets in my van. See you there, Mama."

After Maher had seated Huda in his sleek BMW, he slid into the driver's seat then pulled carefully out onto the dark road; Najila followed in the van. They were soon winding up the side of Mt. Gerizim.

Corinne gazed happily out her window and watched the moon rise.

~22~

Come and See

Maher drove through the outskirts of Nablus up to a small stand of pines that hugged the lower slopes of Mt. Gerizim. After he parked near the edge of the grove, he gently helped Huda out, took her arm, and walked slowly with her toward the trees. "Let me see ... where is it? Little bit hard to find in dark. Ah, yes, here is nice bench. Some ladies can sit there. Huda, wait here, my dear." Quickly he retrieved two small, folding camp chairs from the trunk of his BMW and set them up next to the wooden park bench. "Come, my dear, sit down, please. Chairs are more comfortable for your back than sitting on ground."

Najila pulled the van close to Maher's car. The women got out and followed Najila to where Huda and Maher were sitting. The grove was bathed in a pale, luminous glow as the moonlight seeped through the tall pine trees. Wanting a few minutes to herself, Corinne walked a little distance from the group. She looked down the hill, surprised to see how massive the ancient theater ruins were, jutting out from the ridge below. She thought how Ruth would love doing a show down there on that wide stage arena. Up here, the whole setting reminded Corinne a lot of her "special" night; she hoped she could tell it right.

Najila beckoned to Julia. "Please, sit here on this bench. It is more comfortable than the hard ground with your bad knee." Slowly, Julia lowered herself to the bench, careful of her blue dinner suit. "OK if I squeeze in with you, Julia?" Alicia asked as she approached the bench. "I'd open a vein if I got grass stains on these slacks. Kay, come sit with us. We'll scoot over. There's room for you, too."

Vicky and Najila pulled three, well-worn, chenille blankets from the back of the van and laid them on the grass, after first kicking aside several pinecones. The rest of the women then arranged themselves on the blankets. "These spreads come from my Gran Najet's house." Najila said softly. "She is in my mind when I use them."

Corinne shifted a bit, trying to find a comfortable position on the blanket. She removed her shoes and set them to one side. She felt really nervous, totally out of her comfort zone. Then she noticed that, although the moon was climbing higher, the thick pines created deep shadows; she could hardly see the others at all. Oh, for heaven's *sake*, she told herself. Get over it. You're a big girl. Just tell the story, and don't take too long. They're all probably anxious to get back to the hotel.

Huda and Maher chatted softly as he pointed out the lights of Nablus' new hotel and business district. On her side of the blanket, Najila bit her lip and wondered if she should say something. After all, her mother and Maher did not know these ladies yet—about their stories and everything. Mama would surely think the whole thing was very odd.

Then Inez spoke up, enunciating each word carefully. "Najila, I have loved seeing all the Samaritan sites and learning their fascinating history. It has been amazing how so many of Sapha's words from your grandmother's notebook seem to relate to us. Yet, one of the best parts of this trip has been the chance to tell a little bit of our *own* lives, to have such good places and enough time to share *our* stories. Your kindness has meant so much. I want to give you big hugs and thanks."

Najila gave a huge sigh, and her shoulders relaxed. As she reached across the blanket and squeezed Inez's hand warmly, she saw Huda's head turn towards her.

"Fantastic set-up, Inez," Alicia murmured. "OK, Corinne, out with it. You're like a cat in a sack. You were dying to come up here, so let's hear it—your turn to talk."

Corinne crossed her legs, fiddled with her watch, and played with a pinecone that had rolled onto the blanket.

"Yeah, c'mon, Corinne," Julia said. "Who could ask for a better deal than this? The dinner was fabulous, the air is soft, the night is young, and the moon is up. You're on."

Corinne laughed and ran her hand through her sandy red hair. "Well, I have to admit, I've procrastinated in telling my story because it's a little different than all of yours have been so far. I mean, who's going to believe such things could happen in this day and age? But, after we saw Mt. Gerizim and, then, with the moon coming up tonight, I figured this would be a good time, as in, now or ... oh, pardon me, Mrs. Danfi, Mr. Musallam. I hope this won't be too boring for you, or you won't think it's too weird or strange," she finished in a rush.

"Not at all, Corinne," Maher said kindly. "We enjoy hearing you, is great privilege. Please. We are Huda and Maher–all friends together tonight."

Najila's head jerked up. So it is Huda and Maher now? she thought. And *Rania* introduced them? Aiyee!

"At first," Corinne said, in her soft, Midwestern accent, "I worried I wouldn't be able to adequately describe the event that has shaped my life. After the past few days, I've decided to just tell my story—tell about the miracle and what happened. Maybe, someday, I'll even write it all down."

"Come *on*, Corinne," Norma urged. "Tell us what happened. This is *so* exciting!"

Corinne cleared her throat. "OK, *OK*. Some of you have told your stories in chronological order— your early life, your parents, problems at home, and so on. However, Alicia and Norma started with their crisis first and then connected the dots. So that's what I'm going to do: tell you about the most important thing that has *ever* happened to me. It really wasn't a crisis; it was more like, I don't know, like an epiphany, or a miracle even. After I tell you about that, then I'll fill in the rest, OK?

"It was the spring of 1967," Corinne said, now more relaxed. "and I'd been out of high school for about a year. I was working but still living at home. My sister, Annette, a nursing student, and I decided to attend a Joan Baez concert on Holy Saturday night instead of going to church with our parents. I remember my dad was disappointed that we'd made that decision because his hope was that all his children would remain 'good Catholics.' But faith privacy was part of our family life; my father never asked, and we never volunteered our feelings about religion. We were Catholics; but we never prayed together at home, except at the dinner table, where my father would recite grace quickly and almost unintelligibly: 'Bless us, O Lord, and these your gifts'—some of you know the rest."

Julia laughed. "Nobody could say that grace faster than my daddy. My brother and I used to time him—four seconds was his personal best."

Corinne chuckled. "And I thought my dad was speedy! Anyway, at that time of my life, I was really critical, judgmental, and self-righteous. I'd say I had a definite superiority complex when it came to my parents and most other people of their generation–pretty typical sixties' attitude, I suppose. Also, in spite of having twelve years of Catholic education, I was *very* blasé and had become very indifferent about my beliefs, religion, and a lot of other things. I definitely needed a little guidance in my life then.

"The concert was held at a large university in St. Louis, close to the Mississippi River. I picked up Annette, and we headed downtown. Being with her was unusual because, even though we were close as sisters, we didn't go out together socially very often. I had several friends I normally hung around with, and she had a steady boyfriend who took up most of her free time. I was into black and folk music, and I was anti-war and anti-establishment. Neither Annette nor I were fans of the Beatles and that whole scene. We thought alike on a lot of things."

Ruth stretched her arms over her head and yawned. "I sort of remember all that stuff. I thought about being a hippie, but I never had the time. I was too busy working—just trying to stay afloat."

"Yeah, I understand that," Corinne said. "Well, anyway, we were running late; so, by the time we got to the campus, the parking lot was full. I had to park on the street about two blocks from the concert hall. Once we finally got in, it was a really good concert; it lasted almost three hours. Joan sang anti-war ballads in her clear, beautiful voice. When it was over, we filed out with the crowd onto the college grounds. Although we were exhilarated by the music, neither of us was drunk or high. It was close to midnight; and, as we exited the concert hall, Annette and I were immediately struck by the beauty of the spring night. The full moon was *so* bright that we could see clearly all around us, almost as if it were daytime—sort of like tonight, you know, if we were out from under these trees. I looked around for streetlights, thinking it wasn't *possible* for it to be so bright at midnight. The temperature was perfect: about sixty degrees, and there was a slight breeze. Above us, lovely, puffy clouds floated, stark in their beauty against a navy blue sky.

"As we walked to our car, we began to notice that the sky was changing dramatically. The clouds were moving at an accelerated rate—too fast to be natural. Not only that, but the clouds were all moving *toward* the moon, from every direction: north, south, east, and west." She cleared her throat again, then continued, her voice even softer. "All of the clouds were moving as if they would collide in front of the moon. It was as if the sky was in fast-forward motion. And then ..."

"*What?*" Vicky asked excitedly. "What happened *then?*"

Corinne rolled forward onto her knees and stretched out her arms. "And *then*," she whispered," the clouds formed a perfect *cross*. The edges of the cross were so straight and so exact—they could have been drawn with a *ruler*! The huge, golden moon was at the very center of the cross."

No one breathed.

"We stood on the street, transfixed by this miracle. People around us were gasping, crying, and falling to their knees. I wanted to look at the people and at Annette to see their reactions; but I didn't dare look away from the moon.

It was the most gloriously beautiful sight—and *so* inexplicable! I thought: 'Someone holy has asked God for a sign, and this is his response. I am so lucky to witness this.' It only occurred to me much later that God had meant for *me* to see it. He meant the sign for *me*! I also think it was meant for Annette to be with me to reconfirm for the rest of our lives that it really *did* happen.

"The cross stayed in place for perhaps three minutes. Then it dissolved. The clouds broke away, floating back the way they came, in every direction, until they reached the point where we first noticed their beauty, and then stopped. The sky was back to normal. I looked at my watch: It was just after midnight on Easter Sunday morning. We stood on the street for several minutes, talking to strangers, everyone exclaiming about the miracle of what we had all witnessed. I felt somehow detached, and everything seemed almost surreal." She sat back down on the edge of the blanket and rolled the little pinecone back and forth.

"Thinking back on that night and examining my life later, I identified with Thomas, the disciple who declared he would never believe unless he could put his finger in Jesus' wounds. All my life, I had been given the gift of Catholicism. Oh, I did all the right things but never truly appreciated that gift. Since I was born and baptized into a Catholic family, I took my religion for granted. Now I had faith, but I felt I didn't deserve it. How did I, selfish, indifferent *me*, deserve to know, without reservation, that Jesus exists? That he is the Son of God became an absolute *fact* for me that night." she said softly.

Julia was astounded. "Corinne, in all the years I've known you, I've *never* heard you talk about this or even talk *like* this before. In fact, this is the most I've *ever* heard you talk about *anything*! Who *knew*?"

On her camp chair, Huda squeezed her eyes shut. This *couldn't* be the same thing she'd seen so early that morning in her little garden in Nablus all those years ago. But it was—she *knew* it! She recalled that weekend: all the Easter preparations, excitedly planning for dinner with her parents, preparing the special sweets for Najila, who had just turned nine. Her husband, Nabil, was away. She hadn't known where, he never told her. It was just three months before the war began that June. She had always *meant* to tell someone, to ask others if they, too, had seen that moon, those clouds, that cross. But there was so much tension in those weeks after Easter. People were afraid, they were leaving town. Other things had seemed more important.

On the blanket near the two camp chairs, Najila watched her mother. When Huda opened her eyes, Najila smiled at her, shook her head slightly, and casually laid a finger along her lips. Huda nodded slowly; she realized that Naji *knew* and was asking Huda not to interrupt Corinne's story. Huda's throat grew tight as she remembered how sweet Naji had always been, so considerate of others, just like her papa.

"Corinne," Alicia said from the bench, "there are signs of Jesus' existence all the time—like a thought, a word in the heart, or a person appearing just when you need them. Sometimes, though, I think God does something a little more spectacular, like your special night. Some people call these phenomena of nature. I'm not so sure. I think they're *way* more than that."

"Yes, that's exactly how I'd felt before that night," Corinne agreed. "Afterwards, I kept asking myself: How many people are given absolute *proof* that Jesus is the Son of God? I felt so humble and unworthy, and those feelings continue to this day. Was I given proof because I might not have found the strength to believe on my own? Or did God love me so much—that sheltered, idealistic, innocent young woman that I was in 1967—that he blessed my sister and me with this wonderful gift to sustain our faith for the rest of our lives? I still don't know. I *do* know that, no matter who challenges our beliefs, no matter who argues against our faith, we know unequivocally that *everything* we were taught about Jesus, *everything* we hold dear as Catholics, is founded on absolute truth." She paused to take a drink from the small water bottle she'd brought. "Whew. I need to rest a minute. Going back, telling all this is still pretty emotional."

Najila turned to Corinne. "What an amazing night for you and your sister! You grew up as Catholics, you knew what you saw, even if the reason was not clear. You *knew* that cross in the night sky was very special—maybe a great sign from God."

"You know, Corinne," Vicky said thoughtfully, "there may not have been *audible* words like those Jesus said to Sapha at the well, but you understood the message just the same. The sign was to your eyes and your intellect; but, most of all, to your *heart*. I think you *did* meet Jesus that night but in a slightly different way than Sapha did."

Inez looked up at the sky and sighed. "*Ay Dios mio*, Corinne! You were so lucky!"

"What did she *say*?" Julia whispered to Vicky. "It means, 'Oh, my God,'" Vicky answered.

Corinne stretched out her long legs on the blanket. "You can imagine my surprise when I got Kay's email, giving me the verses about the part where the Samaritan woman mentions the Messiah coming, and Jesus says: 'I am he, the one who is speaking to you.' I mean, I nearly dropped *dead*! What a coincidence!"

"Corinne," Najila said, "the cross was not what you expected; but Jesus was not what Sapha expected either. She wrote that, even after he *said* that he was the Messiah, she *still* was not sure about him."

Huda rubbed her eyes, trying to remember how many years it had been since she had read Sapha's words herself. How long ago *was* it since she had given that little notebook to Naji, admonishing her to keep it in a safe place because it was a family heirloom? Now, Naji was sharing Sapha with all these *foreign* women. Was that good?

"But, Corinne," Inez persisted, "when did you realize

you were not sure about your beliefs? You attended
Catholic school for twelve years; you *must* have had
some beliefs. Maybe you just did not recognize them."

"You're right, Inez," Corinne replied, "but I
didn't recognize a lot of *other* things in those days
either. Oh, I thought I did. Isn't that what every
person in their twenties feels—that they know *everything*? Speaking of, now might be a good time to tell
you about my younger days; so you can know what
came before that night."

She ran her hand through her hair. "Let's see.
I was born in 1950 into a very large, middle-class,
Catholic family in St. Louis. Fifty some years ago,
it was not uncommon for Catholic families to have
ten children. I didn't consider myself unusual or outstanding in any way. We were all high achievers, ex-
celling in school and in sports. I was child number six
in a family of five boys and five girls."

"*Ten* kids? Good *Lord*! Your poor mom!" Julia
blurted. "Oh, gosh, Corinne! I'm *sorry*!"

Corinne laughed. "That's OK, Julia, not to
worry. Anyway, we belonged to St. Joseph's Church;
and all of us kids attended their parochial school. We
were very content; our world was small and protected.
We did not face race or crime issues. Oh, sure, we
knew about bad things because we read about them
in the newspapers; but bad things always happened
somewhere *else*. We didn't even think to thank God
for our blessings. We took our lives for granted and
didn't give much thought to lives or problems not related to our town. My father was definitely the head

of the household, making all the decisions regarding any major or minor issue in our family. My mother was a beautiful woman; but she was abnormally shy, with low self-esteem, and given to depression. Making decisions was difficult for her. I can remember complaining to my sister that Mom always seemed to have a hard time making up her mind and didn't always seem happy. Now that I'm older and a mom myself, I realize she did the best she could, given that she was always so busy with all of us kids—and suffered from depression on top of it. When I think about it, I see that she actually did a *terrific* job because we all got good educations, married well, and turned out OK. That's a lot, isn't it?"

"Yah," Huda said softly. "Is enough."

"My childhood was pretty uneventful," Corinne continued. "I excelled in sports and belonged to the church choir. Those were the two activities, outside of school, that shaped me as a person. I was an average student, doing well in the subjects I enjoyed. However, I lacked guidance at home with self-discipline, study habits, and homework. With ten children, I suppose it was hard for my mom to be vigilant about all of us.

"Fortunately, I was *very* close to my maternal grandmother, who gave me a great deal of affection and attention. She would come to help my mother occasionally. In the summers, I would stay with her in her small, one-bedroom cottage, five miles from our home. Even though, at her death, my grandmother had over one hundred direct descendants, she told me frequently that I was her favorite. My grandmother influenced my childhood the most because, through her, I saw myself as gifted and worthy. When I die, her face is the one I want to see *first!*"

"What a beautiful thought," Kay said gently. "I feel exactly the same about my grandmother, too."

"Anyway, my early life revolved around school, sports, family, friends, and my grandmother. It was happy, but I suspected early on that my mother had emotional problems. I learned to avoid her and/ or obey her quickly to avoid her wrath. She always brags that I was her easiest child to raise because I rarely questioned or challenged her. But she did her best, given her life situation."

"Man," Alicia said, "no wonder you were so good later, when you worked on the crisis intervention phone for your local police. What a perfect job for you, Corinne! You learned to suss things out at your mother's knee."

"Well," Ruth ventured cautiously, "I don't have any children, so what do *I* know, but it seems that having ten kids would be taxing on *any* woman. Maybe what looked like emotional problems might have been just sheer, grinding exhaustion! Lucky you, though, to have a loving granny there."

"Absolutely!" Corinne replied. "My life would have been very different without her. And, besides my grandmother, religion also played a huge role in my childhood. I took what the nuns at school told me very seriously. I remember clearly in the first grade, when Sister Mechtild read an account of the Crucifixion; and I began to cry. She stopped and asked me, in front of the whole class, what was wrong; but I was too embarrassed to admit how touched I was by the story of Jesus' death. During elementary school, I went to confession frequently and Mass every day, except Saturdays, during the school year. I also sang in the church choir until I graduated from the eighth grade."

She smoothed a wrinkle in the blanket. "And, in my early adolescence, when I was about thirteen or so, I began to rebel—I guess most kids do at about this age. Now that I'm older, I can see that it was probably my disrespect for my mom that pushed me into a short, but very defiant, phase. Wanting to be popular, I started to smoke and run around with a fast crowd. I gave up old friends who didn't measure up to the social standards I wanted to set for myself."

Inez chuckled softly. "That sounds familiar."

Corinne sighed. "But my parents had other ideas. They were very worried about me and decided I needed a protected environment. So they sent me to the Heart of Jesus Academy, a private high school for girls run by the Sisters of the Sacred Heart of Jesus. Their campus was small and cloistered from the outside world. Unfortunately, they didn't teach us much about guys, so I remained totally inexperienced, innocent, and gullible."

Julia exhaled sharply. "Wow! That must have set your folks back some *big* bucks—and with nine other kids still at home. They must have *really* been concerned about where you were headed, Corinne."

She nodded. "Yeah, I know this now; but, back then, I was one big ball of *resentment*. Anyway, in spite of this, or maybe *because* of it, once again, my social life took off. On the weekends that I came home, I dated a lot; my goal in life seemed to be how to have the most fun on a Saturday night. I also began to distance myself from God, questioning everything I had ever been told. After I graduated from high school, I got caught up in the anti-war movement; but, because I'd moved back home and had a job working for the local school district, I continued to dress conservatively. So that I could afford to buy myself a car and nice clothes, I paid my parents only ten dollars a week for room and board. My mother was always very interested in what I was doing and who I was going out with. She was very busy with ten kids but had very little life of her own. She was always curious about my life and activities, but she almost never gave me orders or advice."

Ruth leaned towards Corinne. "Girl, you don't know how lucky you *were*! Be glad you didn't have Arlene for a mother. She dished out enough advice for the *universe*!"

Corinne laughed. "Poor Ruth. Anyway, by this time, my sister, Annette, was in nursing school, living in a dorm on the campus of a teaching hospital. We both attended church on Sundays, out of habit rather than desire. Some Sundays, we didn't go at all. In spite of the fact that we had all gone to Catholic school and were members of the

Catholic Church, God wasn't really a big part of our lives. So you can see why I felt so unworthy on that Easter Saturday night. I knew all the rituals and the right words; but it was more duty than faith. I probably would have said that Jesus was the Messiah, but I didn't take it seriously."

"You know, Corinne," Najila said, "Sapha was like you. At her time, most Samaritans thought they knew what the Messiah would be like; and they worked hard to make sure he would find them. But when this ordinary Jewish man told her that he *was* the Messiah, she could hardly *believe* it."

"Right," Ruth declared. "But look what she did then, in spite of not being sure. She forgot her water jar, dashed into town, and told her neighbors that she'd met this guy out at the well who'd told her lots of things about herself; so she thought maybe he might be the Messiah. But they had to come and see for themselves. It reminds me of Mary Magdalene and the Resurrection story. You know, I'll bet those male disciples were really hacked that it was often the *women* who were first on the scene. What can I say?"

Julia flexed her knee and shifted on the bench. "Corinne, that night must have been really super for you; but I need some clarification here. You said that seeing that cross in the sky on the night of Joan Baez's concert let you know in no uncertain terms that Jesus was the Son of God and that everything you ever learned about him was true. But I don't get it. Be more specific, will you? How *exactly* did this happen? Did you have some kind of *feeling*?

Were there *words* in your mind? I mean, how did you go from seeing this cross in the sky to *knowing* that Jesus was the Son of God?"

Corinne nodded. "I'll try to explain, Julia. The revelation from God that night is still so hard to put into words. As the clouds were moving towards the moon, and my sister and I first realized what was happening, my first thought was: This is a sign from God to someone very holy. Perhaps it's for Cardinal Ritter who was the cardinal of St. Louis at the time. Or maybe it's for someone very special who needs a sign to make an important decision, like a religious vocation. I was sure the sign wasn't meant for *me*; I was just privileged to witness it. But, as the clouds formed a perfect symmetrical cross with the moon at the center of the cross bars, I thought: This *is* Jesus. It can *only* be Jesus. This is the sign of Christianity. It couldn't be mistaken for anything else! It was too perfect, too spectacular, and too impossible!

"It was hard to *believe* what was happening even while we were staring up at the sky. Who can control the weather but God? What science, what man-made magic could possibly affect the wind to blow from every direction towards a central point? It was unequivocal proof to my sister and me that Jesus lived and died just the way I'd been taught since childhood. If I could only adequately describe to you how beautiful it was! The sky was navy blue, the clouds were like puffs of new snow, and the cross was brilliant moonlight. I wish all of you could have been there.

The gift of faith that God wants to give to everyone, almost always with no outward sign, was given to me physically. I was unbelievably humbled by the experience. Remember: I was raised in a *very* Catholic environment with lots of religious structure in my life. It was only when I saw that miracle that I recognized that faith was missing in my life. Since then, I say the same prayers and attend the same Masses; but things are different. Maybe I'm different.

"Anyway, the miracle was over with so quickly! Did it really happen? My sister and I stared at each other dumbfounded. Afterwards, I *knew* I was meant to see the miracle. I will always feel unworthy, but I am convinced it was God's intention for me to see it. Oh, yeah, and another thing: I'm basically a coward; and, though I usually try to meet life head-on when problems arise, I gather strength from my faith in God. He's never let me down yet," she said firmly.

"I know the feeling," Alicia said with a smile.

"Anyway," Corinne said, "after that night, life went on. I continued working, then got married after a few years. I stopped working, Dave and I had three kids, we moved around several times, and I went back to work. You know. The usual things. But, ever since that night, I try to put the faith I found to work. It doesn't matter if I'm at the grocery store, swimming in the local pool, or playing bridge— somebody always needs a helping hand. Plus, when I answered the emergency phones in the police department, once I started hearing the troubles *other* people had, I realized how much God has blessed me. My life is good, and I'm *very* grateful."

"I'd say you've done all the right stuff, Corinne," Vicky said. "You saw the sign at night; Sapha saw Jesus at noon. You were a young girl with little faith; Sapha was a woman with little future. Like Jesus' other disciples who had abandoned their nets or their tax tables, Sapha and you both left your 'water jars': your old beliefs, your old ways. You moved forward."

"That's always hard, isn't it?" Norma said, as she stifled a cough. "Leaving the old is so scary and threatening. It's hard to move into the new, the unknown. But, once we find the smallest bit of courage and concentrate only on our next step in *spite* of our fears ... well, you know what I mean, Corinne."

"Yeah, Norma, I do. Luckily for me, everything else in my life has been pretty good. Oh, sure, there have been illnesses and troubles, like my Dave's heart problems, my cancer, things with our kids. You know, the usual stuff in life. But since 'the night,' I can always pull up the memory of that cross and *know* that God really loves me. Oh, yes, and whenever my sister, Annette, and I are together, one of us invariably asks, 'Remember the miracle?' We're bound together forever, not only by our biological sisterhood, but also by that wonderful night so many years ago. I thank God that my sister was with me to witness the miracle, too. Other people have come and gone, but Annette will always be in my life. That, too, was part of the plan. Not everybody is ready; but whenever I hear someone who's searching, I feel compelled to share 'the miracle' of that night. Does that help, Julia? Is that enough?"

"Yeah, I guess so," Julia said with a big sigh. "It must be nice to have a sister."

Corinne smiled and checked her watch. "OK, that's it. We probably should go. Thanks for listening. I hope there are people in St. Louis still trying to explain that night, and I hope other people are listening."

Huda took a deep breath, then rose from her chair. "*Shukran*, thank you, Missus Corinne, for story of life and wonderful night, how you change. Before, I never say anybody either; but I saw *same* cross in moon. It was March 26, early Easter morning in Nablus, before sun comes up. Naji was small girl then, only nine ..."

"Yah, Mama," Najila said softly, "I saw, too."

Huda nodded. "But so much happen in our country then, only few months before Six Days' War in June. I never speak about cross until now. To *think*—if Naji not organize this trip, not share notebook from Gran Najet, if Norma not invite us sit for dinner, then none ..." Her voice broke.

Maher stood up, but Najila reached her mother first. She handed her a tissue, then put her arms around her. "It is OK, Mama. Crying is fine. The stories *are* emotional. I am so happy you came tonight. Come with us tomorrow, too, OK? I pick you up at eight-thirty. We will take our breakfast at the French Corner, then some shopping. After that, who knows?"

Huda hesitated. "Oh, but, I not … well, maybe."

Alicia leaned over and whispered to Corinne. "You're not the only one sharing a miracle tonight. Your story sure brought those two closer."

Corinne smiled. "Sometimes the moon puts everything in a different light, doesn't it?"

~23~

Through the Market

K ay set her coffee cup on the small, wrought-iron table and stretched out on the padded chaise longue, grateful for the shade of a poolside banana tree. This trip was tiring, but she was *very* glad she'd come. Last night, on Mt. Gerizim, had been so incredible!

Behind the hotel, a gardener was mowing the grass. Suddenly, Kay was seven again, walking behind her father, earnestly raking the cuttings as he pushed the old mower. The fragrance of new-mown grass always reminded her of her father. He'd always been so patient—unlike her mother, who was always so busy, so strict, so ...

"Morning, Kay," Julia said as she and Norma emerged from the dining room, carrying mugs of coffee. "Mind if we join you? I'll just park my cup on your table, while I drag over some chairs. Najila said to remind you that we'll be going downtown around nine. I think we're going to have a bite at the French Corner Pastry Shoppe and then hit the market, or maybe it's the other way around. I'm looking forward to both. I hope their croissants are fresh." She drew two white pool chairs close to Kay.

Julia made herself comfortable, then stretched out her arms. "Wasn't that *something* last night? I couldn't *believe* Corinne! She's usually so quiet and reserved. What a story, eh?" She squinted into the sunlight toward the door. "Hey, Najila's here. And will you look at who's *with* her? Well, well!"

Huda and Najila walked across the pool deck; the other women soon came out and gathered around. "Good morning, ladies. I am happy that you all dressed cool for comfort and shopping. I picked up Mama earlier, so now we will drive to the *souk* area. We must park in a car park and walk a bit. First, we look through the old *souk*, then stop at the French Corner, have coffee, maybe little bites to eat, and then some shopping time, OK? The first few days of our trip, I talked to you about ancient times: Samaritan life, culture and religion, and about Sapha. Today, we will look at modern things. Actually, many shops in the *souk* are not so different now from what Sapha saw." Najila smiled at her mother. "And Mama comes with us. If you need help, ask her. She is *very* hard with bargaining."

Norma giggled. "I'm *so* glad you're coming, Huda. There is something I'm hoping to find, and *you* will surely know where I should look." She linked arms with Huda as they walked to the van together, chatting happily in Arabic.

"I'll just run and get my things," Kay said as she got up from the chaise. "I'll be back in three minutes. Please don't leave without me!"

Ruth tapped her watch and grinned at Kay. "On your mark, get set, *GO!*"

Najila tried to be philosophical as she helped everyone into the van. She was very surprised that her mother had agreed to come, but maybe having her along wouldn't be so bad after all. Maybe, finally, she would understand Najila's work.

They drove from the hotel into the old section of Nablus. Although it was early, the parking lot was nearly full. Najila eased the van into a spot next to a palm tree. "Good, the tree makes shade when the sun moves."

"Plus, it's also a great landmark for those of us who are geographically challenged," Ruth declared. "I can get lost in my own backyard."

Alicia laughed. "It's probably good that you were the flight attendant and *not* the pilot."

They followed Najila into the ancient *souk*, past old shops crammed together down both sides of the dusty street. At the first shop, they saw a sheep carcass suspended from the doorway on a black, metal hook, next to a row of partially-plucked chickens. Farther back, a whirring refrigerator case held cuts of fresh meat in various shades of pink and red. Flypaper dangled ineffectively from the ceiling.

Next door, at the rear of the fish shop, Julia saw an old man, sitting cross-legged on a battered cushion; water flowed through a narrow trough beneath his feet. He was casually gutting fish with the longest knife she had ever *seen.* "How does he keep from cutting off his *heels?*" she whispered to Najila.

"Oh, he has done this fifty-sixty years," Najila replied, "plus he is almost blind. But he knows every voice. *Marhaba.* Halloo, Hamid," she called gaily.

From the murky depths of the shop, Hamid waved his knife. "Halloo, Naji. *Keif halek?*"

"*Zeina, el-hamdulillah,* Hamid," Najila answered.

Julia looked over at Norma who translated the old familiar greetings: "Hi, how are you, Naji?" and "Fine, thank God, Hamid."

They passed by a fruit and vegetable shop; Norma and Huda stopped to admire rows of pale green zucchinis and shiny, purple eggplants, next to carefully stacked oranges, lemons, and watermelons. Fluffy salad greens of every kind were arranged next to tomatoes, peppers, and cucumbers. The shop owner quickly cut up a large bunch of shiny, dark red grapes and handed a cluster to each woman. "For lady friends, Missus Huda. You come back, shop here later. I give you best price." His wide smile proudly displayed three sparkling, gold front teeth.

"Najila, could we stop a minute, please?" Norma asked, as they stood in front of the spice *souk.* "I want to get some cardamom seeds; my husband loves them in his coffee." She gave her order for half a kilo, then watched with interest as the merchant set an antique weight on his tarnished brass scale. Crammed together behind him on the floor were huge, open burlap bags of cinnamon; cardamom;

strands of costly yellow saffron; pepper; nuts; a variety of dried herbs; sunflower, pumpkin, and melon seeds; dried peas; white, brown, and black beans; tiny, orange and green lentils; several kinds of rice; and a few strange things she didn't recognize.

Norma looked around and sniffed. "You know, I love where I'm living now; but I really miss this aroma. There is absolutely *nothing* like it. Spice *souks* all smell the same. Sapha probably shopped someplace *exactly* like this. Think of it: two thousand years later and we're still inhaling the *same* spices."

"Hmph," Julia said, as she made a face. "I'll bet you don't want to *know* what's at the bottom of those sacks, Norma. Get the guys at the hotel to freeze your seeds tonight, or your suitcase will be full of critters by the time you get home. You'll be unpacking more than just your dirty socks."

They paused briefly in front of the bread shop and watched the baker—red-faced, swathed in a long, dirty apron, and arms covered with flour. The door of a stone oven built into the back wall stood open. With a long, flat, wooden shovel, he deftly removed freshly-baked pita breads, slid them onto a cooling rack, then quickly inserted the next batch on a second shovel.

Ruth admired his agility. "He's just like a dancer—it's the Bread Ballet."

The baker turned to them. "Madames take pita? Very good, please." He tore several hot pitas into small pieces, placed them on a dented, blue enamel plate, and passed them to the women. Najila thanked him and bought a half dozen. Julia took a piece, blew the flour off, and gingerly took a bite.

Across the street, Inez and Corinne were peering through a dusty window. "This looks like the coffee shop," Inez said. "Come in with me, Corinne." While Inez gestured to the owner, Corinne saw that large bags of aromatic coffee beans–black, brown, green, and pale gray—covered most of the floor space. Several small shelves above the cash register displayed silver coffee pots, gift sets of delicate, gold-rimmed coffee and tea glasses, and boxes of sesame cookies. At the rear of the shop, the owner switched on an old-fashioned metal coffee grinder to prepare Inez's order. He muttered to two old men who were sitting on upturned wooden boxes, smoking water pipes and sipping coffee.

Ruth stuck her head in the door, then stepped back onto the pavement. "Love that smell!"

Gradually, the street widened onto an open area, originally designed as a little park. Now only brown scrubby grass and a few broken park benches remained. Beyond the grass stood an attractive, modern café. The elaborate, gold sign on the sparkling windows announced that this was the French Corner Pastry Shoppe; and all guests were welcome. Several local young women were chatting near the door; one very pretty one was giggling into her cell phone.

As Najila and Huda led the group toward the café,

Kay turned and glanced back up the street. Above the shops, she saw a thicket of black, electrical wires strung helter-skelter, back and forth, from one side of the street to the other. Bare bulbs hung down at irregular intervals. She reasoned that those wires and lights had only been added in the last thirty years, but the street had probably been here for *centuries.* She recalled that verse she'd read months ago at her desk—about walking the ancient paths, knowing the good way, and finding rest. She realized that the people up and down this whole street had been walking these same ancient streets and paths, doing these same things, all their lives—and the people for thousands of years before them. They seemed so happy. They looked like their souls were at rest.

What was the message for her? Was all the fast-paced, high-tech gear of today *really* making her life better? Did she *have* to have the latest Twitter connection? Did she *really* need a new hands-free cell phone—so she could look like a *complete* idiot as she walked along, talking to herself more than she already did? It often seemed like so much electronic narcissism—just one more way to isolate herself. She wondered if she could go back to a simpler life, fewer possessions, maybe living out of a little motor home, stamping books in a library somewhere. She also wondered what her family and friends would say—probably that she was in the beginning stages of senility.

Kay smiled. What the heck? she thought. Wouldn't it be fun? How would she feel if she didn't at least *try*?

Mostly, did she have time? Ah, well, right now, she was going to have a croissant. There's *always* time for that!

~24~

My Food

K ay caught up with the group as they were entering the café. The waiter escorted them through
an arch to a cheerful smaller room off the main
dining area. Small, black bistro tables and chairs
were clustered in front of a large window, where the
morning sun streamed in, bathing the room in warm,
bright light. Two young mothers sat at a rear table,
feeding toast bites to their squealing babies.

"Aren't they *precious?*" Norma cooed. "They
look just like little birdies."

"Najila, see if the waiter can drop those blinds
a little, would you?" Julia asked. "I forgot my sunglasses."

Alicia stood to one side. "Ruth and Vicky, help
me push some of these tables together, so we're not so
spread out, OK? Let's see. There are ten of us, so how
about we make a big oval?"

Huda raised her eyebrows and whispered to
Najila, "Amriki ladies very bold, but still nice." Najila
patted her mother's hand.

Kay took a seat. "Najila, last night Inez thanked

you for the time you've given us for our stories. Today I want to thank you for all the great eating events we've enjoyed. I can't *believe* all the wonderful foods we've tasted since we've been here. Again, your planning has been superb!"

"Thank you, Kay," Najila said. "I am happy you are enjoying the meals. Now, I will order the croissant mix. This shop prepares many different fillings, chocolate is especially good. I will ask for small ones, OK? Waiters will bring bottles of water and take orders for coffee, cappuccino, or espresso—what you like. When we are done here, we will walk to other *souks*. Please— no hurry; we have plenty of time. After shopping, we will return to the hotel to take our lunch. Then you can have a small rest, maybe pack before you leave tomorrow morning. Tonight, after dinner, we will have a celebration at Sapha's well, *insha'allah*. The old monk gave me special permission to enter after closing hours." She winked. "I will bring him a little bag of almond croissants—his favorite."

Huda whispered to her in Arabic and pointed towards the door. "Yah, Mama. *Shukran. Mumtaz.* Ah, ladies, toilets here are clean and the only ones before we go back to hotel. You can find them at rear of the main room."

Ruth gave her the thumbs up sign. "My first travel rule: Never pass up a bathroom."

Huda, Najila, and Ruth had chosen seats that faced the arched doorway, thus giving them all a clear view of the entrance and the main room. As the waiters brought the bottled water and glasses, Ruth noticed that the young girls who'd been outside were now happily showing off their new cosmetic purchases at a table near the door. In a secluded rear booth, the pretty girl sat by herself, stilling talking on her cell phone. Nervously, she tapped her carefully-manicured nails on the table and twirled a large, emerald ring on the third finger of her left hand.

The two babies began to squeal even louder; hastily their mother stuffed them into their strollers and exited through a side door. The noise level in the room dropped dramatically.

When the platters of warm croissants arrived, Ruth chose a chocolate one but set it down after one bite. She wiped her mouth with a napkin, then reached into her tote bag and took out an envelope. After a sip of coffee, she looked around the table. "On our first night together, I told you that, because Beth couldn't come, she sent me her story and some photos as email attachments. In her note to me, she asked if I could read it sometime along our way while we were eating because Kay gave her the verses from John's Gospel that talk about food. I know this is a public place, but now that the babies have left, it's quieter. So is this a good time, Najila?"

"Fine, Ruth," Najila replied. "This is a perfect place for Beth's story: nice chairs, cool air, good croissants, and plenty of time. Please tell us." She motioned for the waiter to bring them more coffee.

"OK. Here, let me pass the photos around first.

That way, you and your mom can see who Beth is; and the rest of you can see how she looks today. I love her new, shorter hair." She handed two digital prints to Najila who scanned them briefly, then passed them to her mother. The photos showed different views of a smiling woman, dressed in jeans and a red blazer, standing in front of the Coliseum in Rome.

Huda studied the pictures. "Missus Beth nice looking, red jacket very pretty also. Yah, I like to hear letter. Any lady so young with white hair must have *big* story."

The group exploded in laughter.

Ruth had another sip of coffee, then took the letter out of the envelope. "All right, then. Here's Beth":

Dear Friends,

Ruth has probably told you by now that I had surgery several weeks ago to repair my right knee. Since it isn't healing very well, my doctor said I couldn't make the trip because I might re-injure the knee with so much walking, etc. After what I've gone through, I sure don't want to do that. I'm sending my story with Ruth, so I won't mess up Kay's plan for the verses she assigned to everyone. Bless her heart—I know Kay has done a super job of organizing this trip for you. How I wish I could be there!

Kay gave me the verses in John's Gospel

when the disciples went to a nearby village to pick up some lunch. Since Jesus
was hot and tired, he sat down by the
well to wait for them. When the Samaritan woman came along, he asked her for
a drink. Then they had this really in-
tense, theological discussion. When the
disciples returned, lunch in hand, Jesus
told them he had *another* kind of food—
that of doing his Father's will.

What were they to think? They were very
perplexed and probably thought somebody else had gotten there first with the
lunch. They didn't seem terribly bright
much of the time anyway. They often
missed the point of what Jesus was trying to teach them—they just didn't *get* it.
Jesus was very patient, though, and kept
teaching them until they got it. Eventually, they changed.

I've changed, too; but it's been a struggle. I haven't always been very bright either. Now I'm being spiritually fed with
a different kind of food, and that's what
I want to tell you about. I'll start with
my early days, so you can see how things
developed. Along the way, God gave me
many opportunities to change. He was
very patient with me, too, repeating the
message over and over, until I got it.

I was born in 1956, in a little town in central Idaho, the same town where my mom grew up. Right after my mom graduated from high school, my folks eloped one weekend across the border to Nevada. They found a little house back in Idaho. My older sister, Elaine, was born a year later. I came along the next year and was supposed to be a boy, named after my dad. We two girls were the apples of our daddy's eye! We were loved and treasured, and we *knew* it. My three younger brothers were born six, eight, and ten years after me, respectively.

During these early years, Dad changed jobs frequently; and we moved several times—to California, Nevada, and finally settling in Minnesota, where I grew up. Dad put in long hours at different kinds of jobs, mostly as a truck or bus driver or doing unskilled labor. He was a good, kind Christian man but was held back by a poor education; he was never very successful. He was the traditional head of our household and made most of the decisions, but they weren't always good. Mom often had to "work around things," as she put it. Dad tried really hard to be a good husband, father, and provider; but he didn't make enough money to support the family, so Mom helped out.

Mom was the one who really ran the family. She was the glue that held us all together. She knitted mittens and scarves for all us kids, made clothes for Elaine and me, took in ironing from the neighbors, did house cleaning for wealthy people my aunt knew in town, had a huge vegetable garden in the summer, and, later, worked extra hours at night as a cocktail waitress. We had a wringer washing machine and hung up the clothes to dry; but we always had bicycles, ice skates, snow sleds, and a toboggan.

We played in the snow in the winter and ran wild and barefoot outside in the summer. We'd go on long camping trips every summer in Dad's homemade wooden camper he'd built onto the back of a pickup truck. Mom painted a sign for it that read: FLYNN'S FUN HOUSE. Mom and Dad would throw all five of us kids back there; and off we'd go to Canada, northern Minnesota, or out west to visit Idaho. All we had was old Army camping stuff, but we sure had fun!

Church became a big part of our lives when Mom joined the Lutheran Church in our town; I was baptized there soon after that when I was four. We were all active in the church.

Sunday school, confirmation classes, and youth group all served in teaching me a reverence and love for Jesus. I've always had faith in Jesus as my Savior and in the Bible as the true Word of God. We all saved up dimes, so we could buy a big family Bible for the coffee table; I can still remember getting my own beautiful, white, zippered Bible for Christmas when I was twelve. I wanted that more than *anything* in the whole world. The main reason I started to take piano lessons was because I loved all the hymns so much and wanted to play them.

However, as we got a little older, all her extra work often took Mom outside the home. I'm sure she didn't want to be gone, but there wasn't much choice—there was just *never* enough money. I was ten when my youngest brother was born, so Elaine and I did a lot around the house and helped my mom to raise the three younger boys. Elaine and I sure knew how to change diapers; feed a baby; and do the laundry, ironing, cooking, housework, and even some sewing. All that equipped me to be an industrious person. Plus, our mom always made us feel important. Over and over, she'd tell us how she really depended on us to help her. We didn't know any different;

it was just how it was. Elaine and I shared the responsibility of taking care of the boys after school and doing our chores, but I don't remember ever resenting it. I never missed out on anything because of it.

Actually, I feel that my childhood was happy; I was given many opportunities. Mom made sure I got to do what I wanted to do. She always arranged rides for me to get to summer marching band practices because the school was about ten miles away, I babysat for the neighbors at night, worked my first job in a department store when I was sixteen, earned my piano lessons by babysitting for the teacher, took French horn lessons, was in the church choir, went to summer camp, etc. I'm grateful to my parents that they never held me back and never tried to restrict me. I was allowed to be in lots of activities and make a lot of decisions on my own. I had a lot of freedom to choose, within the framework of our Christian upbringing.

As I was finishing high school, things began to change. I know my folks loved each other; but they had their problems, too. They didn't always see eye to eye; and they began to argue about a lot of things, money in particular. Mom was a lot younger and smarter than Dad.

Dad. She was also very beautiful, and her work as a cocktail waitress often kept her out late at night. After a while, she met a guy at the club where she worked. Sometimes, he'd stay around to help her clean up at closing time and would drive her home if she didn't have the car. Everything was fine for a long time—they were just friends. Eventually, they had an affair. Dad found out and was just crushed. It was like the life had *totally* gone out of him. They didn't talk about this much with us kids, but I could tell. I don't know if they went for counseling or what. One thing led to another. Other things happened that damaged their relationship even more; and, shortly before I finished college, they finally got a divorce.

Ruth laid the letter on the table and took a big drink of water. She looked a little pale. "Wow. Beth and I are pretty close, but I didn't know all this stuff about her *parents*."

"It's probably not something a person wants to talk about," Norma said tentatively, "but I can sure sympathize with her dad. When my ex sent me back to the States, those feelings of rejection and failure made me feel like my life was over. In a way, it was."

Ruth turned her head slightly as she heard the side

door open. A handsome, thirty-something young man, sporting designer jeans, a lavender polo shirt, and aviator sunglasses perched on his blow-dried, blonde hair, politely threaded his way around their tables. He walked to the arch, quickly surveyed the main room, then joined the pretty young woman in the rear booth. She flashed him a brilliant smile as he sat down and took her hand.

Turning back, Ruth picked up the letter. "I'll go on. It probably gets better."

Right about now, you're probably all wondering why I'm writing so much about my family. It's to show you how blind and dumb I was later. Anyway, I paid my own way through college by working and with scholarships and loans. School kept me very busy, so I didn't see my family a lot even though I was only eighty miles away. Still, we were very close; and I felt secure in my relationship with them. I could bring a whole caravan of kids home for the weekend, and Mom would have the hot chocolate and chili ready for us.

Man, oh, man, I was hot stuff, all right! I showed up at college with my Beatles' records and rock band posters, hip hugger jeans, and platform shoes. I was a "good girl," but I liked to party hardy. I learned how to drink, smoke, dance, and have a good time. I didn't know anything about the potential dangers of the party scene, but God kept me safe. I had a strict moral code when it came to sex, though; and that kept me out of a lot of trouble! I really didn't see any problem with being a party girl *and* a virgin, so I lost a lot of boyfriends because I wouldn't "put out."

I went to a small Lutheran college in southern Minnesota for the first two years. It was great, but I also learned that there were many people who called themselves Christians but didn't act like it. I saw the difference between belief and actions. Although I'd been given a lot of responsibility early, I continued to have a lot of freedom to choose and run my own life. Some of my college roommates had been raised in very strict, tightly-controlled Lutheran homes without much freedom. I don't remember ever envying them!

My problems came later, but hindsight shows me that their roots began while I was still in college. Although I was taught all about religious concepts, I wasn't taught about reality: life's problems and temptations and how to deal with them. Like those early disciples, I just didn't *get it* when it came to *applying* what Jesus said to my day-to-day life.

I met Perry when I was a junior. We soon knew we were meant for each other. He respected my views on sex and religion and, gradually, came to know Jesus. He was confirmed in the Lutheran Church; we were married there in 1978, just before my folks' divorce. That was sad, of course; but their troubles were a long time in the making. For us, it was a golden period of romance, love, and good times. We were finishing college and looking forward to our new life together. Before we met, Perry had led a pretty sheltered life. He had lived with his folks at home until our marriage. So we had a really hard time convincing them to let us drive from Minnesota out to Idaho together, so he could meet my folks; whereas I'd already been on my own for five years. We came from totally different realms of parental authority and control. The best thing we ever *did* was to go to Australia to work for three years, where he became independent from his folks.

Ruth paused for a moment and glanced out the door. She saw that the blonde man had changed places and now had his arm around the girl. Ruth could hear snatches of their conversation. In a strong Texas twang, he told the girl that he was on assignment in Israel with an international hotel chain and that he and his wife would be getting a divorce—soon.

Huda leaned close to Ruth and clucked her tongue. "See pretty girl out there?" she hissed. "I know her family, called Khoury. She married, husband is Salim Shahin, nice, older man. She not get fancy ring from blonde boy. Get only *trouble* from him!"

Ruth sighed. "Sure looks that way, Huda. Now, where was I?" She continued reading.

> Things were fine in our marriage—at first. Our kids came along: Mark in 1980, in Australia, and Bettina in 1982, in Iowa. In 1984, we moved to Rome; and, a year later, I started working as a nurse in an international hospital. I hadn't met you all yet. Soon, we got into the party scene: Perry would stay home with the kids, while I went out with the girls from work; or, sometimes he and I went to parties with some of his colleagues. It was all lots of fun and very harmless—at first.
>
> We weren't aware of it then, but this was when our real problems began. What started going wrong was our focus—it was *outside* our family. We thought only about work and parties and how much fun we could have. The kids were at daycare all week; and, even though we spent the weekend days with them, we

usually went out on weekend nights. When I think about this now, it makes my heart twist and my eyes tear up at my lack of devotion to my sweet children. I didn't even *think* about it then. We thought we were good parents. After all, didn't we spend a lot of time with the kids? But I know in my heart where my focus was: I was interested in my career and in having a good time. Period!

Gradually, more serious things started happening. Satan chose this time to toss a little temptation into my path—to turn my heart away from my marriage, home, and children even further. And I bought *right* into it. I was totally blind and couldn't see it. I was very cocky but also vulnerable, inexperienced, and *incredibly* stupid. I realize that now. What happened next was that I started an emotional affair with the teacher of my Italian class. He was a few years older, suave, and really handsome. At first, he'd ask me to join him for an espresso or a glass of wine after class with other class members. Then, later, it was just the two of us. It finally turned into a physical affair. It was so wild and passionate. Plus, there was the thrill, the excitement, the infatuation, feeling desired, not getting caught—the whole 'forbidden fruit' thing. My concentration was almost *totally* on him for about six months.

I knew it was wrong. But I didn't know how to handle it or where to go for help. I just didn't know what to *do*! I'd been praying and seeking God's help, but it didn't seem to be working. Eventually, I couldn't take it any more—all the lying and sneaking around—I was wracked with guilt, so I broke it off. Then I told Perry.

As long as I live, I will never, *ever* forget the look on his face when I told him what I'd done—what had been going on. We were sitting in our living room. At first, he seemed very calm. Then he suddenly ran into the bathroom and was violently sick to his stomach. When he finally came back and sat down, he looked like a ghost or like he was in shock. He started shaking—had to wrap himself in a blanket–and then he started crying. My big, strong husband—crying like a baby!

"Wasn't I good enough for you, honey?" he sobbed.

I felt like I'd stuck a knife in his heart. I'm sure he felt that way, too.

Things were pretty rocky for a long time. We

were polite to each other, but we slept in separate bedrooms and just sort of co-existed. We continued with our jobs, did stuff with the kids, and kept up appearances. But Perry would often be really sarcastic because he was so hurt and bitter. It was pretty awful. No, it was horrible. Wouldn't you think that, with my family background, I'd be the *last* person to do something like this? That's when Jesus really became important in my life. He began to offer me a different kind of food.

During all this, I was still working in the hospital; and, one day, something happened. Bill, an asthma patient who I'd looked after for several weeks, had some visitors. He introduced me to them. As I left the room, I could hear them praying for him. Later, when Bill was well, he invited our family to come out to his house to visit his family. So we went. What a chain of events that started! They had this big cookout evening; and we met all of these other friends of theirs, all Spirit-filled Christians. We didn't know *any-thing* about that. It was certainly not a *Lutheran* kind of thing, but they were nice people anyway.

Somehow, I think they knew that Perry and I were struggling; but they never said a thing.

They didn't push us to pray, get counseling, or anything. They just loved us and prayed for us. After a time, Perry became close to several of the men; and, slowly, he began to share our problems with them. The wives began to pray for us. They'd invite the kids and me over for a Saturday. Plus, they asked us to go camping with them in a national park.

These new friends soon became the center of our lives. I couldn't believe this was happening. I mean, we needed help so desperately; and then it came—just like that! They were angels to us! Although I was already a believer and was aware of my sin—was searching for help—I didn't realize until much later that Jesus was sending help. He was using these people to speak to me. They never criticized; they just fixed barbeque suppers and listened. And, gradually, our focus changed.

Jesus put these people in my life and used them to teach me—to feed me more about the word of God and what Scripture says about temptation and dealing with it. They taught me to pray, to memorize Scripture, and to apply all that Lutheran doctrine to real life and real problems. They showed Perry and me how people can love and accept each other unconditionally, sin and all, because Jesus loves *us* that way.

I did my part to fight Satan by praying, studying, and memorizing Scripture. That helped me to see things more clearly. Jesus, on the other hand, changed my heart, straightened out my thinking, and helped me to act honorably. Eventually, I *knew* that my old self, my desires, and my old attitudes were gone. I was a dramatically different person from before. I had a new mental attitude and a whole new self. God was helping me, resulting in a new strength for me, and enabling me to do things I'd never done before. I was able to get this other guy completely out of my life. The memory remains, but Jesus took away the sin itself. He forgave me, he helped Perry to forgive me, and he helped me forgive myself.

As a believing Christian, it was *hard* to face those failures and hard to admit what I'd done. I'm glad I'm *writing* this and not actually having to *say* it out loud. But I want to be honest about my life. It is what it is, no matter how I might wish it were different. It was also hard to let go of old distractions—the old patterns. There were also other problems to deal with. Perry had severe feelings of rejection as a child that he had never been able to share with me until that point, so my affair caused him to feel even *more* rejection.

One of the new things I did was to take a hard look at my life. First, I decided I was missing precious time with my kids; so I quit my job at the hospital. Perry made good money, and I knew I could always go back to nursing at some later point. Right then, the kids needed me; and I needed to get my life in order. It was during that time that I met you and joined the study group, too, which helped a lot.

We cleaned house big time. We dropped out of the party scene, gave away our hard rock music, added Christian books to our library, and centered our family life in Christ. Perry and I both learned more about understanding and communicating with each other. I'm happy we made those decisions, but it took almost *six* years before we were back to normal with each other. During that time, we also learned a lot about parenting; I'm really proud of how our kids turned out.

As the years have gone by, I've shared my story with other women. It gives them courage, hope, and concrete evidence that God can help them if they're willing to surrender.

Some folks don't believe that people can change, but my story is proof that Jesus can change a heart and a life!

We've lived in Italy for twenty-six years and now are getting ready to retire back to the States. Since I have degrees in public health and health education, I might do something in those fields again because I really hate all the toxicity in our environment and how it affects health. As long as I keep a clean heart and a willing spirit, I know I'll find the work I'm supposed to do.

Have a great trip, and send me lots of pictures. I miss you.

> All my love,
> Beth

Gently, Kay set down her coffee cup. "What a wonderful letter! How incredibly honest! I can certainly identify with Beth's difficulties in admitting failure. Yet, failure, like death, is a part of life. What's important is to learn from our mistakes and our failures and carry on."

Ruth folded the letter and looked around the table. "At the beginning of this trip, I was all set to take a big step: I was ready to divorce Pete. However, after your story, Norma, and now hearing Beth's again—oh, yeah, she'd told me some of this when we were together in Rome but never all the stuff about how Perry felt and then how *she* felt—I've been sitting here, asking myself, can I *really* do that to Pete? I know it would hurt him. Maybe we could try something else instead, like get some counseling, some help with anger management or improving communications. You know, maybe we could learn how to talk honestly with each other, say what we mean without totally trashing the other person, or find some new things we like to do together—or *something*! There's *got* to be a better way. Life's too short to cause somebody so much pain if there's another way to deal with things. It might take a while, but I'm going to do it. I *want* to do it!"

She glanced at her watch. "Geez, look at the time! We're burning daylight! I'm making a pit stop, and then I'll meet you guys at the door, OK? Let's go shopping."

As Ruth stood up, she noticed Huda glaring at the young woman in the back booth. "Hey, Huda, I'll bet you'll be having a word with her on your way out, eh?" Huda nodded, quickly paid the bill, then firmly took Ruth's arm.

Together, they marched purposefully into the main room.

~25~

Serendipitous Shopping

A few minutes later, Norma followed them. She blinked as she stepped out into the late morning sunshine. "Wait, Huda, let me get my sunglasses; then I'll be ready. I'm sure you can help me find a lace tablecloth. I bought one ages ago in Damascus; but, then, some red wine got spilled on it. No matter what I did, I could never get it out. I gave it to my little niece to play dress-up with; she loves being the bride."

"Yah, Missus Norma, *maffi mishkala*, ah, no problem. Friend have *big* store, sell many fine cloths. Best quality, best price. Missus Beth's story good, eh? I say few words to pretty young girl, tell her forget sexy, blonde boy, think of own life and family. Come, walk this way."

Ruth gave them both a little wave as Najila came out. Thrilled, Najila watched Huda and Norma disappear down a dim side street. She turned as the rest emerged from the pastry shop. "OK, ladies, you will find more shops down this street. We do not have to all stay together. It is now eleven-thirty, so we can meet at my van at one o'clock. Go straight down to the fruit and fish shop street to the car park; you will see the van. I will phone the hotel and say we take our lunch at one-thirty, *insha'allah*."

"*Fabulous*, Najila," Ruth said, as she grabbed Vicky's arm. "C'mon, let's go. I want to duck into that cosmetic shop down the block. I need a new zipper bag for my make-up. I'm a sucker for cute stuff, and I'll bet they'll have a good selection. It's a remnant from my flying days. I always kept those little bags stocked up; I could be ready for a trip in an hour."

Vicky smiled. "Sounds great. Plus, I'd like to find some Ahava creams. I don't know if they're really made from Dead Sea salts, but I bought some before and loved them. Their moisturizer is the *best*! After that, let's stop at a gold shop, OK? I want to look for something a little out of the ordinary."

"See you guys later," Ruth yelled as they headed down the street. "Last one back to the van buys drinks tonight!"

"Hey, Julia," Alicia said, "care to hang with me? I want to check out that next place, the Family Book Store."

"Well, yeah, sure, thanks, Alicia. I'd love to. So, what are you looking for?" Julia asked as they entered the well-lit shop. Several older men were browsing through regional and international newspapers near the front window.

"I'd like to find a book on local flowers. I'm always on the lookout for new varieties." Alicia walked slowly to the rear of the store, stopping at several counters along the way.

Julia worked her way along the wall, down the right side to the back, where Alicia stood. "Wow, Alicia, look at all these shelves—so many nice books; and everything's so *clean*. This guy either does a huge business, or else he has a little whisk broom like Kay's!"

"I know. Right in front of me," Alicia announced, "is a whole shelf of gardening books, all in English. I could spend a whole *day* in here!"

"For sure," Julia affirmed as she waved her arm around. "On that shelf above your head, I can see a copy of *Astronomy in Israel*, in English even. This place is a *gold* mine!"

A small, dark, scholarly-looking man walked quietly up to Julia. "Thank you, Madame. We have largest selection of English books in all Palestine. Many customers from America, Canada, or Great Britain—all come here, want buy English books, magazines, papers, other things. I have in store or make order."

"Super!" Julia said enthusiastically. "You have a *great* shop here."

Alicia looked at her watch. "Let's hustle, Julia. It's already noon, and there are a lot more stores we haven't seen yet." Ecstatic, they paid for their purchases and were soon back on the street.

I want to pop into that fabric shop next." Julia urged. "Would you look at that *beautiful* blue material on the left with the little, gold flecks in it? I've never *seen* fabric like that in the States–and so reasonable, too. I've found this great dressmaker near me in Phoenix. She's very talented and could make that up into something nice for me."

Alicia nodded. "Yep, that's your color, all right," she said, as they entered the store, packed floor to ceiling with hundreds of bolts of fabrics in every hue and texture. "Look, there's Corinne. What's she doing here? I didn't know she sewed. Hey, Corinne, what's happening?"

Corinne was walking slowly up and down the aisles, searching through piles of multicolored fabrics. "Oh, not much. I was just remembering how much fun we had when we read the Samaritan woman's story the other night, where you used the fabric pieces. So I'm picking up a few more bits for my kids' religion classes. They love acting out the stories when we study the Gospels. With a piece of fabric, it doesn't take much to get them going. Plus, they remember the lesson so much better that way, too. Look, here's even a camouflage print for the soldiers. These small pieces won't take up much room in my suitcase; although I did bring an extra duffel bag, in case I got carried away." She grinned sheepishly.

Across the street, Kay and Inez came out of a drugstore and saw that they were next to Jadir's Stationeries. "Oh, Kay, may we go in? Do you mind? I know you want to find a rug; but, as long as we are here, I want to see if they have a map. Maps are a passion of mine."

"Plus, they're so useful for your teaching, aren't they, Inez? I'll bet this trip is giving you lots of new ideas. Of *course* we'll go in. Besides, the rug store is just down there; and I'm watching the time."

In five minutes, they were back on the street, each carrying bags with large, splendidly-illustrated maps entitled *The Land of Israel that Jesus Walked* and bars of fragrant, sandalwood soap that the shop owner had pressed on them as gifts. Kay shook her head in wonder. "These people are *so* polite and generous. Maybe these shops aren't big American malls, but maybe that's OK. They have such a *personal* touch. I *love* that!"

"Yes, me, too. I am so excited about my map! Ah, I see Vicky and Ruth in that gold shop over there. We can join them." Teetering on the curb, they dodged a honking taxi, then hurried across into Nabil's Jewelry.

Nabil himself was slight, his black beard trimmed to a perfect point, his pink, silk shirt perfectly pressed. Standing in the doorway, he glanced frequently at his diamond Rolex, while casually wiping a gleaming Gucci loafer on his white pant leg. His small shop was awash in glittering gold of every kind and price range—rows of earrings, racks of necklaces, chains, and bracelets. Miniature spotlights illuminated the glass cases of diamonds, rubies, and emeralds.

Vicky moved to one of the cases. "Good afternoon, Madame," Nabil said. "I can help you?"

"I hope so. What I'm looking for is a bit out of the ordinary. I'd like to find a gold charm or pendant with the number twelve in Arabic." Nabil gave her a blank look. Vicky then drew the numbers and a necklace sketch on a piece of paper for him. Nabil smiled and shook his head;

but, after a moment, he held up an index finger. He quickly dialed a number on his cell phone, hurried through the usual greetings, asked a few questions, and hung up. "My brother have. You wait, Madame, few minutes, please."

The women spent the time gazing into all the cases, pointing out their favorite pieces. Soon, the door opened; and a younger man resembling Nabil entered. He held a small, red box. "Here is number twelve. Which Madame want?"

Vicky smiled and waved her hand. "I'm the one."

Just then, Najila, Norma, and Huda entered the store. "Good," Najila said. "You are here. We looked in several shops but did not see you. Norma thought you might be here. If you like, Mama can help you with buying."

"*Marhaba*, Nabil, Ahmad," Huda said in English. Her lips were slightly pursed. "These ladies my Naji's group. You give them best, *best* price, OK? Not want I tell your mama."

"No, *no*, Missus Huda," the younger man fawned. "Of *course* price is best, always best for you. Look, Madame, I put necklace here, so you see. Very bee-you-ti-ful. Lady order last month, never pick up. *Much* money." He drew the gold necklace out of the small, red box and laid it carefully on a square of thick, black velvet.

Ruth gasped. "Wow! *Gor-ge-o-so*! That chain is so unusual, and the gold numbers are all outlined in sparkly diamonds. They look kind of weird, though. I see the 'one', but what's that other thing?"

"That's a two," Norma said, as she drew closer to the counter, "as in a one and a two make a twelve. Here, Vicky, try it on. Let me do the clasp for you."

Tears sprang to Vicky's eyes as she looked in a mirror, while Norma fastened the necklace around her neck. "Oohh, this is *stunning*, Mr. Nabil! *Exactly* what I wanted! I'm almost afraid to ask the price."

Nabil looked at the tag and then quickly tapped a series of numbers into his calculator with a flourish. "This piece custom made, *very* good diamonds, so normal price be ..."

"*NaBIL*," Huda hissed, giving him a slitty-eyed look. "*Best* price. *Halas*. Ladies *Amrikis*, maybe send other *Amriki* friends here ..." Her implication hung heavy in the air.

"OK, *OK*, Missus Huda. Only today, just for you, I give best price. Five hundred and fifty."

"Ladies, we *go*! Nabil is *bandit!*" Huda exclaimed with a huff as she turned to the door. "Lady who order necklace not want, now be secondhand, almost *junk*! Shop go down, Nabil. No other peoples here today. Two-fifty. *Halas*."

"Missus *Huda*! Business very bad. Five hundred."

Huda smiled thinly. "My heart, it is breaking. Three hundred."

"And seventy-five." Nabil sighed with a stricken look.

"Mama, please," Najila whispered. "*Halas.* Enough already."

"OK, Missus Vicky," Huda said grandly. "You give three hundred and fifty. Then we go."

Vicky nodded, paid Nabil, and slipped the red box tenderly into her purse. Laughter and applause erupted as the group spilled out the door.

"You were *magnificent,* Huda," Norma said. "I would *never* have the nerve to bargain like that."

Huda beamed. "Hah! Shopkeepers love, like *game* for them, Missus Norma. Come, we go rug shop next. You try there. You, too, Missus Kay. I help. We all friends."

Amazed, Najila shook her head.

What next?

~26~
Take Joy

F our doors down, the sign read: "Ibrahim's Rugs and Optics' Store. Fix Price." Fixed price? Kay thought. This ought to be fun. Still laughing at Huda's steely resolve, the women filed inside. Carpets were stacked everywhere—on shelves and tables, rolled and standing upright, like dark sentinels, in the corners. Piles of smaller carpet squares bore little cartoon signs, suggesting use as tablemats or coasters. One aisle was devoted to the latest model clocks, watches, cameras, tripods, small telescopes, binoculars, lens cleaning fluids, and brushes. A collection of antique coins and bills from many countries lay jumbled in a glass case under the modern cash register.

Drawn by the optic displays, Julia picked up a long, narrow box. She grimaced as she blew off a fine film of dust. "Hey, Alicia—a thirty-power Zeiss telescope! What do you think? Do I need this?"

"Of *course* you need it. It's your very own stare way to the stars. Get it? Stairway? *Stare* way?"

"Yeah, yeah, I get it. And I'm *getting* it. I've wanted one of these ever since I was a little kid and . . ."

"And your mama declared that nice little girls didn't *need* telescopes, right?" Alicia said with a wink. "Well, guess what? We're big girls now, wearing big-girl panties; so we can do *whatever* we want."

"Oh, I don't know if I should; but, oh, what the heck? Why *not*?" Julia replied, her voice growing stronger with each word. "I am, and I can. Besides, nobody's here to criticize me. Wait, here's the lens cap; but where's the instruction manual?"

Near the front door, Ruth and Inez fell into fits of hysteria, as they modeled the latest sunglasses that were hanging from a black, wire rack. Each pair was flashier and more outrageous than the last. "I'm all *over* these," Ruth exclaimed. "So cool with a big hat for those midnight trips to WalMart! I'll get a pair for Beth, too. She'll love that."

Vicky fanned herself as she walked down the center aisle, hoping to find a bargain. Instead, she inhaled the overpowering scent of mothballs. The oppressive heat in the small store, combined with the odor of naphthalene, made her slightly nauseous. She saw that the back door was open, so she made her way slowly toward it; she needed some air. An ancient, electric fan whirred close to a decrepit, metal chair leaning against the doorframe. She sat down, removed her sandals, rubbed her sore feet, and took some deep breaths.

Noticing Vicky's pale face, Najila spoke to the shopkeeper, then walked quickly to the back. An Indian assistant produced another chair and scurried away for cold drinks. The manager gestured helplessly toward the open door and swiped at the chairs with a broken fly swatter, all the while apologizing profusely for the dust. Najila thanked him and sat down carefully. "All OK, Vicky? Not sick?"

"No. I'm fine, really—just a little nauseous from that heavy mothball smell. The fresh air helps."

"Ah, fine then. So, are you happy to be in Palestine? Is the tour all right?"

"It's been great, Najila; and I've loved every minute. You've done a *terrific* job of guiding us. There are so many things to see around here. I wish we had more time. That seems to be the story of my life. I always try to pack too much in and am forever running out of time. But look at you—you never seem to be rushed."

"Thank you. I am happy to appear so. Actually, I was a nervous wreck, with much worry and hurry-hurry before your group arrived. But things are going OK, and everyone is so nice."

"For sure. These are really special women. It's been terrific to reconnect with them all again. I'm actually a little sad that we're almost at the end. Plus, Najila, I've loved getting to know you. I'm *so* impressed with what you've done with your life. You seem like a woman with a great deal of common sense and courage. You're always upbeat, and you seem very happy. I like that. If you have a few minutes, I'd like to share some things with you."

Najila blushed. "Thank you. I try. I was not always; but, as Ruth says, life goes by very fast. So I want to spend mine in a good mode—no, wait, I think it's 'mood,' right? Please tell your story now, Vicky. I would love to hear it. Maybe the other ladies come along, or maybe not." She sat back in her chair.

Vicky fanned herself with her hat. "Either mode or mood will do, but I think you mean 'mood' here. This is kind of a strange place–a shop for rugs and sunglasses—but it fits me pretty well actually. Like a carpet, so many things are interwoven in my life; and I see things differently now, ah, with new lenses."

She propped her sunglasses on the top of her head, then rubbed the bridge of her nose. "I'll get right to the point. You told us how you've dealt with the good and bad in your life, so how or when did you ..."

Just then, Ruth squeezed around a stack of rugs. "Here she is, guys. I *thought* I heard your voice, Vick. Oh, sorry—is this a private session, or can we crash the party?" Julia, Alicia, and Inez stood behind Ruth.

"Nah, nothing's private here. I just needed to sit a bit. That heavy-duty mothball smell was really gagging me, and you guys were busy shopping. Then Najila came, and I started talking. Imagine that! Anyway, pull up a rug or a box and join us."

After he returned with the drinks, the alert Indian assistant quickly assessed the situation and brought out a stack of white, plastic chairs from a storeroom. "Madames

sit here, please. I get more drinks. You like tea or
Pepsi?" He bowed and promised to return soon with
their orders.

Vicky took a sip of her Pepsi, then set the can
on the floor. She fished a piece of paper from her
handbag. "We've heard about the Samaritan woman;
but I think I'll recap the verses Kay gave me, so we're
all up to speed, before I tell my story." Vicky read:

> Do you not say, "Four months more, then
> comes the harvest"? But I tell you, look
> around you, and see how the fields are
> ripe for harvesting. The reaper is al-
> ready receiving wages and is gathering
> fruit for eternal life, so that sower and
> reaper may rejoice together. For here
> the saying holds true, "One sows and
> another reaps." I sent you to reap that
> for which you did not labor. Others have
> labored, and you have entered into their
> labor." Many Samaritans from that city
> believed in him because of the woman's
> testimony, "He told me everything I have
> ever done." So when the Samaritans
> came to him, they asked him to stay with
> them; and he stayd there two days. And
> many more believed because of his word.
> They said to the woman, "It is no longer
> because of what you said that we believe,
> for we have heard for ourselves, and we
> know that this is truly the Savior of the
> world."

She slipped the paper back into her purse. "There's a lot in those lines, more than meets the eye. We'd all agree that there's plenty of work to be done, that we've all sown and reaped in our own ways, and that we've benefited from what others have done for us. But rejoicing? Being happy? That wasn't always on my radar. But, after some things happened to me early in my life that left me frightened and angry, I realized I had a choice: to get bitter or better. I've been finding new chances, new fields to reap and harvest, ever since. I'll try to follow that thread as I tell you about my life."

Inez turned to Vicky with a big smile. "I was hoping to hear from you. You always have such *unique* views on things."

"You're kind, Inez. There are some who'd choose a different word than 'unique,' but that's OK. Although a lot of my life has been good, I've known a few hard times and had some bad stuff happen, too. I'll start with a scary little event that happened in Mexico, while I was still in college. Of all the experiences of God I've had, *none* was more powerful than that one for learning the existence of evil. It helped me to understand and accept my early days and to improve the later ones."

"May I join you?" Corinne said as she slid into a chair.

Inez moved her chair a bit, widening the circle. "Ah, good, Corinne. Vicky has just begun her story."

Vicky rubbed her nose again. "This may sound a bit

like sci-fi, kind of hard to believe; but it actually happened. It was the summer between my freshman and sophomore years in college; I was doing an intensive Spanish language program in Guadalajara, Mexico, offered through an Arizona university. One fine, Sunday morning, wanting to practice our Spanish, my American roommate and I went to Mass in a lovely old church. While waiting for the service to begin, I decided to get a closer look at their beautiful statue of Mary; so I walked over, knelt down on the flat, wooden board at the base of the side altar, and bowed my head. It was peaceful and quiet, and everything was fine.

"Suddenly my body temperature dropped. I got ice cold—felt like I was freezing! I couldn't stop shivering. As I looked up at Mary's statue, the room started spinning. I was dizzy and nauseous; I braced myself against the kneeler and hunched forward, breathing through my mouth. My chill then became a flash of searing heat, and the nausea increased. My legs were shaky, as I staggered out of the church into the fresh air.

"I sat on the curb, my head in my hands, wondering what I'd eaten that caused all this. My mind flashed ahead, thinking of the days I'd lose being sick. I was so mad at myself! Now I'd picked up an intestinal bug after having spent two months in Mexico without so much as a stomach cramp! My roommate joined me and insisted we take a taxi home. I agreed and stood to wait in the shade of the church. Pretty soon, I'd cooled off; and I realized that I felt absolutely fine. So we went back in to Mass, which had just started. We sat in the very last pew, just in case I had to make a quick exit. Everything was fine until time for Communion. As I stood in line and moved slowly forward, the nausea returned, increasing the closer I got to the altar. I wanted desperately to step out of line and leave the church; but I just *couldn't*. It was like—oh, I don't know—like something was *holding* me there, like my sandals were nailed to the floor. I could almost feel the color in my face draining. My palms were sweaty, and I was positive I'd vomit any *minute!*"

Ruth reached into her tote bag for a tissue. "I know what you mean, Vick. I've felt exactly the same way, when I worked a flight during a thunderstorm."

"When I was little and the Mass was still in Latin," Vicky continued, "I had the habit of repeating the only thing the priest said in English before Communion: 'Lord, I am not worthy to receive you; but only say the word, and I shall be healed.' That was now my mantra as I approached the priest. He said, 'The Body of Christ,' and I replied 'Amen.' The minute the Communion host touched my tongue, the nausea dissipated. I returned to my pew, and everything was fine. No sweating, no dizziness, no problem. Go figure. Still, I thought I had some kind of weird, intestinal bug; and I was afraid it would strike again."

"Isn't that the *worst?*" Julia said as she unwrapped a nut bar. "I just *hate* it when I get the travelers' trots."

Ruth rolled her eyes. "Geez, Jules!"

Vicky stifled a laugh, then took a long drink of her

Pepsi. "Afterward, my roommate and I discussed our plans to go shopping in the art district north of the city. Naturally, I was a little worried; and I wanted to go home. Then my roommate said something alarming—that, perhaps, I had encountered the devil in that church. *WHAT*? I said she was *crazy*! After all, I'd studied enough about the teachings of Vatican Two to know that the devil was passé.

"We went on, shopped a lot, and had a wonderful time. Still, the memory of the morning haunted me. We returned to the church the next day after class—just to see. Nothing happened that Monday; but it did the following Sunday, exactly as it had the week before. This time, I was prepared! I was a prayer *warrior* that day! I knelt in front of Mary's statue through the entire Mass. I prayed the Rosary and fought the evil that twisted my stomach, urging me to run from the church. It was a battle I'll *never* forget! The priest saw me struggling. Had he heard my prayers? I didn't know. After he gave me Communion, I was fine–the same as before."

Alicia exhaled a big puff of air. "Wow, Vick! That's straight out of Spielberg. Weren't you *terrified*?"

"I was shaking, even the second time. Those two events were *very* frightening. I've since asked myself many times what really happened then and why. I'd been brought up as a Catholic and went to Catholic schools and a zillion Catholic services. I'd had no contact with the occult, or drugs, or any other things that might have planted a seed that could later grow into this horrific thing. So why did this happen, especially in a *church*? Isn't that the *last* place you'd expect to encounter satanic powers or forces? To this day, I don't really know the answer.

"I just know what happened to me as a result; it was one of my big turning points. The evil I experienced in the church in Guadalajara challenged my faith. I'm a logical twenty-first-century person. I just had a stomach bug, didn't I? What else could it be? I didn't believe in the *devil*.

Hadn't the demons and possessions in Scripture been explained away as psychological imbalance? Wasn't evil just good people making the wrong decisions? So what should my response be? As a little side note, a few years later, when I was in grad school, I heard a lecturer speak on who the devil was in the New Testament. His theory was that the devil loves God but can no longer enjoy salvation and the comforting gift of the Spirit. He said that the devil is jealous of our potential to reach out and be close to God, that the devil's main objective is to prohibit our response to God's call, to get between God and us. Believe me, the prohibition in that Mexican church was very strong on those two days! My gut response was to leave. But I didn't. I didn't run. I even went back."

"Look, here's somebody else who's back," Julia exclaimed, as the shop assistant handed around cold cans of Pepsi from a dented enamel tray. Julia carefully wiped off the can with the hem of her shirt, popped the top and took a sip. He thanked her profusely as she laid a few small coins into his hand.

"A year or so later," Vicky went on, "I knew it was time for me to take the next step. I had to move forward in my relationship with God. Like Jesus in the desert, I'd been confronted with the devil; and my faith grew. I think that there are always people and/or events in our lives that continually challenge us to mature. We either meet the difficulties successfully, or we refuse to respond—we run away. Then we have to face the consequences of our choices. My choice was to be happy."

"I know," Alicia said. "Making even little changes in our lives can be a huge challenge. Peoples' fears are often too great for them to do that. Old habits may be painful; but, like an old sweater, they're comfortable because they're *ours*. So, people just stay stuck. If they could only realize that God is always with them, wanting to help them, it might be easier."

"Uh-huh," Ruth mumbled. "But they don't, so it isn't."

"Absolutely," Vicky said strongly. "It wasn't until that encounter with evil that I really saw how God had *always* been with me, had *always* taken care of me, no matter what had happened. It was then that I began to move toward a more adult relationship in my faith. I began to be grateful—for everything. The evil that day in Mexico pushed me to look deeper. I came to understand that, had I not responded to the devil by toughing it out, accepting the challenge, staying in that church, even going *back* to that church, my faith would have shriveled like those pressed

flowers in my high school yearbook—a memory of my
youth. Ha! Speaking of memories, here's a bit of useless trivia for you: My parents, my daughter, and I
were all born on the twelfth day of the month. Plus, we
are all four the eldest, three generations of twelves—a
big number in our family."

Julia spoke up importantly. "I know some *other* big twelves, too! The ancients knew that the moon
and the sun both go through twelve stations, the signs
of the zodiac. They also knew that there were twelve
northern and southern stars, twelve months of the
year, and ..." She paused for breath.

"And that there are twelve tribes in Israel,
twelve patriarchs, twelve minor prophets in the Old
Testament, twelve disciples of Jesus, and twelve gates
in the Book of Revelation, to add a few," Vicky added,
with a laugh.

Ruth raised her two thumbs. "You guys are
regular wicked-pedias. Super! Now we know why
you wanted that 'twelve' necklace, Vick. It's *your*
number."

"Right. Anyway, on one of those auspicious
'twelve' days, I was born in a small town in central
Illinois. I arrived a bit early because my mom slipped
and fell on an icy step. She doesn't remember much
about that day, only that the ether in the delivery room
made her nauseous. She's told me she was proud of
me and loved me. But, when her high school friends
came to visit, she was embarrassed by her state of
fallen grace. Teenage pregnancy is never easy. I don't
think she's been able to shake the shame, even after all
these years. Even when I was little, I was pretty aware

of my alien status. I tried hard to compensate and fit in, but my relatives still think of me as something odd. They know who I was born to; but, whenever they see me, they want to poke me and pull my hair, just to see if I'm real.

"I guess I should clarify things a bit. My family probably holds some kind of record for multiple marriages. So, Sapha, with her five husbands: no big deal. My mom's mother was married three times; and my grandfather was married seven times, twice to my grandmother. He had six children. My grandmother abandoned my mom to my grandfather after their second divorce."

"Geez, Vick," Ruth said sympathetically. "And I thought *my* family had problems!"

Vicky sighed. "Yeah. I know this all sounds complicated, but it figures into what happened later. Don't bother to remember it all—there won't be a quiz! Anyway, according to my mom, Granddad's wives were jealous of her and abused her, as did Granddad whom she hated. Sad to say, the day he died was cause for celebration for my mom. Wife number seven placed my mom, a high school sophomore, into a Catholic boarding school, where she stayed until she became pregnant with me and left to marry my father. After I was born, my parents rented a house in that little Illinois town; my dad worked at the local electric plant. My mother's family, her brothers and half-brothers, lived in the next town over. My brother, Joey, came along thirteen months and ten days after me. I love my little brother. He's a cool guy; and we were always close, even as teenagers."

Vicky picked at a scab on her hand. "I was three when my parents divorced. One day, my mom just up and left the family. So Joey and I lived with my father and my grandparents on a farm near another tiny town, about a hundred and fifty miles south of Chicago. I can still see the wooden plank sidewalk, the new bank down by the highway, and the cemetery nearby. But guess what? Three years later, when I was six, my mom showed up, totally out of the *blue*, and abducted Joey and me from my grandparents' home. I remember sitting in her car, not exactly sure who she was. We sped by the playground of the school I was to attend in a few weeks. I thought, 'I'll never get to play on the monkey bars.' That was like the end of the world for me. I *loved* monkey bars!

"Twenty-four years later, Mom sat on the sofa next to me and told me where she'd gone those years when I lived with my dad and his parents. She held my hand while she explained that she'd had an affair and became pregnant. My father *cruely* rejected her. She told me that her lover would have married her and accepted my brother as his own but not me; the man wanted no daughters. So, for my sake, because of her love for me, my mother told me she'd given up a life of happiness with the only man she would ever truly love. She expected me to be grateful for her sacrifice, sympathetic to her pain. I wasn't."

"Good *grief*, Vicky!" Alicia exclaimed. "I can't *believe* you're just sitting here so calmly, telling us all this. I'd be crying my *eyes* out, if it were *my* story!"

"Yeah.   Well," Vicky replied bitterly, "been there, done that. The weird thing is that, later, my mom was shocked and hurt when I expressed absolutely no interest in meeting my half-brother, Danny, the illegitimate son she bore and gave up for adoption during the period she was missing in action. About ten years ago, Danny, who's a year younger than Joey, did the search thing and found her. Then he moved with his family to Tucson to be closer to her. She was less than thrilled, but what could she do? Nonetheless, she said she would never forgive me for my lack of regard for her sacrifice; she never has."

"*Ay Dios mio*," Inez murmured. "I know about difficult mothers."

Vicky dangled a sandal from her big toe. "Anyway, to pick up my earlier story, after my mother had abducted Joey and me, she moved the three of us to a larger town closer to Chicago. There we lived in abject poverty in a ratty, two-room, walk-up apartment. My mother worked at a steak house at night, at a café during the day, and at a laundry on her days off. Not surprisingly, during this time, she developed a bit of a problem with alcohol and amphetamines. Joey and I were left on our own—a lot. At the grand age of six, I became a whiz at making peanut butter and jelly sandwiches. My father, my mom's brothers, and the social services department finally tracked the three of us down. I've never understood why my brother and I weren't returned to my father. Finally, Mom stopped leaving us home alone."

Najila had tears in her eyes. "How terrible for you, Vicky! Your mama worked so hard, but to leave you children alone? I cannot *imagine!*"

Vicky shrugged. "I'm sure you can't. I've spent many sleepless nights wondering those same things. Anyway, my mom then farmed Joey out to stay with the family of one of her boyfriends. Shortly after that, she contacted her mother whom she hated almost as much as her father. I was sent to live with Grandma Susan for the next two years. She and her husband were alcoholics, but I didn't know that. All that mattered was that Grandma's house was a safe place, and I wasn't frightened or alone when I was with her."

"You must have felt that way a lot when you were a kid," Corinne said.

"Yep. Now that I have children of my own and I think of all the things that *could* have happened to Joey and me during those years, I want to cry—or scream with rage! But it's over now. With God's help, we survived; and I've decided to move on. But, it definitely left a mark. Anyway, my mother then dated lots of guys while considering reconciliation with my father. Funny—when *she* was the one who'd walked out on him, why would she *want* to go back? Why would he *take* her back? Frankly, I think she lived in a dream world. She told me once she was 'a slave to love.' *OK!*"

"Maybe this was her response to her own tough

past?" Julia asked. "Being abandoned so often, she was always looking for love?"

"Could be. Unfortunately, when I was seven, my father and grandfather died exactly a week to the day of each other. My father was killed coming home from the electric plant one night. A semi-truck hit him, head on. I never saw much of my dad's family after the funeral. It was as if Joey and I were bad memories, best forgotten. After my granddad's death, my grandmother moved to Tennessee. I saw her only once, years later, when I was eighteen and went to visit her for a day. We really didn't have much to say to each other.

"Five months after my father's death, my mother married Tom when she was expecting my sister, Kerri. The nuns at my school thought I was impervious to their little barbs regarding my mother's sudden wedding. I wasn't. I knew. My baby sister, Louisa, later completed our family foursome. She was born twelve months and eighteen days after Kerri. I was eight, and Joey was seven. Tom had been married twice before and had three daughters from his first wife and one daughter from his second. He moved us, his new family, to a big house on the nice side of town. My mother hired a professional decorator, shopped at expensive boutiques downtown, volunteered at school, and drove a Cadillac. We even had a housekeeper and a nanny. Life was looking good. Alas, it didn't last."

Alicia stood up and moved toward the door. "Yeah, I know that dance—two steps forward and fifteen back. Listen, I'm stepping outside for a smoke. Keep talking, Vick, I can still hear you from out here."

Vicky nodded. "Four years later, Tom lost his business; and we moved from our big, beautiful house in Illinois to twenty-five acres on the outskirts of the Tucson city limits. Tom and a business partner built a mobile home park on a dirt road at the edge of town. My mother was terribly angry about the loss of her cushy life. Before we could move to Arizona, Tom was required by law to legally adopt Joey and me. We went to court, talked to the judge; and, when it was all over, I had a new dad. Tom was one of the best gifts God *ever* gave me.

"Happily, our family thrived because my dad's new business thrived. It was a great time in my life. During Catholic elementary and high school in Tucson, I was a cheerleader, gymnast, student council representative, good student and an all-around popular, happy teenager. I worked part-time jobs to pay for my many activities and my car insurance. Tom was jubilant at my graduation! My folks gave me some pretty, southwestern Indian jewelry and a set of yellow Samsonite luggage, and I left home."

"I know that luggage!" Ruth hooted. I got the *same* stuff!"

"After trying several universities in Arizona, I finally settled on a college in San Diego; I entered as a sophomore and studied theology and philosophy. Very slowly, my eyes started to open. It was during those courses that I saw it had been the Divine who got me through those tough early years and, later, gave me the courage to conquer them and put it all behind me. I am one hundred percent certain that, without God's help, we would not have survived. Period.

"And after that experience with evil in Guadalajara, when I was helped a *second* time, I knew God was really *there* for me. There was a *reason* I'd lived through all those things; and there was something *else*, something *more*, I was supposed to do. This may sound airy-fairy, but that's how I felt. So, I figured that I had to do my part and learn what it was that I did best and then do it—you know, respond to my calling. I got really excited. I *wanted* to do this because I was so grateful for having been rescued–not once, but twice. I was so happy just to be *alive*, so I started looking for my calling.

"I'd loved elementary and high school; college was just as great. I worked my tail off. I graduated with honors, then did advanced work in systematic theology at a university in Montreal, thinking this was my call. I even began the doctoral program in the theology school at the University of Denver. Then love came along. I married Jack and left the program shortly before the birth of our daughter, Janna. I taught high school religion and theology classes before we moved to Rome, where our son, Steve, was born a year later. When he was about two, I organized a little preschool at our house for my own and a few neighborhood kids. That was fun; those little kids were *so* cute."

Vicky smiled broadly. "Around that time, I started attending services at the English-speaking church, began teaching a church history class at the center there, and then met you guys. I *loved* our study group!

"As our kids got a little older and more mobile, we did lots of neat things in and around Rome. Whenever Jack had a few days off, we traveled all over Italy: to Venice, Ravenna, Florence, as well as to Austria and Switzerland. We'd hop on the trains with the kids, and away we'd go. I couldn't believe our good fortune to be living in Europe. I was really sorry when we moved back to the States."

"I hear ya'," Ruth said wistfully.

Vicky looked at Ruth for a long moment. "That reminds me: I forgot to tell you about a really sad thing. After twenty-five years of marriage, my mom and Tom divorced. He and I had been really good friends for a long time. Mom got tackier than usual and reminded us both that, since I was not Tom's *real* daughter, he no longer had an obligation to parent me. When I didn't comply with her new 'custody' arrangement, she felt I had betrayed her. She refused to speak to me for the next five years. Weird, eh? Somehow, I moved on."

"Before you move on *too* far, may we join you?" Kay asked, as she walked up with Norma and Huda. "After she helped Norma with a tablecloth, Huda was *brilliant* when I finally chose my little blue carpet. We've been up in the front, haggling with the manager. With Huda's encouragement, I got the absolute *best* price. I hope we're not too late."

"No, it's fine," Vicky said. "I've got a bit more yet. Please have a seat. Look, there are even three chairs left. That assistant guy is good. He's probably the one who *really* runs this store."

Najila looked around her. "It is nice that our last story is here, with all these hand-woven carpets; since Sapha was a weaver, too. She would be happy we are here. Today we come full circle."

"You know," Vicky said, "before their divorce, I used to think that Tom ran things. Now, I'm sure all of that was handled by my mother via emotional manipulation and various levels of abuse and abandonment. She blamed Tom for everything wrong in her life, yet she had us all dancing around in circles to her every desire. *Nothing* was ever good enough for her. You probably all remember, before the days of guilt and parental scarring, the buzzwords were 'character development.' My mother promised me that the more I endured, the stronger I'd become. She said I'd thank her some day for her tough love. She's proud of my independence, my self-reliance. Huh! She doesn't want to know how frightened, lonely, and isolated I felt. To this day, she still takes credit for who I am, boasts to her friends about how hard she worked to mold me! In spite of my brother and sisters' troubled lives, she uses me as proof that she hasn't failed as a mother. I hope that, someday, she'll find peace and happiness. I'm trying really hard *not* to be like her.

"Two years after their divorce, Tom married a fourth time. My dad had many great qualities, but choosing a woman of character as his wife was not one of them. Barbara was extremely jealous of my sisters and me and did everything in her power to drive a large wedge between my father and his three closest daughters. In mid-January, 2000, shortly after their tenth wedding anniversary, my father fell into a deep depression. Long story short, he took his own life a month later. Since I'm the designated 'religious' one of the family, I planned his funeral Mass and even did one of the readings." Vicky's voice caught. "I will always miss Tom. He gave me so much love and taught me so much. I'm glad his pain is gone."

Ruth slipped her arm around Vicky and handed her a tissue.

"As I tell you all this," Vicky said, as she wiped her eyes, "I can see now that my childhood was actually *miraculous*! It was filled with people who loved and cared about me, people who were not blood related—not family. The greatest of these non-relatives was Tom who adopted me by necessity. I respected and loved this man as a father and friend. His suicide was really tough, and it took me a long time to recover. Sometimes, I think he's still with me."

Alicia ground her cigarette out and returned to her chair. "Losing your dad *is* hard."

Vicky nodded, then looked at her watch. "Oops! I'll talk fast. After we left Rome, in 2002, and moved back to the States, I went to paralegal school. Earlier, I had wanted to go to law school before I discovered my love of philosophy and theology. Twenty years later, I decided to check out the law profession before making that hundred-thousand-dollar investment. Smartest thing I ever did! The required paralegal internship took place at the District Court close to where I lived; after graduation, I worked for two district court judges for three years. I thought *this* was my call. At first, I loved the job; but the weight of other people's troubles, the constant negativity, and the hostile environment stressed me to the max. My boss sensed my withdrawal. He attacked my pride and questioned whether I was tough enough to 'handle' it. God knows, I'm *Super Woman*! So I fell for the bait and stayed much longer than I should have. A few months later, after my yearly 'well woman' physical, I walked out of the doctor's office with a lump in my breast, a dead thyroid gland, an infection in my uterus, and a wickedly-high white blood cell count. I gave my two-week notice.

"Then I pursued another dream and began to write a novel. I've already told you about *Theodora's Mirror*. I thought *this* was my calling, so I wrote daily for two years. By then, the kids were in high school and starting to attract troubles. I mean, it was like they had *magnets* on their belt buckles! What a time we had! It was hard to be grateful when they were both caught in a rip tide in Mexico and nearly swept out to sea; or when Janna rolled her car to avoid hitting a deer, had to be extracted from the wreck, and almost died; or when she was injured in a school lab accident; or when she wanted to abandon her college plans and marry a persistent boyfriend; or when Steve did the usual teenage rebellion things for way too long. Somehow, they survived; we all survived. But, I'm telling you, letting God take care of my kids was *hard*."

Inez's big, brown eyes looked puzzled. "But God took care of *you*, did He not?"

Vicky chuckled. "Point taken, Inez. Yes, over and over and over again. Since college expenses for our kids were mounting up, I went back to law firm work. Because of my prior experience, I moved up the corporate ladder quickly and got higher-paying jobs with more responsibility. I managed legal departments for several large satellite companies, ending up as Director of Workforce Compliance; I made a lot of money. Ha! You'd never know it to look at me today; but I used to wear suits, worked ten to twelve hours a day, had a staff reporting to me, attended meetings non-stop, and was tied to my phone twenty-four seven. But, honestly, I've never felt legal work was *totally* my thing. In my fifteen-year career, the paychecks were the best part. How stupid is *that*?

"Then, not long after she graduated from college and married, Janna started having a series of weird ailments. There were frequent trips to the Emergency Room. All kinds of doctors did all kinds of tests; she was one sick young woman. She was finally diagnosed with lupus. During that time, I volunteered with a friend at the local public television station in their Super School News program.

We would help middle-school kids prepare a news show for actual broadcast. That was fun, mostly because it took my mind off all the crises with Janna. I prayed constantly—worked myself into a complete praying *frenzy*! I finally realized that God was up to the task of taking care of her and that I could not, by sheer *will* and prayer, change the plan that God had for her. Then I remembered to be grateful, for *everything*. Now, believe it or not, in spite of incredible odds and life-threatening medical challenges, Janna has a miraculous baby boy and is getting on with her life, as am I, thankfully.

"Najila talked about Sapha a minute ago. I think she must have been afraid, and then grateful, too. She experienced her growth in faith after just one encounter with Jesus. She doubted, then, believed, assumed risk, overcame her fear, and finally spread the word. She ran back to town, and told the townspeople what had happened. Because of the changes they saw, they believed her. Then, when they met Jesus in person, they believed he really *was* the Savior of the world."

Julia washed down the last of her nut bar with a big gulp of Pepsi. "OK, Vicky, so Sapha knew some theology. You said you also studied theology in college and grad school, you've taught religion classes, and you taught those neat church history classes at the center in Rome. Do you ever think about going into some kind of ministry—I mean, now that your kids are grown and all? It's not something *I'd* want to do, but maybe *that's* your calling."

Vicky leaned down to remove a pebble from her sandal. "Funny you should bring that up, Julia. You know, I've been a Catholic all my life and have gone to parochial schools through the graduate level. I love the Mass, the liturgy, the rhythm of the church calendar, and the saints. I think, when you're a kid, organized religion functions to affirm the little voice of God in our heads, the one that says you are precious and that God loves you. However, looking back, I think that the most valuable lesson I learned from organized religion when I was young was to be wary of any person who professed to have the power to withhold God from me. Sadly, that includes most of the Catholic clergy I encountered as a child and many today. Given the current state of the Catholic Church, having women in charge might be a really good thing. But any proselytizing, preachy Christian soldiers, hell-bent on judgmental jihad, turn me *off*; so I steer a wide path around them. I found God on my own, not through any of them.

"I love to tell people about the saving love of God, but I'd be a hypocrite if I said Christianity was the only ticket to union with the Creator. I see organized religion, be it Christianity, Judaism, Islam, Buddhism, Hinduism, Shintoism, Taoism, etc., as a necessary evil that needs to be *strictly* regulated by a wide variety of straight-thinking people. Then there's the fact that my vision of God doesn't fit any mold. I'm too liberal and flexible for most staunch, Christian literalists; what I say is often refuted. Some people say I'm not a true Roman Catholic. I've been verbally attacked, even called a messenger of the devil. Isn't *that* a riot, given the Guadalajara deal? I'll never give up my faith, not even to become an ordained Episcopal priest, something I've considered. Things could always change, of course; but for the moment, I've no plans for any formal ministry. I might teach another church history class. Maybe that's my call because I love telling people about the good, the bad, and the ugly, and, mostly, the constancy of God's love, in spite of people's *incredible* stupidities."

Huda laughed. "Same problem here, Missus Vicky. Religion not always about God. Many peoples much stubborn, always think *own* way best."

"Don't forget, Vick," Alicia added, "you've helped a lot of people, especially in those church history classes. Those fields were ripe for the harvest: You sowed, and they reaped. First they heard your words, then they heard Jesus' words. Then they went on and shared with others all over the world. *Big* ripple effect there!"

Corinne finished her Pepsi and then gathered up her purchases. "Or, given all that you've already done, Vick, maybe your new calling *could* be to relax and kick back a little. Maybe do some more kids' TV shows, find your dreams, finish your book, and regain some balance in your life. Going through an experience like you did with your daughter probably left you really wiped out, too. So take some time to take care of *yourself*. Much as we all hate to admit it, we're not twenty any more."

"And," Norma said enthusiastically, "although your

mom responded so *negatively* to all her problems, you've chosen the *positive* route. I know you'll continue it with your writing!"

Vicky smiled. "Thanks, Norma. I have a friend who always closes every email with 'take joy.' I try to do that now. Everybody says 'take care,' don't they; but 'take *joy*'? That's cool. Sometimes it was really hard not to blame God or to beg for a reprieve. It would have been so tempting to let life beat me down. Over and over, God gently reminded me how blessed I was; things could have been *much* worse. Now my goals are: stay with it, don't run, don't abandon myself, and be grateful. When I respond like that to God, my spiritual life just bubbles up, like a spring in the desert, and saturates everything with living water. This all started when Jesus sat at the well and waited for Sapha. I know he waits for me, too. So that's all. Guess we should head back to the hotel now. I've got some packing to do."

Huda stood up. "Now, ladies, we go back to van, then take lunch. You go first, Naji."

As they trailed behind the others to the front of the store, Kay put her arm around Vicky. "Oh, my dear, I know *just* how you felt—what you went through. That's *exactly* how it was with my son, Chris. I never knew from one day to the next whether that would be his last. I could do nothing to help him. Me—Mrs. Always in Control. I just had to trust that God would, however he chose to do it. But it was so hard to let Chris go. Eventually, after a lot of time, I did get through it. So maybe," Kay said gently with tears in her eyes, "you don't have to decide your next step or calling just yet, Vicky. You've always been such a hard worker, such a go-getter, full of plans and projects. Like Peter, at every challenge, you got out of your boat—and you walked on water. But do you know what happened when Peter and Jesus both got back *into* the boat? The storm died down."

Up ahead, Huda turned to face them. "Yah, Missus Vicky, plenty storms in life when you little girl, then with own kids. But daughter not die in ocean waves, or car or school accidents, or with bad boyfriend. She not die with lupus either."

Huda reached out and patted Vicky's arm. "Such good story. You very strong woman, Missus Vicky. Evil not touch you. Daughter like you—she touched by God."

~27~

Last Night–First Day

N ajila had told Mr. Hamid they were going out to the well by eight-fifteen, so dinner had been served earlier than usual. Kay now sat on the edge of her bed, checking things off her list. Tonight was their last night, and she wanted *everything* to be perfect. Vicky was in charge of the prayer service. Check. Alicia said she'd gotten a little gift for Najila. Check. Hopefully, she'd also remembered something for Huda, who'd turned out to be such a big help. Plus, she seemed to have a different attitude toward Najila's work now. Norma will do something with water. Check. Julia said she'd help with the set-up and clean-up. Check. Kay read through the list once again. She didn't want to forget anything.

She carefully capped her pen then laid it and her list down and thought about the afternoon. I'm glad they finally got the pool filled; that swim before dinner was marvelous. I do hope my suit will be dry by morning. The young chef outdid himself at dinner again, and the waiters were *so* sweet— singing us a little farewell song in Arabic. Oh mercy, it's eight already. Time to go. I want to stay on schedule.

As she hurried out into the parking lot, Kay was happy to see that the others were already gathered near the van. After setting a hibiscus flower afloat, Norma took a few final photos of the pool, the front of the hotel, and Mr. Hamid, looking smug behind the reception desk.

Once they'd all climbed into the van, Najila asked, "All ready? Then we will go. The old monk said he would open the front gate at eight-thirty and would only stay five-ten minutes. He goes to his bed early. He is a very nice man but sometimes a bit grumpy."

Soon, Najila parked across from the stone wall outside Jacob's Well. Norma pulled out her camera but stayed on that side of the road. "Quickly," she said. "Arrange yourselves on either side of the gate. Najila, you stand in the center, like you're opening the gate, OK? You, too, Huda. Ah, perfect. Let me take just one more."

"Hey, Norma," Alicia called, "come take my place here on the end, then give me your camera. I'll get another shot with you in it. We don't want this to look like you weren't really here, do we? Thanks for always remembering to do this. Memory moments slip by so fast."

Soon they were inside the courtyard, and the old monk latched the gate firmly behind them. He bowed and smiled his gratitude when Najila handed him the bag of almond croissants.

The setting sun was still visible through the large opening behind the altar. A light breeze stirred the fragrant roses and jasmine vines along the stone walls.

But, somehow, things seemed different.

"Here we are again," Vicky said softly, "in this wonderful oasis of peace. But look, Najila—*look* at what the monks have done for you!"

Tears welled in Najila's eyes as she turned around. The entire courtyard had been swept clean and straightened. Construction equipment had been pushed to a far corner and covered with old blankets. The unfinished stone altar was spread with a fine, white cloth edged in delicate antique lace; an arrangement of yellow roses dotted with red hibiscus flowers stood in the center. At either end, two large, beeswax candles, anchored in sand, glowed inside tall, wide-mouthed glass chimneys. A pitcher of water and twelve crystal glasses stood to one side, while a dozen white, plastic chairs were in a semicircle in front of the altar.

"Nice," Julia said. "Very nice. Our job just got much easier, Kay. But why are there *twelve* glasses and chairs? Who else is coming?"

"Maybe Sapha will show up," Ruth murmured. "Wouldn't that be a kick?"

Please take a seat, ladies," Kay directed briskly as she moved to the front of the altar. "Unbelievably, our time in Samaria is almost finished. After seeing so many of the places Sapha might have lived and walked, Najila and I thought it would be fitting to finish our tour back here at the well, where it all started. To those of you who spent the afternoon making plans for this little celebration, I say thank you. Now, I'll turn things over to Vicky."

"Thanks, Kay," Vicky said as she consulted a small piece of paper. "We've put together an informal service that we hope will summarize our experience here and say a huge thank you, not only to Kay for getting us off the dime and organizing everything, but also to Najila for giving us such a magnificent tour here in this Holy Land. I know I speak for all of us when I say that our lives will *never* be the same. We'll start with Julia, who's chosen our first reading."

Julia walked deliberately to the front of the altar, stood close to a candle, and then opened her small Bible. In a slow and carefully-modulated voice, she said, "This is Isaiah 12:2-6":

> Surely God is my salvation; I will trust,
> and will not be afraid,
> For the Lord God is my strength and my
> might; he has become my salvation.
> With joy you will draw the water from
> the wells of salvation.
> And you will say in that day: Give
> thanks to the Lord, call on his name.
> Make known his deeds among the na-
> tions; proclaim that his name is exalted.
> Sing praises to the Lord, for he has done
> gloriously;

Let this be known in all the earth.
Shout aloud and sing for joy, O royal
Zion, for great in your midst
Is the Holy One of Israel.

As Julia made her way back to her chair, Vicky looked directly at her. "Perfect choice, Julia. It was so appropriate for where we are and what we've done. Those words have it all: hope, praise, promise, and instruction for us. Plus you read so beautifully."

Julia beamed.

"And now, because we're in this special place tonight," Vicky said, "Norma has a word about wells and water."

Norma walked to the center of the altar. The light from the two candles gleamed on her dark red hair. She coughed a few times then cleared her throat. "Some years ago, I attended a retreat. At the end, we had a little prayer service called 'On Being a Well.' One woman read Sapha's story from John, too; but, I have to tell you," she said with a giggle, "it wasn't *nearly* as effective as Corinne's little play we did. Then there was a prayer about being a well today. It said that each person *needs* a well—we all need someone who helps us, gives to us, and fills us, no matter *what* we're thirsty for.

"It also said that each person is a well, that we can all give things: hope, encouragement, understanding, joy laughter, and just life—of one kind or another—to others.

So, during the last few days, when we've been at this well and around the area, getting to know Sapha, her life, and her people, I've asked myself a few questions. What if I were sitting by the well with Jesus and the Samaritan woman? Did she know him for what he was? Would I? What would I ask him? What really happened when the Samaritan woman went to town?"

Julia had tears in her eyes. Norma's questions were very penetrating.

"What and who are some 'wells' in my life?" Norma continued. "When and how can I be a 'well' to others? When do I ask Jesus for living water? What happens when I do? What living water have I received recently? What have I done with it? Is it moving, flowing out to others, or has it gone stale and stagnant? Anyway, now might be a good time to have a drink of the real thing before we leave, as a little reminder."

Norma then went to the side of the altar, picked up the pitcher, and filled one glass. She gave the glass and then the pitcher to Vicky, who drank the water, and poured some into a fresh glass. Then Vicky gave that glass and the pitcher to Corinne. Norma passed out glasses, and the pitcher continued around until each woman had drunk a glass from one neighbor and filled the glass of another. Norma then returned the glasses and the pitcher to the corner of the altar. She nodded to Kay and sat down.

"What a wonderful living parable!" Kay exclaimed as she turned in her chair to face the group. "I'll think about being a well every time I drink a glass of water from now on. But that's the *point*, isn't it, Norma? Anyway, ladies, as Najila said this afternoon, we've come full circle; and what long and difficult roads we've all traveled! We've learned that we weren't alone. Since we heard earlier what *might* have happened to Sapha, what she *might* have done after she left the well, I'd like us to take a few minutes to *briefly* say what might happen to us—what we'd *like* to do, once we leave here. Tomorrow's departure is very early, so there'll be no time for this then. And, since I brought it up, I'll start.

"This has been the most extraordinary journey of my entire *life*. I hadn't been in remission very long and wasn't at all sure I could make it. But I wanted to come, so I *did*. I'm *so* glad you all came, too. Each one of you is such a *gift* to me. I'm also thrilled that we learned and saw so much with Najila and Huda, our wonderful guides and friends. What I'd like to do," Kay said with a little grin, "is to get that camper and make some trips around the western United States. I'm going to stock it with a selection of children's books and get some cards made that say 'Reading Together' or something similar. When I hit a town, I'll hand out my cards and ask at the local clinic and churches for names. Then I'll visit the kids with catastrophic illnesses. My son loved reading, so I'll be doing this in his honor. In spite of all the deaths and losses in my life, when I felt so sad or lonely, I've realized I *wasn't* alone. I don't want these kids to feel alone either. I may be a gray-haired cancer survivor, but I've still got a few good miles left in me! Oh, and, before I forget, though I sent you one earlier, I put together a hard copy list of everybody's home and email addresses; so we can all stay in touch during our travels the next few weeks. Pass these along, would you, Vicky?"

Vicky laughed as she sent the lists down the row. "You're really excited about this, aren't you, Kay? But it's a wonderful idea. I know I wasn't alone during the bad times of my life either. Although there's often evil around, how we choose to respond makes all the difference. Each time I meet a challenge and make a decision to move forward instead of remaining stuck in my past, I know it's because Jesus is with me. You'll be with me too, Najila."

In her seat at the end of the row, Najila blushed and shyly ducked her head.

"My plans," Vicky continued, "aren't quite as well formulated as yours, Kay; but what I'd like to do is to keep writing and finish my novel. For now, that's a good choice because, besides being something I'm really passionate about, it frees me up to help my daughter, if and when she needs me. I'd also *like* to do something I did years ago—help kids to produce their own TV shows. And, if I can find all my old notes and a venue, I'd love to teach some church history classes again. That's way easier and more fun than doing legal work."

"Well," Alicia said pensively, "it would have been easy to have remained stuck in my past, too, bringing up my kids like I'd been raised. That solitary hospital room time taught me that, no matter what was happening, I *could* control and change my attitude. When I asked for God's help, it always came, right on time. Since Jim's nearing retirement, we're almost done in Rome; and we'll be going back to the States. Besides getting settled in a new house, I think I'd like to get a part-time job working for a landscaping business and maybe try out some ideas for computerized garden design. Later, if the boss was willing, I'd like to take a few bright kids and teach them about gardening and how to love the earth and its calming effects. It might give them a profession, too. Who knows?"

"Oh, Alicia," Norma said, laughing. "That's so exciting! It's like Outward Bound for gardeners! That sounds like so much fun. Could I come and work with you? You know how I love flowers. Like you, I was in 'solitary' too: first, when my first husband sent me back to the States, and, later, during cancer treatments. But my prayer groups sustained me. Once you learn how to ask for help from God and from friends, who would *ever* want to go back to trying to do everything yourself? So what I really want to do is to organize prayer and meditation groups for cancer survivors in hospitals and churches in my area. How does the name 'Living Well' sound?"

"It sounds perfect," Julia said. "I went to a group like that during my chemo. It helped me a lot. Nobody knows what you go through during all the stages of the illness—the treatments, the sickness, and the losses—like somebody who's already been there. It's comforting to be with people who understand what you're talking about. They don't try to fix you; they just listen and are *there*. I think I want to keep going with the volunteer work at our local museum and maybe get more involved in the astronomy department—like giving after-school or summer classes in astronomy for kids. I love astronomy, and I want to teach kids to love it, too. Since I live in the Wild West of Arizona, I could call the classes: 'Shoot for the Stars.' What do you think?"

"Julia, I love that name!" Inez said. "Think of the possibilities for your logo. Like you, I have had some bumps in my life; but, once I decided that I liked my new life, my new self image, and my new relationships with my family and friends better, I took the actions necessary to make these changes permanent. Mostly, I took better care of myself.

"And guess what? When I took better care of *myself*, then I could take better care of everyone *else* around me. I do not have to repeat the same destructive patterns that I had seen earlier. For today, anyway, I feel God is there and does care for me. Sometimes, I think God has helpers—like all of you. Your lives, your stories, what you have all done on this trip—everything has been a picture of how God loves us. My big dream is that my husband and I will build a house, maybe near Milan. After that, I would like to find a way to use my psychology degree a bit more. There is a need in Milan for young women to get some direction to change their lives. Since my Italian is growing better, maybe I can help them."

Ruth smiled. "Terrific, Inez! What a great way to use your past training! I now know, without a shadow of a doubt, that *I* want to get back into a community theater group. I *love* doing plays, so why should I keep depriving myself by saying I'm too busy? Then, there's something else, a little more personal, that I want to do. I want to make copies of my mom's diaries and share these with my brother and sisters. They were pretty young when she died, and they didn't know her as well as I did. We learned who Sapha was because of what she wrote, so my siblings can learn who our mom was because of what she wrote in those diaries. I wasn't up for this for years—it hurt too much—but now I can. Her diaries were a gift to all of us. And, hey, since yesterday, I've been thinking: Do I realize that God's given Pete as a gift to me? Oh, yeah, he wasn't always exactly what I *thought* I wanted; but he *has* taken awfully good care of me, even when I didn't deserve it. Besides, he makes *really* good cheese biscuits! So, if I change my attitudes and stay with him, maybe we can totter into our golden years together. What a hoot!"

"You know, Ruth," Corinne said, "I ask myself almost *every* day why I was given the gift of that sign that night. I never looked for that miracle, and I've never felt I deserved it. Yet it happened. Probably none of us *deserves* the wonderful things that have happened to us—that we've talked about the past few days. Maybe that's what grace means— that God loves us and wants to help us and take care of us in *spite* of our failings, our stupidities, and our meanness. Right now, I'm happy with my life. Dave and I have a small house in a small town, we have many friends, and we do a lot of things together. I like teaching religion classes at my church, playing bridge, swimming and biking, and spending time with our family. I might write down my experiences of 'the night' or even try to *paint* it. Who knows? I don't have any big plans; but if something comes along, I'm open." She nodded to Vicky, who then motioned to Alicia.

Alicia stood up and called Najila and Huda to the front. "We are so grateful for all the things you've done to make this trip a huge success, Najila. The hotel was great, the food was fabulous, and the tours were amazing. Best of all was hearing directly from Sapha. We've all stayed at good hotels, eaten great meals, and taken tours before; but we've *never* heard from a real live biblical person before. So, to insure that we're not the *only* ones to hear this, I've gotten you a little help." Alicia handed Najila a package wrapped in gold paper. "I couldn't believe the guy at that little bookstore had this, but he did. Now you'll have no excuse for not telling *everyone* about Sapha. Go ahead, open it."

With nervous fingers, Najila carefully unwrapped the package, then handed Huda the paper. "Look, Mama, a new book: *Guide to Book Publishers, Editors, and Literary Agents*. Oh, *shukran*, thank you, Alicia. Thanks to you all. You know now what my future plans are."

"Sorry it's a 2010 edition," Alicia said, "but it's the only one he had. It should work to get you started. Huda, we've also gotten a small gift for you. We have all *loved* your help, your understanding, and your humor so much these past few days. So here's a little something for you to use when you do this again for the *next* group. You might want to set the box on the altar and open it there."

Huda smiled broadly as she laid the gold wrapping paper aside then gently unwrapped the inner tissue paper. "Ah, water pitcher—*crystal* water pitcher—for pass along, eh? Such good idea. Swedish brand, very fine crystal. *Shukran*, Missus Alicia. You get best price?"

They all broke into peals of laughter.

"Oh, Huda," Alicia cried. "You're the best. *You* are priceless."

Vicky was still smiling as she opened her Bible. "I'll close with Psalm 126."

> When the Lord restored the fortunes of
> Zion, we were like those who dream.
> Then our mouth was filled with laugh-
> ter, and our tongue with shouts of joy.
> Then it was said among the nations, the
> Lord has done great things for them.
> The Lord has done great things for us,
> and we rejoiced.
> Restore our fortunes, O Lord, like the
> watercourses in the desert of the Negeb.

May those who sow in tears reap with
shouts of joy.
Those who go out weeping, bearing the
seed for sowing,
Shall come home with shouts of joy, carrying their sheaves.

Kay stood up. "Well, ladies, we are done. We've
traveled, talked, walked, cried, and sighed. Tomorrow, we're leaving. Take all your belongings; and,
mostly, take *joy!*"

Najila walked to the edge of the altar, next to
a candle, and held up her hand. "Thank you, Kay.
Thanks to all of you. You made this, my first real tour,
a brilliant success! You were always on time, gave me
your attention, your gratitude, help, new plans, and,
mostly, a new mama. Sapha wrote of her experience
with Jesus by well. Then I translated Gran Najet's
notebook, so I could tell you what Sapha wrote. Before you leave, here is her last page":

> And I have written so that you may come to
> believe that Jesus is the Messiah, the Son
> of God, and that, through believing, like me,
> you may have life in his name.

"I wish you good flights and good life. I wish
you well. Now, please blow out the candles, Vicky.
We will go back to the hotel. The boys have a small
surprise for us."

+++++++++

"Man," Alicia declared to Kay as they walked to the hotel parking lot, "last night was just one of those nights that go on *forever*, wasn't it? First there was the celebration at the well, then the party back here, with all those great snacks and even *champagne*! We've really raised the bar for Najila's next tour group. I hope they'll get the royal treatment we did!"

"Yes, this whole trip has been *amazing*," Kay agreed. She checked her watch. "Hmm, it's almost seven. I hope the others will be along soon."

"Here, let me help you with your bag, Julia," Norma said as they came down the path. "I see you're limping a bit this morning."

"Oh, it's nothing, really," Julia said. "After all, I'm going to have to schlep it myself, once I get to the airport; but thanks, Norma. When Mr. Yousef comes, you can help me lift it into his taxi. That will be great."

The front door of the hotel banged open as Ruth, Inez, Corinne, and Vicky all spilled out onto the porch, loaded with luggage, tote bags, and purses. "Listen, you guys," Ruth shouted, "let's do this again real soon and not wait another ten years, OK?"

"Louder, please?" Alicia said mockingly. "You'll wake the *dead*, Ruth!"

"Quickly, boys," Mr. Hamid scolded, "come, come, not make ladies late." Led by Mr. Hamid, the waiters hurried out of the kitchen, once again carrying trays laden with small white boxes and plastic water bottles. "Missus

Najila not ask, but you ladies might wish small bites for drive to Tel Aviv. We pack little breads and fruits from breakfast buffet, some cheeses, one-two sweets from last night. Please to take one—my compliments."

"Oh, *shukran*, thank you, Mr. Hamid," Najila said as she and Huda came out. "What a good idea! Now the ladies will not be hungry on the journey back. Your snacks are *much* better than airport food. Now, before Yousef comes, Mama has some special words for you ladies."

From the top step, Huda turned to face the group. "One, I say you I help Naji with publish Sapha's writings. Two, when I am young girl, my mama, Gran Najet, always say me this before I make trip. She gone now; so, in her place, I do. Say you Arabic, then Naji say English." Huda raised her right hand over the group:

> The Lord bless you and keep you;
> The Lord make his face to shine upon you, and be gracious to you;
> The Lord lift up his countenance upon you and give you peace.

When Najila had finished giving the blessing in English, Huda spoke. "God say this blessing to Moses, is *very* special for Samaritans. Now *you* special, too. You well women."

Kay's eyes were brimming. "Oh, Huda, thank you so much. I've *never* had a finer blessing! Thank you, too, Najila. The tour was *superb*. We loved it, and we love you both. And, look, there's Mr. Yousef, right on time. Perfect! It's just seven. Come on, ladies. Gather your things. It's time to say good-bye."

Amid many hugs and tears, the women bade farewell to Najila and Huda. "Don't forget to write," Norma called. "I'll send you my photos, as soon as I can."

Once again, they managed to stuff their luggage and themselves into Mr. Yousef's dusty, old taxi. "Julia, you take the front seat this time," Kay said. "Your knee will be more comfortable."

The sun was just coming up as Mr. Yousef slammed the doors and got in on the driver's side. As he roared out onto the road, Julia looked in the side mirror and smiled. At the corner of the hotel, a small, stone water jar lay to one side.

Maybe it was Sapha's.

Historical Notes

Even after 2,000 years, there is still great interest in the Gospel of John. Many scholars agree that the Gospel could have been written in Ephesus or another large city in Asia Minor with a large Jewish population between 85 and 105 AD. It was possibly a mixed community with many Gentiles because the author explains many things that Jews would have known.

Authorship could have resulted not from an eye-witness, like John, son of Zebedee, or John Mark, or from a special disciple called the Beloved Disciple, but from group input, like a Johannine (John's) school in Ephesus, Palestine, or Syria. Or perhaps it was from the disciples of the Beloved Disciple and other teachers within this community, with the final structuring and editing done by a single, very-talented individual.

The Gospel is divided into two parts:

Chapters 1:1—12:50—Book of Signs—
Jesus' confrontation with the world
Chapters 13:1—20:31—Book of Glory—
Journey to the father, when Jesus' hour arrives

This gospel is very different from the other three synoptic (meaning one or common view) Gospels. It is almost like a novelette, full of dramatic scenes. Major themes are first expressed in the prologue, which functions almost like a musical overture. Many opposites: life/death, light/darkness, belief/non-belief, acceptance/non-acceptance, insiders/outsiders, plus other concepts, such as the pre-existence of Jesus, truth, and "the world," are all introduced. The rest of the Gospel is a working out of all those themes.

The theme of water is also very prominent. First, the Pharisees and John the Baptist talked about being changed by baptism with water. Then there was the great Cana story with Jewish ceremonial washings and Jesus changing water into wine. The Samaritan woman's story highlights the doctrine of "living water," her encounter with Jesus bringing many changes for her and others. Although a supper before the feast of Passover is mentioned, there is no narrative of the institution of Communion; a foot-washing ceremony is described instead.

Unlike the other gospels, there are no parables, only long discourses and episodes or vignettes: John the Baptist, Nicodemus, the Samaritan woman, the woman caught in adultery, the man born blind, Mary and Martha, Mary at Bethany, Mary Magdalene, Thomas, Peter, and the Beloved Disciple. Five of the major vignettes are about women. This is very unusual, given the ancient time and place this Gospel was written. In the first century, most women in biblical lands could not write, nor were they written *about*. This is the only New Testament book considered possibly written by a woman.

Three important literary devices used throughout the Gospel are misunderstanding, irony, and symbolism. Many characters just don't seem to *get* it; but the audience and readers *do* get it, thanks to help from the narrator. The author was very creative in having his characters' words mean more than what appears on the surface. Almost everything seems to stand for something else. Many, if not most, statements or terms in John's Gospel, where the Samaritan woman's story appears, have been given symbolic meanings. Scholars acknowledge that when John says something, it can often have at least two or three meanings.

But Jesus' statement, concerning the Samaritan woman's five husbands, has frequently been interpreted *literally*. Many writers have then added their own opinions and prejudices as to the reasons for her many marriages. She has been the victim of centuries of abuse, unfavorable publicity, and misinterpretation. In the sixteenth century, John Calvin wrote that she had been stubborn and disobedient, thereby forcing her husbands to divorce her, with her later turning to prostitution. Other writers talked about her shameful, immoral past, labeling her as a sinful woman, having only short marriages or long affairs.

It is extremely unfortunate that many scholars through the years have perpetuated these myths. They reached the conclusion that, because Jesus said "for you have had five husbands, and the one you now have is not

your husband," that her morals were low, she was
loose and promiscuous, that her situation was irregular, or that the five marriages were her fault.

In Old Testament times, the town well was a
local gathering place where women went, not only to
draw water for their families, but also to meet their
friends—maybe trade a bit of gossip. There are several early stories about man meets woman at a well
and they marry: Isaac and Rebecca, Jacob and Ra-
chel, Moses and Zipporah. In this Gospel, man meets
woman, but they *don't* marry. The author often used
such switches to alert readers that something different, something special was happening.

Samaritan beliefs were somewhat different
from those of the Jews at the time of Jesus. Samaritans used only the first five books of Moses, calling
those books "the Law." In the fifth book—Deuter-
onomy—God had promised to raise up a prophet like
Moses from among the brethren. The Samaritan hope
was that this prophet would come to them. Another
hope was that this prophet or *taheb* would say that
their mountain, Mt. Gerizim, was the correct place to
worship and not in Jerusalem, as the Jews taught.
This was because Samaritans felt that Mt. Gerizim
was the spot on which their ancestor, Jacob, had his
heavenly vision. They also believed that this *taheb*
would locate sacred religious utensils—serving dishes, bowls, plates, etc., hidden away in a cave on Mt.
Gerizim—and also find the rod of Moses and some
manna.

However, both Samaritans *and* Jews of the first

century were very restrictive about what should happen in a private or home environment and what was, or was not, allowed in public. For women, almost everything of any importance happened only at home—*the* sphere for women. Men, on the other hand, held forth in public. In many towns, there was even an elected official—a man called a *gynaikonomos*—whose job it was to see that men and women behaved themselves in public. Women generally had no problem with this.

So it was completely *unheard of* for men to talk with women in a public place like Jacob's Well. It was even more shocking that this conversation took place between a Jewish man and a Samaritan woman and that he would ask her for a drink. All these things were considered serious pollution by both groups, which could account for the returning disciples being very surprised to see Jesus in conversation with the Samaritan woman.

Some writers say the Samaritan woman wasn't an actual person; but that this was a "type" story, that John "wrote her back" into the time of Jesus, to validate the conversion of the Samaritans from his time. It is possible that the Samaritan woman might stand for women who were missionaries in the early days of Christianity, or for one woman in particular who was instrumental in the conversion of the Samaritans in John's community later. With forty-two verses, it is one of the longest stories in any of the Gospels. Although unnamed, the Samaritan woman is now immortalized forever.

Whatever truth the author of John intended, the story line in his Gospel shows that Jesus did not criticize; and the woman did not apologize. She did not deny her past, but Jesus also did not condemn her present and future. She asked intelligent, theological, and pertinent questions, was answered with integrity, and treated with respect.

Her growing faith and excitement that she had met and spoken with a mighty prophet who might just be the Messiah allowed her to forget her water jar and leave her former routines. She moved beyond her social and cultural boundaries to announce her discovery to her townspeople. She invited them to share in her joy. Fear of derision did not get in her way. She stepped out in faith, she was believed; and, thus, through her, many others "came to him." They had heard, and now knew, that "this is truly the Savior of the world."

The Samaritan woman's story portrays how Jesus was accepted by the despised and the desperate, while at the same time being dismissed by the intellectuals and the outwardly religious. Like other apostles, her faith motivated her to action. She witnessed to her townspeople: "Come and see. Could he possibly be the Messiah?" It is interesting to observe what happens to faith in each episode, why some characters, like the Samaritan woman, move toward a deeper faith in Jesus, while others move away, choosing indifference or even rejection.

Was the Samaritan woman a real person? Or

was she simply a literary device? We just don't know. What we *do* know is what John wrote, what John wanted us to know about this woman and about Jesus. It is not necessary then, to clean up, sanitize, rationalize, or symbolize her story. Jesus accepted her as she was, she accepted his gift, and her life was changed forever.

For the Samaritan woman and the contemporary women, discovery of the source of their individual "living water" was a turning point. They realized that Jesus, God, a Higher Power, or the Divine accepted them and loved them unconditionally. They were thus free to let go of the damaging past and were empowered to build a new future.

Acknowledgments

A book is always the fruit of many minds. My editor, Danelle McCafferty, is incredible! She has eyes on stalks! With gratitude, I received comments and encouragement from Barbara Bowe, RSCJ; Jeanette Lucinio, SP; Carolyn Osiek, RSCJ; Judith Bennett, Monica Chappell, Susan Duncan, Terri Hale, Vevonna Kennedy, Lisa Kochinski, Irene Lewandowski, Laurie Orth, Dr. John Pilch, Dr. Judith Reid, Verlon Stone, Carol Tilley, Dr. Samia Williams, and Ron Wooten-Green. Special thanks go to my husband who urged me to begin this project in 1999. He shared his insights and acerbic wit, cooked gourmet meals, and unsnarled my computer.

The following authors have influenced me greatly: Mary Ellen Ashcroft (*Spirited Women: Encountering the First Women Believers*), Marcus J. Borg (*Jesus: A New Vision–Spirit, Culture, and the Life of Discipleship*), Thomas Brodie (*The Gospel According to John*), Raymond E. Brown (*The Community of the Beloved Disciple*), R. Alan Culpepper (*Anatomy of the Fourth Gospel: A Study in Literary Design*), Peter Ellis (*The Genius of John: A Composition-Critical Commentary on the Fourth Gospel*), Elisabeth Schuessler Fiorenza (*In Memory of Her*), Robert Kysar (*John–The Maverick Gospel*), Bruce J. Malina and Richard L.

Rohrbaugh (*Social-Science Commentary on the Gospel of John*), Vashti M. McKenzie (*Journey to the Well*), Carol A. Newsom and Sharon H. Ringer (*Women's Bible Commentary*), Dr. John J. Pilch (*The Cultural Dictionary of the Bible*), David Rensberger *(Johannine Faith and Liberating Community)*, Sandra M. Schneiders (*Written That You May Believe*), Bonnie Thurston *(Women in the New Testament)*, and Ben Witherington, III (*Women and the Genesis of Christianity*).

The story of Sapha, the Samaritan woman, is based on factual information gleaned from available sources. I have endeavored to reconstruct her life and give her a persona, to the best of my ability. Any errors are my responsibility.

Ladine Housholder
February 28, 2012

Discussion Questions

Introduction and Background: The Samaritans and the Samaritan Woman

1. Read 2 Kings 17:1-41. What is the main theme?
2. What were some of the sins of the Israelites? Do we do some of the same things today?
3. What happens when we try to worship more than one God? Who, or what, are some of our foreign gods or idols today?
4. Read John 4:1-42. What is your reaction to this story? Why do you think it was preserved and included in the Gospel?
5. How is each main character or set of characters presented: Jesus, the Samaritan woman, the disciples, and the townspeople?
6. Are there certain people, or groups of people, that you tend to avoid in your life? Why do you think this is so?
7. What was the main thing Jesus did for the Samaritan woman in this story?
8. What was her reaction? Can you share a similar situation from your own life?

Chapters One—Five

1. Have you ever acted on a dream, vision, or message you received? What was the result?
2. When have you undertaken an involved task that seemed personally overwhelming at first? What did you do?
3. Where are you in your spiritual growth: moving forward or standing still?
4. List some characteristics of Kay's that make her a good leader for this trip.
5. What are some things that make Najila unusual, given where she lives? How did she take care of herself, following her husband's death?
6. What motivates Najila to get into the tourism business? What obstacles does she have, and how does she overcome them?
7. What made the Rome study group particularly important? Do you belong to a study group? What are its aims and goals?
8. Have you ever received an unexpected gift that came at just the right time?
9. Why was Sapha remarkable? What was going on around her?
10. Upon their arrival in Tel Aviv, what were some of Julia's expectations? How do you react when things don't meet your expectations?

Chapters Six—Seven

1. What was the group's first impression of the Nablus hotel? How was their arrival handled?
2. What was Najila's attitude about changing her agenda? Is it easy for you to make quick changes in your plans? Is flexibility an important asset?
3. Do you think that some people, like Julia, attract bad luck; or is it only a coincidence?
4. What do you do when you find poor service or maintenance?
5. What do you learn about the nine women at the first night's dinner?
6. What are some of their differences?
7. What are some things that bind them together?
8. Why have they made this trip? What is each woman seeking?

Chapters Eight—Ten

1. What was your general impression of the Samaritans and their history?
2. Imagine yourself sitting by the well with Jesus and the Samaritan woman. Did she recognize him? Did she know him for what he is? Would we?
3. What things were initially important to the Samaritan woman? What did she ask Jesus? What would you ask him?

4. Why is it important to look beyond the surface—
   at people or situations?
5. Describe some of Kay's losses.
6. Why did these seem so overwhelming?
7. What was her initial reaction to well-meaning
   comments from friends? Have you ever had a
   similar experience?
8. What help have you received when you sutained
   a great loss in your life?
9. List some of the steps Kay took to regain her
   serenity in life. Can you suggest other things
   that have been helpful to you, in similar situations?
10. How did Kay's early life experiences prepare her
    to be a good leader?

Chapters Eleven—Thirteen

1. Why does Najila go to great pains to relate his
   torical background at each site in Sebastia Park?
2. Do you think history repeats itself? In what
   ways?
3. Describe some of the many times Ruth thought
   she was the wrong person in the wrong place.
   Do you ever feel like this?
4. Why did Ruth choose to show photos of her family and herself as part of her story?
5. How did the death of her mother affect Ruth?
6. List some of the things that made Ruth's adolescence difficult. Are you familiar with any of
   these things?

7. Why was it so hard for Ruth's father to care for the children on his own?

8. Jesus said to the woman: "If you knew the gift of God." What are some of God's gifts to you? Was it easy to recognize them?

9. Then Jesus continued: " ... you would have asked him and he would have given you living water." What living water has God given you recently? What have you done with it? Is it still living—flowing out to others—or have you allowed it to become stagnant?

10. Why was Ruth considering divorcing her husband, Pete?

11. What were Huda's objections about Najila's work?

Chapters Fourteen—Sixteen

1. How did Alicia handle her near-death experience? Have you ever been in a similar situation?

2. List some important things that happened during Alicia's four-month bed rest.

3. Describe the relationship between Alicia's parents. What was the catalyst for her mother's decision to finally step out on her own? Why was this difficult?

4. What was Alicia's underlying problem? Are there secrets in your life that are keeping you disturbed, uncomfortable? What are you doing about them?

5. How was Alicia a partner in her own healing?

6. Who was Photina, and how did her story originate?

7. What picture do you get of Julia's early years at home? In what ways was her life similar to Sapha's?

8. What was the major problem for Julia throughout her life? What messages did she receive from her family concerning this? Were those messages helpful to Julia? How do injunctions from our past often color our present?

9. What role did religion play in Julia's life? Why did her father's views on religion change? What was Julia's reaction to these changes?

10. How did Julia handle all the medical problems that befell her family? List some other ways people handle their illnesses or handicaps. What may account for these differences?

11. What are some of the suggestions the other women make to Julia? When is it time to let go of our parents? Is this an easy step?

12. Have you ever had a new "calling?" What have you done about it? How is it working out?

Chapters Seventeen—Nineteen

1. What do Kay and Vicky suggest to Najila? What was Najila's first reaction?

2. How was the civil war raging outside a metaphor for the war raging in Inez's home? What were some of the problems in her early life?

3. How did Inez internalize these problems? What were some of her harmful behaviors?

4. Describe some of the changes Inez experienced as a teenager. What was she being asked to do at home? Have you ever found yourself in this situation? How might these early years have influenced her career choice?

5. How did Inez receive help for her problems, her addiction?

6. List some of the positive behaviors Inez now practices.

7. What are her future goals and plans?

8. What was Najila's attitude about cultural slights or restraints? Have you ever adopted a similar attitude?

9. List some of the main beliefs of the Samaritans. Why was Mt. Gerizim so important to them?

10. What did Sapha, and then Jesus, say about this mountain?

Chapters Twenty—Twenty-two

1. Describe Norma's early home life. What kinds of strengths did it build for her?

2. How did Norma handle her unexpected divorce? Do you know others who've been in her position? What was their response?

3. In Norma's opinion, which is worse—cancer or rejection? How did Norma receive help in both areas?

4. Do you belong to any support groups? In what ways are they helpful?

5. What was Norma's most important attitude?

6. How did Norma handle the situation of the surprise guests at the restaurant?

7. How did Alicia and Ruth handle Rania? Do you know anyone like Rania?

8. Discuss Najila's feelings when she saw her mother with a man.

9. Have you ever experienced an extraordinary occurrence, such as Corinne witnessed, or a special dream? What did you do about it? Did you share this event or dream with others? Why or why not?

10. Why was Corinne so close to her grandmother?

11. How might Corinne's early experiences with her mother have given her special empathy on the police department crisis hot line?

12. Following her unique experience of "the night," how does Corinne now try to live?

13. Why was Corinne's "night" also special for Huda?

Chapters Twenty-three—Twenty-five

1. Why were these *souks*, or markets, so interesting to the group?

2. Discuss your thoughts about the benefits or distractions of modern technology. Do you, like Kay, ever long for simpler times? What actions have you taken to simplify your life?

3. How did Beth's early life prepare her for her careers in the caring professions as a nurse and teacher?

4. Describe other situations where it might be easy to become "too friendly" with someone of the opposite sex.

5. Do you know anyone who's been in Beth's shoes? How did it turn out?

6. Do you think Beth's letter and the little drama in the café between the young Palestinian girl and the American man affected Ruth and her decision about Pete?

7. Was Huda the right person to speak to the young girl? How can we know whether to act/ speak or not? When can advice be helpful? Hurtful?

8. What are some patterns in your life that might need changing? Have you been able to rebuild areas in your life? What help have you had with this?

9. List some of the surprising purchases the women made on their shopping trip. How was each woman's purchase special for her needs?

10. Describe Huda's bargaining technique. Have you ever tried that? What happened?

Chapters Twenty-six—Twenty-seven

1. Do you relate to anything in Vicky's story: her early life with various relatives or her fears?

2. How would you describe Vicky's mother? What might have been early influences in her mother's life?

3. How was Vicky able to overcome her "tumultuous background?"

4. How did Vicky handle the strange supernatural occurrences of evil during that week in Mexico? Have you ever experienced a similar occurrence? What did you do? Did you tell others about it?

5. Discuss the theme of abandonment that runs through Vicky's story.

6. Was the advice given to Vicky at the end of her story good?

7. What were the high points of the final ceremony out at the well? Why was Norma's living parable appropriate?

8. What changes did you notice in Huda's behavior? How might those affect her relationship with Najila?

9. In what ways was this trip beneficial for Najila, Huda, and the whole group?

10. List some of the plans each woman has for her future.

11. How are *you* different today than you were ten years ago? In looking back, what changes do *you* see?

12. What new ideas for your own life have you gained from this study? What steps will you take *today* to implement them?

About the Author

Ladine was a member of Bible Study Fellowship while residing in Arlington, Texas. Many years of life and travel in the Middle East later gave her special insights into the similarities to first-century biblical settings. While a student in a graduate program at Catholic Theological Union in Chicago, she

Ladine Housholder standing next to Jacob's Well in the Palestinian city of Nablus in the West Bank.

journeyed with CTU groups to historical sites in Turkey, Greece, Jordan, and Israel, experiencing and photographing the areas of ancient Samaria: Sebaste, Shechem and Jacob's Well, where the Gospel of John says that the Samaritan woman met Jesus.

Music has also been prominent in Ladine's life. She has been a private piano instructor, professional accompanist, and duo-pianist for fifty years. She has designed and presented numerous piano pedagogy classes plus has served as music director and vocal coach for many theatrical productions.

In 2006, Ladine completed an English translation of a book detailing the witch persecutions in 1590 in southern Germany, where she now lives.

QUICK ORDER FORM

☎ **Telephone orders:** Call 434-906-6926

▭ **Email orders:** monica@copperteapotpub.com

▭ **Web orders:** www.copperteapotpub.com

▭ **Postal orders:**
Copper Teapot Publishing
P.O. Box 4492
Charlottesville, VA 22905-4492
USA

Please send _____ copies of *The Well Women.*

Name: _____

Address:_____

City: _____ State: _____ Zip:____

Telephone:_____

Email address:_____

SALES TAX: Please add 5.3% for books shipped to Virginia addresses.

SHIPPING:
U.S. (Media Rate): $3.30 for the first book and $0.70 for each additional book.
APO/FPO/DPO: $6 for the first book and $3 for each additional book.

_____ books at $15.95 each	$_____
+ 5.3% sales tax (for Virginia residents only)	$_____
+ Shipping	$_____
TOTAL	$_____

METHODS OF PAYMENT

If ordering by mail or by email--
❏ Check (made payable to **Copper Teapot Publishing** and sent to the above address)

If ordering online--
❏ Credit/Debit Card: Visa; MasterCard; Discover; Amex or ❏ PayPal

Made in the USA
San Bernardino, CA
22 October 2014